MADELINE'S JEWEL

MADELINE'S JEWEL

Joy –
Thanks for the
great conversation.
Hope you enjoy!
Barb
Dimich

Barb Dimich

Cover photo and design for Madeline's Jewel by Barb Dimich

Library of Congress Number: 2004093728
ISBN: Hardcover   1-4134-5898-X
               Softcover   1-4134-5897-1

This book was printed in the United States of America.

To order additional copies of this book, contact:
Xlibris Corporation
1-888-795-4274
www.Xlibris.com
Orders@Xlibris.com
25344

In Loving Memory of Phyllis Church

Friend, you gave everything, wanted nothing
and captured my heart in the process.
You were my inspiration, my true believer.
I cannot grieve my loss,
but cherish the moments, the laughter, and the smiles.
I cannot shed my tears of sorrow,
but will remember you in each tomorrow.
That little dash between the dates
is significant of our time apart.
So, my dear friend, I know the day will come
when we once again reacquaint.

Also by Barb Dimich

Superior's Jewel
SEALed Fate
Concealed Judgement

ACKNOWLEDGEMENTS

THE ORIGIN OF the Apostle Islands Trilogy came long after my first visit to La Pointe and Bayfield, Wisconsin. With a desire to put many ideas into one simple story, this trilogy came into focus after a phone call to Lori Hinrichsen of Madeline Island's Chamber of Commerce. Best friends Katharine, Michelle and Nicole emerged as three heroines. Lori without your knowledge and guidance of the area and people, I could not have finished the Apostle Islands Trilogy.

To George Toman of the La Pointe Police Department, after chasing you around fourteen miles of rock, I can't thank you enough for filling in the gaps on Wisconsin law, crime scene investigation, the tours and the intriguing 'inside info'. In many ways, our chat iced the cake for an amazing finish.

I am especially grateful to Nori Newago, President of Madeline Island Historic Preservation Association for your assistance in locating the owner of "Song of The Pioneers" by Elvera Myhre. A special thanks to Elvera's granddaughter, Virginia Lofrano, for permission to use the song that your grandmother wrote. As the story emerged, each verse in Song of the Pioneers became an integral part of the trilogy.

A gracious thank you to the Reiman Family and their friends for bailing my car out of one muddy mess then inviting me into your magnificent retreat overlooking 'the big lake'.

Special thanks to Alice Cadotte for the historical facts and reference materials, as well as Linda Ohlandt who shared more cultural tidbits of the area.

Thank you to Roger Lenz for your gun expertise and the patient explanations, and to Rudy Sterbenk for detailing the necessary boat info that I needed throughout the stories. *I hope that I got it all right.* Your help was extremely useful but your friendships will always be invaluable.

Barb Dimich

PROLOGUE

SHE WAS TWENTY-EIGHT that warm summer night he strolled into the Red Rock Tavern. Suspenders supported a pair of bib-top overalls, which had seen the better side of hell. His rugged face looked like the sole of an old army boot. Weather-beaten in a handsome way Michelle Callihan thought as she stared at him with longing. His golden brown hair was tangled and matted carelessly and reminded her of elflocks. Sloe-brown eyes with a Robert Mitchum, sleepy-eyed gaze sidetracked from his shabby appearance. But when their eyes connected, she observed a spark of some indefinable emotion that lasted only an instant. It unbridled static charges and feverish excitement inside of her. The allurement of that exchange convinced Michelle her waiting and wanting were about to end. He approached her table and quite openly studied her. An impish, hopeful grin signaled his approval. Derek Gunderson introduced himself and they talked and danced the night away.

Through the days and weeks to follow, private dinners and picnics on secluded beaches were typical things to do at the start of a new relationship. The surprise came in the unexpected ways he pressed her with relentless enjoyment. He feigned an interest in her passion for old movies and handpicked her favorite wild flowers to fill her crystal vases. But when he began rummaging through her novels and even read one or two, she felt wrapped in a silken cocoon of euphoria.

Her affection deepened and intensified until Michelle fell in love. Her heart sang with delight when Derek finally proposed. The waiting and years of preparation had been worth it. Vivid childhood recollections included a gown highlighted with a halter-style bodice and basque waist overlaid in Venise lace. Embroidered threadwork trimmed the skirt with a chapel-length train flowing from shirred satin. Pearl beads and fabric roses decorated the crown headpiece veil. Her long, dark hair styled up revealed pearl droplets on her lobes while opera gloves added an exquisite finish. Life-long friends Katharine and Nicole were bridesmaids and her sister's children were the ring bearer and flower girl. The fantasy included riding to the church in a horse-drawn carriage with the clippety-clop of hooves. The trick was to figure out a way to transport a horse across Lake Superior. Michelle pulled it off successfully—*success was extremely important*—then her storybook wedding played out into the perfect royal ceremony.

Derek's devotion continued when they dashed away on a Jamaican honeymoon. Bottomless peace and satisfaction consumed Michelle throughout the week. They had brunch in bed on sterling silver trays with doily decorations, lounged on sandy white beaches in the afternoon, feasted on evening dinners and aroused their love with Champaign moonlit ocean dips. The perfect start for a wonderful life together.

But, she found out much too late.

The abrupt change in his personality began the week they returned from Jamaica. His moods veered sharply to anger. A raging temper flared quickly. Chills hung on the edge of every word when his violence emerged. Michelle thought the torture crushing her serenity would pass. She believed the man she fell in love with would return. But his behavior only worsened. So did the incredible fear that embedded itself deeply within her soul. Until today, she had no idea her successful business and life-long dreams were crumbling to fibs and deceit. The exchange of sacramental vows and his promise of eternal love was just a cover-up.

Michelle shook uncontrollably. Her heart thundered inside of her chest. Tonight had been the worst beating. Fear and anger twisted around her ragged breaths. It gnawed away her shriveling confidence. Derek was a cheater. He was a liar and a thief. But most of all he was an abuser. How could she not have seen through his disguise? Michelle wept aloud, rocking her trembling body back and forth. Hot tears slithered down her face in stinging pain.

He came close to killing her tonight.

She shuddered inwardly then mustered enough strength to lift her tortured soul off the edge of the tub and stared at her degradation in the bathroom mirror. He'd hacked off her long, beautiful hair with a steak knife. Bruised eyes were commensurate with the swelling of her mouth and jaw. Her youthful glow had vanished alongside the destruction of her impeccable life. The agony felt like a nightmare frozen in time and she was stuck inside the cold, piercing ice. This wasn't a nightmare she silently told her battered reflection. This was real. Michelle choked back another uncontrollable sob and gently dabbed a washcloth at blood from a cut above her left brow. It stung, but the ache in her heart hurt more. *She had failed.* She was never more wrong about anything or anyone. Her marriage to Derek was a travesty. Unable to deny the facts or the misery of the haunting events, seething rage mounted inside of her. Her husband had cost her everything. He had lied, stolen from her, and stripped her of deep pride and dignity. Ignoring the mocking voice inside that wondered why, she would rid herself of him forever. Then an even more terrifying realization washed over her. How would she keep the rest of the world from discovering her humiliation?

Song of the Pioneers
by Elvera Myhre

Mad'line Island, Beautiful Island, I love the
name with all my heart. It was here my dear
   old father came to live and do his part,
to carve a home from the dreary wildwoods,
   to grub and dig, to chop and build.

O there is no other island so dear to me as thou art.
   Mad'line Island, Beautiful Island,
   I love the name with all my heart.

CHAPTER 1

Eighteen Months Later

GOLDEN LIGHT POURED down from a cloudless sky. A woodsy aroma mingled with the scent of sweetened apples. Shiny classic hotrods and streetcars lacquered the brown grassy field as bright and picturesque as the harvest of autumn trees. In the background of a scene perhaps stolen right out of Norman Rockwell, the Apostle Islands speckled Lake Superior's magnificent blue water with nature's paintbrush.

Not far away while dad checked out a time-honored Chevy, brother and sister engaged each other in a deliberate dispute. Other men drooled over untouchable dreams while their children scampered playfully around the classic displays. The scene was crammed with picnickers, sleeping babes and a mother scolding her youngster for jumping on the bumper of a '51 Ford pickup. Who could blame the kid when the vehicle beckoned and seduced in a way only an automobile enthusiast would understand?

The man taking it all in stopped to check out the cranberry red truck himself. A close match to the one he already owned back in Boston, this vehicle was a man's choice during his grandfather's generation. Today, ownership of a classic car was an expensive hobby. Those who couldn't afford it, concealed their feelings of envy.

Unfortunately, the twinge of desire enclosing his own heart had nothing to do with a passion for old cars. Nor did those demons of desire center on his worldly success. Surrounded by the sensuous allure of Bayfield's apple festival, those dancing demons consumed him with solitude. The imposing scenery only provoked his private thoughts of happiness, family and home. The poverty was as critical as a condemned building's need for structural redesign.

He shuttered inwardly at the thought and refused to dwell on personal loneliness. Nodded at several as he strolled through the crowd, then, halted abruptly. *There she was.* Stunning and gorgeous like he had imagined. His pulse pounded eagerly brewing up to an erratic summer storm. His mouth watered with silent thoughts of drooling as he gazed across the grassland at her and beamed approval. While her beauty was intimate magnetism that tugged at the core of his soul, the movement of his feet increased with the beat of his heart.

He stopped a few yards away from her to admire the car of all cars. She was a 1934 Ford Cabriolet pick-up, and the one grandfather repeatedly said was lost to hard times. With a blueprint inspection of the amenities—dust hood, dual horns, rumble seat, cowl and tail lamps, chrome plated windshield—he beamed approval a second time. Renewed excitement ruled him as he checked out the taupe interior, the most important feature. Ford had changed the color in May of '34 from the standard brown Bedford cord to taupe. Any other shade would lack authenticity grandfather said. That point turned the search for this vehicle into a steadfast three-year love affair. And one where time was running out. The car was half of a fifty-year anniversary gift to his grandfather. The other half of his gift, a plan in progress and not without additional delays, would delight his Grandma-ma, barring no more interference from Michelle Callihan. The supervisor on La Pointe's Town Board provided many obstacles from the start. He suspected her fight against this project would progress to the end. He learned that from his right hand man, Billy Abbott. Sent here to scope out the area, Billy's investigation proved worthy when he returned and advised of Callihan's ability to create snags. Snag was a mild version of her grit. She flat out rejected his idea of a mall on the island, which he couldn't dispute. She refused to hear any revised plans, literally quoting their strict zoning codes to him. Much to his dismay, the Town Board agreed with her. But he didn't give up. He never gave up.

Thanks to Billy, he had the facts, statistics and documented history of the area. He also had photographs of the tavern from top to bottom along with color glossies of the entire island. The photos were the inspiration to his second proposal. Memorizing every detail in the pictures turned out to be a fantastic study for him to compare with the Red Rock Tavern history he heard about many times. Nonetheless, two years of setbacks with the Callihan woman came at his expense. Running short on time and long on annoyance, he broke off his connection with her and the Town Board and went to the owner of the tavern, Ted Evans. Evans blew a glee gasket over his proposal, quickly secured a deal with him to recreate the historical ballroom and guaranteed the Town Board would unanimously agree to the reconstruction. Unfortunately, not all did. Callihan still held out as long as possible.

Personal staying power beat her out. For every argument she presented, he trounced her with a counter argument. An architect's job demanded inventive effort. And if he could figure out the guts of any inaccessible structure, he could damn well overcome the whims of an unsatisfied woman. He bombarded her skepticism daily. Blueprints inside and out, paper plans of schematic evidence, detailed photographs with diagrammatic drawings of every section of the tavern drawn to scale made a paper trail between Madeline Island and Boston. In the end, his legal department wrote her that no one would ever be able to see or tell that the present-day Red Rock Tavern had once stood alone. She finally conceded, but he knew her vote to proceed came with undue reluctance and he preferred total unity.

The third obstacle, and one not in his control, forced him to reconsider the entire deal. Carter Taylor, the Town Board Chairman, called to advise him of the ghastly murders on the Island that began in July. He felt shellacked by the events when the serial killer shot Ted Evans. Searching for a plausible reason to continue, his parents reminded him that he wasn't a quitter and he put Billy

Abbot to work again. When Evans contacted him during his recovery to reassure him of the capture of the killer—rather, he was shot and killed—he agreed to proceed.

Tomorrow's groundbreaking gave him four months to perform a miracle for his grandparent's fiftieth wedding anniversary. It left barely enough time to frame and put the walls in place before winter set in. He would have to push the subcontractors hard, get his own hands dirty to meet the timeline and pay the extra costs for a timely completion. All for a grand celebration of fifty years of marriage. A cynical inner voice cut through his thoughts. His parents would also reach that plateau. Genuine love evaded him and he'd never be as fortunate. He decided long ago *convoluted* described relationships adequately, so why bother with it. Grandmama didn't agree with him. She said marriage was elementary and tantalizing. *"No problems too big, no conflict too difficult when shared with your lover,"* she repeated too much for his liking. He didn't believe it.

"You try too hard. When you find her, she won't care if you are rich or poor," his grandfather said. Several women had proved the wise old man wrong there, too. *Nope,* he thought, the right woman did not exist.

The sun's glare off the Cabriolet's chrome bumper brought him back to reality. He removed a piece of paper from his shirt pocket and compared the vehicle identification numbers.

"Billy, you've earned yourself a tidy bonus this time," he muttered.

"She's a beaut, ain't she?"

Shifting casually, a coarse-looking fellow stood behind him. Fifty and then some, the man had beady little eyes that contradicted a large, heavy body. Elevated brows and a long gaze exposed an eagerness to deal. The man's pig-like eyes bared personal excitement to bait him in and swindle more money out of him. How well he read the putz. The eyes always gave away a human's deepest desires.

"You the owner?" he asked.

"Don Farley. Built her from the ground up with all the original parts."

"That right?"

"Yep. Took me a couple of years to do it."

"Mind if I check under the hood?"

"Not a' tall."

Concealing his elation, he lifted the car's bonnet, stalled several minutes and gently closed and re-latched the cover. As he turned to face Don Farley, he swiftly sidestepped a wad of chewing tobacco the local spewed out from the corner of his mouth. He learned, with Billy's help, that Don Farley was a thorough man with a deep affection for old cars. His own affection ran deeper.

"How much do you want for her, Mr. Farley?"

"I'm a fair man. I've labored over her day and night."

"Name your price, Mr. Farley."

"Sixty-seven, five."

"Fifty-seven, five."

"Sixty-five," Don Farley shot back.

"Fifty-nine, five! Not a penny more."

"Sixty-three, five," Farley countered.

"Sixty!"

"Sold!"

"Mr. Farley, you've got yourself a deal."

Don Farley's beady eyes widened.

"I'll have a cashiers check drawn up immediately along with the paperwork to transfer title of ownership."

"You driving her outta here?" Farley asked, discharging another wad of chewing tobacco.

"I've made arrangements for storage."

"You know," Don Farley taunted, "I would've taken your first offer, Mr.—what'd you say your name was?"

"You should know, Mr. Farley. I would have paid your full price. Baines. The name is Travis Baines."

CHAPTER 2

A CRISP AUTUMN morning with vibrant colors, Mother Nature's first frost came later than normal. It fingered Madeline Island with gentle wisps of white. Quaint serenity encompassed the early morning. Tourists were gone from La Pointe until next summer, putting the town back to a submissive population of a couple hundred.

Michelle Callihan glanced in her rear-view mirror. A pretentious smile, indeed strained, and mortared there since last Friday, reflected back. Teardrops she kept hidden in her heart had turned to stone a long time ago. Just because she forfeited her own contentment with life, she couldn't begrudge her best friend's happiness. Nevertheless, Katharine's marriage to Mac Dobarchon made the weekend too long and direly depressing. Like always, Michelle refused to dwell on her own disappointments.

This minute, she was late for the groundbreaking at the Red Rock Tavern.

With her acceptance of the voted in position as a supervisor on La Pointe's Town Board, she never gave much thought to the amount of valuable time this job would suck up. A post generally requiring simple town decisions had been doing exactly that. It kept her away from the landscaping business she had re-fostered with pride and care. All her precious free time had been dedicated to the old coot who owned Baines, Incorporated. Today she would meet the architectural firm's entrepreneur for the first time in two long years of controversy. She couldn't wait to get it over. It wasn't that she disliked people. On the contrary, she loved working on group projects. *Usually*. Rage engulfed her when the bastard cajoled Ted Evans into building a ballroom adjoining the tavern after the Town Board unanimously voted out a commercialized shopping center on Madeline Island. She felt sure financial influence had persuaded Ted, and Baines had plenty of it. She was concerned with the way he convinced Ted to accept a proposal without Board approval first. The unknown reasons a doddering old fool wanted his designs on Madeline Island disturbed her. What was his motive? Was it foolish whims of a pretentiously rich jerk with nothing better to do? Regardless, she would continue to protect her island from the impulses of richness. She would give no one rights to change the Islanders or the land, and despised those who tried.

With exception of her college stint to obtain a Bachelor of Forestry, she had spent her entire life preserving the unblemished area. Born and bred here, she cherished La Pointe's quaintness, loved the way Lake Superior surrounded the island town with demure magic. The history alone dated them back to the 1400's. The importance of it identified who they were and she would let no man mess with that history. Mr. Travis Baines of Baines, Incorporated could care less about the historical significance of the Apostle Islands. And that ticked her off more than her money did. More than how he wormed his way onto the island. A thorough investigation of him and his company provided long lists of proven achievements and high recommendations, too. His company was a world-renowned architectural firm. When the Board insisted on a unanimous vote, she had no choice but to concede. Though he won the battle to mess with one of the precious jewels of the Apostle's—*her island*, she would make damn sure he followed every zoning and building code right down to crossing his t's and dotting his i's in the dirt.

Navigating the corner and heavy machinery on Red Rock Road up to the Tavern, Michelle instantly spotted her gregarious friend standing in a foursome. Nicole was dressed in her newest ensemble. Her honey-gold, long hair glistened in the morning sun as she amused three men with sociable conversation.

"Definitely a Type B," Michelle muttered.

Big, bold, Carter Taylor and his mustache with matching battle-ship gray hair stood next to Ted and a guy wearing a yellow hardhat. She wondered if Ted was up for this. With noticeable weight loss after taking a bullet in the shoulder, his pinkish skin had been zapped of it's normal color. Michelle parked her car next to a black sports car. Briefly admiring the Ferrari, she shut off the engine to her cobalt blue Mustang and scanned the entire area for the old man. Several workers and contractors also sporting hardhats stood around guzzling caffeine.

"Figures," she huffed, sliding out of her car. "Jerk doesn't even have the decency to show up today."

"Michelle," Carter called out as he and Ted met her half way. "We're still waiting for Ed Harris from the Island Blazer and somebody from the Bayfield Weekly to get here. Grab some coffee inside and I'll introduce you to Travis Baines."

"Ted how are you feeling? Are you sure you can handle this?"

He rotated his shoulder and winked at her. The twinkle in his dusty blue eyes conveyed his excitement.

"The doc fixed me up fine. I wouldn't miss this for the world. Come on let's get you that coffee."

*   *   *

Travis Baines had never known any woman to drive a vintage car much less own one. He learned quickly if cars weren't showy and expensive women cared even less about them. The '69 Ford Mustang spiked his attention immediately. The blue color reminded him of a flawless, extraordinarily preserved precious stone. But the critical moment came when Carter called out to the female exiting that mustang. His world flip-flopped and sucked the wind out of his sail. *The dream has to be my nemesis.* The moment he finally met the dogged Callihan he expected a frumpish-looking administrator wearing a tasteless business suit. He was wrong and all he could do was gawk at her with complete surprise on his face. Michelle Callihan was slender and graceful. A real lady in shimmery gray slacks and a delicate jade-colored sweater with heeled pumps that enhanced a look of loving to pamper self. Her polished glide exposed enormous self-confidence. Although he didn't get a good look at her eyes, he recognized the faintly golden flesh of her face. And shocking as that familiar face was to him, he knew it would compliment immense green eyes and long dark lashes.

"She's one of my two best friends," Nicole said. "If you'd like, I can introduce you."

Baines forced himself to acknowledge the woman standing next to him. "Call me Travis. And, yes. I would appreciate meeting her, Ms. Jarvis."

"I'll introduce you on one condition. You must call me Nicole."

"Deal."

"Nicole, we got a problem and I need you inside," Ted called from the Tavern's door.

Carter and Michelle exited, moved toward them and stopped a few feet from them.

"Ed just arrived," Carter said. "Michelle Callihan . . . Travis Baines. Travis . . . Michelle. I'll be right back and we can get this show on the road."

Travis removed his sunglasses. "We finally meet, Ms. Callihan."

"Mr. Baines, I prefer Michelle."

The attractive features he admired moments ago were a deceptive cover to the icy tone in her voice. Her posture overflowed with bitterness, but he'd dealt with far worse in his line of work and extended his hand anyway. Obstinacy forced her to focus everywhere but at him before she eventually reciprocated.

Jesus! Her flesh is colder than her personality. A problem in need of immediate settlement, he began, "Michelle," and stopped when her name rolled off his tongue the way a fine car rolls off the assembly line.

"What?" she snapped.

She flashed him an impassively cold stare from emerald green eyes that were more amazing than the one's in his vision. For a moment, he examined her carefully. Her eyes darted nervously back and forth. "This is a done deal. You have my assurance that the ballroom will meet with the Town's specs."

"You can bank on it."

"I already have. After the thorough background investigation you did on me and my company, I'd expect nothing less from you."

"And I'll expect the same thoroughness from you," Michelle retorted with a raised chin and cool stare.

"I guarantee it. I'm a businessman who examines every aspect extensively including the people who work with me or for me. I've studied the history of the Apostles, Madeline Island and the Red Rock Tavern in detail. As I've already advised you in writing, you will not know the ballroom never existed when I'm finished with this project."

"You've never been more wrong about anything in your life, *Mr. Baines*. I'll know."

She tossed down the last of her coffee and crossed her arms tightly. Deliberately guarded, it gave him the impression she needed protection from him. Upon his closer inspection, a distant, timid expression lay dormant behind the cold emerald green of her eyes. Her dark hair swung about her proud shoulders. It reminded him of finely spun silk from the Orient. On the outside, she appeared delicate, fragile. He couldn't decide whether it came from youth or vulnerability and assumed something other than this project had caused the obvious pain he observed in her eyes. Sadly and unwanted, it yanked and wrenched him in two.

"We're all set for the digging," Carter Taylor called out from several yards away.

The next thirty minutes photographers from both papers snapped off numerous shots while reporters captured history in the making. They spoke to and scribbled quotes from Baines, Carter, Ted, the engineers and general contractor.

Michelle stood alone. She glanced from man to man feeling like a misfit in a place where she spent her entire life. Drained of mastered discipline, she wished for solitude right now. With all the inquiries she made on Baines Incorporated, she never thought to check out the detail of his age. Her embarrassment turned into sarcasm, and she now dissected the man in the hardhat behind sunglasses she wore to hide her private thoughts. A big wheel and king of his domain, the architectural jerk had triumphed. While the boys played with big toys and shoveled the first scoops of dirt, Baines had insisted they wear hardhats, too. Hers was too big and kept sliding off. She swallowed back an acid lump at the base of her throat as the obnoxious noise from machinery reverberated in her ears. She couldn't watch the destruction of beautiful trees, tossed her hardhat and returned inside the tavern.

"Hi, Hayden."

"Hey, Michelle."

The bartender was a jolly fella in his forties with a whistling fetish, and probably started his day earlier than he did most. "Did Nicole get her problem taken care of?"

"You betcha. She's getting used to Gypsy calling in sick."

Michelle eased onto a barstool as Hayden wiped the wood-enameled bar top. Already clean, she assumed he performed the gesture more from habit. "Why doesn't Nicole just fire her?"

"It's not that easy to get help in here. How you doing? You want something to drink? Coffee? Juice?"

"Coffee if you have it."

"We've got everything. Ted wants Baines' men satisfied."

"I'll just bet he does," Michelle muttered when Hayden walked away to retrieve the caffeine she truly needed less of.

Nicole bounced in through a six-paneled swing door that separated the kitchen from the bar most referred to as the lounge. "Hi, hon. You gonna be okay?"

"Fine! Peachy! Why?"

"I knew you'd be shocked when you met Travis. I was after hearing everything you've said about him."

"Yeah, whatever."

"Hon, everyone's extremely confident this will work when it's done. It's also going to improve the tourist season."

"Fast buck, Nicole! That's all anyone cares about. Tell me what will happen to our privacy if what you say is true. Other jerks will show up wanting to make La Pointe and Madeline their winter wonderland. People like Travis Baines with a shitload of money are gonna come in here enticing people like Carter and Ted."

"Michelle—"

"They'll buy up every inch of land and destroy the bountiful trees just so they can build elaborate houses they'll spend three or four months a year living in, *if that*! Where will the history of the Apostles be then, Nicole? And how will you feel when more money-grubbing people like Travis Baines, who aren't even from this area, start moving onto the other islands with fax machines and cell phones? This won't be a haven anymore. It'll be a second office for the filthy rich to claim as a business expense on their taxes."

"Michelle."

When Nicole finally nodded, Michelle spun around on the stool. She gaped into a pair of the fiercest grayish-blue eyes she'd ever seen. Trusted even less. Baines' lips were stretched tightly. In two strides, he moved in closely, peering angrily at her. It forced Michelle to flinch.

"Let's get something straight right now, Mizz Callihan! I am *not* some money-grubbing rich bastard with a cell phone on me that I use as a tax write off. Dare I tell you a jerk like me with a shitload of money is the *least* of your problems! Barely eight in the morning, I've just encountered my second crisis of the day!"

Cowering under the sound of his explosive voice, Michelle sensed whatever his second problem was she was his first. When he stepped closer and pinned her between him and the bar, panic engulfed her.

"Nicole," Travis barked hotly. "I need a phone to call the police. Ours aren't hooked up yet and my backhoe just uncovered a young girl's body."

CHAPTER 3

TAUGHT ANGER CONTROL no matter what the cause, Travis fumed silently while he studied the blueprints and schematics with the general contractor. His thoughts raced dangerously. Waiting for anyone annoyed him. Twenty precious minutes had slipped away since he called the police. Time would be lost and result in cost overruns. That really annoyed him. He swung sharply around when a squad car pulled onto the job site. He followed Carter and Ted headed toward the red-haired, solid-built man exiting the white vehicle.

"Where is she, Carter?"

"Chief, we just started clearing away. The backhoe operator saw her and stopped. Chief . . . Travis Baines. Travis . . . Gage LeNoir."

Both nodded, shaking hands. "Carter, did Nikki or Michelle see her?"

"No. They're inside. Come on, we'll show you."

Travis tagged behind the two men around to the north side of the Tavern. He stopped several feet from the body and gagged on the obscene odor. An onslaught of graphic words spewed out of the police chief's mouth and Travis wondered how anyone survived this kind of work.

"How long will this take, Chief?" Travis asked.

"As long as it takes the Ashland County criminal investigator and the medical examiner to do their thing. They're enroute."

"Do you know her?"

"She hasn't been here long," he said.

"That's not what I asked you, but how can you tell?"

"The cooler weather's delayed decomposition."

"You don't think this is the doings of a copycat to the others?" Carter then asked.

"What's he talking about?" Travis asked.

"Won't know until Del and Gus go over the scene," Gage replied. "Carter, I'll need your cooperation since Joe went off to study forensic medicine and Mac's on his honeymoon with Katharine."

"I was informed the serial killer had been shot dead," Travis said.

"Copycat means exactly what it says," Gage told him.

The in white uniform shirt cop avoided direct answers and examined the area in search of something. A clue? Evidence? What? On the eighth day of October, Travis did not like the odds or their implications. Billy Abbott had checked into those murders for him. David Patriot was a psychotic serial killer who began his killing spree over two years ago in Green Bay, Wisconsin. He killed in July, October and December. He lured sixteen-year old Native American girls in with drugs and liquor, kidnapped them then murdered them slowly with poison in a ritual ceremony. It took some digging, but Billy discovered some died from the lethal chemical while a poisonous seed from a plant killed the others.

The dismal look on the Chief's face told Travis that copycat probably wasn't what he was thinking either. Someone had screwed up big time, which meant the serial killer was still on the loose. He glanced at the dead girl. The killing wasn't over. And he couldn't afford costly delays or a loss of time this late in the season.

"Carter, did anyone find a liquor bottle anywhere nearby?" Gage asked.

"No, nothing. Why?"

"I need everyone to back away from the scene so nothing else is disturbed."

"Chief, I won't interfere with your investigation, but can you at least give me an idea of how long this will take?" Travis asked.

"Leave the backhoe where it is. They'll need to examine it for evidence."

"I asked you a question. How long is this going to take you?"

"You know what, Baines? I'm fresh out of staff and answers. The M.E. and crime lab are coming over from the mainland and they'll be here when they get here."

"I'll knock off work and have my men get—"

"Baines. No one is going anywhere. I'll need statements from everyone that's here as well as a list of all your employees and anyone involved in this operation. Tell your men to wait inside the Tavern."

"You're not suggesting one of us had something to do with this are you?"

"This girl's been dead a lot longer than you or your men have been here, but I still need statements from everyone, including you."

Travis whistled sharply then ordered, "Everyone inside the Tavern. You're still on the clock and the police need your cooperation. The sooner we get this over with, the sooner we can get back to work."

The police chief retrieved a roll of yellow tape from his squad and began wrapping it around the location of the dead girl. "Need help with that?" Travis offered.

"Why not. Take this roll and start on that end by the tavern. Secure it around tree trunks thirty yards from the center point of the victim. Try not to touch anything."

They met half way. The morning heating up from the sun a shiny glare blindsided Travis. "What the . . ."

"Here comes the Crime Lab," Gage said, walking away.

"Chief. I think I just found what you were looking for," Travis called to him. The glare came from a liquor bottle in the brush.

"Don't touch it!" Gage yelled back.

"Chief, what've you got?" Gus asked.

"Gus, Del, that's Travis Baines. They started construction on the tavern and found the body a short time ago."

"Is it the same as the others?"

"Identical. Baines just located the bottle over there where he's standing. Can you wrap this up quickly so his crews can get back to work?"

"Ah, the new ballroom," Gus said, scanning the scene. "You bet. We'll do our best."

"Thanks. I'll be inside taking statements from his crews. Lemme know when you're done."

*   *   *

Nicole rambled on about the dead body, but Michelle refused to lend an ear. Ever since the yellow hardhat set foot inside the tavern to announce the discovery—she blinked. Her own reflection in the mirror behind the bar said she was pale as a fish. She felt like she was going to hurl and inhaled deeply. "Nicole, I need a cigarette."

"No you don't, Michelle."

Yes, she did! Alongside feeling like a four-star asshole, how could she have been stupid enough to mouth off the way she had? "You could've at least warned me he was standing there," Michelle blasted, caring less about the fairness of venting her nervousness.

"Hon, I tried but Travis waved me off. Besides, I really thought you saw him in the mirror here."

"Well, I didn't!" she shot back sharply.

"Here he comes now with Gage. I'm outta here. I've got work to do since Gypsy isn't coming in for her shift."

Coming up on Michelle's right, Gage said, "Michelle, Nikki, neither of you can leave here until Gus and Del are done outside."

"Gage, I have client appointments this morning."

"Tough, Michelle. I will not let either one of you relive what you went through this summer. Call and change 'em. Nikki, I need to talk to you."

"I heard you," she responded coolly. "We aren't to leave until you're done outside."

"Privately, Nicole. *Now*."

"Fine." Her back to the bar, Nicole glanced at Gage in the mirror. "Follow me."

Michelle swallowed hard when they left. A web of firm control encircled Mr. Baines Incorporated. From the charcoal-gray mirror she had ignored until today, they eyed each other. He stood there with his broad chest and powerful shoulders, the hardhat perched on the top of his head like a king's crown.

Except for Hayden washing glasses at the other end of the bar, they were the only two in the room. Michelle sucked in a deep breath and swiveled around on the stool to face the man she insulted. "Mr. Baines, I'm sorry you overheard what I said."

"But you're not sorry for what you said, are you?"

"No. No, I'm not. I can't help what I feel inside. I've spent my entire life protecting our Island because it means everything to me. I love the Apostles and I cherish the history here. I'll never stop blocking outsiders from trying to move in and take over. This is all I have left."

Peculiar curiosity covered his face on her last declaration. Michelle squirmed slightly, sucked in another quick breath. "As you said, Mr. Baines. This is a done deal and I'll have to take your word that you won't commercialize the tavern. Since we'll be working together, I'd like to patch things up between us."

"You mind if I sit down?"

Michelle knew how to be bold at a distance. She could even be direct. But she had no idea how to control the internal fears up close and personal and shifted nervously. "I guess not."

"Regardless of your other flaws, I admire your forthright honesty."

Casually, he moved toward the barstool and straddled it as if he owned it.

"Mr.—"

"Michelle. There is no way I'm going to work with you if you keep calling me Mr. Baines. It makes me sound like an old man. Call me Travis and I'll accept your apology."

She quickly trapped an involuntary grin by covering her mouth with her fingers.

"That's the first genuine smile I've seen on you since you arrived here this morning. Don't cover it up."

Removing her hand, she began, "Mr.—" when he zapped her with a prolonged glare from under the brim of his hat. "I assumed Travis Baines was a crotchety old man."

"Really? I figured you for a frumpish maid in a tacky polyester suit."

"You thought I'd wait on you hand and foot?"

"No more than you thought I had one foot in the grave."

His mouth split into a wide grin. Amusement flickered in the gray eyes that met hers. Their thoughts similar, she couldn't resist laughing then said, "Friends?"

"Friends," he replied.

"What?" she asked when he examined her longer than necessary.

"Tell me why, when a smile looks good on you, do you plaster a phony grin to your face with sheetrock screws?"

"I make it pretty obvious, don't I?"

He nodded, waiting.

For a long moment, she looked back at him then said, "I can't answer that."

"Okay. Then tell me about your '69 Mustang."

"Not on your life, Travis Baines. You may have gotten your hands on my island, but you'll never get your hands on the Stanger."

He choked on the coffee Hayden had placed in front of him. "You're not only claiming ownership of the island, but you named your car?"

"What's wrong with that? Men name their toys all the time," she flipped off.

Travis swiveled and leaned an elbow on the bar, facing her. "I can't argue with you on that. Nevertheless, I assumed a woman's level of interest in cars stopped at price and color."

"Assuming all women are the same is your first mistake, Baines."

"What's my second?"

"Never assume anything about a woman. The minute you do, she'll change her mind."

"Because it's her prerogative?"

"You catch on quick."

"How long have you had the 'stang?"

"Since getting my drivers license. I worked through school and saved up. Offers are tossed my way every year during Bayfield's car show, but it's not for sale."

"So you keep it for sentimental reasons, not the fact that you're a car buff?"

The thought of confessing to him that the car was the only thing she had left after her ex finished her off flickered through her with gut-wrenching terror. The Mustang was one of a few things she kept out of Derek's name and with good reason. "Would it matter either way?" she countered.

"No, it wouldn't. You've kept a fine piece of machinery in excellent condition. And that, Michelle Callihan, tells me a lot about you. So, tell me what Gage meant when he said you and Nicole weren't going to relive what you went through this summer?"

Michelle toyed with the coffee cup she had drained for the second time. "Nicole and I, along with our best friend, Katharine, took a boat out to Michigan Island one day."

"Katharine the police officer?"

She sat back, instantly surprised that he would know that, and then nodded. "Katharine went off to sketch the lighthouse while Nicole and I went walking along the shore. We discovered the second murdered girl when Nicole tripped over the body."

"You are kidding aren't you?"

"Afraid not."

"I've heard stories, but tell me how they finally caught this guy."

"Following an upheaval in Katharine's career and desperately seeking a way out, she quit her job and came home to this horrible mess. As I said, the three of us discovered the second victim, but Katharine was with her brother when Joey found the first victim.

To make a long story short, and one I don't care to relive the vivid events of, the police chased him all over the place. Then Patriot trapped Katharine inside a rented bungalow here on the island and set it on fire. She shot and killed him in self defense."

"Was that when she was shot?" he asked.

"No. We were all sitting outside at the funeral of the third victim when Patriot opened fire. God, we all thought we lost her that day until we learned Katharine's injury wasn't nearly as bad as Ted's. I was sitting next to her when it happened and heard bullets whizzing by. I still have nightmares about it."

"And in the middle of all that, you've had to deal with me."

Michelle sat upright. She looked at him for several moments. "Yes."

"I guess it's my turn to apologize."

"For what? You didn't know."

"I'm sorry you had to go through everything that you did. I'm a persistent man when I want something. I pursue it relentlessly until I get it."

"So you're a spoiled little rich kid, is that it?"

"I call it determined. Tell me something, Michelle. Do you despise all men who earn a tidy income? Or do you just spurn me?"

All men! Income has nothing to do with it. He steepled his fingers and continued to watch her from the bar mirror. "It's offensive the way the rich use their financial influence to take away someone's heritage for personal gain."

"Then it's not my money that offends you, but the fact that you believe I'm swindling you out of your ancestry because I want to add to the Apostle Island history?"

"Let me clarify something with you. You do not offend me. And I could care less about your money except for the fact that you obviously have enough to buy off people with it. As to your last point, don't you mean change our history?"

"Not in the least. Architectural history has always been a part of history in general. Sometimes even the most important part."

"Why do you have a need to change what already is?"

"It's not changing what is, Michelle. It's adding to our ancestors for our offspring. Why do you feel we should become lost in the past rather than setting high goals for new achievements?"

"The past is where I came from. Trying to change what is, can and does lead to serious mistakes."

"It sounds like we're talking about more than architectural history here."

Too startled by his suggestion, Michelle didn't have any worthy objection and drew in a deep breath. She fought hard not to tremble. With her own mile-long list of historical failures to cling on to, the barrier wall thickened around her.

"It's not a serious error if an architect is fully aware of the emphasis he places on production that has the most positive visual quality. For centuries, architecture has been a practical art providing shelter and serving human needs."

"The only practicality is to serve man's pocket book," she snipped.

"I wonder how the Egyptians, Greeks and Romans before Christ would feel about your statement because they chose to pay more attention to pyramids and temples than they did housing. Do you think for one minute they would have spent years doing physically difficult labor if they would have had one iota of our simplest technology?"

"Isn't that contradictory to your practicality of providing shelter and serving human need? The pyramids of Egypt provided shelter for the dead. And some of the greatest architecture was intentionally built to serve gods rather than man."

"Michelle, before Christ it was more important to the Egyptians to shelter the dead than the living. It's a relatively simple concept in their climate. By serving their gods, man has served his religious needs. Don't you want to be part of the making of history for your children and their children be it through choice or style, or the endeavors of religious beliefs?"

Travis Baines made a point she couldn't argue. When her life took on monumental disaster, she lost sight of what the future held. She gave up. Failing miserably at one of the only two things that meant everything to her, the word *failure* had been branded across her forehead. Aidan and Elisabeth Callihan had made it clear divorce was unacceptable. How could she possibly go forward without support of any kind? Just thinking of it had shattered her.

Travis nudged her in the arm. "You still with me?"

Michelle jerked abruptly. Horror twisted around her heart. The only human touch she could tolerate was from Nicole and Katharine.

"What's wrong?" Travis asked.

Her breath seeped out of her slowly until she squeaked out one word. "Nothing."

"Michelle, I'd like to hear and learn more about you. Say yes to dinner with me tonight. Then I'll tell you all about my ancestry and why I'm here. It might surprise you."

Abruptly, she hopped off the barstool. "No thank you. I've made other plans. Please excuse me, I have phone calls to make."

She took flight faster than a cougar going in for the kill. Travis wondered how she could hate him that much for being here. He swiveled on the barstool as the door to the Tavern opened and Michelle smacked into the man entering.

"*Omigod!* Mac! What are you doing back here?"

"Are you okay? Did I hurt you?" he asked, catching her arms.

She shifted uncomfortably, backed out of his grip and glanced sideways at Travis Baines. "No, I'm fine. Where's Katharine? Is everything okay with you two?"

"We're great. We had to come home. Katharine's been sick with the flu since we got on the boat. She's at home in bed."

"Oh, how awful. The poor thing. Nicole and I will go see that she's okay."

"Michelle, I talked to Del and Gus outside. Where's Gage?"

"He's around here somewhere. It's starting up again and Gage won't let Nicole or I leave until they're done outside. How can this be happening again? I thought it was over."

"Who's the guy headed this way with too much interest in you?" Mac asked, stepping in front of her.

"Travis Baines," the man said extending his hand.

He traded handshakes. "The ballroom. I'm Mac Dobarchon."

"The Green Bay hero."

"My wife's the hero. I work with Gage now. Did you find the body?"

"I was there." The out-of-uniform cop was tall, lean-muscled and sheltering Michelle the way bear do their cub. "One of my machine operators found her. Gage is questioning my crew in the restaurant area."

Mac nodded, shifted slightly. "Michelle, everything's gonna be all right. Go find Nicole and wait this out with her until we tell you otherwise. They'll be done out there soon. Baines, follow me."

They headed for the dining room. With no alternative, Michelle located Nicole in her office and informed her of Mac and Katharine's return then used Nicole's phone to call clients. She rescheduled the entire day for later in the week. Needing to be alone, and with the wait, she found a corner table downstairs and sat where no one would disturb her.

Travis Baines gave her plenty to think about—things she chose to stuff and lock away in an attic. Her mother and father had drilled her incessantly. They wanted explicit details surrounding and leading up to the divorce. They asked nothing of the marriage and that's when she thought it better to keep her burden private. She refused to explain and received a childish scolding alongside their ridicule for not making her marriage work. The words were engraved in her mind.

"My God, didn't we teach you better?"

"Marriage isn't a game you walk in and out of on a whim."

They didn't leave out their thoughts on the fact that she had failed either. The fiasco *she created* didn't come from anything they ever taught her. Without their support and understanding, she couldn't tell them what Derek did to her. Long before she ever took her vows, the ramifications of divorce were drilled into her.

Michelle glanced at the door when Baines and his men exited the Tavern. She would never go out to dinner with him or any other man. She felt achy, exhausted and so tired from the private burden she carried that everything made her nerves throb. She needed more time to ease the pain and to erase the internal fear.

"Here you are," Nicole exhaled. "They're done outside. Sheila came in and will cover until four. I fixed up a little something for Katharine and we can go there now. Mac doesn't want us to say anything to her. He wants to tell her himself about the girl they found. Did you get a hold of everyone?"

"Yeah. Let's get as far away from here as possible.

CHAPTER 4

"Nicole, you can't barge in now that they're married."

"Doesn't matter, it's locked," she replied pounding on the door. "I hope Katharine's okay."

"She's probably asleep. What did Gage want to talk to you about back at the Tavern?"

Without answer, Nicole pounded harder on the door until it opened. Katharine's stunning red hair was soaked and dulled dark from sweat. She stood wobbly on her feet, clutching the door with her hands for support in an oversized jogging suit that brandished a Green Bay PD logo.

"Oh, hon, you're really sick," Nicole crooned. "Mac stopped by the Tavern and told us. What a horrible way to start your honeymoon."

"How'd the groundbreaking go, Michelle? Did you finally meet Travis Baines?" Katharine asked while gripping her stomach.

"Fine. Yes. We didn't come over here to discuss it either."

"Katharine, Travis is not an old coot like Michelle thought. He's young, virile and remarkably gorgeous."

"How young?"

"Near our age. You should've seen the way he noticed Michelle when she pulled into the lot this morning at the tavern."

"He was interested in my car!"

"Uh-huh," Katharine replied, forcing a smile.

"We're here to help you, not discuss that jerk. Come on, let's get you in some fresh garments and back into bed. You poor thing. We brought you white crackers and seven-up."

Katharine moved in an oxen-gaited manner around stacked and unpacked boxes as Michelle held her arm to the bathroom. "Damn this stuff sucks! I've never been sick a day in my life and I've been puking for the past forty-eight hours. Well, on and off for a couple of weeks actually," she added in afterthought.

"Sweetie, you've been through a lot the last seven months of your life. It was bound to catch up to you. I'm sure you're still weak from the gunshot wound to your arm and all that smoke you inhaled in the fire. You need to drink lots of fluids."

"When did you get so motherly?"

"Taking care of Sylvie's kids, Shalee and Brendan. Can you balance on the edge of the tub just in case you need the toilet? I'll help you wash up."

"Yeah. I've set up permanent camp here since we got back this morning."

Michelle wet a washcloth with cool water then stuck a thermometer she found in the medicine cabinet under Katharine's tongue. Gingerly, she washed her girlfriend's face and handed her a towel after removing the sweatshirt. She withdrew the thermometer and studied it for a minute. "Katharine, your temp is normal. Have you had any diarrhea?"

Shaking her head, she mumbled, "I'm just nauseated and can't keep anything in me."

"You having any cravings?"

"No! I've got the crud," she blasted sarcastically.

"Have you had any severe stomach cramping?" Michelle asked.

"No. Why?"

"Katharine, when was your last period?"

"I don't remember. You know me. They've never been regular. Why?"

Gingerly she felt Katharine's forehead as a backup to the thermometer. "Sweetie, I don't think this is the flu. I think you're pregnant."

Katharine's face paled light bulb white and she slipped off the tub. Michelle caught her, suppressing a giggle. "I'll call the doctor and Nicole and I will take you in to find out."

"Are you crazy? That's impossible!" Katharine screeched.

"Are you telling me you and Mac haven't had sex yet?"

"Well, no . . . of course, we've had sex."

"Then why on God's green earth would you think it's impossible for you to be pregnant?"

"Well, I just . . . it's . . . I guess it's a good thing we got married right away. How long have I been pregnant? How can you tell?"

Michelle broke into laughter. Katharine examined her for the answers with a wide-eyed expression. "I wish Mac could see you right now. You're so stunned, you look precious."

Nicole stuck her head in through the bathroom door. "How's she doing?"

"Nicole, we need to call the doctor."

"Why? What's wrong?" she asked, moving into the bathroom.

"I think Katharine's pregnant."

"*Great balls of fire!* Are you serious? Katharine's really pregnant?"

"Well, since the girl doesn't know how the birds and the bees work, I want the doctor to confirm it. But yeah, I think our best friend is going to have a baby."

"Ah geez," Katharine groaned. "Now the saucy twit is gonna start crying."

"I'm sorry. I can't help it. This is positively wonderful. And the best news we've had since they found that girl's body this morning."

Katharine sat upright. Michelle swung around bluntly. "*Nicole!*"

"What body?"

"Oh shit," Nicole croaked out and shrunk back.

"What girl's body?" Katharine demanded. "What are you talking about?"

"I better go call the doctor," Nicole muttered, turning.

"Freeze, Jarvis! Tell me what girl's body they found. And where?"

"I'm sorry. Mac wanted to tell you. It's another sixteen-year-old. At the groundbreaking this morning. I didn't mean to let it slip out and now if you're pregnant . . . oooh, K-Katharine, I'm so sorry. Mac's gonna be furious with me."

"Is it the same as the others?"

"Gage thinks so."

"Help me get dressed. I have to see for myself."

Michelle grabbed her arm. "No you don't. Nicole, dry your eyes and go call the doctor. Then call Mac and tell him what you did. Do not tell him why you did it. Katharine, the only place you're going is to the doctor."

"Callihan! Nobody tells me what to do."

"Katharine Dobarchon! You're white as a ghost and using the sink to support yourself. If you're pregnant, there's no way I'm letting you involve yourself in this murder. So help me, I'll call Mac myself and tell him what I suspect if you fight me on this."

Riled up and in no mood for any crap from either one of them, Michelle stood firm. Katharine wobbled slightly as she eyed her waiting for a reply.

"This is frightening, Michelle."

"What's frightening? Pregnancy is a natural part—"

"Michelle! The shock of your diagnosis comes from one scary fact. I was probably pregnant the day I almost died in the fire."

"*Omigod!* That's the most horrid thought you could ever have."

"You guys, I've been hurling for over a month. I never once considered I might be carrying Mac's baby. Fine, call the doctor. But don't call Mac. I understand why he wanted to tell me himself."

"That's more like it," Michelle said smugly. "Now lean on me and I'll help you into some clean clothes. Nicole, make us a doctor appointment. And you," she looked at Katharine, "stop thinking such awful thoughts."

"Katharine, I really am sorry," Nicole said. "My mouth is always getting me into trouble."

"You're right, but we still love you. Come here and give me a hug."

"I love you both and I really hope you are pregnant."

"Damn, if I'm gonna feel like shit for the next nine months, my doting husband won't have a heart or eyeballs left when this is over."

Michelle chuckled. "If you've been puking as long as you say, it's less than that. And wait til you get over the morning sickness and start craving the strangest combinations of food."

Katharine studied her. "How the hell would you know, Michelle?"

"Sylvie went through it both times with Shalee and Brendan."

When Nicole went to make the call, Michelle assisted Katharine into the bedroom for a change of clean clothes.

"Cough it up, Callihan. What gives?"

"About what?"

"Baines, Inc. I can tell something happened and it had nothing to do with the man liking Brian's Mustang."

Michelle finished tying Katharine's tennis shoes and plopped on the bed alongside her. "I was inside the Tavern spouting off to Nicole about him and his goons taking over the island when he walked in and heard everything I said."

"It couldn't have been that bad."

Nicole entered the room, confirming, "Oh it was bad all right, Katharine. She called him a money-grubbing rich bastard with a shitload of money. The earliest I could get you in was two o'clock. They told me to keep juices and fluids in you since you've been throwing up so much. Here, hon, try the seven-up and see if you can keep it down."

Katharine took the glass, sipped and studied Michelle. "You didn't really say all that, did you?"

"And then some," she replied, flushing miserably.

"He must have said or done something to upset you."

"He's there. I don't need anything else."

"So, he's not really an old man with one foot in the grave like you had hoped?"

Nicole eased in on the other side of Katharine, crossing her long shapely legs. Michelle wanted to wring her neck for bringing up the subject of Baines and blabbing anything about him.

"Katharine," Nicole sighed, "this guy might just be hotter than Mac."

"Not possible. Is he nice?"

"Beyond words. We had the opportunity to chat before Michelle arrived and poof," Nicole snapped her fingers. "Just like that I lost his complete attention."

"Bet that broke your heart," Katharine teased.

"Yeah, a little," Nicole confessed.

"This is ridiculous!" Michelle heaved herself upward. "Nicole, you're nuttier than a fruitcake! And I'm not talking about this anymore."

"I'm not crazy, Michelle. I know what I saw."

"Fine! Knock yourself out chasing after him. I'm not going back to the tavern until they're done destroying it!"

Katharine tapped Nicole's arm as she readied to spout off a response. They waited, watching Michelle wring her fingers together until her knuckles turned white. "What else happened, Michelle?"

"Nothing. I apologized and that was it."

"Michelle, I recognize fear at sixty paces. If Travis Baines didn't upset you, then cough up what really happened between you and Derek. Is there more than what you've told us?"

She bundled her arms tightly and stood in front of the window more annoyed than afraid now. "I'm not talking about something you both already know."

Katharine forced herself up, hung onto her equilibrium and slowly made her way toward Michelle. "Girlfriend, I'm a cop. Remember, I've always been able to tell when you weren't divulging everything to us."

Michelle whirled around. "You're also butting into something that I'm desperately trying to forget ever happened to me. Now back off and don't ever ask me about it again! You owe me that, Katharine." Her eyes jerked angrily. "You too, Nicole. And you can stop interfering in my love life. I don't have one and I don't want one. If you want that dipstick architect, he's all yours. As far as I'm concerned the man never existed."

Too weak to stop Michelle from bolting full speed out of the bedroom, Katharine stood in the middle of the room while Nicole hummed, "But you definitely need one, girlfriend."

CHAPTER 5

O F ALL THE places Travis went to in the world, he never had the opportunity to rent a genuine log home. The exposed beams, all-natural interior and Cathedral ceilings of this very secluded place conveyed a distinct ambiance he instantly liked. Two bedrooms down and a loft upstairs provided plenty of space to set up an office, too. Without further thought, he signed the rental agreement. He now recalled feeling seduced at the time of signing. As though he completely lost his ability to negotiate the weekly rate. With the peace this place offered, price didn't matter.

Dusk nearly done, he sat on the forty-foot ponderosa porch of the Pine Cove Retreat listening to an autumn breeze shovel slow-rolling waves against the rocky cliff. Raised on the East Coast Travis saw a million sunrises over the Atlantic. He rarely saw spectacular sunsets like the one that just dipped and scuttled quietly beneath the reddish-purple horizon moments ago. Kicking back after a drawn-out day, glittery stars now swam softly out of a royal blue sky. He thought there was magic here. Enchanting magic that quickly found a way to grip his mind and heart. It called out, tempted and controlled him in a way he had never experienced or expected. The powerful enchanting pull provided him with the same allurement of a sexual tug. And the same loneliness and confusion that welded together into one upsurge of devouring yearning. Regardless of the peacefulness, he found it all vaguely disturbing, glanced at his watch.

With the time difference between Boston and Madeline Island, his parents wouldn't call for a couple of hours. The first workday had been consumed with trouble. They lost three hours this morning with the groundbreaking and uncovering that girl's body. The Island's police chief saw to it that things were wrapped up quickly, and his faithful crew willingly worked late to make up for lost time. Drain tile, footings, foundation, sill plate and end joists were the first necessity. Once done, the framing could begin before the weather turned on them. An architect never ignored the charms of weather. But, if their luck held out this season, they would have several more weeks of this nice stuff. Told on numerous occasions Lake Superior could change at any moment alongside how cold a good Northeast wind could get here, the last thing he wanted was to be caught red-handed without a roof and walls. It would be merciless on his crews, too. He sincerely hoped tomorrow would be a more prosperous day.

Throughout the planning stages, he weighed the cost difference of having materials brought over intact against constructing roof trusses and the like on the island. As much as he wanted hands-on doing every part of the labor himself, cost and time beat out his personal desire. The trusses were being ferried over already intact. The best in the business had been retained to do the rest.

Savoring the taste of his Golden Gate Julep drink, Michelle Callihan's words played over in his mind now. After their morning conversation, he was content with his decisions. She would be just as satisfied as he was at the completion of this job. In spite of weather and shortened deadlines, the work would be done precisely to specs.

Travis drained his glass and lifted himself up, went inside. He couldn't erase Michelle's large and innocent emerald green eyes from his thoughts. Her outward appearance exposed potent strength and determination, but those haunting eyes hid fear and panic. He almost believed Michelle Callihan used humbleness to conceal the real emotion he observed. Distrust.

Although she and her friends had been through a lot, he doubted her suspicious nature was a result of finding a dead body.

Although grisly adequately described that poor girl his crew uncovered, once in a life was more than he cared to deal with it. He shuttered inwardly. How must those three women have felt alone on a deserted island upon the discovery of human sacrifice? Obviously scared, but he couldn't help wondering what other devastation had reduced Michelle to lack the faith she did in everyone. She couldn't possibly feel accountable for the murders, or hate him as much as she showed.

Refilling his glass from a pitcher of fresh-made julep, the ringing phone said his parents were home early. His mother had a wonderful voice, gentle and clear.

"Hi, honey. How'd the first day go?"

"Hi, Mom. Is Dad on the extension?"

"Right here, son."

"After several grueling hours of delay, the guys agreed to work a couple of extra hours."

"Why the delay?" his father asked.

"What happened, Travis?"

Affectionate concern and strength blossomed out of Rosemary Baines' words. "We found a young girl's body on the site. The police chief believes its related to the others."

"Is it going to halt the project more?"

"I don't believe it will, Dad. The police took statements from everyone as quickly as possible. La Pointe residents are as excited about the ballroom as I am. Any further stoppage will only increase the current anger. The police are doing everything they can to help the job run smoothly."

"Good. Is everything set with the classic truck you found?"

"It's in storage. Billy will make sure it's here when the time comes. Dad, he deserves a bonus for this one. It's a perfect match."

"Whatever you think is appropriate."

"Honey, what about the Callihan woman? Did you work things out with her?"

"Not at first. Mom, she has the same big green eyes I've told you about. They'll make you think you're gazing at priceless emeralds."

"Really?" she said with interesting surprise in the tone of her voice.

"Yes. And I've been anxious to tell you, Dad. She owns a vintage '69 'stang she's kept in mint condition. I can't wait for you to see it. The Apostle Islands and Madeline are everything you've both said and more. I just watched the most embracing sunset I've ever seen."

Phillip Baines chuckled quietly and told his son, "I'll be just as anxious to see her car, Travis, as I am to meet this woman. Your mother and I are leaving in the morning for Italy. You have our numbers if you need to get a hold of us for anything."

Travis nodded as if his parents could see him. "How are Grandma-ma and Grandfather? Did they make it to Florence without any problems?"

"Yes. Nor do they suspect a thing, honey. We'll make sure to keep it that way. Your father and I have told them you're off on another job and you would call them as soon as possible."

"I'll call after you arrive in Florence. Give them my love and enjoy Italy. You'll both think Florence splendid no matter what time of year it is."

Temperamental weather never hindered his parent's travel plans. The delays gave them an excuse to snuggle up in each other's company and thrive on seclusion from the outer world. For him, he'd take the weather over being stuck inside anytime.

"We will, honey."

"We love you, son."

"I love you both."

Travis disconnected. Heaviness centered in his chest like an old wound that ached on a rainy day. He frequently wondered why he was an only child when his parents loved each other more than they loved their own life. He sat in lonely silence ignoring the extraordinary void—been doing so for many years. But he couldn't let it pass tonight. Why was tonight different from any other? He shook his head regretfully.

"Because Baines, old man, all that love and family value your parents and grandparents provided for you has made you recognize your own needs."

He couldn't blame them for personal defeats. They did their job. They enlightened him to the qualities women preferred. So why was he still single. Bullheaded came to mind. So did his demanding ways, but then he didn't take over the business because his father was tired of working either. A successful business was important.

He owed those traits to the man who taught him the business—a business that had nothing to do with MBA's, PhD's and Bachelor of Architects but everything to do with distinction. Phillip Baines taught him the craft of dealing with people and pride of ownership. His father, after obtaining a well-deserved degree, founded Baines, Inc. from the ground up then built up a list of clientele who respected the name Baines for its moral qualities as well as its superior designs. Now semi-retired, Phillip Baines held a CEO position and had given his only child full command of the company. A company that carried its name proudly and stood for integrity and virtue. In the architectural business, Baines, Inc. maintained a pedigree of outstanding excellence the whole world recognized.

He would never do anything to destroy that, but then the business wasn't the problem. Recalling the first time he took an active interest in becoming an architect, both agreed not to change the name to father and son. Changing the name would not alter the blueprint of excellence above all the others in the business. The name had already established a reputation for outstanding values. The extreme quality of their designs always came first, but endorsing satisfaction with clients as well as within the company carried the utmost importance, too.

The cry of a loon distracted Travis. He neglected to turn the lights on inside, and a full white moon now illuminated the rooms of the rental. The surroundings corroborated his loneliness, which was where his problematic thoughts began—*there she was again.*

Travis picked up his drink and shuffled over to the door. He scanned the area in search of something he couldn't see. The crying woman who haunted his sleep wailed softly now with a Lake Superior breeze swaggering intimately in through the open windows. He peered out into the comfortless night, listening. Spears of white light streaked the blackened water beyond the cliff's edge. The crying stopped as quickly as it started and the persistent pierce in the middle of his chest had possession of him. He needed to figure out why as much as he had to unravel a repetitious dream with a mystified meaning.

When she cried out softly a second time, Travis whispered back, "Who are you milady and why do you weep so?"

CHAPTER 6

THE REDUNDANCY UNNERVED her. Michelle glanced in her rear view mirror as she drove away from the last Madeline Island proprietor. Though she couldn't prove what she couldn't see, each time she went from one client to the next she felt certain someone was following her.

"I'm headed for the loony bin," she told her reflection in the mirror when she looked again.

She trembled inwardly at the thought. She had seen too much, witnessed too much pain, but in the end, proved to herself that she was immune to everything. The rebuilding of her business was evidence of that. The owners of Madeline condo's and rental homes raved about her plans and designs. One by one, word had spread quickly and within two years of beginning Scenic Landscaping, she had signed contracts with all but one. Except for losing the Carriage House account when it burned to the ground in August, Josie Stewart's father, Bert Hanson, chose to do his own landscaping for Hanson's Inn. Michelle strongly suspected the animosity the three best friends had with Josie geared his decision.

It didn't matter. With the restructure of her business a year and a half ago, new contract terms and conditions included spring renewal, summer maintenance and fall cleanup. Now contemplating taking her business to the mainland meant hiring help for the growth. With more than a dozen business contracts an employee seemed to be the only answer. Those annoying lords of the lawn consumed the mounting hours. Unsightly to any garden, no matter how attractive the design, weeds controlled how much time she spent on landscape preservation. Pruning controlled the rest. Then there was the dominating spodosol soil. Very common to the cool, humid areas of the Great Lakes coast, Madeline Island's acidic soil, known as the dreaded red clay and sand, had low fertility.

It didn't help a few years back when they went through unusually warmer temps, and the working season extended itself. The prolonged warmer weather, along with the weird weather pattern changes took away from the winter break she gave herself each year. The entire country had been in a warm-up to the point Lake Superior had dropped ten inches. Some blamed it on global warming while others blamed it on the year of El Ni-ño. The fact was that changing topography since glaciers first formed the Great Lakes had actually forced the lake to rise causing new problems of land erosion. Now, the biggest complaint she heard lately was the increased population of deer. Deer made their way over via winter's frozen lake. The whitetails ate anything, especially in late winter and early spring. The annoying critters destroyed gardens and new growth of cedar, white pine and hemlock. Not to mention the way bucks stripped the bark off the trees. They rubbed the velvet growth between their antlers against the trunks to rid themselves of the skin and hair.

With a long exhausted sigh, Michelle thought forward to a much-needed winter break for the first time since the inception of Scenic Landscaping nearly ten years earlier. The off season would give her time to think. Not totally convinced to pay someone else to do manual labor, she had to be certain hiring an employee was the right choice. The work had to be faultless. She also needed to trust the person she hired and glanced in her rear view mirror once more on her drive to Mrs. Chernak's house. Saundra Chernak was her only residential contract. La Pointe folks preferred to plant their own property and those who needed guidance with designs and plans paid by the hour. Mrs. Chernak, who opted for a full contract, was the last reschedule from Monday. Her client would undoubtedly chatter on about the murdered sixteen-year-old girl, too. The other clients did. After four days of listening to nosy concerns, the weekend couldn't come fast enough. She'd curl up with a good novel and her orphaned cat, Keeker.

Michelle parked the car in front of the quaint Cape Cod. Actually, she mused, the house was plain and simple. The gable roof was the only part that gave it a Cape Code appearance. The wealthy woman thrust the screen door open.

"Watch out for the doggie do-do, Michelle, darling."

Michelle exited the Stanger and met her client half way. Mrs. Chernak was a woman whose presence exposed her privileged circumstances. Immaculate and preen in a fall pantsuit there wasn't anything artificial about Mrs. Chernak. Prominent cheekbones gracefully aided her aging process, as did her smooth skin. The good Lord had willingly handed over a sleek and sinewy figure as well, which gave Mrs. Chernak the appearance she was ten years younger than her age of sixty-three. Carefully applied make-up complimented the woman's blue-gray chignon and her elegant taste in minimal, yet priceless, jewelry. Widowed and childless, Saundra Chernak prevailed as Scenic Landscaping's happiest customer. The only distasteful thing about Mrs. Chernak was her fragrance abuse. Michelle believed the refined lady must have gallons shipped in just for bathing.

"Mrs. Chernak, thank you for being so patient this week," Michelle said, heeding the earlier warning to sidestep a fresh blob.

"Michelle, darling, you look worn out. You're working yourself way too hard like you did awhile back."

Her client's subtle hint was curiosity. She had a tacit response and recalled as a wedding gift, Saundra paid to have a horse and carriage brought up from North Carolina. She was insistent there was nothing like the Old South. Following her marital farce, Mrs. Chernak's alert greenish-blue eyes said she knew the divorce was rough. What her favorite customer didn't know was the marriage had been rougher. Scenic Landscaping's first customer lent an ear and did so only once when Michelle refused to discuss the subject. Mrs. Chernak never mentioned it again, until now.

"I am a little tired. I see Secunda's been running wild and free again."

"Adeline Girard must think I'm the heel of the Island. I know Gage is tired of my complaints, but that selfish pet of hers dug another hole in my backyard. I'm sure to bury bones from one of his latest trophies. That product you sprinkled around the plants the last time you were here didn't work. Secunda obviously can't smell and the unpleasant odor made me sick."

"Have you given anymore thought to a fence or planting a living barrier of uncomfortable shrubs to deter pets?"

"Fences are so unsightly. If I have to install one, I'd at least like it to compliment the style of my home. I can't seem to find anything."

"Perhaps you should speak to Katharine Dobarchon and see if she would draw a design for you. She's very good at seeing what others can't. Then you could have a fence specially made."

"Oh! Do you think she would do that for me? I hate to intrude on newlyweds especially now that she's pregnant."

Anxiety spurted through Michelle. She hadn't spoken to Katharine or Nicole since Monday, but the news of Katharine's pregnancy spread rapidly. She was delighted when Nicole left a message after the doctor's appointment to confirm Katharine was eight weeks along. Regardless, guilt overflowed inside of her for the way she yelled at her two best friends that day.

She swallowed and found her voice. "Katharine will go stir crazy cooped up through the winter. She might welcome something to do. I can talk to her if you'd like. If she agrees, we could have it done, shipped and ready for spring installation."

"Won't she and Mac be overwrought with the construction of their new house and preparing a room for the baby? Not to mention Mac and Gage are working on another murder. Land sakes this is horrible! Just horrible what's happening on the island."

And there it was, Michelle mused, shifting uncomfortably.

"Oh dear, now I've done it," Saundra clamored. "Dear child, we won't talk about that. Tell me how the construction is coming along over at the tavern instead. You were there for the groundbreaking."

Groundbreaking, Baines, Inc., being shot at, murdered young girls, La Pointe residents always watching, wondering about her divorce, and now the strangest feeling that someone was tailing her. Michelle couldn't take anymore. Her stomach ached again. Her eyes burned dryly from sleeplessness. She pressed two fingers to the bridge of her nose and inhaled. "Mrs. Chernak, I haven't been at the tavern since Monday. I don't know how the construction is going and right now I need to get to work on winterizing your yard."

"Darling, you're exhausted. I can see you haven't been sleeping well. Come inside and we'll have a cool glass of lemonade with some fresh baked sugar cookies. My yard can wait until next week since winter won't be along for some time."

"I doubt the meteorologists with their Doppler Radar would appreciate your prediction."

"Oh, pooh. I can give a better forecast just by looking out my window. The yard can wait. Now come inside and relax."

"But we've already had frost and that isn't good."

"Nonsense. You need your rest. Besides, it's unsaintly warm for working hard outdoors today. In fact," Saundra fanned her fingers in front of her face, "I'm overdressed."

Michelle lacked the strength to argue and followed her client inside. An hour later, and completely mellowed, she promised Mrs. Chernak extra visits at no charge for the inconvenience this week. She would head home after two more stops. She needed to apologize to Katharine and Nicole for blowing up on Monday. She would go to Katharine first, find a way to apologize then discuss drawing a fence for her chipper Southern Belle. Before she pulled away from the house, Michelle checked her rear-view mirror yet again. She saw no one, but the uneasiness loomed.

*   *   *

"I knew this wasn't over!" Mac exploded.

"I agree," Gage said. "Everything's identical to seven out of the nine victims. This one died from paraquat poisoning. The only two things we don't know are the location of the liquor bottle before Baines' men started working and the name of the victim. Where do we go from here, considering?"

"Considering that Patriot is dead?"

Gage nodded.

"We go with Katharine's theory that Patriot was working with someone. I don't believe he was a copycat."

"What about a cult?"

"That's too organized, there would be more involved. I contacted Cole to let him know. He'll talk to the Profiler and return to assist us since this appears to be related to the Green Bay case. The captain gave him the go ahead."

"He's coming here?"

"Uh-huh. Why?"

"No reason," Gage muttered. "You're keeping Katharine out of this, aren't you?"

"She didn't like it, but yeah I ordered her to stay out. I told her I'd cuff her to the bed every morning before I left if she sets foot anywhere near the station or the case."

"Did she haul off and slug you?"

"She tried. I'm bigger."

"I can't believe my little sister is having a baby or that I'll be an uncle."

"You know, for the first time in my life, I do not want to work a homicide. I want to be home with my wife."

Gage stood, filled his mug with old coffee and drained the pot in Mac's cup. "Then let's go nail ourselves a killer and close this case fast. I've been giving our deadly chemical, paraquat, my full attention since Monday."

"And?"

"Remember how we once thought Patriot might have been spraying marijuana plants with it?"

"Yeah."

"I checked further and found out that paraquat is used by the highway departments to kill roadside weeds."

"Here on Madeline?" Mac asked.

"Nada. More on freeway systems and single lane highways."

"So?"

"Guess where Curt Stewart works," Gage said.

"Highway department."

"Actually, Ashland county, but same difference since its road construction. So I checked."

"And they use paraquat."

Gage nodded.

"I don't know. Curt was stunned the day Katharine and I questioned him. And his alibis did check out."

"Do you really believe it's coincidental that Curt works for Ashland County and they've had two reported paraquat thefts in three-gallon increments in the past three years with the dead bodies turning up here?"

"What I believe is that's a whole lot of premeditation."

"It's never been recovered either."

"Did they suspect Curt Stewart?"

"They had no reason to."

"An outside job?"

"Don't know," Gage said.

"There's just one problem with your theory," Mac said.

"What's that?"

"Ashland County is a helluva long way from Green Bay."

"Keep one crime far away from the real crime, which leads me to one other individual."

"Sibling Kevin."

Gage nodded. "The questions, Mac, are did Kevin really know David Patriot? If so, how? When did they meet? Where? How was Kevin Stewart able to steal this chemical? Did he steal it for Patriot"

"He could've had a copy of his brother's key made."

"Aren't county keys marked 'do not copy'?"

"I never have liked him since I saw him put his hand on Katharine," Mac said, standing. "Let's go roust the sonovabitch and find out. After all, he did lie about never having been to Green Bay."

"Wait a minute. When did he lay a hand on my sister?"

"The first night we had dinner together at the Tavern."

"You told me he harassed her."

"She dropped him to his knees," he said, recalling the incident. "I stepped in when he started mouthing off to Nicole. Told him what I'd do to the nerves in his body if he didn't leave."

"Nobody messes with my sister or her friends!"

"So, you wanna be good cop or bad cop?"

"Bad cop!" Gage spit ruthlessly.

CHAPTER 7

LOVE AND PREGNANCY agreed with Katharine. Michelle never saw her looking more radiant or happier in their entire lives. The baby was due in the spring. The newlyweds had hoped the house construction would be complete before Thanksgiving, but it was moving slowly. At the mention of drawing a fence for Mrs. Chernak, Katharine's interest increased and Michelle passed along Saundra's phone number.

Upon expressing her regret for Monday's explosion, Katharine played cop and interrogated her. Michelle avoided a reply to the questions, but left with their friendship intact. The answers were unimportant and belonged in a past she wanted to forget ever existed. Now, as she drove to the tavern to beg Nicole's forgiveness, annoying apprehension swept through her gut.

She quick-checked her rear-view mirror once more and gasped. "*Omigod!* He's back!"

Her heart thrashed savagely inside her chest with the unforgotten horror. Michelle slammed the brakes. The red car behind hers stopped just as suddenly, turned around then peeled off in the opposite direction. Sucking the life out of the air around her, Michelle gunned the blue Mustang in the direction of the Tavern. The tires screeched loudly rounding the corner onto Red Rock Road. Braking hard a second time, the car skidded to a stop and Michelle jumped out, bolting toward the tavern's entrance.

"Michelle!" Travis yelled and jaunted over to the car she left running with the door standing open.

"Nicole! He's back!" Michelle yelled frantically inside the tavern.

Customers in the middle of conversations stopped, sat up, peered curiously. Some stood quickly with an interest in the disturbance. Nicole rushed out from the kitchen. "What is it? Michelle, what's wrong?"

Her hands clenched into fists, her breathing still rugged, she exclaimed, "Nicole, he's come back! I saw him. He was following me. He's back!"

"Hon, take a deep breath and tell me what happened. Who's back?"

"Derek! He's come back."

"Great balls of fire! Hayden, get me a brandy. Quick!"

Nicole wrapped an arm around her and steered her into the dining room. She guided her to a corner table nudging her onto a chair then yanked out a second to sit beside her.

"Michelle, calm down. Take a deep breath then tell me what happened."

Her fingers twisted together tightly. She grabbed the snifter Hayden set on the table and guzzled the brandy in one gulp. Her insides heated instantly. She tried to speak, but her voice wavered. Agony swam neurotically through her body and Nicole embraced her shoulders a second time.

"Hon, what happened?"

She spewed out, "I've spent the last four days finishing up my fall clean-up with the inns. For the past two, I've felt like someone was following me—*especially today*. I just left Katharine's and was on my way over here to apologize to you for blowing up on Monday. That's when I saw him. He was driving behind me. Nicole, Derek's been following me. I stopped, but he turned around and drove away fast."

Her voice broke, and she cried, "Oh, God, Nicole! I can't go through this again. He took everything including my dignity."

Hugging her tight, Nicole whispered, "Hon, we're not gonna

let anything happen to you ever again. You're safe and you're staying with me tonight. You've got keys and can go to my place now."

"I can't," she said in a choked voice. "I'm too scared to be alone right now."

"You can hang out here, but I've got the late shift tonight. I'm gonna go call Gage and Mac."

"No!" Michelle screeched, clawing at Nicole's arm. "You can't tell them. What will they think?"

"Listen to me," she ordered, taking Michelle's trembling fingers. "Mac and Gage won't think badly of you. Nobody will. You never deserved this and I should have made Frank take care of Derek a long time ago. Michelle, we all love you, Gage and Mac included. Nobody blames you for what happened."

She forced herself to settle down and replied in a suffocated whisper. "Nicole, you can't tell my parents."

"I won't."

"They think the divorce was my fault because I wasn't a good wife. That I failed at my spousal duty. They'll insist I go back to him. Promise me you won't tell them."

Hugging her again, Nicole murmured, "I promise, honey. I'll never breathe a word."

Lovely, delicate, perfect, he thought. And scared to death. Travis hung back watching and listening. Michelle never saw or heard him when he called out to her in the parking lot. What had her ex done to cause so much fear he wondered. What did she mean he took everything? How did an ex husband strip her of dignity? He didn't know how to interrupt, or if he should. When she left the Mustang running, he shut it off and removed the keys. Now he didn't have to. She stopped squeezing her eyes shut. They popped open and she tossed a hate-filled glare at him.

"*You!* Do you always lurk and listen in where you don't belong?"

"No. I wasn't—I didn't mean to. You left the keys in the 'stang with the engine running."

"I'm sorry," Michelle muttered hastily.

"So am I, Michelle," he said quietly, handing her the keys. Reversing direction, he walked out of the tavern.

"Listen," Nicole said, standing. "I have to get back to work. The dinner activity has died down so sit as long as you like. I'll bring you a menu and you can order something when you're ready."

Michelle nodded and modified her position, tucking one leg under the other. After several moments, she stood. She needed to walk, and meandered through the lounge to the dance area and sat near the back windows to watch a dozen crewmembers in plain view working diligently. Cement flowed swiftly pouring the beginnings of the foundation. Right alongside the hired hands, Baines was in the middle. That surprised her—thought he was more the type to bark out orders while others labored like slaves.

Travis and others smoothed the fill the cement mixer dumped. Another hardhat controlled the flow of concrete into the footings. Maybe she *had* underestimated Baines. Intrigued, Michelle stood and went outside to watch. The general contractor approached and handed over a hardhat.

"Put it on," he yelled over the groan of the cement mixer.

Michelle did, staying out of everyone's way. Each man had a job to do yet all worked together. Some had removed their shirts, including Baines, and their backs were tanning in the fall heat and sunshine. Muscles moved symmetrically under skin glistening with sweat that drained directly from brawn.

She moved over to the construction trailer. Blue prints were in plain sight on a table set up outside. Curiosity forced her to flip through the pages, but after several, she began to study them with heightened interest. The initials T.P.C.B. were scrawled on the bottom right. She and Travis Baines had more in common than she cared to admit. She wondered what the P and C stood for and why he had two middle names.

When she came to the interior floor plan, she merely stared at the paper. Gifted with the ability to visualize a birds-eye view of any set of plans, the add-on would enlarge the dining area and increase the size of the kitchen. The lounge and old banquet room would remain the same. An additional smaller bar would service the new ballroom. The awakening experience left her reeling. Michelle flipped back through the bluish-white pages until she found the outside design again. Her breath caught in her throat. He hadn't lied. The tavern's appearance would remain identical to its present appearance.

"Does it meet with your approval?"

She whirled around and felt her face flame hot. With a hardhat secured between his bare chest and arm, the golden hair on his arm was lighter than his sweat-drenched head. Gray cement flecks covered all of him. Oddly, a fascinating sparkle radiated from his gray-blue eyes. "Travis, these are wonderful! I didn't know you did them yourself. I mean, assuming you are T-P-C-B."

He nodded. "The P is for Phillip after my father. The C is for Cadotte after my grandmother as in Julia Cadotte."

"Cadotte? She can't be your grandmother! You can't be related! It's not possible—*she died*. Baby Julia was—" her voice broke off in mid sentence. She was helpless to halt her embarrassment and removed the hardhat before it fell off her head.

"Anything is possible," he said, smiling. "Julia Cadotte Perry is indeed my grandmother on my mother's side and she is very much alive."

Michelle fell silent. She thought about the plaque near the tavern's entrance. The original building was constructed in the late 1800's. It was a memorial to Chief White Crane and Michel Cadotte's granddaughter Julia Warren. The only *plausible* explanation was the name Julia had been passed down through the generations. Her face flushed more with humiliation. Why didn't she check *his* background?

"Travis, I'm sorry. I didn't know you were related, but it certainly does explain a few things. You must think I'm an idiot."

"What I think, is that we spend entirely too much time apologizing. But I also enjoy the way you protect my ancestors. If you'll have dinner with me inside I'll explain everything, including the reason I'm here."

"*No!* Thank you."

He took the hardhat from her hands. "Michelle, I admit I overheard you inside with Nicole and I apologize for that, but this is just dinner."

Nowhere to go until Nicole finished her evening shift, what could it hurt? "I'll buy mine and you can buy yours," she answered too quickly.

"Deal," he said, smiling. "Just give me a minute to remove a layer of cement. I'll be right back."

Just as he swung the door of the trailer open, they both glanced skyward then at each other when a moan whispered nigh on a breeze.

CHAPTER 8

"HOPE YOU DON'T mind work clothes. My others are back at the Pine Cove Retreat."

Michelle smelled soap when Travis jumped out of the trailer wearing a clean t-shirt and faded jeans. He did more than wash up as noticeable by his hair. The damp mounds of layered waves reminded her of nutmeg. The expression in his pearl gray eyes seemed to plead for friendship. He hadn't bothered with a razor and she wondered how often he wore the bristly-guy facade at the office. Strong bones made his face interestingly worn. As much as she hated to admit it, Nicole was right. Baines looked ruggedly handsome in a kind-hearted way. A pair of loafers put his large effective stance several inches above her height. His hands weren't office smooth either like the executive she had him pegged for. They were ironbound and sturdy—she stopped. "I'm sorry. What did you say?"

"Do you mind my attire? Is it okay for dinner?"

"No—I mean yes."

"Well, which is it?" he asked, chuckling.

"It's fine. The Tavern is known for casual and informal," she said, annoyed with herself for checking him out.

"Good, then let's go."

As they walked, Travis asked, "Were you really able to read those blueprints?"

"Yup. Not nearly as professional as yours, but I need to be able to design for my landscaping business."

"I'm curious," he said, directing her towards the entrance. "Do you actually do blueprints like we do in the architect business?"

"Some landscapers do. I wimped out and am afraid to admit I rely on computer software programs. Others prefer freehand and paper. My expertise is with numbers rather than drawing the lines."

"Footage and yardage I bet, giving you a very profitable business."

She stopped suddenly. "You investigated my business?"

"Of course. You and everyone on the Town Board. Admittedly, what I learned about you was the first of many surprises."

Nervousness spilled over. Had he learned how she nearly faced bankruptcy? She assumed he did background checks on all of them—it was fair turnaround—*but on her business?* She continued toward the entrance and he opened the door letting her proceed.

"Tell me about your numerical expertise," he said.

It took extra effort to face him, but Michelle did. Tenderness flowed out of his gray eyes with a gleam of interest she didn't want to acknowledge. "I was always a whiz at math," she said entering the tavern. "I can get square footage, diameter and circumference faster than most using a calculator. Katharine is the artist. Travis, you should see her sketches. They're so life-like and filled with such emotion. I don't know how she does it."

"If her sketches are all it takes for you to suddenly spill over with life, I'd like to see them sometime."

"There you are! Michelle, I've been frantically looking for you."

"She was outside with me," Travis replied. "It seems that my opposition has taken an active interest in my construction site."

"Really? Then I must let you in on a little secret. If Michelle was snooping around, you have her undivided attention."

Michelle toasted Nicole with a glare-filled expression.

"Thanks for the advice. I'll take her interest any way I can get it. I want her thinking my way."

As the two shared a laugh, Michelle muttered, "If you keep

talking about me like I'm not here, you'll lose my attention just as fast."

"Too late," Travis told her. "The look in your eyes says you're hooked. Nicole, we'd appreciate it if you could seat us at a quiet table."

"I'll do that." She winked conspiratorially. "I just need to talk to Michelle privately. It'll only take a moment. Would you mind?"

"Not at all."

When Nicole nudged her to a corner, Michelle said, "I see what you're concoct—"

"Listen, hon. I called over to the station and talked to Mac."

"I wish you wouldn't have done that when I told you not to."

"Michelle, I love you too much to let anything happen to you again. Mac said if Derek does anything you're to call immediately and they'll handle it discreetly. He also told me that unless Derek does do something, he's pretty much free to roam the island."

"Fine. Now that you've wasted your breath, is that it?"

"Just one last thing."

"What?"

"I'm glad you're giving Travis a chance."

"I'm not."

"He really is a nice man and entirely too hot for words. Now let's go find a table where you can sit back and relax in his company. Then you'll spend the night with me."

"Wishing for my heart to change is a moot point, Nicole"

"I don't think so, girlfriend. Follow me," she said, gliding away.

"One giant hormone with only one thing on her mind," Michelle grumbled then followed the saucy twit who was already out of earshot. *I must be crazy! The tavern is where I met Derek. This is a mistake, but I have no other safe place to go right now.*

"Travis, with the tourist season over things won't be busy in here tonight. I'll keep you and Michelle out of the flow of traffic."

Travis acknowledged with a smile and nod, waited for Michelle then followed both women.

"Here we go. This corner will be quiet. The server will be over shortly with menus. Enjoy your meal."

"Thanks, Nicole. I'm sure we will," Travis replied.

Michelle plopped down with her back to a wall before Travis could assist her. He slid onto a chair opposite and watched her. Who wouldn't the way she fidgeted nervously? Hitching her hair behind one ear, she wondered what was going through his mind. As the waitress approached their table, enchantment for Baines blazed out of the girl's eyes.

"Would you like a drink?" Travis asked before the waitress did.

Michelle shook her head and made introductions. "Beth, this is Travis Baines. Travis, this is Beth Johnson. And I'll take a Pepsi, please."

"Hi, Beth. Nice to meet you. I'd like a Golden Gate Julep if you can stir one up."

A speechless Beth regained her composure, but not her natural color. "Would you like your julep with grenadine or maraschino cherry juice?"

"Maraschino, please."

"Do you prefer lemon or lime juice in that?"

"Lemon. Tell us, Beth. What do you recommend off the menu?"

"My personal favorite is the chicken penne pasta. Our special today is broiled or pan fried scallops. I'll have Hayden fix the drink to your liking, Mr. Baines, and bring Michelle her Pepsi. I'll be right back with your drinks."

"You were testing her," Michelle said when Beth escaped poise re-intact.

"Yes, you could say that. I didn't acquire my status by making assumptions about anything or anyone. I'm not perfect either, but I do strive for perfection. The only way to achieve success is to ask questions, or as you say 'test' people."

Interesting Michelle mused. She once felt that way until her emotions were deadened to complete erasure. "So what else is in that?"

"What?"

"Your drink. What's in it?"

"It's non-alcoholic. Pineapple, lemon or lime and orange juice with either grenadine or maraschino cherry juice. Alcohol inhibits my mind and clouds my brain."

"Then you don't drink?"

"I've been known to toss back a few, but I like being in total control." Glancing around the restaurant, he said, "Nicole is very good at what she does here. I've yet to be disappointed with the service or the professionalism of her staff."

"And I bet you had her checked out as well."

He chuckled. "You'd win that one. I found everything to be above the standard acceptance as you just witnessed. She trains them very well."

Michelle hid her excitement. She and Katharine were just as thrilled with Nicole's success. Starting as a waitress in the bar and then the restaurant, Ted saw Nicole's potential. He sent her off to training seminars upon promoting her to manager several years ago.

"You're right. She truly loves what she does. In fact, she's adamant about the subject. It's almost like this is her own child and no one dare to criticize it."

Travis leaned back in the chair. "You're pretty amazing yourself."

"What makes you say that?"

"With your own share of heartache you make it very clear you don't begrudge your friend's their happiness."

Stirring uneasily in the chair, she said, "Travis—"

"You also have the most amazingly brilliant green eyes I've ever seen. They change shades with your moods, but they're always smaragdine, the other name for emeralds."

And he was in love with them. And her flesh. He wanted to caress the satiny gold he dreamt of—

"We were talking about Nicole," Michelle huffed.

Travis cleared his throat. "That's quite a trio of friends. Katharine the artist and protector, Nicole the congenial one in the social and business world, and you, lover and defender of land and heritage."

Too surprised to do more than nod, Michelle wondered how

he had figured them out that quickly. Finally asked, "You've met Katharine already?"

"She showed up here earlier this week looking for her husband. No offense, I liked her immediately. But Mac's got his hands full with that one."

"Indeed, you've met Katharine."

Beth returned with their drinks and took their order. When Travis leaned forward casually propping his elbows on the table, Michelle leaned back in her chair. A probing query came into his eyes and she immediately felt awful. If her life had been normal, she wouldn't have reacted or thought anything of his gesture. "I'm sor—"

Waving her off, he asked, "Tell me, do you come from a large family?"

New flutters swept through her. She hadn't thought about that specific weekend in long time as it came back to mind in vivid color. And not a natural liar, another pang of guilt seared her thoughts. Tasting her Pepsi, Michelle quietly said, "Travis, I wasn't entirely honest with you before."

He stared back in waiting silence.

"I didn't really save up to buy the Mustang. It belonged to my brother, Brian, who died in a boating accident on Superior when he was eighteen. Brian always said the color of the Stanger reminded him of jeweled stones. It was his pride and joy. He loved that car. I wanted it, knowing I could keep his memory alive by maintaining its condition. I'll never part with it."

Nope, Travis thought, it wasn't just her eyes. He was in love with all of her. He knew it Monday when he first spotted her. Now he understood the line he'd heard all through life, when you meet her you just know. He realized instantly of the need to tread lightly in order to convince Michelle Callihan of the same.

"Travis?" Michelle queried.

"I'm sorry," he said, recovering. "Truly sorry for your family's loss and my greed. I liked the car the minute I saw it. Was Brian older or younger than you?"

"Brian was the oldest. I have a younger sister, Sylvie who lives in Bayfield with her husband and their two little dumplings, Shalee and Brendan. The kids love spending a weekend at Auntie Michelle's house because I get to spoil them rotten."

"Really? How do you do that?"

His face and eyes lit up like the Northern Lights so prominent in the area. Creases around the corners of his mouth added to the now obvious rugged charm Nicole talked about. "Kids are easy to please. They love taking the ferry over from Bayfield. We bake cookies and swim at the beach. I let them stay up late watching videos and eating popcorn. They love playing with Keeker." Michelle chuckled, thinking about it. "Although I'm not so sure he feels the same about them."

"Who's Keeker?"

"My cat. I found him on the roadside one day. He was drenched and quivering. Practically starving. Nobody claimed him so I kept him."

Travis lifted his glass to sample the drink and set it down. "I bet you always have some small toy wrapped and ready for the kids and Keeker."

"Yes. How'd you—"

"Ahh, Michelle. You have the makings for a wonderful mother."

"That won't happen. One marriage is enough and the subject is not on the table for discussion. Tell me about your family."

"I'm an only child which doesn't make a lot of sense to me."

"Why's that?"

"My parents are very much in love. I always thought they'd have more. I once had hopes for a brother or a sister."

He leaned back in his chair, his voice lowering. Emotion played with his face until traces of despair snuck into his hardening features. Had Michelle not been apathetic she might have understood the difference between having lost versus never having.

"My parents love me just as much," he said after a moment. "A day never passes that they don't express their affection. I feel the same about them and my grandparents. Family is very important."

But *their* love's not the same Michelle silently filled in, wondering if Travis knew how the sound of his voice tainted his words. Their meals delivered, she said, "Tell me about your grandmother, Julia."

His face brightened and the already familiar, wide grin returned.

"Grandma-ma. She's a vivacious, high-spirited woman who doesn't take crap from anyone except my grandfather. I would imagine it's because she wants him to think he's in control. That aside, they fell in love the night they danced in the Red Rock Tavern ballroom. Grandma-ma loves dancing. She speaks frequently of the evening. She says the moment she fell in love, she chased grandfather until he caught her."

Michelle swallowed the food in her mouth fast before she choked. "What a priceless thing to say. But Travis, the ballroom burned down many years ago."

"I know. Their fiftieth wedding anniversary is in four months. I want to give them something with meaning."

He toyed with his food and Michelle waited, sensing there was so much more he wanted to say.

"It began three years ago upon discovering myself at a crossroads. The business was doing well. I'd been everywhere, done everything and still I lacked fulfillment. Of what I had no idea. Then things started to happen and for awhile I thought I was going crazy."

Michelle wondered why, but kept silent.

"I started working harder. So many hours Mother and Grandma-ma were worried. Their voices clearly exposed their concern. The only times in my life that they reprimand me are when they fear for my health or safety. One night, working late in the office, the birth of this idea became clear. I'd been hearing about the Apostles and Madeline Island all of my life from my mother. Grandma-ma also speaks avidly of the area and is a distant descendant to Michel Cadotte, Sr. Four greats to me they've said. Her maiden name is Cadotte and Michel Cadotte, Jr. was her great-grandfather. He built the Red Rock Tavern, which did include a ballroom. With both my grandparents having strong affections for dancing, their first date was in that ballroom. Both tell the same story of how he took her to the ball in a 1934 cabriolet he saved every penny to buy then through bad fate, lost his prized possession. I finally located the classic car at Bayfield's car show last—" He stopped. "I should say, after a lengthy search I located it before last weekend. The cabriolet and the ballroom are my gift to them. Since the burned down ballroom was never reconstructed, I've done some tweaking and redesigned it as closely to the exact specs as possible. So you tell me, what better way to celebrate fifty years of wedded bliss than to recreate the duplicate night their lives came together."

A wad of something stuck in Michelle's throat and her response came out in a hoarse whisper. "Oh, Travis."

"Now you understand how Grandma-ma was Julia Cadotte until she married Ronson Perry. Her father was Joe Cadotte and son to John who was son to Michel Cadotte, Jr. Joe named my grandma-ma after Julia Warren who died at the age of five months. Joe Cadotte is also the individual who re-built the second Red Rock Tavern after the first one burned down. But they never reconstructed the ballroom with it."

If she thought she was a four-star asshole a few days ago, the number just doubled. Not to mention, the tears she let turn to stone wanted freedom. More astounding was the fact that she suddenly felt a sense of new fulfillment. Michelle gulped hard. "Travis, why did you originally want to build a mall here when you are part of the history and ancestry?"

He laid his fork down and took another drink of his julep. "The idea of recreating the ballroom didn't come to me at first. I wanted something here for Grandma-ma. I just didn't know what. That's why I sent Billy Abbott. After his first trip, I realized the mall was all wrong. I know it didn't seem like it at the time, but I'm very grateful for your convictions and Billy Abbott's thoroughness. He discovered the car I'd spent three years searching every continent for, and adequately informed me of your strong objections. I'm not here to destroy what already is. I'm here to adjoin history to an old memory for grandparents I'm deeply fond of. I never really wanted to change what is, I wanted to add to it."

"Why didn't you just tell me—the Board, this in the beginning?"

"It was personal. I don't normally mix business with pleasure. Besides, I enjoyed dealing with your spunkiness. Grandma-ma will love you when she meets you. For that matter, my parents will, too. I plan to have a grand celebration here for their anniversary. Nicole has been very kind in preparing the details."

"Nicole? She knows your reason for building the ballroom?"

"Only that there's to be a fiftieth wedding anniversary party. The history doesn't seem to fascinate her the way it does you."

"What about your father? Is he from here as well?"

"My father knows nothing of his past. He had no parents or siblings and spent his life being bounced around the foster care system in Minnesota. He made up his mind to do something with his life and went to college where he met my mother, Rosemary. They married after graduation and had me the following year. I was born in Superior before they moved to the East Coast. It was the place to be in the architectural business. Then he started the company and made a name for himself."

Michelle leaned back in the chair. "Well. You certainly know how to make a girl feel stupid. Travis, I'm not only sorry you overheard me blowing off steam Monday. I'm sincerely apologizing for what I said."

Oh yeah! Most definitely, he was in love with her. "You aren't to blame completely."

"I should hope not, but had I not been . . . never mind."

"Michelle, anyone can recognize their mistakes. Those who have the courage to admit to them are born winners. I should have told you. I wouldn't be bending over backwards to beat the weather clock now if I had."

"Ted getting shot prolonged the situation more for you. What can I do to help move this along?"

"You're good on a computer, right?"

"Yes."

"We need someone to oversee building materials and scheduling. Make sure they're right, delivered on time and not damaged. You could work from the trailer. We're set up with fax, extra phone lines, internet capability, the whole works. You'd be working with Jerry, the general contractor, subcontractors, engineers and me. You'd make sure the plumbers and electricians and other subcontractors are here on time."

"Travis, I don't know a thing about building materials or construction."

"Everything's detailed explicitly. I'll teach you the difference between 2x4's and 2x6's, explain a floor joist and a wall stud, and show you a truss versus a gable. It will save us a lot of time if the materials are here when needed as well as the subs. It'll also eliminate the potential for cost overruns. If you're available tomorrow, I'll show you how we operate."

Watching him curiously, she decided the man certainly didn't waste time. Though he seemed to have a lot of confidence in her no matter how incapable she felt, she suspected she walked right into a setup. Her vow not to become involved shattered. At last, she had strong urges to be a part of this project and a happy feeling soared deeply into her soul. "I have one contract appointment on Wednesday. Otherwise, my calendar is clear. Tomorrow would be good."

"Great. Then it's all set, Michelle. You're going to be involved in adding to the history you're so fond of. There's one more thing I'd like to learn."

"What's that?"

"What do you like to do for fun when you aren't working? You know, relaxation."

"Old movies. Katharine Hepburn. I love Cary Grant in *The Bachelor and the Bobbysoxer.* 'I once knew a man.'"

"'What sort of a man?'"

"'A man with a . . .'" Michelle stopped. "You know it?"

He nodded.

"I love watching Cary Grant fall in love while trying to bail himself out of the mess he gets into with the judge's little sister. I laugh wholeheartedly when he's conned into those races during the picnic with the guy who already has the hots for the judge. I haven't seen that movie in a long time. I've started rebuilding my collection—"

Her mouth twitched with the memory. The lively excitement she felt quickly plunged. Panic replaced her exuberance. Michelle fought the internal struggle to keep her pained emotions in check.

"Milady, what is it? What's wrong?"

"Nothing," she said, rotating a piece of silverware in her hand.

"Michelle, I'm not going to hurt you. Please, talk to me."

A loud argument coming from the Tavern's entrance distracted both of them. Michelle looked around Travis when he turned to see.

She whispered, "*Omigod. It's him.*"

Travis looked back at her then stood. "Wait here."

In long strides, he skirted tables through the empty dining room to the entrance. Nicole was toe to toe with two men who'd made their way to the bottom of a whiskey bottle.

"Is everything okay?" Travis asked.

"Kevin, I've had it with you coming in here every night causing trouble. And Derek, you're not welcome in the tavern much less on the island."

"You can't refuse me service!"

"I can do anything I want. Both of you get out of here now."

"I'm not going anywhere until I talk to Michelle."

"Michelle wants nothing to do with you," Nicole informed him.

"I'm not leaving until I talk to my wife!"

"She's not your wife anymore!"

"The hell she ain't, bitch!"

"The hell she is." Nicole ripped back. "Leave now or I'm calling the police."

"Why you—"

Travis was quick. He grabbed the guy's arm, thrust him into the wall and snarled. "Don't even think it."

"What's going on here, Nicole?"

"Mac, you already know Kevin Stewart. That's Derek Gunderson," she pointed accusingly. "They've been in here drinking whiskey and getting too loud for the crowd. I've asked them both to leave nicely. Now I'm demanding they leave."

"Why's Travis got him pinned against the wall?"

"He started to come at me and Travis intervened."

"Nicole, you want him arrested for threats with the intent to assault?" Mac asked.

"I never touched the bitch! You can't arrest me!"

"Listen here punk. You threatened her—"

"And I'm a witness," Travis growled, keeping the slimy bastard who hurt Michelle nailed to the wall.

"And she can have you arrested," Mac informed him then gave the Stewart brother a hardball gaze. "I'd be very willing to oblige her and book you for the night. Any threat is also entitled to a restraining order forbidding both of you on the property."

"I didn't threaten her!"

"Maybe not tonight, Kevin. Have you forgotten about our little run-in awhile back?"

"No sir. Haven't forgotten your visit the other day either."

"Nicole, it's your call," Mac said.

She shook her head. "Just usher them both out."

"You sure?"

She nodded.

"Well, boys this is your lucky night. I'm strongly suggesting you both go home and sleep off your drunken binge."

Travis loosened his grip and they hurried out without another word.

"Nicole, call me if they come back. One warning's all they get. Where's Michelle?"

"In the dining room. We were having dinner," Travis answered.

"Thanks for your help, Travis. Go on back—" Nicole stopped, turned and looked into the lounge when another argument ensued. "It's Friday night and that's Josie and Curt at it again. They've been slugging back beer all night and ripping each other's throats out. Thank God we're only open for another hour."

When Mac followed Nicole into the bar to resolve the escalating quarrel, Travis headed back to Michelle. He'd fought off another need when Gunderson went for Nicole's throat. More disturbing than that were his thoughts about the violence he observed in Gunderson's eyes. No wonder Michelle lived in fear. He didn't have to imagine for very long the hell she must have endured during the marriage. What he wanted just got tougher and he thought of his grandma-ma. She'd been telling him for years he had a voice as smooth as silk and could talk the devil into going to church. This venture was going to take more than smooth talk, and right now, he had no idea how to proceed.

He stopped at the table expressionless to his thoughts. Michelle's eyes were big and round and anxious. Ever so beautiful.

"Is he gone?"

"They're gone," he reassured, sitting down.

"They? Who else was out there?"

"Some guy named Stewart."

"Kevin Stewart. They hung out together. This is awkward and I don't want to talk about it. It's humiliating . . ."

"I know, Milady."

She swiped back a tear from the corner of her eye. Everything about her made everything Travis did automatic, effortless. He re-stood, took a step then stopped when she drew back. Instead of lifting her into his arms for comfort, he stepped back.

"Michelle, you don't have to talk until you're ready. But you must know, I'll never hurt you."

CHAPTER 9

"GAGE, WHAT DO you know about Derek Gunderson?"

"Not a lot. He was married to Michelle for less than a year before they divorced. I didn't know the reason for the divorce until Katharine told me. He's not from around here. Why, Mac?"

"You see the logs from Friday night? The call to the Tavern? He and Kevin were giving Nicole a hard time. Baines had him pinned against the wall when I got there."

"Yah. I read it along with the dispute between Curt and Josie. I've told Nikki to sign a complaint so we can do something with those drunks."

"I'll see if I can work on her. Did you get copies of Ashland's theft reports?"

"Right here." Gage picked them out of a pile, handing them over.

Mac scanned the one-page reports hastily. "According to these, the thefts happened in broad daylight."

"You sound surprised."

"Pretty risky taking three gallons of paraquat out of a County garage in the daytime, don't you think?"

"I'm more surprised there was no forced entry. It still tells me someone had keys since the doors are always locked. Mac, there's something else that's bugging me."

"What's that?"

"Some of the characteristics of a psychotic serial killer. For one, Patriot was never hospitalized."

"Yeah, I had the same question awhile back. The Profiler told us if Patriot was having delusions, he would have to show signs of harming himself before they'd lock him up. But having delusions didn't necessarily mean he would inflict injury on himself."

"Can this Profiler be wrong?"

"Anything's possible. However, she had too many things right about his childhood without knowing who he was."

"What about her notations here about wanting domination, manipulation and control over others? You never did find anyone who actually knew him except his mother. Did she ever notice any unusual behavior?"

"To some degree. The mother was sympathetic because of the abuse he received from his father."

"Was the mother abused?" Gage asked.

"Never admitted to it, but I'm inclined to think so. Gage, I agree there's some fault in the Profiler's assessment and asked Patriot's mother if she ever thought he heard voices. She flat out denied it. Most likely out of protection. But other things don't jive either, like the complex motives that are supposed to make finding him difficult. The guy left a print at the scene of my niece's homicide . . ."

Mac believed he had profited the most from Katharine's love. She helped him comprehend that Clarissa's death wasn't his fault. He loved her in more ways than she could explain. "If it hadn't been for that latent, we wouldn't be any closer. Does leaving a print mean he really wants us to catch him? I don't know. And why'd he go after Katharine with a weapon versus kidnapping and drugging her? We also haven't located any tarps or the paraquat."

"Circumstances? Katharine got in his way just by being in the wrong place at the wrong time. We now know there's someone else but I think Patriot knew this person. I also think that individual enticed him into the crime because they knew he was delusional. We can even explain away that the voices in his head told him to use abrin. I'd think that leans toward domination. Doing it his way. The problem is, we have zilch for leads. I personally think Patriot was only guilty of two murders. Someone else actually killed the other eight victims and whoever that person is, that's our serial killer."

"You believe the middle Stewart sibling is at the *bottom* of a nameless list?"

Gage half shrugged.

"Let's pay this Gunderson character a visit. Check him out. Find out what he's been doing the last couple of years. That one is filled with too much hostility for my liking."

The station's door opened and Cole entered. "Hey, Mac. How's married life?"

Mac stood and reached across the desk to shake hands with his ex-partner. "Good. Damn good. Katharine's pregnant."

"You sun-of-a-gun. Congratulations." Cole faced Gage. "Chief, how's it goin?"

"If you would've caught this bastard before he got out of Green Bay I wouldn't be working around the clock now."

"Ouch! Mac, you put up with that everyday?"

"He's more worried about competition," Mac goaded then ducked when Gage threw a book at him.

"Competition? What for?" Glancing from Mac to Gage, Cole said, "Ah, you've nothing to worry about. Believe me, that beautiful blond flat out refused me."

"Nicole ain't stupid," Mac muttered.

"Just for that, you're buying me dinner tonight. I'm starving."

"You're always hungry, Gilroy. What'd the Profiler have to say?"

Cole invited himself to a chair, and said, "She's sticking to her original report with two exceptions. The first being Patriot was working with someone and became the copycat. The only other fact she's adding is the compulsion he has to kill over time, which might come from accumulated hostility. She's now convinced the killer is someone who has a history of frustration and becomes obsessed with trivial problems."

"That contradicts what she said about Patriot looking for a father figure," Mac said.

"Oh great. A Profiler who changes their mind." Gage poured himself coffee and offered some to Cole.

"Thanks," he said. "The obsession with trivial problems could be as insignificant as misfiled forms or letters escalating the hostility to kill. Anyway, you get the idea."

"Our federal tax dollars hard at work. Any sort of killing is hostile," Gage grumbled.

"Gilroy," Mac huffed. "I hope you didn't come all this way to tell us something we already know."

"Hey, don't shoot the messenger."

"If our real serial killer stays on schedule we've got less than three months to find him. We're gonna work backward and start with the theft of the paraquat from Ashland County. Cole you're in plain clothes. How do you feel about digging up what you can with the Sheriff's office on these thefts?"

"I'm on it. I'll start with the employees and see what I can find out. If there's one thing I've learned, somebody always saw something."

"Good. Start tomorrow when they open their doors. They've got around two hundred employees total."

"Mac, do a background on Gunderson. See what you can dig up. Do not let him anywhere near Michelle."

"Count on it," Mac said, explaining why to Cole.

"Then work with Cole interviewing the employees and I'll cover your shifts."

* * *

Michelle stepped outside of the construction trailer to watch the work crew. The plumber had already hooked up water to the existing main. The shipment of 2x4's for framing confirmed, the trusses would arrive Monday next week, framing subs on Wednesday and the mechanics man was scheduled Friday to install a new furnace and AC for the entire building. With the exception of one cool day of rain, the weather was holding. The foundation poured last week, men drummed their hammers installing the floor joists. She never knew those perpendicular boards to a floor were called joists or 2x10's either. Ceiling joists were 2x6's on this site because of the span of the building Travis said.

After her first day on the job, she went home with a dreadful headache from all the noise. The subcontractors and inspectors overwhelmed her—keep the inspectors happy everyone adequately informed her, too. The job couldn't go forward if the work had flaws. La Pointe's strict zoning fell into sync alongside the fire codes when she actually saw what and why. She smiled to herself. No way would she have known whether Travis had done something right or wrong without his interpretation of the codes to her.

Wednesday, her presence of mind returned as she winterized Mrs. Chernak's yard. Today singing saws were a rhapsody of harps to her ears. In fact, she was in a chipper mood. Travis had praised her when she caught a mistake on window figures against the blueprints. The dimensions on the glass doors, which would lead outside to a patio, were incorrect. Immediately after verifying with the general contractor, she called to cancel and re-ordered. The woman had been a tad pert with her, but she dictated the supplies would be on time since it was their mistake. The company guaranteed no delays but she would stay on it, checking every couple of days. The roofers would show up following the framers. Optimistically, she discovered herself anticipating every aspect of the new construction.

Loud voices coming from the tavern's entrance distracted her and Michelle looked to check it out. Josie Stewart and a woman with light-colored hair were laughing as they went inside. Josie wore leotards under a long shirt, and the other woman wore spandex shorts and a matching top. A fanatic about exercise and vigorous workouts, Michelle wondered why Josie would waste a beautiful fall day drinking inside after sweating up. Especially when alcohol contradicted weight watchers.

Her attention went back to the construction crews, and one

more time, Michelle analyzed only one man behind her sunglasses. The brawn in his arms and shoulders glistened gold from the autumn suntan. Patiently unruffled the entire week, Travis adjusted to problems and delegated easily. She knew from watching and listening, a long list of ethics and values were etched into his mind. He fretted little over making good impressions—didn't have to since everyone already respected him. All week, she heard the workers acclaiming their admiration for the architect. As she watched the physical strength he put to a hammer, she quickly figured out that Travis Baines thrived on hard labor. He expected no more from his men than he gave of himself.

"Hey, Michelle. How's it goin? Anymore incorrect dimensions?"

She smiled at the general contractor. "Hi, Jerry. Not yet. I came out to watch the way you guys make construction appear simpler than it really is. You never seem to get bored with doing the same thing over and over either."

"That's because each site is different. It's comparable to a maze or a puzzle and I get to figure out all the pieces."

"He's good at what he does, isn't he?"

Jerry glanced in the direction she was looking and nodded. "Travis is not only the best at what he does, he's a good man. His company is superior to anyone else. Every man here, including myself, would work for nothing with the guy." Winking, he added, "Don't ever tell him I said that."

"Don't tell me what, Jerry?"

"I'm busted," he whispered to Michelle. "Just flirting while you work up a sweat."

"If you want me to keep signing your checks, you'd best not be thinking anything concerning Michelle."

"He's protective to," Jerry told her with a twinkle in his eye. "Travis, my man, it'd be worth a job's pay. You'd better keep an eye on her. Later, Michelle when the boss isn't eyeballing you."

"You're the one I'm gonna keep my eye on. Remember that old man."

Snickering, Jerry turned to leave. "Might be older than you but at least I don't have purple thumbs."

"Just keep walking, Jer."

Reflexively, Michelle looked down at Travis thumbs.

"Since you're refusing a paycheck, I'd like to take you somewhere tomorrow for the great job you've done this week. You saved me a bundle of money by catching the window error."

"Where?" she asked.

"Hun-uh. It's a surprise."

"Shalee and Brendan are coming for the weekend. I forgot until my sister called that I had promised them awhile back. We're going to the lagoon to rent a boat if it doesn't rain."

"Are you baking cookies, too?"

Childlike wanting flashed in his eyes and was noted. Thankfully, her eyes were still covered with shades, otherwise, they might betray her thoughts right now. "Maybe. Why?"

"Sounds like fun. Can I come?"

Bowled over, Michelle asked, "Are you sure you want to? Brendan can be hell on wheels some days."

"It just occurred to me that I've never seen where you live. Yes, I want to come. And Brendan and I will have a man-to-man talk if necessary."

Michelle stared at him all sweaty and breathing strength. No one would ever know he was a corporate man and owner of a world-renowned business.

"Michelle, it'll be innocent. You've got nothing to worry about."

She gulped back an itty-bitty lump of desire she started feeling earlier in the week. "It's not that. I figured the last place you'd want to be is around kids after working as hard as you have all week."

"Milady, you figured wrong. I'd love to spend the day with all of you. What time shall I come over?"

It was the second time he used the name Milady with her. Made her wonder why and where it came from. His begging eyes exposed the eagerness of a child, distracting her thoughts. Her tongue worked faster than her brain when she said, "I'm meeting Sylvie in the morning over in Bayfield around ten."

"Great. I'll meet you at the ferry for the nine-fifteen. Would you have dinner with me tonight?"

"I can't. Nicole has the night off and Katharine's feeling lonely because Mac's been working long hours on that murder case. We've made plans this evening."

"Girl stuff." He grinned. "You have fun and I'll see you in the morning."

"Michelle!"

Jerking, she swung around and observed a pair of hard, angry eyes. She wrapped he arms protectively around her. Derek was unrestrained and approaching fast. His voice was harsh with rage, it was mean, and it meant trouble. Travis moved protectively closer, but no matter who stood between her and her ex's temper, the fear inside weighed her down like a steel glob inside her stomach.

"I never signed any goddamn papers! In my book that makes us still married!"

She knew this day would arrive, and the steel weight just gained ten pounds. Her arms came undone and she cut loose. "No we're not! You were served with my petition but never bothered to show up for the hearing. Wisconsin has a no-fault divorce law. The marriage was irretrievably broken based on facts I presented."

"Wisconsin is a community property state. You owe me!"

Michelle glared at him then spit hotly, "For what? You demolished everything you hadn't already stolen from me!"

Derek lurched, she wobbled backwards, and Travis took one step halting him with just his presence.

"Brian's car! It's half mine. Give me the car or pay me what it's worth. Elisabeth agrees I deserve something for my suffering since you filed for the divorce."

Stunned by his proclamation, Michelle's back stiffened. Her hands clenched tightly into fists near her sides. Derek's temper when crossed was uncontrollable, but this was the last straw.

"You slimy snake. You may have ruined everything else in my life but you'll never get your filthy hands on his car. Get away from me or so help me I'll have you arrested for harassment."

"This ain't over you little whore."

That's it!

Travis clenched, swung and planted his fist into Derek's jaw. Michelle jumped back and watched her ex hit the ground quick and hard.

"Now it's over!" Travis hissed, taking Michelle's elbow and hastily steering her into the trailer.

CHAPTER 10

CEASELESS QUESTIONS BATTERED away inside of Michelle.

"How dare *she* tell Derek he deserves Brian's car!"

If not for being scared of her ex and enraged with her mother, Michelle would go over and ream Elisabeth Callihan a new butt hole. First, she needed to figure out a way to hide the Mustang— Derek would steal that, too. *Why did her mother think her ex deserved any part of Brian?* Didn't his memory mean anything to her?

Fighting with will, she hadn't shed a tear since that last night Derek came close to killing her, but she lost the tight control and broke down into hysterical sobs in front of Travis. She still couldn't explain anything to him and Travis didn't push her for details. Nevertheless, he wouldn't let her leave until she calmed down then became insistent that she make a police report. When she refused, he called Katharine and Nicole to inform them she would be late.

Michelle sniffed, wishing she carried tissues in her purse. Parking Brian's car in front of Katharine's house, she checked her eyes in the rear-view mirror. She could do nothing about the red swelling and exited the vehicle. Nervously glancing over her shoulder, she was locking the car when both women came barreling out of Katharine's house. They met her half way with worried faces.

"Hon, what happened? Are you okay?"

"Michelle, he didn't lay a hand on you did he?"

Gulping on the ache in her throat, tears blinded her again. Michelle swallowed back more sobs, shaking her head in response. They hugged her snugly then guided her into the house. She didn't feel worthy of their comfort. She was a wretched human being who had brought dishonor and condemnation to her family and probably her friends. Inside the house, Katharine tossed a chocolate covered cherry into her mouth as Michelle just stood there feeling numb and utterly alone.

"Mac and Nicole filled me in on the incident last weekend at the Tavern," Katharine said. "Tell us what happened tonight."

In a broken whisper, she said, "Neither of you need my problems."

"Hon, your problems are our problems. We love you and we aren't letting you go through this alone a second time."

"She's right, Michelle. I talked to Mac and Gage and they're with you a hundred percent. But you have to tell us what happened so we know how to fight back legally."

Why, she wondered, standing motionless in the middle of the room. The pain ran so deep, she clearly recognized herself as completely inadequate. *Didn't they?*

"Michelle, we feel the hurt you're experiencing. It pains us both, me more, to know I wasn't here when you needed me. I'm here now. We both are," Katharine said.

"I need a beer and a box of tissues," she muttered.

"With ice. Coming right up," Nicole responded.

Michelle sniffed and looked at Katharine quizzically. "You must be over the morning sickness."

Katharine snuggled into a corner on the couch and tossed another chocolate into her mouth. Michelle inched over and joined her with an ungraceful lurch then swiped a piece of candy.

"You were right about the cravings. I've never been one for sweets, but here I sit eating these damn chocolates and peanut butter and jelly sandwiches. Mac thinks it's a girl because of all the sugar."

"Katharine, you look radiant and beautiful. I've never seen you this happy. I can't dump my problems on you."

"Michelle, friends are supposed to carry the burden when we can't carry them ourselves."

Nicole returned with iced beer and a seven-seven for herself. "Katharine, you need milk," she said, handing her a tall glass. She took the vacancy on the other side of Michelle. "Katharine's right. We'll never let you go through this alone a second time."

"I can't do this," she sniveled. "Your plates are both full."

"Yes, you can," Katharine told her.

Michelle guzzled her beer as Katharine set the chocolates aside, gripped the arm and couch back, shifted her body to face Michelle and crossed her legs.

"Come on girlfriend, spill your guts."

Nicole mimicked Katharine and plunked the box of Kleenex in Michelle's lap. "I'm sorry I've never been a good listener like Katharine, but, hon, I do love you. Let us help you."

Michelle held the glass rim to her lips and sipped her beer. After several seconds, she yanked out a Kleenex and dabbed her eyes. So debilitated from carrying the load alone, she finally caved.

"It was awful," she whispered. "After awhile, the emotional hurt covered over the physical pain of his fists. There were many times I thought he was going to kill me."

She glanced at Katharine through teary eyes. "The last time it happened, I had to cut my hair because he whacked it off with a knife."

Nicole groaned and Katharine wrapped her arms around Michelle's shoulders with one silent thought; *indeed, she was going to kick ass—big time!*

"I have no idea what I ever did to make him go off the way he did. It didn't start until after we got back from Jamaica. It was weird the way all of a sudden he started to find fault in everything I did. The meals were too cold, too hot, not to his liking. I spent too many hours at work or not sharing the funds from my business. Oh hell, sneezing, coughing, peeing at the wrong time of day set him off. Usually a night out drinking enhanced the violence," she told them, smothering another sob.

"Usually?" Katharine asked.

Michelle nodded.

"How many times did he do this to you?"

Too many, she thought, and the memory of the raw, pent-up horror of physical abuse and fear overpowered Michelle. Tears seeped uncontrollably down her cheeks. Her restraint collapsed and Michelle bawled. She cried hard until she had no emotion left inside of her—the hate, guilt, the anger, and the shame—until she felt as hollow as her voice sounded. Both women held her snugly until the racking inside her body subsided and her sobs turned to a whimper. All had yanked tissues repeatedly from the box. With a handful of Kleenex balled in one hand, Michelle blew her nose with another.

"He almost killed me that night. I was so scared. I thought I'd never see either one of you again. I knew what would happen when I confronted him about stealing money."

"What money?" Katharine asked.

"From Scenic Landscaping. The bank had called and left a message that day. They said I was overdrawn. I knew it was impossible. I hadn't written any checks. When I called them back, they told me I had exceeded cash flow and withdrawals for the month. It was the excessive dollar amounts from my line of credit and ATM fees causing the overdrafts. At first, I argued with them, told them I rarely used my card. I'd written a check that week for supplies and it bounced harder than a spiked football."

"Why didn't you come to me if you needed money," Nicole asked.

"I didn't know I needed money! I made a trip over to Bayfield the same day and they showed me their records. I was livid and asked to see our personal accounts. He drained our savings account and Scenic Landscaping of more than forty grand."

"Michelle, you didn't put his name on your business account, did you?"

She shook her head and blew her nose again. "No. Somehow, he got a hold of my ATM card and the PIN and made the cash withdrawals. I was steamed up all day, but I didn't care, nor had I thought about what his reaction would be. Scenic Landscaping is *mine*—he had no right to steal that money. That night, he'd been with Kevin and came home drunk. Stupidly, it was rage making me lock horns with him. In a violent rampage he destroyed everything in the rental. My crystal vases, my old movies, everything, before he went off on me with his fists. When he grabbed that knife, then me it was too late for any recourse. I thought for sure he was gonna stab me and kill me but he started hacking away on my hair. He shouted and yelled then pounded on me some more. When he was done, he just left as he always did. It was the last time he ever laid a hand on me. In the middle of winter, I packed my clothes and went to a motel here. The next day I left the Island and went to Ashland. I couldn't let anyone see my face and hair."

Anger spewed over inside of Katharine. Nicole had been silent far too long and Michelle felt her disappointment. Believed they both thought less of her than she already thought of herself. She'd given up on herself and they would desert her as well. Gulping down a golf ball-size lump in her throat, she realized telling them was a huge mistake.

"Do you know if he came back to the house that night?" Katharine finally asked.

"I'm sure he did," she said quickly over her choking, beating heart.

Nicole stifled a sob, grabbed another tissue, wiped her eyes and guzzled the last of her drink.

"I left a note telling him I was filing for divorce. I hadn't legally changed my name on the business credit card yet. I used it to hire an attorney in Ashland. He took pictures of my bruises and filed the preliminary papers. He made me see a doctor who said I had a mild concussion and stitched up a cut over my eye. Now Derek thinks he's entitled to Brian's car because he says my mother told him. But he's not! I made damn sure of that."

"How did you do that?" Katharine asked. "Wisconsin *is* community property."

"Under Wisconsin law, Brian's Mustang fell under an inheritance. It was mine before I ever met Derek. The attorney had me change the title to Sylvie's name as additional protection."

"Does Sylvie know what happened to you?"

Shaking her head, Michelle muttered, "I told her I was divorcing Derek and didn't want him to get the car. She understood."

"What about your mother and dad?" Katharine asked.

The questions were automatic and so were her answers. "They hounded me to learn what happened. I tried to explain but they believed the fault mine for not making the marriage work. Divorce is inappropriate. I've stained their family name. They've accused me of being inadequate."

When Michelle started to sob again, Katharine embraced, hugged and tried to soothe.

"They aren't quite as hard on Sylvie, but since Brian's death they have little to do with either one of us."

"What did they say when you told them what Derek did to you?"

"After I explained to them the first time he hit me, they didn't believe it and didn't want to hear about it. They sent me back to him. I never told them about the last time."

"What happened next?"

Michelle yanked more tissues and blew her nose again. She sucked in another ragged breath. "You're so mechanical at this, Katharine."

"It's important to know all the facts, Michelle."

She didn't understand why, but continued. "The day of my court hearing, Derek never showed up. It took the judge about five seconds to read everything, see the photos of my injuries and label the marriage short term. He granted my petition for divorce."

"What about the place you were renting? Whatever happened to the slimeball? When I first came home, you said he left the island."

"I called what's his name and broke the lease on the rental. I lost the deposit and told him he could clean it out himself. After my bruises healed, I went and stayed with Sylvie until I could figure things out—where to live for starters. The only good thing through the entire process was the fact my attorney owned the house I'm living in now. He said he'd been thinking about selling it and would rent it out to me until I got back on my feet. He gave me first option to buy, which I did, saving us both real estate fees because he did all the paperwork."

Katharine linked her fingers with Michelle's. "You haven't told us where Derek went."

Michelle squirmed when Katharine's intense blue-eyed stare connected with her own eyes. Her throat felt raw and the words came out in a whisper. "I paid him off."

"You did what?" she exploded, dropping Michelle's hand and scrambling off the couch. Pacing the living room carpet, Katharine demanded, "How much? How could you, Michelle after everything he did to you? Is that why he didn't show up in court?"

"I'm sorry," Michelle screamed. "I know I'm a failure at everything! God knows my mother and dad have said it enough. But I did not pay him not to show up." Michelle took a deep breath and shouted, "I paid him two grand to show up and sign the damn divorce papers! He was a drunk and a gambler! He gambled all my money and lost it! I have no idea where he went after I paid him! I didn't care. He was gone from my life! Now the bastard has come back for more!"

Katharine stopped pacing when Michelle crumbled in an onslaught of heavy-duty sobs. She slid onto the couch sheathing her protectively. "Sweetie, I'm so sorry. I'm not blaming you for anything. And you are not a failure. I'm livid with what that son-of-a-bitch has done to you."

Had she not been so distraught, Michelle might have noticed Nicole's odd silence. Had her muscles not been screaming with pin-cushion twinges, and tears glistening steady streams down her cheeks, she might have noticed Nicole was in a vacant trance as two more stood and watched in the shadows.

"Is this a private party?"

Katharine shifted, looked, blurted, "Mac!"

Michelle flinched, and Nicole nudged her up, guiding her to the bathroom.

Mac moved swiftly and kissed away his wife's tears. "Honey, you remember Travis?"

"Yeah, hi." He nodded as Katharine asked, "What're you guys doing here? I told you it was ladies night out."

"Travis stopped by the station and told me what happened at the construction site. We were checking up on you three."

Mac glanced at the closed bathroom door. "Katharine, we heard the whole story. We came in during the first round of tears." He snuggled her into his arms. "It broke my heart so badly I almost cried myself. Princess, you're the only one who can convince Michelle to sign a restraining order."

"Dammit, Mac! She didn't deserve any of this. If I *ever* see that slimeball, you know what I'll do to him. I won't hesitate."

"Princess, what you'll do is too good for him. I already told you, this one is all mine."

She leaned into him, wrapped her arms around his neck, and planted a deep kiss on his mouth. "God, I do love you, Dobarchon. I'll convince her and call you. Now get out of here before she comes back."

"Geez, they're at it again," Nicole said, exiting the hallway. "I'm sure Travis does not want to watch you two kissy-facing."

"A man never knows when he might pick up a pointer or two." Travis half smiled. "Besides they're kind of cute."

When Michelle came out behind Nicole, Katharine ordered, "Leave. Now."

"You three behave yourselves. Gage already warned me about your shenanigans."

Before Katharine could recant, Mac planted a deep kiss on her mouth, then he and Travis vacated.

Seated in the squad car with his mind on a pair of tear-stained emerald eyes, Travis was somber. "Mac, if you don't handle this, I swear as God as my witness, I will."

"Travis, I worked homicide many years. I'll tell you what I told my beautiful warrior in there. I hate wife beaters more than I hate murderers." He glanced over, recognized the look, and asked, "Have you heard Mikala yet?"

"What?"

"Never mind," Mac said, starting the squad car. "Travis, Michelle needs patience and understanding, and eventually she will come around. I know, because Katharine did."

CHAPTER 11

T RAVIS ROLLED OVER, fisted his knuckles under his chin and watched a morning sky lighten over Lake Superior. A gentle rain during the night left a fresh autumn scent blowing in through the open window. Foggy dew misted plant life delicately. A quick-rising sun would vaporize and burn off the precipitation. With the weather holding for the ballroom, some of the crew already volunteered to work the weekend to finish installing floor joists. The mesmerizing call of loons and several other species of chirpy birds, he had no idea what, woke the world with careless merriment. A deer ambled across the dampened grass, stopped to nibble, cast a curious expression then loped away. In the twelve-mile drive between the Retreat and the construction site, semi-tame animals roamed the island like they had part ownership of the rock.

He shifted restlessly incapable of blanking out the previous evening. The misery of Michelle's crying eyes haunted his thoughts all night into morning. He dreamt of her and the horror she had endured. Lurking in the kitchen shadows last night to listen, Mac's heart wasn't the only one that had broken into pieces. His split wide open. How could parents cast out their own? Didn't Michelle's mother and dad understand what she went through? Amazingly, as he watched the three women, he realized something. They had a special bond between them. Like sisters, or pair of old comfy shoes you couldn't toss out. The connection between them went beyond fondness and friendships. Watched over and protected each other is what they did. How many times in his younger years had he wished for a sibling? The prevailing loneliness he always felt with not having brothers or sisters was rooted deeply inside of him making it difficult to ignore what he observed last night, and had lived without.

Travis looked up through the window. The same mantra cry that prowled his sleep every other night was at it again. It reminded him of Hinduism and the Veda, an entire body of Hindu sacred writings. There were four Hindu religious books in the Veda. The Rig-Veda, the Sama-Veda, Atharva-Veda and Yajur-Veda. The Hindu chanted or sung the Veda as in an incantation. What he heard now was definitely a mysterious chant.

He shook his head and groaned. Hearing something he couldn't see was insane.

Travis grabbed his cell phone off the nightstand and glanced at his watch. Dialing overseas to Florence, the seven-hour time difference made it one in the afternoon in Italy. Waiting for the connection, he swung his feet over the edge of the mattress and looked at his knuckles. He should have punched a lot harder on the bastard, but when Michelle cowered, he instantly regretted his actions.

After several rings, the Villa's recorder kicked in and Travis left a message. Throughout the night, he figured out how to resolve his problem. It meant unveiling his surprise early. Grandma-ma would be delighted to be part of the ballroom's construction. He dialed more numbers and made reservations.

After a quick shower, he started a pot of coffee. Travis poured and drank a glass of orange juice while he waited. He studied the ballroom's blueprints one more time. Everything was perfect and back on schedule.

Now all he had to do was teach Michelle how to love again.

And he was not a man who gave up—ever.

*   *   *

Travis arrived at the ferry dock before Michelle and purchased two walk-on tickets. Stepping outside in tantalizing fall sunshine, he saw her drive up and waited while she parked. Her eyes were clear. They dazzled and harmonized with the green birth of Balsam needles as she exited the Mustang. If he hadn't witnessed last night's confession, he never would have believed it. The fear disguised and hidden from the world, her eyes greeted him with the same genuine smile curving a copious mouth. Her hair was swooped back in a soft greenish ribbon. Dainty emerald stones graced subtle lobes he never noticed. She moved with glass-like practice, yet a graceful gait exposed a carefree nature. The overall package made him aware he could never fully know the depth of her suffering. He just wanted to hold her and give her reassurance she would never experience pain again.

Instead, he smiled, greeting her, "Good morning. I bought two tickets."

"Good morning." Her smile faded. "Travis, about last night—"

"Michelle, don't."

She shuffled her feet nervously and moved in an awkward manner.

"You've nothing to apologize for," he said straightforward.

She shoved her sunglasses onto her face and glanced toward the lake. He assumed with hope of finding comfort in Superior's calm waters. The shades couldn't disguise the questions that seemed to pummel her.

"You heard everything, didn't you?"

She squeezed her purse between her arm and ribs and finally lifted her head. She glanced briefly at him and shifted uneasily a second time. He nodded, hesitated, spoke as she turned away. "I'll never hurt you, Michelle. All you need do is give me a chance to show you. I'll prove to you we aren't all like him."

"Katharine and Nicole said the same thing last night. They used Gage and Mac as examples. I've always looked to Gage as a replacement for the brother I lost. They convinced me to sign a restraining order and called Mac to start the paperwork."

"I think that's the right thing to do," he said quietly.

"Mac was so kind and gentle when he came back. I remember feeling envious because Katharine had found such an extraordinary man. Travis, last Friday when Derek showed up while we were having dinner . . ." she clutched her fingers together. "I'm still afraid."

When she turned back, he said, "I know."

His heart liquefied when an infinitesimal look of hope smuggled through her mask of uncertainty. He knew he'd broken through the first of many barriers. "Just a chance. That's all I'm asking you."

Travis held out his hand and waited for her to take it. With slow, deliberate wariness, she accepted. Gradually, he enclosed his fingers around hers and they walked the length of the dock. Boarding the ferry, they took a seat on the upper deck. When he offered his hand a second time, she laced her fingers with his and he squeezed reassuringly. During the ride over to Bayfield, he sensed her anxious chatter was a result of her own discomfort.

"Did you know Lake Superior was once called Lac Superieur au Lac Tracy? Actually, different people called it both names. I believe at the same time."

"Neither sounds Native American."

"French after Alexandre Prouville marquis de Tracy from the 1600's. He was a lieutenant general for all French possessions in North America and responsible for negotiating peace with the Indians in order for the French to have shorter passage through the Great Lakes to do their fur trading. The name *Superieur* was initiated by the French concept that the lake was the uppermost of the chain of Great Lakes. Later, the English kept the name because of Superior's size."

She definitely relaxed more when she could speak freely of the history she seemed to retain with ease. All Travis could do was feed her fondness. "How did they come up with the names of the islands? I've heard there have been changes there, too."

Michelle nodded. "Through the centuries their names have changed several times. It's due partially to the fact that some of the islands that were once visible are now submerged. As far back as the late 1800's there were, and still are twenty-two islands. The others are assumed to have been sandbars. The twenty-two you're looking at were originally called the Twelve Apostles based on the first mission here. The Holy Ghost Mission. It was when a guy named Schoolcraft visited Chequamegon and discovered more islands than Apostles that he renamed the islands the Federation Group. He named each individual island after the States in the union."

While Michelle recited the names of twenty-three islands to the twenty-four states the historian divvied up, Travis' excitement elevated just from listening to her. Again, she said the names would change. Present day, Michigan and York Islands were the only Union names to stick throughout the decades.

"How and when did the name changes take place and stick?"

"I can't recall when, but Hermit Island came from a man named Wilson who was actually a hermit on the island. Raspberry, which is Katharine's favorite, came from the Raspberry River. And Sand Island was named after the Sand River. The others except Stockton were named after natural objects or locations." ·

"Devil's Island is a natural object?" Travis asked curiously.

Michelle chuckled. "No. Devil's is a super natural name. In fact, the Ojibwe shunned the whole Apostle group. It wasn't until the nineteenth century that an Indian would even stay overnight on Madeline unless protected by the French or British. They feared Devil's Island so much they named it after their evil god or devil, Matchimanitou."

"What?"

"Matchimanitou."

"Okay," he said unconvincingly. "Is it true that Madeline Island has had more name changes?"

"Sure is. The Chippewa called it some native tongue word that meant woodpecker. It was also called St. Michael, LaRonde Island, Michael's Island after Michel Cadotte himself, and Middle Island. And of course you know how it became Madeline after Esquaysayway, who was born in this vicinity."

"Tell me."

"The naming of the island, Madeline, was a dedication to her life. Her real name, Esquaysayway was Native American. She was Chief White Crane's daughter and christened *Madeleine* by the priest in Sault Ste. Marie who officiated at her wedding to Michel Cadotte. When she and Michel returned to La Pointe, Esquaysayway presented her christened name to the island. Chief White Crane decided this island would bare her name in his daughter's honor."

"How is it that you can retain all this historical information?"

Michelle studied him through her sunglasses for a moment. "It's in my blood. I've lived and breathed the area since the day I was born. It's like driving the same road every day. You just know it."

Travis carried the rest of their conversation never letting go of her hand. He talked of his travels throughout the world and the places he went because of his career, his love of vintage cars and his home in Boston.

"What's it like? Living on the East Coast? Living in a large city?"

"Everything is at your fingertips. You've only to drive a couple hours north, south or west and you're in another city or state loaded with history and architectural structures depicting the birth of our country."

They looked at each other both feeling matched enthusiasm about what they each knew so well. Although a fleeting moment, each was content with the way things were for the moment, the way they might want it to stay. Total satisfaction.

"How come you don't have a Boston accent?" Michelle asked.

"Endogwen."

Michelle removed her sunglasses and stared at the man sitting next to her. "What?"

Travis laughed. "It's Ojibwe. It means, I don't know."

Startled and amazed, she asked, "You know the language?"

"Grandma-ma has taught me some. She speaks it fluently. I only dabble in it. It drives my mother and grandfather crazy because they never learned. They don't understand why Grandma-ma bothers when she's more French than Native American."

"Say something else."

Travis thought for a moment. "Nin minodee."

"It sounds like fanciful music and magic rolling off your tongue. I can almost hear the native drums from centuries ago. Tell me what it means."

Her eyes were bright and alive, eager, like trauma had never confronted her. "I have a large heart," he told her then caressed her knuckles with his thumb. "Michelle, I want you to have no doubts about me."

She examined him, explored his face for a moment. A deep yearning glimmered from the depths of her troubled eyes.

"I want to believe you, Travis."

He smiled, thinking about it. "That's a start."

They stood together. The ferry had docked and they were last to disembark, walking off hand-in-hand. Michelle saw Sylvie tidy as a pin, thin and tall with her precious husband, Harvey, and their two honeybunches, Brendan and Shalee. She sighed quietly over forgotten dreams and wishes. Sylvie was happy and that's what mattered. The kids saw her first.

"Auntie Michelle. Auntie Michelle."

Both children ran toward her, jumping into her arms. "My little dumplin's. Gi'me hugs and kisses."

After numerous hugs and more kisses, Michelle squatted and let each child stand.

"Can we play with Keeker when we get there?" Brendan begged.

"Do we get to go swimming?" Shalee asked.

"Keeker is anxious to see you both. And I was thinking about a boat ride at the lagoon for starters?"

Both squealed as Brendan jumped up and down. "Yeah, a boat ride. Do we get to stay up late, too?"

"We'll see. I brought a friend with me today. This is Travis. Travis this is Brendan and Shalee."

Squatting down and smiling at the little girl, Travis said, "Hello, Shalee. Aren't you just the cutest little muffin. How old are you?"

"Hello, Travis. I'm five."

He shifted slightly. "I bet you're older than your sister, Brendan."

"How'd you know that? I'm six and a half."

"A little bird told me. So what do you think? Should we row or get a motor with that boat?"

"Auntie Michelle always makes us row. I think we should get a motor with it."

"Then a motorboat it is but only if everyone wears a life jacket."

"She makes us do that, too."

"Auntie Michelle is a smart lady." Travis looked up. "What do you think, Auntie Michelle, rowing or motorboat?"

Michelle ruffled the top of her nephew's light brown hair. "Tell Travis why we always get a rowboat at the lagoon, Brendan."

Kicking a rock, he huffed, "Because there aren't any motors there. Guess you and I have to row, Travis."

"I think we can handle it, little buddy." Winking, he asked, "Whaddaya say?"

Brendan fisted his hands on his hips and eyed his sister and aunt. "Yeah. The two of us can take care of the girls."

Michelle covered a giggle and Travis said, "Brendan, you're a brave and bold young man."

"Hey, Sis, how's it going?" Sylvie called out approaching with Harvey. "Mother called with the latest news update. You sure you're up for the kids this weekend?"

Michelle knew what that meant. Their mother had called Sylvie and told her Derek was back. Undoubtedly, Elisabeth Callihan also added to the gossip on the latest murder. Neither did she miss the inquisitive expression on her sister's face upon seeing Travis.

"I'm sure she did, Sylvie, and we'll talk about mother some other time. Travis, this is my sister Sylvie and her husband, Harvey. This is Travis Baines, the architect doing the ballroom add-on to the tavern."

"Nice to meet you both." Travis and Harvey exchanged handshakes.

"I'm helping him out with ordering and scheduling since I'm done for the season with Scenic Landscaping."

"How's the ballroom coming along?" Harvey asked. Glancing briefly at his two children, he added, "Heard about the delay the first day."

"Set us back a couple of hours. We're right on schedule and will stay there if winter holds out."

"Weather's been good, but it's hard to tell around here. Few years back the temps stayed in the sixties through December. Has Gage figured anything out yet?"

Travis shook his head as Brendan jumped up and down eagerly.

"Auntie Michelle, can we go now?"

"We have to wait for the next ferry, precious, and buy you and Shalee tickets."

"But it's already here. We're gonna miss it."

"Michelle, we bought their tickets," Sylvie said, handing them over. "If you don't mind we're going to Duluth."

"Go on, go," she insisted.

Sylvie leaned over her children. "Gi'me honeybunches." The kids hugged their parents, as she told them, "Both of you listen to Auntie Michelle and we'll see you tomorrow night. I love you both."

"Love you too, Mom and Dad," they chanted in unison.

"Here's their clothes and stuff for the weekend. I put a phone number in the side pocket. They had a late, rather large breakfast" she eyed her offspring, "and should be good for a couple hours."

Michelle swung the strap over her shoulder. She took each child's hand and envied her sister walking away with Harvey's arm around her shoulders.

"Looks like we can board," Travis said.

"Travis, can I sit next to you?"

"Sure can, little buddy. Take my hand."

"Auntie Michelle, I love riding the ferry."

Michelle glanced down at her niece. "I know you do, dumplin'."

On board, they climbed the iron stairs to the upper deck and found seats near the life rail a second time. It didn't totally surprise Michelle the way both kids took to Travis. Brendan had a very balanced personality and was fun to be around. As far as discussing intelligent situations and reasons, she always talked to him like an adult. He just seemed to require it. With an abundance of courage and confidence, he always wanted to do the right thing. Shalee's eyes were chock full of affection and a need for love. Helpful and responsive, she rarely let just anybody hold her. So watching through her sunglasses, Shalee creamed Michelle with surprise when she crawled into Travis' lap. He willingly took her niece, wrapping a protective arm around the child's small torso. He provided the necessary nurturing Shalee required. Michelle felt an odd tug inside her chest, and decided Shalee's concern with where she fit in the group didn't hold water to Travis' charm.

She thought surely their social butterfly personalities would talk both his ears off by noon and he'd not only be ready to leave he would take flight. That theory was blown out of the water when she heard him promise Brendan a showing of the heavy machinery at the Tavern in the afternoon.

Walking off the ferry twenty minutes later, Brendan pulled her aside to whisper, "Auntie Michelle, I like him."

"Oh you do, do you?"

He nodded his head vigorously and ran to catch up to Travis. Once off the dock, Travis came to a stop and looked at Michelle. "Guess what?"

"What?"

"The Ferrari's a two-seater." Flashing a devil-may-care grin, he said, "Looks like we take the Stanger and I get to drive."

"I don't think so."

A sappy puppy-dog expression produced a second laugh out of Michelle.

"Please, Auntie Michelle, lemme drive. Can I, please?"

"Yeah, let Travis drive," Brendan insisted.

However futile it may have been, Michelle looked to her niece for help. At the ripe young age of five, the kid who was sympathetic, helpful and responsive turned on her.

"Travis," Shalee said without giving it thought.

"Milady, you're outvoted."

"By my own flesh and blood no less."

"The keys," he said, flashing a broader smile.

"Well, then. I'll just drive the Ferrari."

Leaning closer, he said, "Deal, but not today. Today we all go in your car, and I'm driving."

He took the keys from her hand, the clothes bag off her shoulder and placed it in the trunk. After ushering the kids into the back seat and buckling them in, Travis waited for Michelle to be seated in front and closed the door. Walking around the Mustang, he got in and let out a zealous groan when his knees rammed the dashboard. Michelle cut loose with laughter and Shalee giggled heartily.

"You both laugh at my misery," he muttered.

"She's *my* girl," Michelle murmured, directing Travis where to go.

Within a half-hour, they were unloading kids from the car and life jackets from the trunk in a gravel parking lot.

"Travis, the boats are down those stairs and we get to cross a bridge and walk to the other side of the lagoon."

"Let's get this P-F-D on you, Brendan."

The child stopped, looked, asked, "What's that?"

"Brendan, wait for Shalee," Michelle ordered.

"A gentleman always waits for the ladies," Travis told him.

"My dad tells me the same thing."

"And your dad is right," Travis affirmed. "Real sailors call these personal flotation devices, or a P-F-D. Now let's get this one on you."

Brendan traipsed back kicking rocks along the way and let Travis put it on. "You hear that Shalee? I'm a real sailor and this is a P-F-D."

Michelle hid a grin as she stooped to retie Shalee's tennis shoe after securing the bright orange lifejacket around her niece's body. She rose and took Shalee's hand. "Thank you kind gentlemen."

"You're welcome, pretty ladies."

While Travis led, Brendan played tour guide. In a matter of sixty seconds, they heard a rambunctious story of previous adventures at the lagoon. They walked down the first set of stairs and stopped on the landing.

"Auntie Michelle, can we go swimming?"

"Afraid not today, Shalee. The water's cooling down."

After Travis scanned the area checking out the scenery, he continued downward toward the wooden bridge Brendan had indeed described down to the last two by four. To their left, Lake Superior spanned out from a sandbar. Right was a swamp-grass lagoon with boats stacked on the bank near the bridge and water's edge. Madeline Island's enchantment sustained a new breath of life.

And as quickly, it perished.

Travis came to a jarring halt so fast Brendan bumped into him. Michelle collided with Brendan. Gawking long enough, Travis spiraled around, lifted Shalee into his arms and seized Brendan's hand swinging him around to face the stairs. Looking directly into her eyes, the laughter was gone from the soft pearl-gray color of his.

"Take Brendan's other hand and follow me. Don't take your eyes off of me."

His taught voice chilled through to her bones. Wordless, Michelle did as Travis requested.

"Kids, I have a better idea. What would you both say if we go have ourselves a spot of ice cream? Afterward I'll find us a motorboat instead of a rowboat."

"What's a spot of ice cream?" Brendan asked.

"Make that an ice cream cone," Travis answered, chuckling now.

Both cheered, "Yea!"

When Travis rushed them up the lumbered stairs, Michelle's heart rate accelerated faster. She and Brendan barely kept up with his long hurried strides back to the Mustang.

"Michelle, get them in the car. I have to make a call."

Travis moved away, pulling a cell phone out of his pocket. By the time Michelle had both children in the back seat, he had disconnected.

He moved swiftly, snapped the car door shut, and told her, "There's a body lying on the bank."

"*Omigod!* No! Not another one!"

"Gage and Mac are on their way but we have to wait for them."

CHAPTER 12

AN ENCOURAGING HUG might help Michelle, but the idea of physical touch destroyed any further thought. Travis' brows were drawn together in an agonized expression. His eyes clung to hers, analyzing her reaction.

"Michelle, you and the kids can't stay here. Nor do I want you left alone either. Use my cell phone and call Katharine or Nicole to come and get you. I'll drive your car to wherever you are as soon as they finish talking to me."

"I can't. Katharine went to their new house today and Nicole's working."

"Come on, let's go," Brendan whined, knocking on the car window from inside.

Travis opened the door and leaned in. They had removed their PFD's. Two squad cars pulled in and skid to a stop. "Hang tight, little buddy. I'll be right back."

Brendan twisted around and peered out. "Auntie Michelle, I need to talk to Gage. Can I?"

"Not right now, sweetie."

Shalee scooted forward and squealed. "Gage!"

Brendan propped himself up on his knees to watch out the back window. "Who's that man with Gage? Where's Joe?"

Michelle slid in sideways on the driver's seat. "Do you remember Katharine from my wedding when you were my ring bearer and Shalee was a pretty flower girl?"

"Yeah."

"Well, that's Katharine's husband, Mac. He works with Gage now."

"What happened to Joe?"

"He decided to go back to school and Mac took his job."

"Auntie Michelle, I like Travis better than Derek. Can we go now?"

"Me too," Shalee stated as Michelle's thoughts wondered briefly. How would Shalee even remember Derek? Who was the dead girl Travis saw?

"Where're they going? I wanna go with Travis and Gage."

"We're gonna wait here, Brendan. Then we'll go have ice cream at Frosty Blues."

"Yippee, Blue Fross."

"Shalee, it's Frosty Blues," Brendan told her. "Say it the way your supposed ta."

Shalee crossed her arms, firmly stating, "Blue Fross."

"Hey, big guy," Gage yelled, moments later when he and Travis returned. "Did you come over on the ferry by yourself?"

Brendan scrambled eagerly and squeezed out through the seats. "Gage!"

Before Michelle could stop him, he bolted. Gage grabbed him flinging him into the air.

"You've sprouted like a bean since I last saw you." Gage propped him in the crook of his arm, and said, "Man, you're getting big! Where's your sister?"

"In the car with Auntie Michelle. Are you going on the boat with us?"

"Not this time. But if you listen to your aunt and Travis, I told Travis you guys could take my speedboat out tomorrow. How's that?"

"Really?"

Travis and Gage walked to the Mustang and Gage answered, "Really. But you have to guarantee me you'll behave."

"You promise?"

Gage nodded.

"Wow, cool! Shalee, Travis is gonna take us on Gage's speedboat tomorrow."

"Gage!" Shalee squealed again and pinched through to get out. Scooping her into his other arm, he said, "Where's my hugs?"

Both children wrapped their arms around Gage's neck. He loved them both from the beginning and Michelle pondered the reasons why he hadn't married and started his own family. She always believed he would make a wonderful father.

"That's better. Now scoot, back into the car and go with Travis and your aunt." Waiting until the kids scrambled into the back seat, Gage asked, "Michelle, you doin' okay?"

When she nodded, he said, "Travis, we'll talk later. Bye kids."

"Bye, Gage," they hollered.

Travis walked around to the other side with Michelle. "Are you sure you're okay?"

"Did Gage know who she was? Was she another sixteen-year-old?"

"No, they didn't know her and she was an adult."

Travis opened the door, waited for her to slide in, closed the door and walked around getting in on the driver's side. Seated, he looked over his shoulder. "Okay. Let's go have ourselves some ice cream." Before starting the engine, he took hold and embraced Michelle's hand reassuringly.

"Travis, do you know how to drive Gage's speedboat?"

"Together you and I can figure it out. How's that?"

"Cool. After ice cream can we see where you work?"

"Absolutely."

Driving in silence to town, the kids settled down in the backseat. Michelle's spirits sank. Grief and despair tore at her heart. Who was the dead girl she wondered. How did she die? Who killed her? When would the killing stop? The growth of a painful knot in her gut surrounded the ceaseless inward question until they reached Frosty Blues.

"Auntie Michelle, I have to go."

"Okay, dumplin' as soon as we get inside. What about you, Brendan?"

"No, I'm good. I'll stay with Travis."

The kids ran toward the entrance, chattering between themselves.

"I think the three of you should stay with me," Travis said.

Anguish peaked and shattered the last shred of Michelle's control. "We'll be fine!"

"It has a loft with two beds and two bedrooms on the main floor."

They reached the front door and Travis opened it, letting all proceed.

"Why, Travis?"

"Just think about it. I'll explain the reasons later," he said, steering Brendan toward a vacant table. "What are you having, little buddy?"

"Can I have anything I want?"

Travis nodded and sat.

"A banana split with extra cherries on top."

"What do you think the ladies will want?"

"Shalee likes strawberry but you better ask her. Auntie Michelle doesn't eat ice cream."

"She doesn't? How come?"

"Once I heard her say it's not good for her hips."

The child's bluntness bowled him over and stifling an urge to laugh, he asked, "Do you think we should tell her what she's missing?"

"I've tried. She won't listen."

"Won't listen to what?" Michelle asked, returning and lifting Shalee up onto a chair.

"Your nephew tells me you won't eat ice cream because it's not good for your hips."

If Michelle hadn't already eased onto the chair, she would have fallen over. Travis' mouth was quirked with humor. Laugh lines crinkled his eyes. She gaped at him critically then looked at her nephew. "Brendan Joseph Hood, when we get home, you and I *will* have a private talk about eavesdropping and repeating what you heard."

"*But, Auntie*, you told me never to lie. And Travis asked why you don't eat ice cream."

"Well, now," Travis said, turning up his smile a notch. "He's certainly got you there."

"Then I believe Travis is the one who needs to be taught manners, Brendan. Nonetheless, we *will* have that discussion later."

"Little buddy, looks like you and I are headed for the doghouse."

Leaning over Travis whispered into Brendan's ear. Brendan hopped off the chair, bounced around the table and gave Michelle a tight hug. "I'm sorry, Auntie, I won't do it again."

"I'm sorry too," Travis said, apologetically. "Are we forgiven?" *How could she not?* "This time, yes."

"Travis has to hug you like Brendan did to make it stick," Shalee told them.

"Yeah, Travis. Otherwise you aren't really sorry."

"I'm positive your aunt knows I'm really sorry. Brendan wants a banana split. What would you like Shalee?"

"I want strawberry with fudge sauce."

Michelle mouthed, 'thank you'.

Travis mouthed back, 'you're welcome' then took her hand under the table for an instant. The comforting gesture astounded Michelle only because she felt some odd sense of new hope.

"Here comes the waitress. You may both tell her what you want. Brendan, ladies first."

An hour later ice cream devoured, constant chatter between brother and sister going strong, they walked over to the Tavern's construction site not far from Frosty Blues. Travis listened to the children then good-naturedly answered questions ranging from construction equipment to zebras. Satisfied, the kids skipped, ran and jumped playfully before Brendan took off running and Travis took off chasing. Brendan was quick. He hurled himself up on one piece of heavy equipment and climbed inside. Subsequent to a firm one-to-one with Brendan, Travis lifted Shalee and let both kids sit in the cab of the backhoe.

The playground at Tonka Bay Beach is where Travis revealed the reason they should stay at the Pine Cove Retreat. Mac recognized the dead woman when he broke up an argument between Curt and Josie in the Tavern last weekend. It was the same night she and Travis had dinner together. He told her that Derek was at the top of Gage and Mac's list of suspects. They wouldn't confirm or deny that he had strangled and stabbed the woman.

Downright miserable, Michelle closed her eyes and walked along the shore. Travis had good intentions. Safety seemed uppermost in his mind. Considering all her options and his request, the truth persisted. She couldn't refute evidence that her ex was a murder suspect. If she didn't heed caution, harm could come to her niece and nephew.

Opening her eyes, she had walked a distance away from the trio of man and children. She gave into the children's insistence and let them play near the water building sandcastles. Travis occupied their time for now. Michelle removed her loafers and socks, rolled up her jeans and mimicked Katharine's habit of pacing the shore back and forth. Watching them, Mr. Baines Incorporated amazed her in many ways. All he asked her to do this morning was give him a chance to prove he wasn't like Derek.

But how could she?

Derek had once amazed her, too. Did it for two years, she mused wading through the water. Travis owned a reputable business. Derek went from job to job with blameless excuses for his lay-offs and firings. The screw-ups were invariably the fault of others. She glanced back—*Travis didn't indulge in drinking*—watched a scene she never once experienced with Derek. A smile ruffled her mouth. Travis had removed his shoes, yanked his jeans tightly up on his calves and buried his ankles in mud and sand with her niece and nephew. She didn't know who was laughing harder, the kids or him. She had no idea what they thought was so funny, but their elated giggles melted her heart into mush. Michelle exhaled and headed back.

Coming up behind them, she said, "Okay, we'll do it."

All three looked up and Michelle giggled then broke into incredible laughter. They had smeared their faces with mud.

"Auntie Michelle," Brendan coaxed. "Come here and see what we found. This is way cool."

She walked around the trio and a huge castle they constructed with Travis' expertise. Leaning over to look, Brendan swabbed his pudgy hands across her cheeks.

"You little monkey," she whooped. Michelle quickly scooped two handfuls of mud from the hole and dropped one on top of Brendan's head and the other on Travis' head.

"Oh, Milady. You have just waged a war."

Travis grabbed her ankles and pulled her into the mud and water. Shalee squealed and Brendan smeared her with a bonus mucky blob. Michelle wiped her eyes with the inside of her shirt and nailed both man and child with a hefty shot of mud pie. Good healthy laughter exploded out of her. The awakening experience left her reeling for more and she grabbed two more handfuls, swung and received same in return. She laughed until her sides ached and the chains that held her prisoner far too long, broke.

"And you call yourself an executive," she teased when Travis wound up, tossed and threw a large splotch across her belly.

"Well if it ain't Mr. Corporate America and Ms. Meticulously Detailed out for their afternoon mudslinging."

The four stopped, turned, stared stupidly.

"Katharine!" Michelle scrambled out of the castle's moat and for all the good it did wiped her hands on her jeans. "We were just—they were building castles—and covered—"

"Callihan, it's all right." Katharine grinned. "It's about time you cut loose and had some fun. Please, continue."

She started to walk away and Michelle yelled. "Wait! Katharine, would you go get us some towels at my house? A lot of towels?"

"Sure. I'll be back in a few minutes."

Michelle shifted, looked back at the three of them and shook her head. "The mud pie crew is what you three look like."

"You're part of this crew," Travis replied.

She giggled then said, "Brendan, remove your shirt and rinse yourself off in the water. Travis, do the same while I help Shalee."

"First things first. Kids did we have fun?"

"Yes!" they shouted.

"Good because I have new plans for us after we clean up. Now do as your aunt told you."

They did and Travis stood. "Did you really mean what you said?"

Michelle sighed, wanting to believe the mud-covered man was a saint. "I can't doubt Mac and Gage or let anything happen to my niece and nephew. We need to stop by my house first. I'll give the kids baths and check on Keeker."

"Just run in and bring the cat along. You can take baths and showers at the Retreat."

Helping Shalee, she said, "We all need clean clothes and Keeker won't adjust in a new place. I just need to feed him."

Each washed off as best as possible by the time Katharine returned with towels. The remaining mud wiped off, Michelle covered the seats and floor of the Mustang before she allowed anyone into her car. She mentioned the plan to Katharine and they stopped for the Ferrari on the way to her house. Michelle gave Travis fresh towels to sit on and two hours later, they were bathed and ready to go. Trailing him to the Retreat in the Mustang, Travis showered while they waited, and late afternoon, they were off again taking the 'stang across the big lake on the ferry.

With little understanding of how Travis had done it, the evening turned into a night geared around the kids and Pizza World. They indulged on an enormous buffet of assorted pizza slices, appetizers and cold drinks. Brendan and Shalee played at least six different pinball machines. Travis also played the machines before and after the kids made seven jaunts through an enclosed moonwalk. Laughing, giggling, they stuffed their bellies with food to breaking point then made it back to Bayfield in time for the last ferry over to Madeline. Shalee and Brendan crashed in the backseat long before.

"Michelle, if you're worried about your car, I can help you out."

"How?"

"I have a storage garage not far from here. We could put it there and you can drive my car."

"What would you drive?"

"A rental."

"No, Travis. But thanks for offering."

Silence loomed in the car the last fifteen minutes of the trip to the Pine Cove Retreat. Travis stopped, got out and lifted Brendan out and Michelle took Shalee. A tired little girl whimpered briefly but wrapped her arms and legs around Michelle as she carried her inside.

Travis came down the stairs and took Shalee out of her arms. "It's okay, muffin," he said, kissing her temple when she whimpered again.

Michelle followed him up to the loft and stood between the twin beds. He had already removed Brendan's shoes and shirt and she did the same to her niece. She leaned over giving each a kiss on the cheek. "Sweet dreams, dumplin's."

Brendan's eyes fluttered open, and he mumbled, "Thanks, Travis."

"You're welcome, little buddy."

Travis took Michelle's hand and led her to the landing. The light he flicked on when he entered the rental dimly exposed the downstairs. She stared at him for the longest moment until something intense flared between them. "Y-you made their day. Thank you."

"What about yours?" he asked, feathering her cheek with a thumb.

His gray-eyed gaze was as silky as his caress. Michelle barely nodded. She fought off her own resistance to him when he stroked her cheek a second time. Something in his manner had been soothing her all day, but this moment, a fresh stirring in the pit of her stomach sent shivers along her spine. He traced her lip, her mouth and scrolled her bottom one out. Lowering his head, their brows touched. Tenderly, he held her face between his hands, brushed her lips slowly as if savoring the taste of her mouth. Her lips quivered and desire dissipated her need to retreat. He gave her mouth tentative kisses then showered her chin with more. Warmth tingled her flesh everywhere he touched her. A curious swooping pulled on her innards. Michelle struggled with a silent battle of will. It had been too long. Yearning incited a hot ache that began in her throat and swelled throughout her body and soul.

"Michelle . . ." Travis whispered.

His breath hot with hers, she inhaled slightly.

Pressing his lips to hers, Travis took her mouth. Moist, pleasing, soft, he would do everything within his power to unlock her heart and unite it with his. He drew back leisurely. Her lashes fluttered. He tucked her waist in his arm and maneuvered downstairs with her. Nothing ever felt more right to him.

CHAPTER 13

GAGE JERKED UPRIGHT in his chair. He fisted the blur from his eyes and glanced at his watch. His neck ached with a kink the size of the Great Lake surrounding Madeline. Now seven on Sunday morning, he dozed off around four, or five, and figured Mac was in the back catching some shuteye himself. Unfortunately, his small little island town now had its fifth homicide since the end of July. That in itself was an inexplicable travesty, a horror movie with him as the main character, a bumbling idiot incapable of solving one homicide let alone five. A blunt, unknown instrument caused the death of the woman Travis discovered at the lagoon yesterday. She was strangled and brutally stabbed. This homicide of a white female, mid to late twenties, and not a La Pointe resident, was unrelated to the serial killings.

Gage pushed himself up and went to make coffee. Katharine called him a greenhorn when they discovered their first serial killing victim, Sherry Martin. Second, Jennifer Wicket . . . third, Jessica Henderson . . . fourth, Jane Doe. He certainly had no claim on that title anymore. The latest victim, Jane Doe number two, came without name even though Mac recognized her from the night he broke up an argument between Curt and Josie Stewart at the tavern a week ago. Last night, they interviewed the couple but neither remembered the woman's name. At least that's what they said. And they weren't coughing up where the middle Stewart sibling and Gunderson had disappeared to either. In fact, deliberating the

whereabouts of Kevin Stewart and Derek Gunderson and their
involvement, neither had been around since the last incident
between Michelle and Derek. The night Travis came by to inform
them about Derek's threats to her.

He and Mac then spoke to Mark Stewart, the youngest brother.
He hadn't seen Kevin or Gunderson and maintained he did not
know the dead woman. Hayden, the bartender, who had called in
the disturbance the same night Derek decided to pay his ex-wife a
visit, didn't know the victim's name either.

"Damn drunks," he sputtered to himself.

Estimated time of death was somewhere between late Friday
night and early Saturday morning. No weapons were located, let
alone the unusual instrument used to slit the victim's throat. Del
would provide him with the details. But until both Del and Gus
got back to him with their findings from the crime scene, he needed
to reserve judgment. He couldn't. Rage almost choked him with
heinous crime out of control in his town.

Sticking his head into the room where they set up cots a few
months back, Mac wasn't there. Gage went to get water for coffee
from a sink in the conference room and took the carafe back to the
office. He glanced over his shoulder when his dad entered the station.

"Gage, your mother was worried when you didn't come home
last night."

He knew better and tossed coffee grounds into the basket.
"Mac and I worked until around four. I must've dozed off and Mac
probably went home."

"Folks are in an uproar. Have you got anything?"

"Not yet. Still waitin' for Del and Gus."

"Who was she?"

"Dunno. It's not related to the others."

"What does Mac think?"

He avoided eye contact with his dad and dropped to his chair
more from aggravation than fatigue. Ever since he offered his
brother-in-law the job, the new father-in-law made it clear he
thought Mac was the more capable cop.

"We aren't saying much until we get results on the evidence. Should have it in a day or two."

"Dammit, Gage. In my thirty-five years we never had a homicide."

He reacted angrily to the challenge in his father's voice, heaved upward, launching the chair to the wall with force. "You think this is my fault?"

"I didn't say that. I want to know if what you're doing is going to solve and stop these murders."

"We're working on it!" Gage pilfered a cup of coffee, thrusting the glass pot onto the hotplate.

"I hope those scowls plastered on your faces are just one more father-son dispute and not another murder," Mac said entering the station.

Both men grunted, neither verbalizing their thoughts.

"Well, then mornin' to the both of you."

"How's Katharine?" Frank asked.

"She's irritating the hell out of the subcontractors on the house. She wants to be living in it before Thanksgiving."

"That's my Pumpkin. My son tells me you don't have any leads on yesterday's homicide."

He heeded Gage's dagger-filled look by saying, "And he's right. Until we see the M.E.'s report and get the findings back on the evidence, we don't have a lot."

"Anything I can do?"

"Yeah, keep Town folks out of our hair."

"I can do that," Frank said and left the station.

"Katharine's right," Gage huffed. "He is a jerk. What have you got there?" he asked, pointing his mug.

"I conned Nicole into whipping us up some breakfast."

"Christ, that woman works 'round the clock!" he heaved out, refilling his mug.

"Maybe if someone gave her reason not to, she wouldn't."

"Meaning what?" he barked now and seared his sergeant with a heated glare.

"Ah, the famous blue-eyed stare. Katharine doesn't get away with it and I sure as hell ain't gonna let you either."

"Then get off my goddamn back!"

"Whatever."

Tossing a Styrofoam container at Gage, they ate in silence to rejuvenate their strength rather than their dispositions. Belly full and primed with caffeine, Gage asked, "Cole checked in?"

"Called last night. He's about a quarter of the way through the list of county employees. He's checked out a couple of leads but nothing yet."

"Cindy in the front office is bitching about all the taped statements he's sending back. What about Michelle's restraining order?"

"I sent my report to the County Attorney and asked him to give it some priority. He'll call Michelle when it's ready to be signed. And if Cindy doesn't like her job, tell her to find a new one."

"Where do you think those two disappeared to?"

"Derek and Kevin?"

Gage answered with an impersonal nod.

"Probably Bayfield since Gunderson isn't signed in anywhere on the Island. I'll keep an eye on Kevin's place in case either shows up there."

"Mac, you really think Gunderson—"

Halted by the phone, Gage picked it up. "Gus . . . yeah. What've you got? Uh-huh." He grabbed a pen and started scribbling notes on a ruled tablet. "That right? What? A three-year-old? Shit! Yeah, we'll check it out right away. Good work. Later."

Gage disconnected. "Sonovabitch! Let's go, Mac. I'll explain on the way."

Not five minutes later, Gage parked the squad in front of the La Pointe motel. He and Mac found the owner inside the office.

"Hey, Gage. What's up?"

"Mornin' Charlie. Need to know if a Maryann Graham is staying here."

"Yup. Checked in week or so ago with a kid. They're in room ten. Whatcha need?"

"Can you let us in there? Think she may have left the child alone."

Moments later, Charlie opened the door. He and Mac proceeded after they told Charlie to wait outside. With guns drawn, they entered slow and cautious. Blinds and drapes were pulled to darken the room from the early morning sun. Mac covered the bathroom as Gage walked past, advancing slowly into the room.

His heart jumped to his throat.

Trembling and curled up between pillows and blankets on a queen size bed was a fragile little girl with the curliest blond hair he had ever seen. The room vacant of others, he holstered his weapon and smothered the rage he felt having his Ruger pulled in front of the child. Her large eyes, swollen from crying, looked blue in the dim light.

"Mac, get the light. Its okay, sweetie. We won't hurt you. Are you Caitlin?"

She balled her hands in front of her quivering mouth. Fluffy golden waves bounced on her head as she nodded.

"My name is Gage. I'm a police officer—"

"I want Mommy," she wailed.

The bulge in his throat grew and he gulped hard. Big teardrops streamed steadily along the child's stained cheeks. "Are you hungry, Caitlin?"

Those feathery curls danced with her bobbing head.

"Lets get you dressed and take you to get some breakfast. How does that sound, Caitlin?"

"Where's Mommy?"

Sick, fiery gnawing squeezed his heart. It was potent and it was growing. How would he tell what appeared to be about a three-year-old that her mother was murdered in the lagoon and abandoned like garbage? He didn't need to reserve his judgment any longer, either. Gunderson just became his number one suspect and not because anger mangled his gut. Latents from a beer can discovered at the crime scene belonged to both Gunderson and Maryann Graham. It was the first solid piece of evidence since the killing began. He couldn't wait to aim the barrel of his P85 at the bastard who'd hurt Michelle and now killed a stranger in cold blood.

Gage held out his hand and waited for Caitlin to take it. "Come on, sweetie. I'll take care of you. Where's your daddy?"

"I don't have one," she sniveled.

"Well, well. What have we got here?" Mac asked.

The child scrambled into Gage's arms and not wanting to scare her, he calmly asked, "What is it, Mac?"

"Just something that'll make your day. Some heavy-duty drugs and paraphernalia."

"Okay, you handle it. I'll take care of Caitlin. Secure the room when I leave and contact Gus to process it."

He had second thoughts about dressing the child and yanked a blanket off the bed to wrap her in it. On a Sunday, it would take until tomorrow to get someone from Social Services over to the Island to take the child into custody. Although the need infrequent, his mother's home provided foster care in emergencies. Thankfully, when his dad was the police chief, he planned that one rather wisely.

CHAPTER 14

APPETITE AND PEACE were gone. It began so long ago with the first feelings of affection. The thudding heart, sweaty palms and twitchy nervousness filled life with sleepless nights. The anticipation of his or her every move, thoughts of every spoken word, and waiting for the final climax were symptoms of a disease called love. It tasted like honey.

Then the complexity of suffering arrived. The unbearable hurt put the serial killer in a dark place where dismissing human value ran deep—*deceitful witches*. To ignore that murky gloom of betrayal was dangerous. It tasted like vinegar.

The killer twisted hard, breaking the seal of a new bottle of Johnny Walker Black liquor, filled an old-fashioned glass three-quarter full and slowly sipped. The alcohol had the flavorful quality of an antiseptic. It stung the pipes going down. But it was good.

Executioner of life was a deserving title, the killer mused. It went well with the hunt for those thieving bitches all trapped inside their lusty greed and salacious cravings. The chase was a game that provided enough power to destroy. Especially to the ones with bronze flesh and hair so dark that it shone like black oil. They look at you all innocently with their large brown eyes as if they really care, but they don't. Their guiltless disloyalty is as physically painful as the loss of love. At least the honey-vinegar taste of revenge provided a feeling of something other than envy— desire to make them suffer the consequences of their lies.

The killer refilled the glass, considering the overall plan thoughtfully. To murder in cold blood felt like an injection of an erotic love drug. A strong aphrodisiac pumped into your bloodstream. The act of killing had physical power that overflowed with the anxious sensation of a first kiss done amidst passionate waves around the ankles. It left an agreeable, yet peculiar taste in one's mouth and was the prelude of better things to come. It was like foreplay before the act of intercourse. Murder aroused. It possessed. It thrilled with potent hunger.

But the ceremony of death had to be planned.

The Almighty One selected each sacrifice in prelude to the ultimate finale. Only he could summon each sacrifice for service. The service was a ceremonious presentation, a purification set up for his grace's standards. The standards were set extremely high and performed with precision. The ritual, called a matin, commenced within the first canonical hour. The stroke of midnight. There were seven total hours. The canonical hours were for devotion and prayer to the Almighty One. That was his ecclesiastical law and only he had the authority to change it. With the body of rules in place, the Almighty One's promise of love would follow eleven days after the summer solstice. Sixteen days after the autumn harvest, Almighty One gave his matrimonial pledge. However, if a seed was planted prematurely, it must be aborted two days behind the Almighty One's birth and prior to carrying out the ritual. Not the birth of *their* sanctimonious God, but the birth of the Almighty One.

Only the killer, who had been chosen by the Almighty One, could execute the ritual procedures. After the capture of each, the ceremony began by tainting the golden flesh with holy water. This dissolved the sacrifice of sins and re-nourished their souls. The next step was to feed the sacred pea and by so doing replenished stolen virginity. Devoted chanting of the Morning Prayer followed. Chanting proved the killer's loyalty to the Almighty One and provided the necessary atonement of the sacrifice. It was considered worshipping to the Almighty—

"Be damned in hell if not pure!"

The killer twitched and downed the liquor. The Almighty One, also called Father—he liked to be called Father—did not tolerate shame. To shame Father meant unworthiness and disgrace. He believed a night of inflamed passion and fervent promises was a poisonous pilfering of virgin flesh. It was sinful and sins could not be forgiven. Father forbade the act of trading nasty favors.

"Be damned to hell for your impurity! You will be cleansed of your infection!"

The voice cutting through the silent thoughts was an enormous command. The killer shuddered and guzzled the liquor straight from the bottle this time. The voices, not just one anymore, were increasing in volume and numbers. Sometimes they were harsh and raw, hardening ruthlessly, sometimes there was contempt sparked by resentment and disappointment. They all spoke, some screamed, but they surged together frequently. The killer could no longer hear or decipher the call of the Almighty One.

Draining the golden solution from the liquor bottle, the killer blotted out the powerful declarations, and reflected back on the latest accolade. She proved to be a superb sacrifice. Dark shadows in her eyes held such a pensive shimmer. To watch the fear swell within in her had provided such an immense pleasure, too. With the end of her days on earth nearing, she cried out for salvation. She pleaded and begged for redemption. Her final prayers that it be over were possibly the most erotic emotion the killer ever felt. Alas, the Almighty One answered the plea of the sacrifice and accepted her soul into his kingdom.

As quickly as the deed was done, all pleasure ceased.

Disappointment settled in the pit of the killer's stomach. The dates of the ritual were three, and three must be handed over to the Almighty One every year until none remained to plunder what did not belong to them. But it was no longer enough to take just three a year. The act of murder had become animalistic greed for more carnage. The need increasing with each execution also delayed the taking of the ultimate sacrifice. The killer retrieved a second bottle of liquor and filled the glass.

Screw the canon laws! Her time is up!

The killer thought about it, grabbed a knife and sliced a finger. The blood dripped to form the words. *Death to the brazen slut with golden hair.*

Just one more sacrifice for the Almighty One and then Father *will* take her.

CHAPTER 15

MICHELLE ENDED HER call with a subcontractor and leaned back in the chair downing another Pepsi. Framing began Tuesday and the roofing subs were all set. Within a week and a half, Travis told her, the addition would start to blend with the rest of the building.

She sighed. The weekend with her niece and nephew and Travis was adequately revealing. As images replayed in her mind, Travis was as captivated with the kids as they were with him. Sunday afternoon on Gage's speedboat, Travis came through with his promise, and let Brendan sit in his lap to steer the boat. 'Awesome' Brendan kept telling Travis. They docked in Bayfield and ate dinner before Sylvie and Harvey returned for their children. Shalee cried when the time came to go home. Brendan was a stoic little hero except for the perceived sadness displayed in his eyes. Her heart did that little flipping thing when both her dumplin's hugged and thanked Travis for a great weekend. The warmth and affection coming from her niece and nephew unmasked unexpected tears. Nearly two years now, she hadn't genuinely laughed, cried or enjoyed anything as much as she did the past weekend.

Michelle fingered her lips, remembering the touch of Travis' mouth on hers Saturday night. He kissed her just the once, but the real shock came with her own twittering pangs of desire. With her mind made up a long time ago, the thought never occurred to her that she might experience those feelings again. An ache sparked by one unforgettable kiss, the strength of passion was starting to overpower her personal decision. She couldn't give herself to any man a second time. *Could she?*

Not a chance she realized when her thoughts shifted to the chilly conversation with Mac and Gage. They stopped by the Pine Cove Retreat on Sunday to warn her about Derek. Evidence suggested that he did murder the woman at the Lagoon. In that telling moment, her blood went frigid while goose bumps wormed their way along her arms and spine. Although Derek had disappeared, they were justly concerned for her safety. He wouldn't stop until he got what he wanted. Money. In the meantime, panic had camped out in her throat with their warnings. It was a decisive moment, a horrific thought, but she had once escaped his punishment. Travis stood by in silence, his face stricken, a worried expression filling his eyes.

Sunday evening after they returned to the marina from Bayfield with Gage's speedboat, Travis pleaded with her to stay at the Retreat. It was a lousy excuse. She missed her black furball and tossed justified gibberish at him about being away from Keeker for extended hours. She flat out refused to stay alone with Travis. Couldn't do it no matter how much genuine concern he showed. The deep-rooted fears of Derek's abuse geared her firm decision.

Michelle pushed herself up out of the chair. Living this way was exasperating and she went outside to watch the crews. Newcomers stood with Travis. Two women and two men shifted spontaneously when he turned and smiled at her. Travis moved in her direction and all four followed.

"Michelle, I'd like you to meet my grandparents and parents."

"Win gwanatch oshkinjigoma."

"Nin kikendjige," Travis responded. "They're green like flawless emeralds, Grandma-ma."

"Here we go, Dad."

Michelle studied the woman who spoke the native words while Travis introduced Julia Cadotte Perry. She was undersized and beginning to thicken around the middle as grandmothers sometimes do. A pert little face beheld petite features. Feathered hair that might pass as silk spinning fiber was snow colored. Travis definitely had his grandmother's waves.

Travis' mother, Rosemary introduced herself and extended her hand waiting for her to accept. Michelle hesitated, interest increasing, while the attractive woman eyed her curiously. After several silent questions concerning what Travis told his family about her, she accepted Rosemary's sturdy shake. Contrary to her firm grip, Rosemary Baines was elegant and gorgeous in an uncomplicated way. Long limbed like the man standing behind her. There was a hint of Native American heritage in Rosemary's high, exotic cheekbones, too. They glowed with rich warmth.

"Mrs. Baines, it's nice to meet you."

"My God! He was right, Phillip."

"Excuse me," Michelle said.

"Michelle, my apologies. You're the first woman my son has ever talked about. He told me your eyes were endowed like emeralds. His description is extremely accurate. I'm pleased to meet you as well but you must call me Rosemary. Pay no mind to Travis and his Grandma-ma when they speak Ojibwe either. We don't. This is Travis' father, Phillip, and my father, Ronson."

"Hi, Michelle. Nice to meet you. Please, call me Phillip."

Vaguely disturbed that Travis would talk to anyone about her, Michelle fought to control new emotions regardless of how much Rosemary reminded her of Nicole. Sleek, tall, fast talker to name the obvious. Phillip Baines was staggeringly handsome, dignified and large with an athletic physique. Travis definitely had his father's aristocratic features she mused, exchanging hand gestures with him. "Phillip, you must be very proud of Travis."

A relaxed mile-wide grin cued his agreement. Ronson Perry, the quietest of the four, patiently waited until she faced him. Travis' grandfather had a long and firm appearance. Horse-faced, Michelle decided, with just a hint of pleats creasing the corners of supple pleasant eyes. Ronson advanced and cupped her hand between his kissing the back.

"Our grandson was right again, Mother," he said to his wife. "Indeed, she is a very beautiful woman. Michelle, would you do us the honor and join us for dinner this evening?"

"I have to apologize for being at an extreme disadvantage here. I wasn't told that you were coming but it's obvious you've all been told about me."

With a sideways glance, she scowled at Travis who just flashed his father's smile and winked at her. The black Ferrari went from zero to sixty incredibly slower than it took her to figure out she was on display for their examination.

"Didn't I tell you she was full of spirit?"

"My dear son," Rosemary said. "We already knew that just by the way she's kept you hopping."

"Travis, give your grandfather and dad a tour. Rosemary and I want to talk to this girl out of male earshot."

"As you wish, Grandma-ma. Men, I think we've just been ordered to get lost."

"That we have," Phillip said, and kissed his wife's cheek.

Rosemary responded then kissed her son's cheek as well. Travis hugged his grandma-ma, telling her, "Behave yourself. Her scowl just told me I'm in the doghouse."

The three loped away as Travis excitedly began pointing at the structure in conversation.

"That boy never ceases to amaze me," Julia murmured.

"Nor his father and me," Rosemary replied.

"Imagine the planning and thought he's gone to just to make Ronson and my anniversary extraordinary."

Enthusiasm or not, he could have at least told me he was going to make an early announcement, Michelle thought. A sidelong glance at the two women, new and unexpected warmth surged through Michelle. Moisture rimmed Julia's blue-gray eyes and Rosemary had snuggled an arm around her. With a thorough examination of mother and daughter, another hidden longing begged for release. The constant yearning started after Brian's death when her own mother relinquished all affection. She and Sylvie rarely hugged anymore either. The tragic loss of a brother and son blew apart a household once filled with family love. The irreversible damage simulated her marriage to Derek. Then a terrifying realization washed over her. She'd kept her failures to herself, never told Elisabeth and Aidan Callihan the details of Derek's destruction because both wished to mourn their dead son—Michelle jerked when an arm encircled her waist. She stiffened more when Rosemary gently tugged her in closer.

"I have to tell you, Michelle. When you opposed my son's plans I found myself admiring a woman I'd never met."

She blinked, felt her cheeks heat up. "Why would you?"

"Travis is not a stubborn man by nature, but he's certainly persistent. He knows what he wants and always receives whatever he sets his mind to. This project is important to him. You actually had him worried. Then those tragic deaths indeed had him considering throwing in the towel. Phillip and I talked him out of it and I'm very glad we did."

"If your son had informed the Town Board of his reasons in the beginning, I would have bent over backwards to see it through."

"He told me what you said."

Amongst many other emotions came a deep sense of shame. It worsened when Rosemary laughed and patted her arm.

"Dear, you have nothing to be embarrassed about. I've taught him better manners. I also let him know what I thought of his eavesdropping." Rosemary chuckled more. "Michelle, it's a very rare day when anyone opposes my son or his scrupulous plans."

She wanted to curl up and crawl into a hole.

"You seem to have done exactly that. Men need to be put in their place every now and then. Don't they, Mom?"

"Absolutely. As long as you allow them to think they're in charge, it can be accomplished with little effort."

Michelle's defenses subsided a little, recalling what Travis had told her about his grandma-ma and a new thought struck her. "Mrs. Perry, you might be exactly the right person to fill in some historical blanks. Would you be willing to help the historical museum? Like telling them what Julia Warren died of at such a young age?"

"It's believed diphtheria or small pox. I don't rightly know. In those days people feared death and rarely spoke of their pain and grief."

"Some still won't," Michelle muttered. Dubitable looks from both women then prompted her to say, "My brother's death at the age of eighteen tore our family apart. My mother's grief has shut out my younger sister and me."

"It must be very difficult for you both to live in the shadow of your brother," Julia said. "As arduous as it is for a mother to lose a child one would think a parent would worship the ground of offspring left behind."

"Mrs. Perry, I apologize. I didn't mean to spoil Travis' surprise by talking about my personal grief."

"You've spoiled nothing! Sharing your emotional pain with us is an honor. It says you trust us and I'll hear no more apologies over sorrowful words that come from your heart."

Michelle broke their embrace when a quick breath of utter astonishment nearly choked her. She had never talked about that life-altering weekend with anyone but Nicole and Katharine. Lately, her guts were spilling over. Oddly, it felt good. Talking also eased the upset stomach she'd started having with too much frequency.

"And stop calling me Mrs. Perry."

"Yes, ma'am. With a condition. I'd really appreciate any help you can give the museum."

"My dear, there's certainly no need to negotiate for a piece of my past. I would be honored."

"Mrs.—"

Michelle stopped abruptly when Julia's face flashed her grandson's intentional expression. "Julia, we would appreciate anything you can share with us. I'll introduce you to Cathy. She'll love talking with you."

"I think I'd enjoy that myself. I want to see how things have changed around La Pointe. Sadly, it's been too many years since we left. We just never found the time to come back."

"Are the four of you staying on Madeline or in Bayfield?"

"Travis made reservations for us here," Rosemary replied. "My son is very thorough and takes excellent care of all of us. He scheduled and booked the Leer to fly us from Florence and got us a rental car as well."

"Booked the Leer?" Michelle questioned, now understanding why a rental would have been easy for him if she put the Mustang in storage like he wanted her to do.

"Phillip didn't mind traveling the commercial airlines. When Travis took over the business, he decided a company jet was a necessity. He hates waiting in airports. For that matter, my son hates waiting for any thing or one."

"Then you've just arrived from Italy?"

Both women nodded.

"Perhaps you'd like to rest. If I take care of a few last minute things today, I'd be available to show you anything you'd like tomorrow."

"That's a wonderful idea. I know Phillip and Dad will be here with Travis all day. Phillip won't admit it, but he misses the onsite work."

"Yes, Michelle, we'd enjoy a tour of Madeline very much. I for one would like to rest before dinner this evening."

"Then it's all set," Julia said. "We'll see you at seven tonight."

When Michelle's jaw dropped, she quickly closed it but a bit too late.

"Mom, you just told Dad not to be so pushy. We've taken up enough of Michelle's time for one day. Perhaps she has other plans this evening."

"Fine, have it your way. We'll meet you here at eight in the morning."

"Julia, please do not use guilt tactics on me when you haven't given me a chance to accept or decline Ronson's invitation to join you. You're wasting your breath and time. Now, I'd certainly enjoy your company this evening, but we'll have to meet here at eleven since I already have an early morning commitment."

Although neither woman appeared offended by her directness, Michelle felt sure she did exactly that. Poised is what they were, and measuring her up . . . *with satisfaction?*

"Eleven will work well for us in the morning," Rosemary responded. "Will seven be good for you this evening?"

"Yes that will be fine. I'm looking forward to it."

"All right then. We'll get out of your way and go tell Phillip and Dad. They'll both be quite pleased."

*   *   *

On the first ferry out of dock the next morning, Michelle was enroute to the Ashland County Attorney's office. The Assistant County Attorney had called yesterday to tell her the complaint for a restraining order against Derek was ready to be signed. Once the papers were endorsed, she could have her ex arrested for any contact he made with her in any way, shape, or form Mac explained to her.

Michelle snorted out a cynical laugh. "Who are they kidding? Derek's extremely violent and vicious. He murdered that poor woman!"

Did they really believe a restraining order would stop him? Jittery as a mouse trapped by a cat, she scanned her circumference before sliding out of the Stanger and locking the door. Ever since she caught Derek following her from Katharine's house, she'd become neurotic about extreme caution. The grating pain in her shoulders had returned as well, and climbing the stairs to the top deck of the ferry, Michelle tilted her head side-to-side to stretch the muscles. *I can't keep living this way* she mused moving toward the ferry's life rail. She leaned against the iron and found soothing comfort in the slightly ruffled waves. They rolled systematically under another glorious blue sky. The cooler air on Lake Superior was an indication of the change of seasons to come. Would her life change for better or worse she wondered.

Exhaling a heavy dose, she had always prided herself on patience, logic and independence, but had forfeited stability since the divorce. While practicality filled her life with detailed routine, hard work and monotony, trepidation filled her heart and mind. The good her parents once taught her to see in people was a waste. The depth of their wisdom only led her to gullibility and manipulation. If she hadn't been easygoing and flexible, she never would have suffered as much as she had. Maybe if she had been less trusting of Derek, her physical abuse would have been someone else's story. With a lot of ifs and maybes in her life, she couldn't change the events or the alteration of her life. Her tarnished innocence and fear of Derek far exceeded her dread of loneliness.

Feeling the presence of someone behind her, Michelle didn't just glance. She whirled around. "Sully!"

"Mornin' lassie. Tis early for an excursion. Business on the mainland?"

Mellow, golden-brown eyes studied her with wary concern. He placed a tattered, unlit pipe between his teeth and lips that were surrounded by a gray-bristle beard. "I have an appointment in Ashland."

"Yer worried, lassie. Care to dump those troubles on old Sully's broad shoulders?"

"Your awareness is comforting. And thanks. But how do you always seem to know?"

"I told Katharine the same not long ago. Tis in yer emerald eyes. Tis a color missing that once matched the mighty pines of the Apostles. Aye, the sparkle's gone and anxiety replaces it. They weep with sorrow as Mikala does."

Michelle peered at the aging man she'd known all her life. With tours done for the season, Sully worked the Island Queen ferry until it, too, was docked for the winter. During summers, he loved playing tourist guide on the Island Princess where he narrated a ghost story of Madeline and Michel Cadotte's three exquisite daughters. Each child adored by their loving parents, Katrina, Nicolina and Mikala were graced with jeweled eyes he said. He forever told the legend of how the daughters were each murdered by medicine men on the night preceding their wedding vows. Sully captured visitor's attentions with a less-than-accurate pledge of why the jeweled eyes were a sacrament to the medicine man's divine creator.

Michelle knew better. True, there'd been at least six children, maybe eight, born to Michel Sr. and Madeline. The most noted in history of those children were Michel Jr., along with two sisters Mary and Charlotte who married the Warren brothers. Mary was the mother to Julia Warren who died at five months old. Although the library and museum had nothing more, there had been mention by way of a letter of a third sister, Jozette Cadotte. Hopefully, Julia Perry would know something about her. And though Sully continually fascinated visitors with the incorrect details, no Cadotte daughters were named Mikala, Nicolina or Katrina. He then told how following the death of her third daughter Nicolina, Madeline Cadotte went into seclusion on the largest of the Apostle Islands and was never seen or heard from again. He beefed up the story with fictitious facts of how the Native American wife died of mourning within a year of her third and last daughter's death. In honor and dedication to the renowned woman, Madeline Island was named. The truth was Esquaysayway, daughter of Chief White Crane, married Michel Cadotte, Sr. in Sault Ste. Marie because there were no priests on the Island. The Native American wife never went into seclusion. But, like others, Michelle always thought that someone would some day construct a statue in Madeline Cadotte's honor. The woman who gave her name was certainly deserving of a monument guarding the gateway of the Chequamegon Bay on the southeast side of Madeline Island in La Pointe.

That aside, Sully's version continued by informing passengers of bridal gifts Michel had for Katrina, Mikala and Nicolina but never received on account of their murders. Through years of storytelling, the largess of jewels had been drastically twisted into large treasures of gold-bearing medallions and coins the French fur trader brought with him from France. Both Michel and his father, Jean Baptiste Cadotte were fur traders. Neither dabbled in gold or jewels. Strangely, Sully's fable didn't end there. With his allegation of tragic deaths and haunting ghosts, he informed tourists that the three fictitious daughters had been heard crying on various islands throughout the Apostles. An expert by repetition, he convinced everyone the three daughter's ghosts would weep loudly until their lost dowries of jewels were located. Three women must also unite in island marriages to their soul mate before the ghosts went to rest in peace.

Sully studied her purposefully. A ridiculous smile filled his eyes and face.

"Lassie, Katharine didn't believe either. But look at her now. Tis a sight ta behold with a twinkle back in the blue twinning Superior."

"Sully, I know you and Katharine *think* you heard Katrina."

"Aye. I was there at Raspberry. We heard Katrina together." Squinting with one eye, he said, "You've heard Mikala, haven't ya, lassie."

Heat stole into her face as she muttered, "I don't know."

When he tossed her a skeptical look, she mumbled, "For at least a year now."

"Tis not trickery in yer mind, child. Ya must stop resisting and believe again. Open your heart. Let it become as fond as ya are protective of our great island."

"Sully, my heart has no room anymore."

"For the heart and eyes to agree ya must know what yer runnin' to and from. Let Madeline soothe yer soul and Mikala will guide yer heart."

She was running to sign a restraining order against her ex. "For being a wise man, you've certainly missed the boat of accuracy on the Cadotte history. You do realize there never was a Mikala, Katrina or a Nicolina."

"Aye, perhaps. And perhaps tis imagination inside our minds making dreams come true in our hearts. I must go now, lassie."

"All right, Sully. See ya later."

The phrase now used abundantly in the area was picked up from the Native American's because they didn't enjoy good-byes. Michelle didn't mind this goodbye.

When the ferry neared the Bayfield docks, Michelle returned to her car, waited and drove off headed for Ashland. Sully, like Travis and his family, gave her plenty to think about. She was thinking too much and sleeping too little. Out of Bayfield and on the highway, she cranked the tunes and floored the Stanger.

Dinner last night with Travis and his family went well enough. It just seemed everyone doted on her more than necessary. The conversation veered from her business, to the Tavern's ballroom, her position on the Town Board to Phillip's interest in her Mustang. Where did she go to college—how did she like living on Madeline? Oh, the evening was nice all right. Phillip and Ronson entertained with stories of Travis, as did Travis and Grandma-ma speaking Ojibwe. Travis nudged her under the table when the two of them started the native language. It took little time to understand he and Julia spoke the language with the intent of getting a rise out of his mother—it worked. Still, those native words sounded musical and romantic to her ears, even with many Ojibwe words being jawbreakers. As the evening wound down, she had answered more questions about her life than she thought possible to ask.

Arriving in Ashland in under an hour, Michelle located the County Attorney's office with little difficulty. It took longer waiting to sign the papers. With a copy of the complaint in hand, she began the short trip back to La Pointe. How odd she mused on the return ferry from Bayfield. Sully was gone.

Driving off the ferry, she reconsidered Travis' request to give him a chance. Arriving home, prior to picking up Julia and Rosemary for the promised tour, Michelle feathered her mouth recalling the kiss. The restraining order lying on the seat of her car would always be a blatant reminder of her past. She abruptly shifted gears, whipped the Mustang in a one-eighty and headed for the Tavern. She couldn't let it happen to her again. She must tell Travis to give up his little escapade for her affections. It would never work.

Michelle raced onto the Tavern's property. She saw the squad cars first, spotted Mac and Gage with Travis along with Phillip and Ronson. Her heart jumped inside of her chest as she gaped at the structure.

CHAPTER 16

T OTAL DESTRUCTION. THE ballroom framing was smashed, demolished, destroyed. Travis turned, saw her, and rushed over in long-bodied strides when Michelle exited her car. His uncompromising mouth and jaw matched a dark wrath burning in his eyes.

"What happened?" she blurted, then stepped back when he almost took her in his arms. Stopping short, he soothed her with a hand to her shoulder instead.

"Michelle, we've all been worried about you. Mom said you had an appointment this morning."

"I just got back from the County Attorney's office in Ashland. Travis, how did this happen? Who did it?"

"Gage and Mac believe it's retaliation."

"For what? By whom?" Michelle demanded.

"I'd already told them I punched Gunderson last week. We arrived here this morning to discover it."

Unmitigated horror dived into the center of her bones. She wondered if her face exposed the depth of her own panic. Then without warning she knew the answer when Travis gathered her into his arms and stroked her hair.

"Milady, we won't let anything happen to you."

She pleaded in a muffled whisper against his chest, "Why, Travis? Why is he doing this? What did I ever do to him?"

He leaned back, took her face between his hands. "Michelle, you didn't do anything. The man's demented."

"But all the work you've done. The delays this will cause. "How are you going to fix this?"

He pulled away reluctantly and held her at arm's length. "The materials are replaceable. Your life isn't. You can't be left alone."

His anxiety-ridden face quivered her insides and scattered goose bumps along her arms. "Travis—"

"Michelle, listen to me. I'm not asking you to stay with me but you can't stay alone any longer."

"Why, Travis?"

He stepped back, ramming his fist into the palm of his other hand. "Because, damn it! This time he threatened *your* life!"

She remained motionless for a moment then reached, laying her hand on his bunched fists. He stared back, a lethal calmness in his eyes.

"We—Mac found a note nailed to a two-by-four."

Her hand dropped. "Where is it? What did it say?"

"Michelle," Nicole exclaimed, flying out the Tavern's entrance. "Thank God you're safe! Hon, I've been so worried about you!"

"I'm fine," she replied. "Travis, I asked you a question."

"Don't do this to yourself."

His quiet words felt like the stillness before a brutal storm, but she insisted. "I want to see it. Show me the note now!"

Gage and Mac approached and stopped in front of her. Mac handed over the note in a plastic sealed evidence bag. "It's not signed,"

Ripping it out of his hand, Michelle recognized Derek's bad hand immediately. Fear clumped and stuck in her throat. She slithered backward, paced, thought, and relived the last vile night with Derek. New images grew in her mind, and her heart refused to stop thumping inside of her chest. Her breathing shallow and quick, she bit her lip rereading the scribble.

You're next bitch! Pay me or die.

Phillip and Ronson joined them and the five men stood waiting, watching her. Rage, more than any other emotion, coiled inside of her now. She shifted, gazed at Brian's Mustang. "It's his handwriting. He's after my car."

Retrieving the evidence, Mac asked, "Why the car, Michelle?"

"It's a '69 Mustang with all the originals. It'll easily sell for twenty-five grand to the right buyer. Maybe more," Phillip told them.

"It was an inheritance after Brian's accident. He wants cash not the car," Michelle retorted tartly.

"Wisconsin is community property with a few exceptions. One is inheritance," Gage explained. "Michelle, we did a background on Derek. He's a hundred grand in debt to a loan shark in Vegas."

"Oh, well, there's a surprise," she snapped angrily.

"He's already killed for less and he won't stop until we arrest him."

"Won't stop killing or stealing!" she blasted.

"Michelle, you can't stay at your house alone," Gage said.

She inhaled a deep breath and quietly told them, "I'm not running this time."

"She's staying with me," Nicole responded.

"Nikki! She's not staying with you! Neither one of you are safe."

"Why me?" Nicole wanted to know. "That jerk doesn't give two hoots about me."

"Maybe not, but I won't risk it. You can both stay with Mom and Dad."

"I will not impose on your folks or anyone else," Michelle said with grave deliberation.

"Me either," Nicole said, stepping closer to Michelle.

Gage's visage an affronted frown, Michelle realized his upset came out of fear for their safety. His anger was more obvious than the first sign of insult. His glowing eyes looked like savage fire bulging out of the sockets. Grit teeth, iron jaw, protruding neck veins, his mouth tightened into a stubborn line. She glanced at the others. Travis's face was a dark mask. Before today, she never saw Mac's eyes filled with black vengeance. Even Phillip gawked at them with some disbelief. If Ronson Perry felt anything for the situation, he appeared to be the only rational one deep in concentration.

"Gage is right," Mac urged. "This guy is dangerous and I believe he'll go after anyone connected to you, Michelle."

"What about Katharine? She's pregnant. Aren't any of you worried about her?"

"Katharine's a trained police officer and can take care of herself," Mac replied.

"My father, grandfather and I agree with them," Travis said in a controlled voice. "I don't care where you stay, but the two of you *won't* be left alone."

Michelle's restraint nose-dived. "I've had enough! None of you, not Derek not anyone is chasing me out of my home ever again. Nicole can stay with me if she wants to, and this discussion is over!"

"This is insane," Gage growled, swung away, took a step then turned back. "You two are so fricking obstinate!"

"I want to talk to these lovely ladies alone," Ronson finally said. "It's clear what's going on here. Would you gentlemen excuse us?"

Travis grunted and followed Mac and Phillip. Gage went along, but kicked a broken 2x4 with the toe of his boot sailing it through the air.

"We could always drug them with sleeping pills like we did to Katharine after she was shot," Mac said.

"Don't tempt me!" Gage spit hotly and sent another split 2x4 reeling through the air off his boot toe. Missing a worker by inches, he yelled, "Sorry!" when the guy toasted him with a nasty glare.

"Give Ronson a few minutes and he'll talk sense into them," Phillip said.

"Dad, Gage is right! What the hell are they thinking? I've had face-to-face confrontations with the son-of-a-bitch. He's brutally vicious. Michelle doesn't stand a chance!"

"Agreed, but you're all too obvious. Haven't you learned you never tell a woman what she can and can't do? She'll fight you every step of the way. Travis you should know how your grandmother *thinks* she's in control. That's because your grandfather lets her think it."

"Is that what you do to Mom?" he retorted.

"This has nothing to do with being in control," Gage blasted. "It has to do with keeping Michelle and Nikki alive. I should lock them up in a county cell until this is over."

Ronson ambled over, and said, "Won't have to. I convinced them to stay with your parents, Gage. Phillip, I called Rosemary and explained why Michelle can't tour them around La Pointe today."

Heads jerked around when Katharine screeched her beat-up Buick to a halt. She hopped out gaping at the shambles. "I just heard and came to see for myself. It's worse than I thought."

"What'd the doctor say?" Mac asked, meeting her and kissing her temple.

"Everything's fine—he'll see me in a month. Mac, who did this?"

"Gunderson. Michelle ID'd his handwriting from a threatening note he left."

"Is she all right? Where is she?"

"With Nicole inside the Tavern. Have you met Travis' dad and grandfather?"

"No."

After introductions, Gage asked, "Katharine, Michelle and Nikki are gonna stay with Mom and Dad until we nail Gunderson. Would you take them home for us?"

"Of course. Is Caitlin still there?"

"Yeah. Social Services is short on space and since the house is authorized foster care, I told them we'd keep her until they had room."

"I'll take care of it. I need an outlet from yelling at those stupid subcontractors. Nothing personal," she added, looking at Travis.

"What kind of problems are you having?" Travis asked.

After she ran down a long list from foundation and cement slab under the crawl space to window placement and doorframes, he said, "I'll make you a deal. If you make sure Michelle is safe at your parent's house, I'll take a look at everything for you this afternoon."

"You'd do that for Mac and me?"

"After the way I've witnessed all of you taking care of Michelle, I'd do anything for any of you."

She broke into a wide grin.

"What?"

"You're really in love with her," Katharine stated.

Mac interrupted tapping Katharine on the shoulder. "Princess, Gage and I have to go." He then kissed her. "I'll see ya later."

"I love you, Dobarchon. Watch your back."

"I will."

"So, Travis. Have you heard Mikala's cry yet?"

"Who?" he asked of the second person to mention that name.

"Yep. You're hearing Mikala. Mac heard Katrina and thought he was going insane, too."

"What are you talking about?" Travis asked again.

"The ghost, Mikala Cadotte."

"Katharine, does being pregnant make you crazy?"

"Crazy in love," she said with a chuckle. "When you meet Sully, the guy who works the ferry and does the Island Princess tours in the summer, he'll tell you this great ghost story about the Cadotte daughters. Three of them, Katrina, Mikala and Nicolina haunt the islands crying."

Unbelievably convincing, he thought of the grinning redhead. Nevertheless, it was obvious she and Mac weren't going to divulge the entire story. He wondered why.

"Talk to Mac if you don't believe me."

"Will it do me any good?"

Katharine laughed then said, "I really do appreciate you checking the house for us. Mac and I have sunk everything into it. I hate to burden him with these problems when he's trying to catch this parasite. Lemme tell you where it's at and then I'll take care of Michelle and Nicole and meet you over there later. When's a good time for you?"

"I want to go through it without you. Make it four when you show up," he said, handing her a pen from his shirt pocket then the palm of his hand for her to write the directions. "Katharine, don't let on to Michelle."

"Don't worry," she said, writing on his hand. "I like you, Baines. But take some advice. I've seen domestic abuse more than I care to admit. Michelle needs to learn how to trust again. Mac, me, my brother, we're all working on her. It just takes time. She's an amazing person and an even better friend. Mac and I will never let her suffer again."

Katharine finished, prodded the pen back into his pocket.

"I see why he calls you a warrior princess."

"Really? Explain it to me."

It was his turn to laugh at her.

"This is one of those man things, isn't it?"

Bopping her on the nose with his finger, Travis laughed wholeheartedly as Michelle and Nicole exited the tavern. When the two women headed toward them, he watched only one wondering if she realized the many ways she affected him. If he had expected her to give a simple compliance to their requests, he had grossly underestimated her.

"Yup. You definitely got it bad, Baines. You're okay. I'll see what I can do to help."

"Katharine, what are you doing here?" Nicole asked.

"I'm taking you two over to Mom and Dad's. Then I'm gonna meet Travis at the new house. He's offered to check on the problems Mac and I are having with the subcontractors."

"Do you need me to re-order any materials for here?" Michelle asked.

"Jerry and I took care of it. They'll have a new load here Monday. You get settled and don't worry about this. I have to get back to work. Katharine, I'll see you at four."

"Thanks again. And talk to Mac if you don't believe me."

"Believe what?" Michelle asked.

"Nothing. Let's get goin."

*   *   *

After Nicole packed and repacked, Katharine told her to take the essentials. The three best friends carried luggage and Keeker into the LeNoir house. It had been many years, but as teenagers they spent many overnighters in this house. In silent admission, Michelle did feel safer with others around her. In his winsome manner, Travis' grandfather had talked them out of their foolishness he called it. The more she thought about Travis' family, the more she longed for the loving feelings to return to the Callihan household. Retrieving the last suitcase, she recalled the original reason she went to see Travis at the tavern.

"Damn," she muttered. Still unable to give herself completely, she would tell him to give up his pursuit of her.

"What's the matter?" Katharine asked, returning outside.

Michelle yanked the suitcase out of the car. "I just remembered why I ended up at the tavern this morning. I can't do it, Katharine."

"Do what?"

"Travis wants me to give him a chance to prove to me that not all men are like Derek. I can't do it. I went all the way to Ashland to sign that restraining order this morning. And for what. A piece of paper won't stop my ex from coming after me. All the way over and back I kept looking in the mirror and over my shoulder. I hate living this way."

"Do you like Travis?"

She laughed cynically. "He's nice, but so was Derek once upon a time ago."

"Michelle, remember the promise we made to each other at Aunt Suzanne's birthday party? About keeping our hearts open?"

"Yeah. Sully told me the same thing this morning on the ferry. He said for my heart and eyes to agree I have to figure out what I'm running to and from. That I should let Madeline soothe my soul and Mikala will guide my heart. Blah-blah-blah."

"Sully's right. When I came home, I had no idea if I'd done the right thing by quitting my job. What I did know is I was trying to run from my fears. Mac helped me to understand why. All of us are here to help you. That bastard won't stand a chance when Gage and Mac arrest him for murder. He'll be put away for life."

Michelle set the luggage down and leaned against the car, crossing her arms. "What does any of this have to do with Travis?"

"I was running from myself and ran right into Mac. You're running from Derek. Let Travis catch you. Like you told me, I think he might be the right one for you. He cares deeply for you, Michelle."

"I believed Derek cared for me, too. Hell I believed he loved me."

"But you never once heard Mikala all the time you were with Derek. You told me yourself you're hearing Mikala now."

"Me and my big mouth," she muttered. Michelle brushed blowing hair out of her face. "Do you still hear Katrina?"

"Not since Mac and I married. How long had you been dealing with Baines before you met, and I quote, *'the old coot'*?"

"Omigod! It *was* about the same time Mikala started wailing. Katharine, do you really believe the two are related?"

"What I think is that Travis Baines is a good, kindhearted man. If you've never trusted me a moment before now, you have to trust me when I tell you that man will never hurt you."

"How can you be so sure?"

"I spent ten years reading slime on city streets. Whether it's ingrained or learned, I know people. I'm positive Travis will never cause you pain. If you decide never to give him a chance, that's your decision. I also know it'll break his heart, but he'll walk away if you tell him to."

"Look who I found inside," Nicole called out, exiting the house. "This is Caitlin. Isn't she just the sweetest thing you ever laid eyes on."

The child with cotton candy fluff and curls for hair was dressed in matching pink, corduroy pants and sweatshirt. She snuggled against Nicole, rubbing her eyes. A red smudge covered one cheek from a nap.

"Caitlin, sweetie, this is Katharine and Michelle."

She wrapped her arms around Nicole's neck and hid her face in Nicole's long golden hair.

"Paula told me to wake her up. Isn't she beautiful! I think I've fallen in love with her."

"She's a little dolly. Hi, Caitlin. I'm Michelle."

"What will happen to her?" Nicole asked Katharine.

"She'll go into the system and they'll try to place her with a good home."

"They can't do that. Can they?"

"They can and they will. Right now, I have to meet Travis at the new house. Want to ride along, Michelle?"

"I'll take the suitcase inside if you'd like to go," Nicole told her. "You haven't seen their new house yet, have you?"

She shook her head.

"Why don't you come with me?" Katharine coaxed. "As much as I love my new husband I still need female companionship."

"All right. It's not like I'm going anywhere else."

They re-entered Katharine's car and drove without speaking along Madeline Island's east side. A snappy crackle under the tire's rotation coming from fallen twigs out of forest's trees and the monotonous chirrup of various unseen birds were the only sounds. The conversation with Katharine along with Travis' words replayed in Michelle's head. *"It'll break his heart. I'm never going to hurt you. I want you to have no doubts about me."*

What was the point? She desperately needed to devoid her brain of all thought. Willing her mind to shut down, she took in the scenery. Longer seasons and Indian summer didn't prevent the leaves from turning on time. Years ago, when her studies first began, she thought it was fascinating the way leaves changed from green to their vibrant fall colors. It wasn't until later that she learned the alteration in day length is what caused the chemical change in the trees. Leaves began their mutation on June twenty-first, the longest day of the year. The producing of less pigment to that date was what kept their leaves green. With the sun's movement south, making shorter days, the colors began the change, leading to their brightest fall banners. Then she discovered the fall colors were actually present year round but masked by green color matter known as chlorophyll that was essential to the production of carbohydrates by photosynthesis.

This year, there was plenty of bright sunlight, which was also vital to the red pigment in fall leaves. Maples were one tree that turned crimson or scarlet. Birch and poplar prominently displayed brilliant yellow and neither ever deviated to red. The tamaracks, members of the pine family, blazed bursts of sun yellow. Green shades of Norway and spruce, which didn't have prominent transformation, mingled with the changing colors to create a striking view.

As Katharine negotiated the next curve, Lake Superior waves rolled into the Island's sandy banks. Proud-standing spears of deep purple, pink and yellowish-white lupine boasted their presence. Bright yellow, tall buttercups scattered playfully like children in and around the lupine's. Wild columbine were her favorites with red and yellow petals floating off long stems of divided leaves. The delicate displays only bloomed April through June, and Michelle wished she could look at them year round.

Several large family groups of egrets also graced the shore without a care in the world. Michelle wondered what it would be like to have their life instead of the one she held in her hands.

A tad further, Katharine slowed and turned onto a dirt driveway. Michelle hadn't been to the old Carriage House since last fall when she came here to winterize the flower gardens. Charred treetops from the fire that burned the place to the ground a few weeks earlier instantly caught her eye. Shivers consumed her, remembering how close they came to losing Katharine. A couple of deer sauntered in front of the car and broke her thoughts. Katharine waited while the pair decided what they were going to do.

"Have you and Mac thought about renaming the place?"

"No. We haven't had time to do much of anything with him and Gage working almost around the clock on these homicides. There's Travis' Ferrari. Damn, that's a nice car."

When they pulled up alongside and parked, Travis navigated

around building material in their direction. Michelle smiled automatically. He waited until they both got out.

"So, how bad is it?" Katharine asked.

"They didn't like me nosing around and that sent up a red flag immediately. How long have they been working on this, Katharine?"

"Since Mac bought the property in September." Looking up at him, she said, "I don't know if I want to hear this."

"I'll start on the bottom. They haven't done any backfill yet which made it easy to check your drain tile. I tried it out. It works. The footings, foundation, sill plate, end joists all look good, as well as the fill under the crawlspace. But insulation is an absolute requirement between the joists under the subfloor or your heating bill will be sky high in the winter. It appears to me they've used leftover scrap for your wall studs and that says they're probably buying toss outs and making a hefty profit on your money. I used a square to check because it also appears some of your corner studs are off but it's easily fixable if they do it immediately and before the subfloor goes in, which I doubt will even fit into a couple of the corners. Your frame isn't gonna hold if we happen to get a good gust through here anytime soon because they haven't braced it. The last thing I noticed regarding the construction, and without using a square, is that your sills and sashes are all crooked to the naked eye. You're gonna have water leakage and that's if they can even get the windows and doors to fit."

Katharine groaned.

"If they really started six or eight weeks ago, they should have your trusses, ceiling joists, and gable studs in place."

"Travis, in laymen's terms."

"This house should be enclosed with an outside wall and roof this far into the project."

Michelle hadn't seen Travis in this aspect of his job and was instantly impressed with his business manner. He spoke with confidence, and though he taught her a few things about putting up a building, if she knew nothing at all, she would trust him with what he just told Katharine.

"We're not going to be living in it by Thanksgiving are we?"

"No you're not. Let me say this much. You do not want this house without a wall and roof when winter sets in. All the wood will warp from the moisture and you won't be able to get it properly dried out. Where are your roof trusses? They should at least be here by now."

"My what?"

He smiled sympathetically. "Katharine, who's your contractor?"

"Mike from Shelton Construction. Why?"

"I've seen worse, but the work here is really shoddy and you're gonna end up with problems down the road."

"What are we supposed to do? We can't just fire them. All our money's tied up in this."

Travis fisted his hands on his hips and stared at the project. "Tell you what. Let me make a couple of calls and see what I can do. Give those two bozos the rest of the day off and I'll call you and Mac later this evening."

Katharine didn't waste another minute and marched over doing exactly that. While she did, Travis asked Michelle, "How are you doing?"

"I'm more concerned with whatever you're planning. This house means everything to Mac and Katharine. Thanks for helping them out."

He brushed a finger under her chin. "I know, and you're welcome. Have dinner with me tonight?"

"I'm not up for another big evening surrounded by a lot of people."

"Just you and me. Since I still owe you, I'll let you drive the Ferrari over to Ashland or wherever you'd like to go."

She half smiled. "As tempting as that sounds, it's been a long day. I have a better idea. Let me cook up something special at my house."

He studied her for a long moment before he said, "I don't get it. You're too tired to go out for dinner but you want to cook."

"I love cooking. It's much easier than getting dressed up to go out for dinner."

"All right, Milady. Ride back with me and I'll drop you off and pick you up at the LeNoir house after I'm done at the job site. How's six sound?"

"That'll work but you'll have to wait while I prepare it."

"You won't let me help cook?" he teased.

Michelle didn't reply instead she wondered if she could ever relax with him or anyone else again. Katharine returned following the two men who were leaving the property and they all left.

CHAPTER 17

OUTSIDE ON THE steps to the LeNoir backyard, Michelle waited for Travis. Paula and Frank had welcomed her and Nicole warmly into their home. No questions asked and understanding and compassion in their eyes. Their open arms were like massaging the ache out of an overused muscle. Paula's excitement increased with people milling around the way the neighborhood kids used to hang out at the LeNoir house.

She thought of her own parents. They would never greet any of them the way Katharine's folks did. Thinking about the distance Katharine once had with her dad, Michelle debated the unknown reasons parents were harshest on their own kids. There was no easy answer and she sighed.

She desperately longed for a cigarette, too. The more stress invaded her life the more she craved her old habit. Three months had slipped away since lighting up her last one but the urgent need hung on. To distract her thoughts, she gazed over the yard. A tattered, ancient swing-set at the back of the property had lost its sparkle and newness. Regardless, three young girls became best friends. They planned their entire futures with Katharine on the slide, Nicole rolling her scrawny legs in summersaults around the bar, and she swinging high enough to see Superior through the trees. In those days, she and Nicole were the daredevils. In reality, Katharine had taken a cop's job filled with death and doom. Nicole made plans to model the latest fashions in New York City. She, on the other hand, was perfectly content to settle down on Madeline raising a family. All she ever wanted out of life went beyond her own mother's marital preaching.

Unfortunately, real life was no comparison to the repetitive preparations three girls made on many occasions some twenty or more years ago. And though life had changed drastically, it was weird how they all ended up back where they began. She thought it odder that Nicole never left the Island to model, or go to college. She and Katharine had moved on so quickly, Michelle wondered when Nicole gave up her dream. *Why did she give up her dream* was a better question.

She glanced up at a window when Caitlin cut loose with giggles. Nicole was enthralled with the three-year-old. The most attractive of the three friends was also the luckiest. So happy without a care in the world. An only child with jet-setting parents never seemed to bother Nicole either. Michelle recalled what Travis said about not having brothers or sisters. After years of heartache, she decided both were fortunate not to have suffered the pain and loss.

Nicole's laugh carried out through the same open window. The tall slender blond, who turned heads with her stunning guise, worked hard at a job she loved dearly. Michelle didn't understand how nothing ever seemed to faze Nicole. Although her tears came quickly, she was actually fortuitous and very strong emotionally. Everything in Nicole's life was clear and uncomplicated. She loved clothes and men, nothing more, nothing less and had a job that provided both. For the first time since they met as youngsters, Michelle envied her best friend.

Another thought clicked inside her mind. Derek had absorbed so much of her time that new pangs of guilt consumed her. She named them Zip and Zing one night when she couldn't sleep. The emotional companions swallowed her up once more for shutting out her two best friends. Marriage and family had always been at the top of her list of importance. The idea had consumed her daily after Brian's death. With a constant ache of failure in her heart she lost the second. And if the missing link in the trio of friends hadn't returned in July, she and Nicole would have grown even further apart. She would be friendless as well. Zip and Zing would play havoc with that. But reliably, Katharine always did fasten them back together when spats evolved between them. Never mattered what the arguments were about, Katharine kept them harmonized with unity. She had no right to blame Katharine for the distance the way she did. After all, she could have picked up the telephone, too.

Bringing the Callihan family back together seemed—suddenly Michelle realized she needed her parents as much as she needed her friends. *But do they need me? How do I face them to explain what really happened?* She had to figure out a way to stop them from blaming and hating her. The divorce wasn't her fault. Just like Brian's death wasn't her fault. Did they even have a clue what was happening to her now because of Derek? *Do they care that he's threatened my life?* How could they believe she and Sylvie hadn't felt the painful loss of a brother?

With Brian haunting her thoughts a lot lately, she tried to remember him. He had her same dark hair with pale green eyes that changed color in light. He was always there for her and Sylvie, that annoying little grin, taunting and teasing—*would Brian have seen through Derek's disguise* she wondered. Would he have stopped the torment before it began?

"Would you have listened to him, Callihan. You're so determined when you want something—"

"Having a private conversation?"

Michelle jumped and glanced over a shoulder at Gage standing in the doorway.

"Sorry, didn't mean to scare you. Want some company?"

"Yeah, why not," she answered, checking her watch. "Travis is late."

Gage came out and plopped down on the steps with a mug of coffee. "He's just delayed. How you doin'?"

"Fine."

"I'm sorry about yelling at you guys this morning, but you know how much you all mean to me."

She nodded. "Gage, you remember how we all used to hang out around here and play on the swing set?"

He smiled. "For being just as stubborn as Pipsqueak you sure are different, Michelle."

"Why do you say that?"

"You don't ask the questions she always does."

"That's because I want to forget the gruesome details."

"Now where you both are similar is in the fact that I had a conversation with her not too long ago about that same swing-set. Why are you asking?"

"Oh, nothing specific. I was just sitting here thinking how life changes and what happens to all of us when it does."

"Michelle, how come you never came to us when you needed help?"

His question, a fair one, came from nowhere and she thought about it with fearful clarity. "Gage, I'm scared of him. I was afraid of what everyone would think of me when they found out I had failed."

His mouth was tight and grim. Katharine had told her that a lowered sense of awareness wasn't good for normal people much less cops, but the growth of anger spread like wild-fire on his face. She suspected he was working harder to squelch his feelings.

"Michelle, I'm sure Katharine has pounded into you that you are not a failure."

She shrugged, nodded. "Doesn't change what I feel."

"Take a good long look in the mirror, kiddo. You're a great friend and a beautiful woman with a successful business even after he almost bankrupted you. I've never known you to give up on anything. Don't give up now."

"I'm trying, Gage. But I'll never forget the pain or the fear. It's embedded so deeply it's hard not to take flight."

"I hope you know that what he did to you is no reflection on you. Derek committed a crime that reflects on *all* men. Whether you believe me or not, when men beat up on women and children they're doing it because of their own inadequacies. It makes us good guys look like assholes. Guys like Mac and me, even Travis, hate them. And Mac and I *are* going to nail his ass—not just for your sake, but for all good men everywhere."

Michelle studied him for a moment then did something she

hadn't been able to do for many years. She kissed Gage on the cheek. "Thanks for the valiant speech and caring so much."

"It's not just a speech. I'm dead serious."

"I believe you." After several moments, she asked, "Gage, do you remember Brian?"

He leaned back on the steps, adjusting his gun belt. "I'll never forget him. He was my classmate. My best friend. Why?"

"I miss him lots. You know he loved fast cars and fast women."

"He loved his sisters, too. He always said he was gonna win the Indy—"

"And have a harem of beautiful babes waiting at the finish line with wine and roses. He wanted to bed them all," she said, laughing.

"He told you that?"

Michelle laughed harder at his bulging eyes. "Omigod, no! But sisters know things. I also remember how he always took care of Sylvie and me the same way you've always protected Katharine."

"Yeah, I remember. We used to joke about which one of us had to bail the three of you out of trouble more often."

Surprised at first then giggling, she responded, "We didn't get into that much trouble."

"Bet me. You three were always doing something you weren't supposed to. Remember the time you, Pipsqueak and Nikki were stuck over in Bayfield and you called us to come and get you?"

Michelle shook her head.

"You were fifteen and eager to party with a bunch of guys. Couldn't find the place and missed the last ferry back to the island."

"Oh!" she shrieked. "I forgot all about that night."

"Uh-huh." He flaunted a doubtful grin. "Brian and I snuck Dad's boat out and went over to rescue all of you."

"Our heroes," she teased. "But you've obviously forgotten how you both chewed us out all the way back here, too."

"You were only fifteen! That party you went looking for was with college boys."

"I remember thinking at the time that punishment from Mom and Dad would have been far better than listening to the two of you yelling at us over the motor."

"Probably right," he gloated. "We had a pact."

"What?"

"Brian and I had a secret pact, no matter what or where we'd always be here for all of you. I know if the tables were turned, Brian would have been here for Pipsqueak. He'd never want you to give up, Michelle."

She swiped at her tears. "I know. I just miss him so much."

Her tears were his heartache. They would live forever in his agonizing memory of a guilt-ridden weekend. "Michelle, I'm sorry . . ."

"For what?" she sniveled.

"I can't replace Brian for you, kiddo, but I'll always be here to help with anything you ever need."

She'd long forgotten the pet name. "He used to call me that. Kiddo."

Nudging her, he grinned, and said, "I know. Thought it might make you feel better to hear it again."

"It does." She hugged him for a long moment. "Thanks, Gage. You've always been like a brother to me."

Reciprocating the gesture, he told her, "Michelle, none of us will let anything else happen to you and I think your date is here. Go on and have fun."

She looked up at Travis when he stepped outside.

"Sorry I'm late. I had a few things that took longer and I should've called. Paula said you were back here."

Michelle stood up, smiling. "That's okay. Gage was trying to cheer me up and it worked."

"Oh? Should I be jealous?"

"You better believe you've got something to be jealous about," Gage taunted.

"In that case, I better get her out of here quickly."

"Travis, call me if anything comes up. I'll be here tonight."

Michelle went inside and Travis turned. "Thanks, Gage. If I were to pick a brother he'd be you."

Slow to respond, he said, "Just take care of her. She's special."

"That she is."

After good-byes, it took five minutes to drive over to Michelle's
house and less time for Travis to make a decision. He was going to
have a long talk with Michelle. He felt like a bigger jerk each time
he walked in on one of her private conversations. Once more, he
listened in on what sounded like the entire conversation, but was
disgusted with himself for allowing it to happen. And he certainly
didn't like his mother's verbalization on the subject either.

When they entered the house, he asked, "What did you decide
to cook?"

"After you dropped me off, I realized I didn't know what you
liked. I wanted to make lasagna but ran over quick and took ribeye
out of the freezer thinking we could barbecue."

"Ribeye's good. Lasagna would have been better." He removed
a package from inside his jacket. "I have something for you."

Michelle pulled her head out of the fridge and looked at him.
"Travis. You didn't have to do that."

"I know. Remember last weekend when I told you I had a
surprise?"

"Yes."

"I was . . . well, here." He handed her the wrapped gift. "Open
it and tell me what you think."

She set the vegetables on the counter and took the present.
Shaking it first, she smiled when it rattled then ripped the paper
off. "Travis! Where did you find it? How did you know I hadn't
replaced it yet?"

"I took a chance after what you said. Do you like it?"

"The *Bachelor and the Bobbysoxer?* You know I do. I've been
canvassing the entire area for this movie."

Michelle took a step and wrapped her arms around his neck.
"Thank you."

Flabbergasted, Travis automatically encircled his arms around
her. "I'm glad you like it."

Leaning back slightly to look, he gazed into her eyes. She
inhaled sharply. "Please, don't back away. I won't hurt you."

He snuggled closer and slowly showered her jaw and mouth

with trial kisses. He nuzzled his nose into her hair and held her, giving her time to adjust to him. "Michelle, I promise, you'll never hurt again."

He brushed his mouth along her cheek and grazed her chin and lips. When she responded, he examined her emerald eyes once more. Gradually descending, his mouth met hers.

Her knees weakened as his slow, shivery kisses tantalized and persuaded. Her fingers linked behind his neck, she pulled him into their kiss and was lost in her spinning thoughts no longer making sense.

He parted her lips slipping his tongue inside locking her securely in an embrace. Their tongues swirled and stimulated in currents of raging rapids. The kiss deepened and Travis devoured the honeyed sweetness of her unselfish lips. Diving into the curves of her mouth, she emitted a low cry. He already knew he was in love with her, but this moment cast further doubt from his mind. His lips left hers to explore her soft golden flesh and nibble her lobes. "Michelle . . ."

His whispered touch sent shivers through her entire body. Her head went back, he caught it and seared a fiery path along her neck. He tugged her intimately and recaptured her mouth with solidity, offering and relinquishing himself. The sensation was new, delicious, tender and moist, warm and savory. A moan escaped and his name rolled off her lips.

How could he be unlocking my heart?

Travis tilted his forehead to meet hers. "Michelle, I know you're not ready to hear this but I'm in love with you."

Every muscle in her body tensed up and he held her closer.

"I'll wait for as long as it takes you to see that we were meant for each other."

She ripped away from his arms and moved right. "Travis, don't! You're making a serious mistake!"

She swung away from him, grabbed the vegetables lobbing them into the sink, and scoured the crap out of them.

Travis stared at her trembling back for a long time. Finally, he said, "Michelle, I'm not him. I'm never going to inflict pain of any kind on you."

She couldn't dispute or challenge him but huffed out, "Travis, it won't work. Give it up!"

Pushing his hands deep inside his pockets, he deliberated momentarily. "Who's Mikala?"

She whirled around, emerald eyes ablaze.

"You've heard Mikala crying?"

He nodded. "Who is she? Mac mentioned her first and today Katharine told me a little about her."

"Dammit, I really need a cigarette."

She dried her hands on a towel and slumped into a chair at the kitchen table. She spent the next thirty minutes defensively explaining Sully's fable of the crying ghosts and telling him the true history of Madeline Cadotte's children.

"Travis, Mac and Katharine weren't believers before but they are now. What scares the hell out of me is I've been hearing Mikala for . . . well . . ." She swallowed hard. "I've been hearing Mikala ever since you started trying to build here. I'm just not ready for any kind of relationship. Sully told me . . . oh never mind. He's a crazy old man with fanciful dreams."

He sat down opposite her a long time ago, now reached over and covered her hand with his. "It's not crazy. Tell me."

Michelle studied him. Unquenchable warmth, deep longing and curiosity filled his eyes. After a long deliberate silence, she said, "Sully told me I never should have married Derek because neither one of us had ever heard Mikala's cries. Now you're here and she's wailing damn near every day in my ear. I need time. I can't mislead you with false pretenses."

He put the pieces together and just as quickly his own life began to make sense to him. Letting go of her hand, he leaned back to give her space, grinned. "Let me go fire up the grill. Then I've got a story to tell you."

Travis picked up the ribeyes and went outside. Michelle went back to her vegetables. She washed and shredded lettuce then let it drain. "Ghosts are like Santa Clause. They don't exist," she mumbled.

Chopping green peppers, she muttered hastily, "And they certainly don't wail and moan to the living even if they do fly around in sheets scaring the bejesus out of people on Halloween."

Giving a brick of cheese a vigorous workout on the grater, she repeatedly told herself, "The man's full of buffalo crap." By the time she had the tomatoes sliced and diced, her voice overflowed with frustration. "He got beamed up on one of his cranes and forgot to come down."

She threw everything into a bowl and tossed the mess up and down a couple of times. "There's several shingles missing from his roof. And there's just no way he's in love with me." She thrust the bowl into the fridge and began setting the table.

"What a bunch of kitty poop. We haven't even slept together. Why would he, Callihan? The story you just told him is nuttier than a squirrel's breakfast."

Michelle stopped.

Did she want to sleep with him?

His sizzling kisses made her feel like a woman again. And arguing the point when her insides fought her brain by melting down into molten lava flow was absurd. She retrieved garlic cheese bread from the freezer and flicked on the oven. Everyone kept telling her Travis Baines was a nice guy. What would it cost her to trust another man a second time? What would it take her to believe in Travis?

He stuck his head in the door. "They're almost done."

"Take the plates off the table," she said as casually as possible. Moments later, he returned with the aroma of barbecued steak filling the room.

"I hope you like it done medium to well."

"Medium is fine. I hope you like garlic cheese bread and salad. There wasn't time to bake potatoes like I planned. I'll open a can of vegetables if you like. What kind of dressing do you want on your salad?"

"Michelle, relax. You'll learn quickly, I eat just about everything.

French, Italian, Bleu Cheese, whatever you have is fine. Come and sit down."

"There's a minute left on the bread. Do you want anything on your steak and something to drink? I've got pop, or leftover Kool-Aid I made for Shalee and Brendan."

Travis set the plates on the table and walked over to her. He took her hands. "Michelle. Relax. I'm not gonna bite."

She yanked her hands out of his. "Travis, you blew me away by telling me you've fallen in love with me. It's not possible. We hardly know each other."

He stared at her then burst into laughter. "Milady, it is possible." He gave her a quick hug. "Now go sit down. I'm gonna tell you a story."

She had no intention of permitting herself to fall under the spell he cast upon everyone else. The man definitely had a screw loose—no way was he in love with her. He sat down across from her with his father's mile-wide grin plastered across his face. When she finally looked up, the salads from the fridge and the bread from the oven were on the table. Was there anything he couldn't do?

"Three years ago I realized I'd been everywhere and done everything there was to do in life. My designs are all over the world. With Grandma-ma telling her stories about the Apostle Islands since the day I was born, and Grandfather talking about his 1934 Cabriolet he lost to hard times, I decided a special anniversary gift was a necessity but not until after Billy Abbott was here the first time did I understand how special. I explained my plan to my parents and they thought the idea splendid. But then you know this already. Anyway, fifty years of marriage is something to be proud of."

He hesitated for a second, but Michelle felt sure he was leaving something out. He took a slice of garlic bread and added more French dressing to his salad.

"During that year, I began having these dreams that involved a crying woman. There wasn't any meaning or plot to the dreams.

The only visual thing I can remember are tears staining golden flesh and green eyes marred from crying."

Michelle gaped at him with her fork midway to her mouth.

"The more I dreamt about her the less I slept. I began working day and night trying to forget about a woman I didn't even know and a dream that held no meaning. One night I was working late in my Boston office."

He took a bite of the ribeye, chewed and swallowed. "I was wide awake when she began crying. Scared the crap out of me. I mean I'm sitting in this skyscraper on the seventeenth floor at one in the morning and some woman I can't even see starts in with these bemoaning cries. I'd already decided I was going to build on Madeline Island at that point. Then the crying stopped for awhile. That was the first time you put a damper in my original plans. Billy had already informed me about the historical tavern along with your strong objections. Since I always get what I want and knew no matter how much you opposed, I also knew I would fight you every step to get the consent I needed. Now, you can imagine my surprise when I first saw you."

"Why?"

"I'll get to that in a minute. Since I've arrived here, I've heard your ghost, Mikala, several times and thought I was going crazy. But I know you heard her that day at the construction trailer the night we had our first dinner together. We looked at each other, both fearful of telling the other what we just heard. Then Mac mentioned Mikala and then Katharine laughed at me when she figured out I'd been hearing your ghost."

Michelle laid down her fork, grabbed a Pepsi Travis set out for her and slugged back the contents. Slamming the can on the table, she said, "Travis, she's not *my* ghost. I don't believe in ghosts. And Sully's story is a fairytale that doesn't jive with any history. None of what you're telling me makes any sense anyway."

"When has falling in love ever made sense, Michelle? Think about it. Two people meet and become so enamored with the other they float through their days and nights. And some do it for fifty years and more."

She half smiled before her mouth tilted into a sneer. "Travis, people do not fall in love overnight let alone before they meet each other. It takes time. You have to get to know the other person. Besides, I'm not as enamored with you as you are with me."

"Michelle." He said it quietly. "I've known about you for the better part of two years. You're the crying woman in my dreams. After you told me about the three crying ghosts, it became very clear whom I was dreaming about. Though I don't understand it, I'm guessing Mikala's always been with you and somehow, her cries and my dreams are both related to the abuse you suffered. Your ghost has brought us together."

She stared at him for a long moment and finally said, "You're insane, Travis Baines."

He let out a belly laugh. "My mother thought the same thing when I told her about the tear-stained green eyes in my dream. It wasn't until I told her about you that she started to believe me."

"I can't believe you told your mother about Mikala."

"I didn't. I told her about my dreams and described you to her. She saw the resemblance the day she met you."

"So, I've heard," she sneered again and pushed cut up pieces of steak around on the plate, stirred her salad until it was soggy. Propelling herself away from the table, Michelle stood and paced around the furniture.

"Travis, when I met Derek I fell in love with him instantly. I didn't let on to anyone, not at first anyway. I suppose because I'd waited so long for the right man to walk into my life. He wined and dined me, bought me gifts, and my favorite flowers—wild columbine. He was so careful to please me, so gentle and kind. But he never made any advances to get me into bed until we'd been dating for a year. I thought it strange and assumed he didn't love me the way I loved him."

Travis quietly set his fork down and picked up his glass of pop. He leaned back in the chair, propping one foot across the opposite knee. Michelle stopped in front of a window, bundled her arms protectively around herself, similar to the first day he met her, and stared out pensively.

"The first time with him was the anniversary of the day we'd met. I was surprised that he remembered the day considering what I thought. He told me it takes time to learn to love someone. I didn't understand when I'd fallen quickly for him. The entire night was a disaster like two teenagers doing it for the first time. I chalked it up to nervous jitters after waiting so long for him to make the first move. During the following year, it really didn't improve. But, I was convinced of my feelings even when he started drinking a little more. Then the revolving door of jobs began. He always had a reason or an excuse for his lay-offs or firings. The sick part is I believed him. Finally, the day came when he asked me to marry him. It was my thirtieth birthday, and since I'd been planning my wedding forever, we married four months later."

Travis remained silent when she started pacing the floor a second time.

"Oddly, my parents were the only ones who were excited about Derek. Nicole made her spite for him very clear to me. Katharine didn't know him since she lived in Minneapolis. Gage tried to talk to me about Derek but I wouldn't listen. I never do," she said more to herself. "Brian's accident demolished my family to smithereens. I'd made up my mind I wanted to be married and raise a family to replace the one I'd lost. There was no way I was gonna let anyone talk me out of marrying him. Part of me loved him because he told me he had no family. He said he was tossed from one foster home to another. He made it difficult not to be sympathetic."

Michelle stopped and looked at Travis. His face was full of that familiar strength and his gentle gray eyes never left her for an instant. "Anyway, the wedding and the Jamaican honeymoon went well enough. The trouble started shortly after we came back. I wanted to start a family immediately. He blew up in my face and stormed out of the rental we had." Michelle hugged her body and started pacing faster. "He came home blitzed to smithereens around three in the morning and that was the first time . . ."

Travis stood and went to her, tugging her into his arms. She quivered briefly before violent shakes took over her body. Silent sobs shook her so hard he held on tight, stroked her hair, and gently rocked her back and forth.

Sucking in a deep-rooted breath, Michelle whispered, "Travis, I'll never let a man do that to me ever again. This can't work between us because I won't let it."

He shifted slightly and gazed into her eyes. He concealed his anger with gentle strokes to her cheeks. He brushed the hair off her face. "Michelle, you did nothing wrong and I am going to show you what true love is all about. That's why my parents and grandparents are here now. I called them because I want you to see their love first hand."

The heavy lashes that shadowed her cheeks flew up. "You wrecked your anniversary surprise to prove to me real love exists!"

He nodded.

"What a waste and now I'm convinced you really are insane. How could you do that to your grandparents?"

She hadn't bolted for the door yet and he smiled easily. "Because you're more precious to me than anyone else in the world. Besides, Grandma-ma is very excited about watching the ballroom come to life. My dad and grandfather are acting like kids with a new toy, having hands-on during the construction. Michelle, I'll give you all the time you need to be convinced, but I'll never give up my pursuit. Milady, I am very much in love with you."

A smile ruffled his mouth. What was the point of arguing when she couldn't explain to herself the fact that she didn't feel fearful when he held her? Aside from that, he was as determined to pursue her, as she was to dump him.

"I want to know about this bad habit of yours."

"What?"

"Earlier you said you needed a cigarette."

Michelle stepped away from Travis and began clearing the table. "I started smoking because Derek convinced me to. I suppose he got tired of my nagging him to quit."

She carried dishes over to the sink and turned. "It's been three months, two days and twenty-six hours. I still crave them like an addict."

He inched closer. "There's only one way to curb that."

Placing his hands on the counter neighboring either side of her, he leaned and united her mouth with his. Surprisingly gentle, caressing more than kissing, his kiss sent electricity racing through her and she quaked with every tender touch.

"I hope those quivers are excitement," he breathed against her mouth. He made a trail along her chin and jaw, down her neck and back up. "I want to know all things about you. I want *you* telling me everything about you instead of my walking in on your conversation with someone else."

Backed up to the counter, she was hemmed in between his arms. He still hadn't touched her with anything but his mouth yet her entire body had inflamed red hot. The sexual magnetism and the prolonged anticipation was almost unbearable.

"Michelle, you don't *learn* to love someone. It just happens."

Her head rolled back in response.

Travis whispered a trail of kisses the length of her neck. "I want to know all your childhood pranks and every plan you made in Gage's backyard." He came back up, touched her chin and nipped her ear. "I'll never stop loving you, Michelle."

The phone rang. Her head snapped forward and she jerked bluntly. The moment was enlightening when she saw something in Travis' eyes, she never noticed before. It was the same look in Katharine and Mac's eyes when they gazed at each other. He removed his hands from the counter and Michelle grabbed the receiver on the third ring. Handing it over, she told him, "It's Gage."

"Yah, Gage, what is it? . . . Leaving now."

Travis cradled the phone. "We have to go. Someone tried to burn the construction trailer down. Hayden saw whoever it was and chased them away."

"How much damage is there?"

"Gage said there's some."

CHAPTER 18

Travis BROUGHT THE Ferrari to a screeching halt near his job site. Squad cars and fire trucks decorated the construction area in a glow of flashing red. Gray hazy smoke filled the night sky. Patrons from the Tavern stood back while Island residents ventured out of nearby homes. Josie and Curt stood at the front of the bar crowd. Michelle and Travis exited the car while Josie stared with longing at the Ferrari. Travis extended his hand linking his fingers with Michelle's as Mac and Gage approached the two of them.

"How bad is it?" Travis asked.

"There's damage to one end of the trailer but only on the outside," Gage told him.

Travis pulled a key out of his pocket and tugged Michelle along with him. "Did you say Hayden saw who did it?"

"He chased someone away but doesn't know who."

The four of them stepped over water hoses from the Engine and Travis unlocked the door to the trailer. He was inside only moments before he exited. "The phone lines are dead."

They walked around the trailer inspecting the blackened outside wall. Melt down from the heat of the blaze had occurred before extinguishing the fire. A closer examination revealed cut telephone wires.

"Gage, I'm gonna sleep here tonight. Tomorrow I'm bringing in armed security guards since you and Mac have your hands full."

"I've called back my part timers to fill in so Mac and I can work the homicides."

"Gage, this is definitely arson," the Fire Chief said, walking over to their group.

"The accelerant?"

"My nose tells me old fashioned, but reliable gasoline. I'll have a report for you in the morning. Got any idea who started the fire?"

"Yeah, I do. Don, can your guys take prints?"

"Sorry, Gage. We're not equipped with anything but the basics."

"Mac, get on the air and get the Crime Lab over here. Tell them what we got. I want them to go over the scene. We'll tape it off and keep everyone out of here until processing is done."

"I'm on it."

"Gage, I'm taking Michelle to your house then getting a hold of my general contractor. I'll be back later."

"Leave your key in case Gus needs to examine the inside."

Travis handed over the key then led Michelle back to the car. Opening the door for her, he asked, "Will you be okay?"

"It's you I'll be worried about staying here alone tonight," she said, sliding in.

Travis jaunted around the back and got in on the driver's side. "I like that you're worrying about me. It means you're thinking over what I said. Jerry will stay with me tonight until we can get security here tomorrow."

Michelle blew out a breath of air driving her hair off her forehead. "Good."

"I'll call you tonight when they're done," Travis said, pulling up in front of the LeNoir house.

"How will you do that when they cut the phone lines?"

"My cell phone."

Her head jerked sideways. "You emphatically told me in the Tavern that first morning you didn't have a cell phone."

"Darlin' what I told you was I didn't have a cell phone on me.

Who's phone did you think I used the day I called Gage from the lagoon?"

"Never thought about it then. Caitlin will be asleep."

"Then I'll call you in the morning. Come on, let's get you inside."

They exited and proceeded to the door. Before Michelle went inside, Travis pulled her into his arms and devoured her mouth with his. The urgent kiss sang through her veins.

"I love you, Michelle Callihan."

The needy kiss caught her off guard, blowing her senses into fragments. Michelle cleared her throat, pretending not to be affected, but her knees gave her away.

Travis grabbed her, opened the door and nudged her through the threshold. "Sweet dreams, Milady." He pulled the door shut behind her as Katharine and Nicole flew down the stairs.

"You're blushing."

"How bad was the fire?"

Pure hot, desire detonated inside of Michelle while the aftermath of Travis' kiss left her mouth burning, aching for more.

"Michelle . . ."

Would she ever believe in Travis enough to trust him? Have no doubts about him. He made it crystal clear what he wanted.

". . . definitely falling in love."

The answers were difficult, but day-by-day the man was wearing down her self-control. She floated back to earth and shook off her thoughts. Her friends stood there with curious expressions. "What?"

"Nicole, Dad has some beer in the fridge and whiskey in the cupboard. I'll take a tall glass of milk. Michelle has something to tell us and I think it has to do with Travis."

"Great balls of fire! It's about bloody damn time. I'll be right back. Don't start without me. I want to hear every word about that kiss we just witnessed."

"Katharine, what are you doing here?"

Suppressing a giggle, Katharine finally broke into infectious laughter. "Callihan, you're pathetically in love."

"Am not," she muttered.

"Mac is camping out at the station and I didn't want to be alone at the rental. I'm staying here with you guys."

"Where's everyone else?"

"Caitlin's sleeping, Dad's upstairs watching TV and Mom's playing bridge."

Nicole returned and each took a glass and curled up on a piece of Paula's worn, cozy furniture.

"Now, let's hear every detail."

"Someone tried to burn the construction trailer—"

"Hon, we don't want to hear about that," Nicole blurted. "We want to hear about Travis. I damn near fainted watching that embracing kiss he just laid on you."

Michelle knew the exact spot they were watching her from. The three of them used to watch Gage and Brian with their girlfriends from Katharine's bedroom window. She slugged back a large gulp of beer while her adrenalin raced nervously.

"The man's crazy, I tell you. After only three weeks he stood there tonight and told me he's in love with me. I mean for God's sake you can't fall in love overnight. And like that didn't blow me away he says he's been in love with me because of some stupid dream he's been having for two years."

"Great balls of fire!"

"He told you he was in love with you?" Katharine asked.

"Like it's not bad enough that goofy ghost has been screaming at me for a year. Nooooo, now she's wailing at him and that crazy fool thinks it's all related and that I'm the blasted woman he's been dreaming about for however long it's been! He said he recognized the green eyes. And if that doesn't just smack you square in the kisser, he's told his parents and grandparents he's in love with me. He's insane, that's what he is. I tell you Travis Baines is insane. How can you fall in love with a woman you've only dreamed about? It's not possible! And the big dumb jerk has pores that are just oozing with erotic magnetism. Even Shalee fell for him and she's only five! He just worms his way in and takes over with that confounded charm of his. I mean he conned Ted."

"Me thinks she doth protest too much," Nicole said with a giggle.

"No doubt about it," Katharine agreed.

Nicole rose from the chair. "Who wants another drink?"

"I want a peanut-butter and grape jelly sandwich, please. You better bring Michelle another beer."

Keeker jumped into Michelle's lap and began purring, pushed his head against her hand.

"Hi, baby. Are you hungry? Did anyone feed you tonight?"

"Mreow."

"Dad fed him and Caitlin. It's like he's a different man with all the people and Keeker in the house right now."

Michelle snuggled the cat. "Keeker and me just want things back to normal. Don't we, baby?"

"The damn cat could care less as long he's fed and has a home. Travis really told you he's in love with you?"

Keeker's purr was on full throttle and Michelle just nodded scratching his neck. She accepted the second beer when Nicole returned and Keeker jumped down.

"You guys, what am I gonna do? I can't fall in love again."

"Why not?" Katharine asked.

"Because it hurts too much."

Nicole settled into her spot flinging hair over one shoulder. "Michelle, I promised myself I wouldn't say I told you so. Nevertheless, I can't keep my mouth shut any longer. Gage and I tried to tell you Derek was an asshole. You refused to listen to us."

"Oh, sure, Nicole. Go on and rub it in my face. The dirty bastard wants to kill me—"

"I won't argue with you about that. Nor will I sit here and accuse you of being a failure. What I am going to tell you is maybe it's time you listened to your friends. Hon, we all love you very much. But more than that we're concerned for your safety and happiness. Travis is a wonderful man and would never do to you what Derek did."

Nicole gulped her drink then muttered, "Travis would never do to me what Derek did to me."

Michelle was slugging back her second beer even faster and stopped. "What're you talking about? What did Derek do to you?"

Katharine stopped chewing, sat up straight, waiting. Tears were already streaming trails along Nicole's cheeks.

"I swore I was never going to tell you this. It happened long before he ever proposed to you."

Her eyes narrowed suspiciously. "You weren't going to tell me what? What happened?"

"Oh damn. Derek was waiting outside the Tavern one night when I locked up. He'd been inside two-fisted drinking most of the evening. Like always, he and the Stewart brothers were drunk and rowdy. Anyway, Derek left a little before closing. The Stewart's weren't far behind. Normally, Hayden leaves with me but that night he had to get home early. So I closed up alone. I knew Derek was beyond normal intoxication but I didn't know how much until he attacked me from behind. I hadn't gotten the Tavern locked yet when he pinned me against the door and tried to rip my clothes off. I fought him off with scratches and a hard knee where the sun doesn't shine. It took his breath away giving me time to get back inside. I locked the door and called Frank."

Michelle suppressed her rage with the appearance of indifference. Her heart hardened a little more with the erection of her anger and hurt. Suddenly, she stood up, swaying with the effects of the alcohol and made her way toward Nicole. She was conscious of only a slow tortured sob.

"He's hurt so many people. I'm so sorry," Michelle said.

"I couldn't hurt you. That's why I didn't tell you."

Tears welled in her eyes and, Michelle cried, "It wasn't your fault, Nicole."

"I see now I should've told you. It was hard when you were so in love with the guy. Not that it matters, but he did come back and apologize to me the next day which is what solidified my reason for not telling you."

Katharine moved over handing them a box of Kleenex. "What did my dad do?"

"He was furious when he arrived. Derek was passed out on the front steps. I did not want to make a report and I certainly didn't want Gage to know about it either. I just wanted that creep off the property. Maybe if I'd been a better friend and told you what Derek tried to do, none of this would have happened."

"I'll get another round of drinks for you guys," Katharine said.

Michelle sniveled, wiped her nose and squatted on the floor in front of Nicole. "Sweetie, I don't blame you."

Smoothing Michelle's hair lovingly, Nicole said, "Michelle, it was wrong not to tell you. We've been best friends since we could walk and talk. You deserve more than deceit from me."

"Well, that part is true and I'll forgive you, but the rest of it was out of your control."

Katharine handed their drinks over and popped a chocolate covered cherry into her mouth. "Are we okay here?"

"Yeah," they each replied.

"Good. Cuz I think before I'm saddled with a kid on my hip, the three of us should go out for a reunion dinner. Kinda as makeup for all our mistakes."

"I'd love to. Let's do it tomorrow night. Nicole, you have to work?"

"Hun-uh. I'm off for the weekend." Her eyes widened. "Great balls of fire, have I got an idea! Let's make a day of it, lunch, shopping for Katharine's maternity clothes since she's starting to show."

"That she is," Michelle said, looking up at Katharine. "We could even pick up some new baby clothes."

"You mean you aren't giving me a baby shower?"

Each too startled by Katharine's revelation to respond immediately, Michelle finally said, "You mean you want one?"

"When you didn't want a wedding shower, we just assumed you wouldn't want a baby shower either," Nicole said.

"Well, I've changed my mind. It's embarrassing to admit how happy pregnancy makes me feel, but yeah, I want one. The baby stuff is so tiny and cute."

"All right," Nicole said. "It's settled. We'll take you shopping for pregnant clothes, have lunch and plan a baby shower. When do you want to have it? We'll invite everyone."

"Whenever, but in our new house if that's okay."

"What did Travis find out for you on that?" Michelle asked.

"You guys aren't gonna believe what he did. Mac couldn't even believe it, but he's very relieved he won't have to listen to my bitching anymore."

"Don't keep us in suspense any longer," Michelle said.

"Travis is one guy I want on my side every day. He was awesome the way he fired Shelton Construction."

"What? How?"

"That man does not dink around. He bought out the loan by paying them off for their time then called a contractor friend of his—"

"Jerry?"

"I think Jerry helped him. Anyway, this new contractor will be here Monday to go through the house. We didn't have to do anything except listen and sign. Travis handled everything for us. The new contractor will finish the work. Monday he'll tell Travis what it will cost to fix all the mistakes."

"You have any idea how much it is gonna cost you and Mac?"

"Considering the size of our down payment, Travis told us nothing. He's worked it out to cover the contractors until the house is done and then we'll assume the mortgage at closing once the house is finished."

"And you don't have to pay anything extra for fixing the problems?" Michelle asked with surprise in her voice.

"Mac and I reacted the same way. Travis doubted it. He'll let us know after this new contractor checks it out. Mac and I agreed it'd be better to pay the extra now rather than down the road if problems developed. We gave Travis the go ahead and resigned papers."

"Then you're gonna be in the house before Thanksgiving?" Nicole asked.

"Travis told us not to bank on it, but we'll definitely be living in it for Christmas."

"Katharine, that's absolutely awesome," Nicole replied. "Now see, Michelle, I told you he was wonderful."

"Yeah, wonderful," she said into her glass of beer. Too many unanswered questions were adding up to dollars. She was there when Travis ran down the list of problems he discovered. How could it not cost extra to repair them? *What* would it cost to fix them? And where would Mac and Katharine get the extra money from? Michelle doubted they could afford even an extra thousand. After all, she knew the price of materials. She also wondered how Travis got around firing one contractor and bringing in another. Contracts were legal binding documents.

Paula came in at one point, gave them all kisses on the top of their heads then went upstairs to bed. Nicole convinced them they should also take Caitlin shopping with them tomorrow between plans for a baby shower on an unknown date. Halfway through the discussion Katharine decided the occasion required a co-ed party. The guys could hang out in the new rec room while the baby shower went on upstairs. Since the baby wasn't due until spring, all agreed they could barbecue on the new gas grill. Before long, and with no official date set, the baby shower was competing with a house warming party.

Long past one in the morning, Michelle conked out on the floor. Nicole fought sleep as she planned a menu but eventually drowsiness overtook her. She slumped backward in the lounge chair. Katharine smiled, recalling the cosmetic saturation Nicole had performed on her face a few months back. She tabled the idea only because she lacked the makeup. She then retrieved blankets upstairs and upon returning, a smile formed on her face. Papers were strewn across the carpet and her three favorite men occupied the middle of the room with adorable expressions.

After several moments, she whispered, "What're you guys doing here?"

"Came by to check on you. What happened here, Princess."

"It's a long story. But these two went down about ten minutes ago."

"I'll take this one," Gage said, walking toward Nicole.

"I've got this one," Travis said, lifting Michelle.

"Princess, what are you three cooking up now?"

"Well, it started out innocently enough. We went from shopping tomorrow for pregnant clothes to a baby shower to a house warming party to a barbecue. Or something like that."

He smiled then he kissed her. "What did you end up with?"

"I'm not sure other than we're going shopping tomorrow and Caitlin's coming with. But dear hubby of mine, I'll let you know when and where you have to be and how much it's going to cost you."

Chuckling, Mac captured her mouth in a succulent kiss. Travis and Gage stood on the stairs waiting, watching, suppressing the longing in their own hearts.

"Princess, you got your nine?"

"Don't leave home with out. You guys be careful."

Stepping outside they waited until they heard Katharine lock the door. "Mac, you go that way to do a perimeter check. Travis and I'll meet you around back."

Travis followed Gage checking the bushes as Gage inspected windows with his flashlight on the side of the house. "You really think he knows she's here?"

"Travis, a cop never overlooks anything. If he does, he's a dead man."

Finding nothing, they met up with Mac and walked back to the squad cars parked in front. Mac took Travis back to the trailer. He and Jerry, who was already inside, discussed and arranged for the security patrol they used on previous occasions less than an hour ago. The contract his company maintained with Range Security called for four trained and armed men on duty 24/7. Range Security would have their men here in the morning. The phone lines would also be repaired sometime tomorrow.

For a moment, Travis stood outside the trailer to contend with his roller coaster of emotions. He thought for sure that any delays on this project would have come from Michelle—before he met her of course. Never once did he consider cost overruns would occur from malicious damage. Thankfully, he always maintained adequate coverage for any type of loss.

The situations were heating up each day and more than ever, he feared for Michelle's life. The tremor in his jaw told him that much. He tried to swallow back the lump that lingered in his throat. It was a moot point to argue with her about protection. All he could do was be there, or make sure someone was always with her.

The highlight of a disturbing day took place moments ago when he carried his drunken lady upstairs to the bedroom. Easing her onto the bed, Michelle said it to him as clearly as if she were sober.

"Travis Baines you're insane and I think I'm falling for you."

Then she was out. He stood there stunned, not wanting to leave her, afraid something would happen to her. Gage entered the room and reassured him she was safe.

"You worried?" Mac said after checking the area around the trailer.

"Aren't you?"

He shrugged. "Travis, there's two people in that house who are armed. Nobody's getting through, around, or by the one I can vouch for. Tomorrow they're going shopping over on the mainland all day. Michelle is safe. You want to stay here or come to the office with us?"

"I told Jerry I'd only be gone a short while. He's not responsible for the job site. I am."

"Call if you suspect anything."

As the squad car pulled away, Travis stared up at the black sky. It shimmered with stars. The smoke had cleared and Michelle's ghost was making her presence known again.

CHAPTER 19

ONE MORE SECOND of attention from anyone and
Michelle would explode. She squeezed the bridge of her nose with
her finger and thumb. A three-day headache grated on her nerves
as much as the caretakers attached to her hip. Michelle popped
two more aspirin for the fifth time today and spewed out an
onslaught of disgusting words at her empty pop can. She chewed
the aspirin dry and swallowed. Armed guards who patrolled the
job site made her feel trapped. She was overworked by Travis and
over doted on by Grandma-ma. With Nicole and Katharine
overprotecting her, she had not a moment to herself. Mac and
Gage cruised by at least fifty times a day but she gave up counting.
Even Keeker seemed more attached, like Caitlin had become when
Nicole went to work in the evenings. And if they played that song
about the Edmond Fitzgerald one more time, she would throw a
hissing fit. Every year in November it played in memory of the
sinking ship—a reminder of Lake Superior's savageness. Didn't
anyone care what it did to her mind?

Now into the second week of November, no one had seen her
ex, and the ballroom was well on its way with the weather holding.
Normal construction problems cropped up and were handled.
Thanksgiving was less than two weeks away, and Nicole and
Katharine were planning some fricking whoop-de-do with Julia,
Paula and Rosemary. Michelle wanted no part of the planning,
nor the partaking. Several residents had called her asking for help

with the Annual Christmas Boutique and she outright declined this year wanting no part of that either.

She briefly studied the orders she found—Mac and Katharine's house was coming along well with the new contractor and Nicole was in her perky holiday mode. This minute, she yearned to take Keeker home, have a long hot bath in her own tub, be left alone to sleep in her own bed, and get back to the monotony of her routine life.

What was this order for?

Perhaps she sounded ungrateful. But they might just as well have tossed her in a jail cell because she had no fricking freedom to come and go as she pleased. Kevin Stewart returned to the island a few days back without Derek and let Gage and Mac search his house. He swore he had nothing to do with either murder nor did he have any idea of Derek's whereabouts. Mac said his trip-to-Green-Bay-alibi contained holes but they were still looking into it.

Holding the order form in her hand, Michelle swiveled around in the office chair inside the trailer. It was time to take control, to get the upper hand. Once filled with fear and despair, she presently thrived on hostility toward the people who meant the most. She needed to get away, to escape, if just for a couple of days. But if she told one, the others would find out and follow her. If she didn't tell any of them, they'd hunt her down and kill her themselves. Looking again at the paper in her hand, she needed to ask Travis or Jerry what this large order was for.

Then there were her parents. Out-of-control was all she could think of the situation and had wasted her time trying to talk to her mother. The old bat sat prim and proper with her nose hanging in the air. Her mind refusing to listen and her ears refusing to hear. The one and only comment *Mummy* Callihan made stung deeply.

"If you're speaking the truth, which I strongly doubt, then you shouldn't have disgraced this family by marrying Derek in the first place."

Now her parents had escaped for the winter and gone south— had been doing so for fifteen years. Maybe it was easier to stop caring altogether like Aidan and Elisabeth Callihan did. The manner in which news spread on the island left no doubts that her parents had heard about the threats to her life. Did they care? Hell no. Nor was Sylvie at fault because they had shunned her, so Michelle couldn't take out her angst on her only sister either.

Tonight the entire bloody crowd was meeting for dinner and she could care less. She had no appetite with her upset stomachs and headaches and the last thing she needed, or wanted, was to be around the LeNoir and Dobarchon household, Nicole and Caitlin, or Travis and his entire family. She needed to find a way out. She could plead a headache and wouldn't be lying, but then everyone would stay home feeling a need to take care of her.

Today was just one more of many through the years Michelle wished she'd never been born. She trapped her foot on the desk to stop the swivel chair and discovered she had dizzied herself into nausea. Tossing the order on the desk—*those orders were for new materials on Mac and Katharine's house*—she stumbled into the bathroom and heaved out her insides. This had been occurring on and off for a few weeks and positively she was not pregnant like Katharine. She barely flushed the toilet, the room spun and everything went black.

*   *   *

Gage idled away the minutes while Mac finished his call to Cole. The way Mac sounded told him that Cole was slowly progressing through two hundred employee statements without leads. A little over a month since Travis' crew discovered the eighth serial killer's victim, they were no further ahead than when Green Bay PD discovered victim one almost three years ago. Cause of death to the most recent teenager was abrin poisoning. Although they hadn't ID'd the dead girl, Del was positive she was around sixteen years old. If that weren't enough to lose sleep over, December twenty-seventh was creeping up fast and time was running out. The serial killer would provide them with another victim. Katharine had figured out the link to the murder dates, the dirtbag killed on the wedding dates of Madeline Cadotte's daughters, which made no sense to Gage.

Gunderson, their prime suspect on the unrelated homicide, was still running loose somewhere in the world even with a nationwide APB on the wire. Their BOLO highlighted all states from Wisconsin to Nevada with special attention in the Las Vegas area. The info included what little physical they had on Gunderson and the reason he was wanted. Backgrounds couldn't find a blasted thing leading to any location, not a permanent address, nothing. The only reason they learned about the old gambling debt was because the prints came back on a hit out of Las Vegas. Vegas police had arrested Derek on a weapons assault a few years back. He threatened a guy with a knife he owed money to. The report date was prior to the first time he arrived in La Pointe. Mac uncovered the debt with assistance from a Vegas police detective. The debt dates went back even further than the assault charge.

Fingerprints from the note nailed to the two-by-four at the damaged construction site were a match to Gunderson, too. That pleased Gage, but with Gunderson on the move because of the debt and felony assault charge, they were S-O-L. So, Gage wondered, where did the scumbag go the first time he left this area? The answer was a stumper.

Once more, he reread the construction trailer's arson report the fire chief had prepared along with the M.E.'s report on Maryann Graham. Gus sent over his report on the trailer as well. No latents but Gus confirmed the accelerant was gasoline. He and Mac interviewed everyone in the Tavern that night then yanked a few bystanders in as well. Except for Hayden seeing what he thought was one person, everyone said the same—nobody saw anything. They spoke to Curt and Josie and Mark, as well as their parents. Again, zilch and Gage suspected a cover up by all.

When Kevin finally returned to La Pointe, he was hauled in for an all-night drilling on the Graham murder as well as the arson. The middle Stewart told them he went to Green Bay to visit friends. When asked how he could have friends in a city he claimed he never went to, he fessed up to the lie. To prove he didn't have Gunderson stashed, Kevin consented to a search of his house, which proved more waste of time. Their only solid evidence was the fingerprints. They knew an unknown blunt instrument with a jagged edge had killed the Graham woman. Beyond that, they were a day late, dollar short and piss poor.

On a hunch, Mac contacted Green Bay and had them check out the cousin Curt previously mentioned they all visited for a Packer's game. According to her, Gunderson hadn't been there, but Kevin was. Gage shuffled papers, locating the interview Green Bay PD did with Josie's cousin, Janice Anderson. Though strong suspicions said Kevin was lying about Derek, they couldn't get him to spill his guts on Gunderson's whereabouts. Scanning Green Bay's report, it stated Anderson didn't know anyone named Gunderson but she also stated 'in all the times Kevin's stayed here, he's never mentioned anyone by that name'.

'How often does he stay with you?'

'He's here at least twice a month.'

Gage groaned. He completely overlooked the probable fact that Kevin and Janice were having sexual relations with each other. Kevin Stewart had been to Green Bay more than he admitted upon his confession the second time around. Why would he keep the relationship a secret when it could alibi him for La Pointe's latest homicide? The same alibi might also be a finger pointer in the serial killings.

Just then, the dispatcher aired a call to see Jesop Merryweather. It wasn't like his hands weren't already full, now the Island had gone nutso with zealous deer hunters. The old man who constantly complained about the four-legged creatures, made a pet of one by tying a blue scarf around the deer's neck. No one was allowed to shoot the animal and his latest complaints were that hunters were taking pot shots at his pet. Gage answered up advising there would be no response and to let the complainant know that.

Twenty-five hour days, backroom naps and gut feelings had worn him out. No wonder he was missing essential information. It was time to start playing dirty.

When Mac ended his call, Gage asked, "Did you catch the fact Josie's cousin and Kevin are seeing each other?"

Mac grunted.

"Yeah, it's right here. According to the conversation Green Bay had with Anderson, they've been seeing each other for several years. Derek went to Green Bay a couple times a month."

Mac leaned back in the chair and stretched. "Wonder if Josie or his brothers know and why would they keep it from us?"

"My thoughts exactly unless Kevin really is our serial killer."

"Jesus!" Mac jumped forward. "I'll call Harry back and have him drill the girlfriend again on the exact dates. Ten bucks says what's-her-name lies for him."

It just didn't seem conceivable. If Kevin were the serial killer, someone in La Pointe would know something about it. The island was a dumpsite for verbal diarrhea.

"Harry'll get back to us."

"Cole have anything?"

"He has a good idea."

"What's that?"

"He wants us to get him pictures of all the Stewart brothers, Gunderson and Patriot."

"Does he honestly believe Gunderson is involved in the serial killings?"

"Not exactly. The point he made is Gunderson was here with Michelle during the time of the two thefts of paraquat. We've been assuming Kevin is lying about not knowing Patriot, and completely overlooked the fact that maybe Gunderson knew Patriot. He wants to put the photos in a line-up and see if anyone reacts to them. Said he'd have better luck with photos than prodding memories from two years ago."

"But won't everyone there know Curt?"

"I asked that. He said he wasn't going to ask them to ID who they knew but to point out which ones they didn't know. Something about some police psyche course he took back whenever. He said most people are going to recognize a face they've seen even if they don't know the person or name."

"Obviously, this can't be used in court."

"That's right. He said it would tell him who's been hanging around the County garage and who hasn't. And if you think about it, they've all been suspects for one thing or another. We just can't pin a damn thing on these guys without hard evidence."

"I know. Even Gunderson's print doesn't prove he killed the Graham woman just that he shared the same beer with her. But I'm still betting he did it."

Gage filled both their mugs with coffee. "Does Cole need booking photos? Or will any do?"

"Doesn't matter."

"Then a yearbook from my senior year would work. All three of the Stewart brothers are in there. Cole already has Patriot's photo and he'll have to use the Vegas picture of Gunderson. Mac, it bugs me Gunderson doesn't have any drivers license. Don't forget Michelle saw him following her in a car. Did you find out what kinda car?"

"No. You think Michelle might know where he's licensed?"

"Maybe. Right now, I'm thinking we should bring in La Pointe's designated drunks and Mirandize them on suspicion of parties to crime."

"I agree. If nothing else we'll put a scare into them and someone's bound to cough up something."

"How long will it take Cole?"

"He'll try it out on the last sixty people before he takes anymore statements then go back to the first hundred and forty with the pictures. You wanna go pick up the Stewart clan now?"

"What I want is P-C to search everybody's home for bracelets, poison seeds and paraquat as well as the weapon used to kill the Graham woman. And I'd really like a DNA sample on Gunderson considering Gus found semen present in our lagoon vic. Then there's whatever was used to strangle her. But I can't very well get a warrant for all their homes without a connection."

"Is Gunderson a hunter or an angler?"

"I dunno and I really hate for Michelle to relive anything about him, but it appears we will have to question her."

"I think she's stronger than we give her credit for. She'll probably be able to tell us a few things about him."

Emotion ruled Gage, but he said, "You're right. You take the photos and—"

The medical call came out over their portables. "... *unconscious female at the Tavern construction site* ..."

Eyes widened, both men exploded, "Michelle!"

They bolted from the office, jumped into their squads and squealed tires out of the parking lot lights and sirens.

*   *   *

A first responder, Mac popped the trunk and grabbed the jump kit and O-2. He ran to the trailer and met Travis at the door. "What happened?"

"I came in to get something and found her lying here."

Mac stooped, noting Michelle's shallow breathing. "How long's she been out?"

"She's been alone for a couple of hours. Said she had a headache. I don't know how long it's been since she passed out."

Gage entered the trailer as Mac masked her face and started O-2, then cuffed Michelle's right arm to take her BP and check other vitals. They heard the ambulance arriving as Michelle's eyes fluttered and her arms started flailing.

"Michelle, it's Mac. Lie still and breath."

Travis stepped back when two paramedics entered the trailer. He let out a breath he didn't know he was holding. How could he have missed the signs? When he stepped into the trailer and saw her lying in the bathroom threshold his heart stopped beating for what felt like a minute. Gray pallor in her face scared him as he checked her pulse and dialed 9-1-1. While on the phone, he discovered her skin cold and clammy. She had complained of headaches and on occasion, he caught her rubbing her stomach. She blew him off by saying it was something she ate. She justified her edginess the past couple of days with exhaustion. The fear he observed in her eyes had been modified to crimped lines of stress across her forehead.

Travis filed his thoughts and watched Michelle sit up.

One paramedic asked, "Do you remember what happened to you?"

"I was feeling sick to my stomach and threw up. Then everything started spinning and I fainted."

"How long ago did that happen?"

Michelle looked at her watch. She had no clue other than she remembered she was almost done here for the day.

"She's usually done around four-thirty," Travis offered. "I came in about four-twenty."

"Did you vomit up any blood?"

Michelle shook her head. She recognized both Andy and John immediately.

Andy spoke gently. "Michelle, when was the last time you ate?"

She cast her eyes downward feeling heat rise in her face and lied. "Breakfast this morning. We have this big dinner planned tonight."

"We need to transport—"

"No!" she exclaimed. "I'm just tired. I'll take a nap and eat a good meal."

Travis shifted uneasily. Mac and Gage grunted.

"I'll be fine," she said hoisting herself off the floor and giving them all a miserable glare. "I just want to go home—to my home."

"We can't force a transport," John told her, "but we'll need you to sign a release. You should see your doctor immediately."

She snatched the clipboard out of John's hand and scribbled her name where he indicated. The two men picked up their gear and Travis muttered something to Mac and Gage before they all left the trailer.

"Michelle—"

"Travis, don't start. I'm packing up and moving back to my house today. I'm not going out for dinner with all of you tonight and I want everyone to just leave me alone."

She grabbed her purse and headed out the door when Travis grabbed her arm. "Michelle—"

"Let go of me." She looked him straight in the eye. "You've made a mistake by falling in love with me. I do not love you and you'll have to find somebody else to help you here."

She yanked her arm out of his grip and rushed out of the trailer. The sledgehammer blow to his gut didn't hurt nearly as much as the pain he saw in her eyes. Not fear, but pure gripping agony blazed out of those jeweled emeralds of hers. This time, it wasn't emotional, only physical. The Pepsi can and pill bottles on the desk caught his eye. Travis opened the fridge discovering the six-pack he put in there earlier today was gone. She lied about eating breakfast this morning and he knew she seldom ate lunch. When they had dinner together, she rarely finished a meal and he was beginning to comprehend the symptoms. Puffiness consumed her eyes and though she didn't dwell on sleepless nights, she mentioned it occasionally.

Travis grabbed a quick shower and dressed in clean jeans and a flannel shirt. He placed a long distance phone call to a buddy back east. Picking up the aspirin and ibuprofen bottles, Rich Avery confirmed what he suspected and Travis scribbled down notes. He disconnected and flushed the pills down the toilet. Next, he called his mother to tell her he and Michelle wouldn't be joining them for dinner, grabbed his keys and left the trailer. She didn't need TLC and she sure as hell wasn't getting flowers or gifts from him.

*   *   *

Michelle stopped Brian's Mustang in front of the LeNoir house and waited. Sheer exhaustion made her faint. She was never more mortified than when she opened her eyes and saw Mac and the others attending to her. She felt even less relief when she yelled at Travis, and now an argument would ensue with whoever was inside. Exhaling a deep breath, she rubbed her stomach briefly then thrust the car door open and marched into the house.

Much to her surprise, everyone was gone. Michelle dashed up

the stairs and packed her suitcases hurriedly. Lugging both back down, she called out to Keeker several times. When he didn't come, she carried the luggage out to her car. Returning inside, she found paper and pen, scratched out a note to Paula and Frank, and called out Keeker's name as she searched each room.

"Damn cat." She would have to come back for him later, and took flight before someone returned.

The first thing she did upon arriving home was to brush her teeth and rid her mouth of the horrid aftermath. An hour later with classical music soothing her soul, Michelle sunk into a hot tub of bubbled water. A glass of milk from Paula's refrigerator did nothing to relieve the ache in her stomach. A long hot soak and a decent meal snuggled up on the couch watching the video Travis gave her would calm her down. She shut off the telephone, too, because everyone would call the minute they heard about her fainting and read her note.

Leaning back in the tub, she slid into the water until it fingered her chin. She massaged her temples and mellowed for the first time in over a month. The hot soaking diminished the spasms in her muscles, and the mild scent of rosemary had therapeutic benefit that drastically altered her previous mood.

Anger and mortification had caused her outburst. When she opened her eyes and saw their worried faces, she absolutely couldn't stand another minute of protective pampering from coddling cohorts. Yelling at Travis didn't erase the determination that consumed his eyes either. She refused all responsibility for *his* broken heart. She was as explicit with him as he'd been with her. There wasn't room in her heart for any man.

Her bath cooling down and her fingers wrinkled, Michelle took the washcloth and lathered it with a bar of soap. With deliberate ginger strokes, she washed her arms, her chest and neck along with the rest of her flesh, then rinsed. Climbing out of the tub she released the stopper and dried her skin. Checking herself in the mirror, color had returned to her cheeks and her eyes were clear but exhausted. The three CD's were done and the system shut off. She wrapped in a winter robe and slid on her favorite slippers, padding out to the kitchen. The fridge was empty except for eggs, Kool-Aid, Pepsi and canned kitty food she thought for sure had spoiled since she hadn't been home for the better part of two weeks. She took a can of Pepsi and glanced across the room at the door.

The knock was soft and Michelle shoved the refrigerator door shut letting a groan slither out. While debating which one had driven over to check on her, the thought of not answering passed through her mind. The tapping sounded again and Michelle walked over and opened the door.

"Travis, what do you want?"

He moved inside and yanked the pop can out of her hand. "You're done drinking this shit. I brought you something better."

Her mouth fell open and she followed him as he headed for the kitchen. "Why can't you get it through that thick head of yours—"

"Michelle. I'm not here to argue with you or protect you from the evils of your ex." He shoved the grocery bag onto the table and turned to face her. "You've got a peptic ulcer and you're going to start taking care of it."

Her eyes bulged, she gripped her hips with both hands and Travis almost laughed.

"I've got an ulcer about as much as you've got M-D behind your name."

"If you can stand there and tell me that you haven't been suffering heartburn, bloating and pain in your stomach, nausea and that vomiting doesn't relieve some of the stomachache, I'll walk out of here right now."

She sunk onto a kitchen chair, gaping at him. "How did you know?"

"Headaches and muscle aches from lack of sleep and anxiety over a long chain of events has caused your stress. You're taking ibuprofen for the muscle ache and aspirin for your headaches. I'd guess around two dozen a day judging by the empty bottles you leave in the trailer. You haven't finished a dinner we've had together since I met you, and you lied about eating breakfast. You never eat breakfast, or lunch. And I'd bet you're swallowing the pills with a six-pack of Pepsi and a pot of coffee everyday. You've also tried milk which doesn't help."

He gave her a second to take it all in then said, "How am I doing so far?"

Miserably, she propped an elbow on the table and cradled her chin, nodding her head.

He reached over and began removing items from the bag. "Good, I'm staying. For starters, I bought you one each of Mylanta and Maalox. Try them both and use the one you prefer as directed on the label."

She watched as he removed fruits and vegetables, whole wheat bread and several packages of meat from the grocery bag.

"There's no need to overeat nor do you have to live on bland food. I'm fixing you a decent meal and you're going to eat every bite and go to bed without aid of pills. You're not to drink coffee or Pepsi, and you're going to take the antacid for four weeks. If you don't do it, I'll haul your skinny ass to the doctor myself just so I can prove you're wrong and I'm right."

"Travis?"

Angrily, he began putting the extra food in the refrigerator and couldn't make himself face her right now. "What?"

"Can I stay in my own home?"

He stopped, straightened and turned to look at her. His heart couldn't say no to her. The vivid emerald color was back in her eyes. She was so fragile and innocent sitting there in a pale green robe. She belonged with him. He also knew he would never give up trying to convince her they were meant to be together. He harnessed the emotional fact he wanted to take her in his arms. "Is that what you want?"

She nodded her head, confirming it with, "Yes. Paula and Frank are wonderful people but I can't take anymore pampering from anyone. I just want some time and space alone."

"Will you please let me come by and check on you each day? I'll keep everyone else away from you."

Her mouth curved slowly before she bobbed her head in

agreement. "I'd like that. I was gonna watch your movie but I'll eat something first."

Difficult to squelch his excitement, he said, "Go watch it. I'll fix you a meal and bring it to you."

He waited as she stood and proceeded toward the living room with antacid in hand. He wasn't wrong about what she needed. "Michelle?"

She turned, waited.

"I did not make a serious mistake about us."

He swung around, flicked the oven on. He didn't expect a response from her. She sighed, before the soft patter of her feet became muffled in the carpet. He was so damn mad at that obstinate attitude of hers that it took grave endeavors to control his temper. She didn't need her ex around to kill her for money. She was slowly killing herself with bad habits caused from nervous stress. Mildly seasoning a chicken breast, Travis placed it in the oven. He cleaned grapes and strawberries and sliced an apple laying them on a plate with wheat crackers. Next he opened a can of chicken noodle soup and poured it into a pan, placing it on a burner. He washed broccoli recalling what Dr. Rich Avery had told him from the described symptoms and the events in her life he provided in detail.

The little idiot had worked herself up into an open sore in the lining of her upper small intestine or her stomach. Nonsteroidal anti-inflammatory drugs had caused either a duodenal or a gastric ulcer. If she refused to take care of it, the damn thing would progress to the point of hemorrhaging or perforation in the stomach or duodenum Rich told him. Travis turned the burner down on the soup, scooped the broccoli into another pan he placed on a second burner.

He threw her a look over his shoulder as if she could see him. Frustrating is what this was and he inhaled deeply attempting to relax.

Her words *I don't love you* bit hard before he debated whether he should tell her about the night she was drunk and he carried her up to bed. It would do no good, knowing the less pressure in her life the sooner she would heal. He had to dig extremely deep to maintain patience. If she refused to take care of herself he might just strangle her himself.

Travis easily located a bowl and scooped out the soup, subconsciously thinking her kitchen had everything in convenient places when he found the trays. He placed the soup and plate of fruit with crackers on the tray and carried it into the living room.

"Here's the first course. Did you take one of the antacids?"

"Yes."

"Good then dig in. Do you prefer bread or toast with your meal?"

"Bread is fine. Whatever you're cooking smells really delicious."

He cracked a smile then winked before hastily returning to the kitchen. Travis flicked the burner on for the broccoli and began brewing herbal tea. He retrieved a tray of ice from the freezer, dumped it into a glass pitcher, modified the burner to low when the water boiled. The teakettle whistled and after depositing teabags in the pitcher he poured the water, added a generous amount of sugar and stirred the contents. Retrieving a tall glass from the cupboard, he filled it with ice then removed the chicken from the oven. He drained the broccoli and dumped it on the plate, buttered a slice of bread and put the chicken on the plate as well. He took another deep breath, attempting to curb his emotions over her stupid bad habits.

After filling the glass with tea, he carried it with the plate into the living room. He noticed two things. Michelle wasn't watching the movie and she'd eaten everything so far.

"Here's your dinner, Milady. How come you're not watching the movie?"

She accepted the plate and set it on the tray. "I was waiting for you."

He studied her skeptically.

"Travis, this is the nicest thing anyone could have done for me. Thank you. I've been trying to get up the nerve to ask if you want to watch it with me."

He fought the urge to join her with the earlier sting of her words. "I think if you were to see the disaster in your kitchen, you might kick me out. Eat your dinner while I try to salvage the place."

Travis picked up the dirty dishes, turned on his heal and strode out.

Michelle dug into the chicken and speared a piece of broccoli. She thought the soup and fruit had tasted good but this was heavenly. So simple and tasty. The ache in her tummy dissipated for the first since she couldn't remember when. Not liking any sort of tea, she sniffed, frowned, faltered a bit then sipped a small taste. She stared at the glass like it was going to say 'I told you so'. The iced tea was as good as the meal.

Cleaning her plate in record time, Travis was clanging around in the kitchen. She picked up her dishes and walked to the threshold of the two rooms. Leaning against the doorjamb, she became acutely conscious of his large, athletic physique. The outline of his shoulders were strong and strained against the gray-flannel fabric. His light brown wavy hair was cut short in the back. Hunger of a different kind struck a vibrant chord inside of her. Very near the spot he stood in now he had touched her with just his mouth. The memory of his kisses swelled her heart with a feeling she thought had died.

She then recalled something more shocking. Derek wouldn't have been caught in the vicinity of a kitchen. Not even to grab himself a beer. The burden of a nasty cold before they married brought back additional memories. They had to cancel weekend plans. He never showed up, called or checked to see how she was doing. In fact, he didn't bother to ask how she was feeling the following week when he finally did call.

Here was a man standing not ten feet in front of her who cared. A man who proclaimed his love for her to the world. A guy who was positive he didn't make a mistake about his feelings. Without knowing how to give herself a second time, she had to find a way.

"Travis?"

He spun around, his large hands dripping water. "You're done already? I would've come and taken the dishes for you."

"Travis, I'm not an invalid. I'm just a nervous wreck. The meal was delicious. Thank you. My stomach feels better already."

"You aren't cured yet."

He stepped around the table and took the dishes. Michelle put her hand on his arm to stop him from walking away. "Travis."

Confusion mingled with tenderness.

"I'm sorry for yelling at you today and I'm sorry for what I said. I really don't know if I meant it. I don't know if I can love you, or anyone. I need more time."

He set the dishes down to gather her into his arms. Gently rocking her back and forth, he whispered into her hair. "I know, Milady. I know. I'll give you time and space to figure it out. Please, just don't shut me out."

He pressed a gentle kiss across her forehead then met her mouth with his. His plea came through the hardness of his mouth. The intimacy of it soothed her broken soul with a message of trust. Long awaited desire sailed through her veins from head to toe with heedless enthusiasm.

He met her forehead with his. "Michelle, you're the only woman I'll ever love. All you have to do is trust this feeling between us."

CHAPTER 20

O<small>N HER KNEES</small> in a pair of jeans that had seen the better side of yesterday, Michelle decided long ago that God made fall Sunday afternoons for garden putzing. Packer fans would argue fall Sundays were set aside for football. She was a fan, but not today.

Rushing through a chat with her loquacious next-door-neighbor, Mrs. *B. B.* Hardy wasn't any different from the other Madeline Island folks. True to form, La Pointe residents speedily dispersed reports that the police suspected her ex of murder. Busybody Mrs. Hardy wanted itemized details of the murdered women. Took too much for granted, interrupted her own statements even implied secrets were being kept regarding the tavern's construction. True to form she always came back to questions of Derek and the murders. Upon pleading garden work, Michelle suspected when Mrs. Hardy severed herself from the fence that separated their yards, it was a painful amputation.

Taking a slow deep breath, her nerves were shot. Fortunately, gardening became the most therapeutic through the past year plus. A healing process that helped her to think stuff through while nurturing her patches of growth. In fact, she designed, installed and painted an imaginary gazebo while working here in the garden. Next spring she might actually go through with the plan. White scrollwork with trefoil openings to hang baskets of vivid purple fuchsias, a white rod-iron table, the fancy Victorian kind, with

two chairs would compliment the scene. Wood-slat benches along
the outskirts might be nice, too. If she asked nicely, Katharine
might draw a design for pay. With the baby coming, Katharine
reneged on going back to work for Iola Tibbs and Michelle suspected
extra cash would help now.

Breathing in fresh air, she scanned the soil for new weed growth.
Her gardens already cleared and bedded, fall heat detonated the
unsightly buggers non-stop from the earth. She yanked a dandelion
root and smiled. Her stomach was only a mild bother since Friday
afternoon. With plenty of rest the past two nights, her headaches
were gone. Most of yesterday, she lost herself in a sappy romance,
recalled chuckling then as well as now because the spicy heroine
with admirable exploits reminded her of Nicole. Last night she
curled up on the couch to watch the video Travis bought. She
leaned back on her heals. Joyful endings were delightful, but she
had never cried after finishing a book, or a movie. Never wept
before when the judge saw Cary Grant at the airport either. Had
no clue why she cried watching it this time or upon finishing the
book.

The ground examination complete, Michelle collected her
tools. Travis kept his promise and stopped by twice yesterday. He
was in buoyant spirits when he told her he had to beat everyone
away with a two-by-four before he came clean with them. They
had expressed their concerns for her, and he reassured them she
was fine. When he updated her on the construction, his level of
enthusiasm skyrocketed. Reframing was done. Roof trusses and
joists were in place. The walls were being enclosed as they spoke.
That she wanted to see. They then had a leisurely lunch on the
patio. He didn't stay long afterward.

It was difficult to find any fault in Travis Baines. Maybe she
was trying too hard, but who could blame her? Gage, Katharine,
Nicole all thought Travis was a saint. Jerry and the guys working
on the ballroom said Travis was a good man. Travis was the best.
When she called Sylvie after an attempt at talk with their mother,
she was told Shalee and Brendan spoke endlessly about Travis.

Everybody loved Travis. So, why couldn't she do the same? Why couldn't she believe he would never hurt her? His kisses unquestionably made her insides thaw—she stopped, looked, listened. The weeping lament pealed around her. Michelle glanced up at a robin-egg blue sky. Mikala was floating somewhere up there and for a brief moment she felt a warm glow.

The feeling didn't last. Personal longing had taken forever to be fulfilled once before. Could it be fulfilled again? At what cost when accused of failing at one of the two most important things in her life? She lost her confidence right along with the disastrous marriage. To relive the terrifying circumstances a second time would cause permanent damage. Irritated with her parents for their ignorance and inability to see the violence she suffered, she felt more dissatisfied with herself. She wasn't devoid of mistakes either. Didn't her mother and dad understand their heartfelt pain over the death of a child was as potent as her loss of a brother? Not only had she lost a brother, but she joined thousands of victims of domestic violence and lost her marriage as well. She had fallen for Derek's charm—

"Omigod! He reminded me of Brian! My mother and dad must have found a replacement for the son they lost."

How could she not have seen Derek for what he was the same way Gage, Nicole, Shalee and Brendan saw through his false charisma? As if Mikala were sitting next to her like an old friend, Michelle said, "Well, don't that just beat all old girl? Even if my mother can't find forgiveness, I can. And I will forgive her."

Looking up a second time, she squinted into the sun. A breeze blew through the backyard, whispering the ghost's softened cry.

"Michelle, you back here?"

She jumped, glanced over her shoulder and around the crabapple tree. The uniform pants were all she saw at ground level. Rising, Michelle walked over to greet Mac and Gage.

"How you doin' today?" Mac asked.

"Much better, thank you for asking. Are you here with good news or do you want me to come and get Keeker?"

"Michelle, Caitlin loves Keeker. No we haven't found Gunderson either. We need to talk to you. Do you feel like answering a few questions for us?" Gage asked.

Slapping her hands together, brushing off the dirt, she replied, "Of course. But what could I possibly tell you that would help?"

"Lets go inside and talk," Mac said, observing the neighbor peeking out a window.

"Sure. I'll make some coffee."

Leading them inside, Michelle started coffee while Gage and Mac pulled out chairs and hoisted their gun belts before sitting at the kitchen table. Retrieving mugs and pouring herself a glass of herbal iced tea, she asked, "Are either of you hungry?"

"No, coffee's fine," Gage said. "We're here to ask you about Derek."

"His habits," Mac added, "hobbies, stuff like that. Are you sure you're up for this?"

Michelle took the seat between them. "I'll tell you whatever I can. It's not personal against you guys and I really appreciate what everyone is doing, but I want my life back. I want to stop living with the fear."

"Good," Gage said. "That's part of the big picture. Can you tell us if Derek ever hunted and if he owned any guns or hunting knives?"

An automatic gesture, Michelle caressed her hair with a hand recalling the mixture of damage and fright. "He didn't own either that I know of. Before we were married, he went deer hunting once with the Stewart's. He said he loved it and wanted to do it every year."

"Who's gun did he use when he hunted the one time?" Mac asked.

Michelle stood and retrieved the coffeepot filling both their mugs. "I think Curt or Kevin had an extra rifle of some kind. I don't know though." She replaced the carafe and returned to the chair. "Why do you need to know this?"

Covering her hand protectively with his, Mac said, "Michelle, the Graham woman was strangled with nylon rope and stabbed with a large jagged-edged knife. You already know we ID'd both their prints on a beer can left at the crime scene."

She gnawed on her bottom lip.

"Michelle, I'm sorry—"

"No. No, it's okay. What kind of rope and knife?"

"Very thin," Gage said. "Fishing line. Was Derek a fisherman?"

"No. Hang on, I'll be right back."

Puzzled, they watched her go out through a mandoor that led to an attached garage. Returning moments later, Michelle asked, "Would this be anything like the nylon rope that was used?"

They stood and studied the tool. "What is that?" Gage wanted to know.

"I use it to make garden lines. I'm not sure what it's made of but it's sturdy stuff. The other thing I discovered is my pruning saw is missing. I assumed with all the stuff happening I left it at one of the places where I finished up fall cleanup the week construction started on the ballroom."

"What's a pruning saw?" Mac asked.

"It's basically a knife-type saw about yea long." She held her hands indicating less than two feet. "It has a squared-off end with two different size teeth for cutting and a wooden, sorta curved handle."

"And you say you can't find this pruning saw now?"

She nodded her head. "I've looked everywhere. Well, before things started happening. Then just forgot about it."

"Have you got a picture of it so we can see it?" Gage asked.

"Yes, in my gardening books." She set the garden line on the table and went to retrieve the book.

"Whaddaya think? Mac asked, studying the line in the tool without touching it. "Could this be what he used?"

"We'll send it to the lab for analysis. I'm more interested in the pruning saw since Del said she died from the stab wounds, not strangulation."

"True. All he did was render her unconscious by cutting off air to her windpipe."

Michelle returned with a large book open to a glossy photo of the tool. With a quick glance at the picture, Gage asked, "Can we borrow this for awhile?"

"Sure, as long as you like."

"Would you put the other tool in a paper bag? We want the lab to compare the line to the ligature markings they found on the victim. We don't want anymore fingerprints on it."

"Do you really think he used my garden line? How would he have gotten into my garage, and returned it without my knowing?"

"Maybe he didn't. But as long as we're here, let's take a look and see if there's any signs of break-in," Mac said.

After a thorough inspection of the garage doors and windows, inside and out, Gage said, "I don't see anything. Michelle, I really wish you'd come back to the house. Mac and I would feel a whole lot better if you did."

"Gage, everyone has been very helpful, but I can't. Besides, Travis is checking on me twice a day and calls just before I go to bed. I'll go bag the garden line for you."

They followed her back into the house. "There's something else we need?"

"What's that, Gage?"

"The Vegas booking photo is old. You wouldn't happen to have a picture of Gunderson would you?"

"Afraid not. Why?"

"He doesn't have a current driver's license in Wisconsin and we checked Nevada, considering his debt. It'd be helpful if we could spread his picture around to the authorities."

"Oh, well, he wasn't from Wisconsin. He was raised in foster homes in Minnesota and never knew his parents. When I met him, Derek told me he was from Duluth, actually Proctor. I never gave it a second thought he might not have a drivers license."

"You sure?" Gage asked.

"Yes. Why?"

"Maryann Graham was from Duluth, but Derek doesn't have a Minnesota license either," Gage said. "Is there anything else you can think of concerning his past or where he came from that might help us?"

"There was something a week or so before we were married. You knew we were already living together. Anyway, I was doing laundry and learned quickly to check his pockets. I found this paper receipt with a different name on it. White or yellow, I think. I can't remember now. I thought it was a paper drivers license. Thought it strange because I know they have plastic laminated cards in Minnesota. When I asked him about it, he said he found it and was going to turn it into the State. I thought nothing more of it."

"Any chance you remember the name?" Mac added, "Or the city in the address?"

"Not the last name or the city."

"What was the first name?"

"That's what caught my eye and why I thought it was his. The first name was Derek and I hadn't really looked at it until he pointed out the last name wasn't Gunderson."

"Do you know if it was even Minnesota?"

She shrugged. "Sorry guys. I don't."

"Tell us about Madeline Cadotte's daughters and their wedding dates since you're familiar with the history here."

"You want Sully's fairytale version or the historical truth?"

"Michelle," Gage said.

"Well. Sully does make the three ghosts he's named Katrina, Nicolina and Mikala who all haunt the islands weeping until true love happens very believable. But Michel and Madeline had about eight children in real life."

"Tell us about the eight daughters."

"Eight children, boys and girls both," she said.

"I'm only interested in the girls who married. The dates are important. What I need to clearly understand is if July second, October eighth, and December twenty-seventh are possibly incorrect regarding the Cadotte women wedding dates?"

"I can't really say, Gage. What we do know is that Charlotte married twice, Mary once, and no one knows much concerning Jozette. We know Mary and Charlotte married brothers, and one daughter married Leon St. Germain. Michel, Jr. also had at least four daughters. So those dates could be from either family and oddly enough, the months do coincide with several births. What does any of this have to do with Derek? Do you honestly believe Derek is your serial killer?"

"We're still putting all the pieces together," he answered. "About these ghosts you mentioned? What're their names again?"

"Katrina, Nicolina and Mikala. But, Gage, those names along with the story are fictitious. According to Sully Katrina is for Katharine. I'm Mikala and Nicole is Nicolina and I'm positive Sully tells it to increase the curiosity of tourists."

"One more thing. Did you see the car Gunderson was driving the day he was following you?

"Red," she said without giving it a second thought. "A red Honda."

"New or used? Did you see the plates?" Mac asked.

"One of the older models." And with a head shake, she indicated no to the second half of his question.

"Okay," Gage said. "Take care of yourself and call us if you think of something or need anything."

When they returned to the squad, Gage said, "I'm gonna have Pete and Alesha drive by here when they're working. Neither can give us more than one or two evenings a week and Pete will be on duty soon."

"She does look better than she did Friday."

Gage thumped his fist on the steering wheel angrily. "Damn, those three are pigheaded!"

Glancing at the glossy page again, Mac said, "You realize this pruning saw is the murder weapon Gunderson used on the Graham woman."

"And you realize he probably tossed it in Superior. Did you check Minnesota's Department of Public Safety for a record on him?"

Michelle came flying out of the house and Mac hit the automatic switch for his window.

"I just remembered something because I thought about

Katharine at the time. That receipt said Minneapolis and the last name was Guthrie, G-U-T-H-R-I-E. She once told me about a theatre in Minneapolis with the same name—that's what caught my attention."

"Michelle, that's a humongous help," Mac told her. "We'll check it out."

They waited until she was back inside and Gage drove off.

"About your question, Gage. Katharine told me if Gunderson had any ID, he'd be in the system forever especially if he was revoked or suspended in Minnesota."

"Is there any way they can do a cross check on names. You know like when a woman changes her name through marriage?"

"That would be on his driving record as well. Assuming he'd been caught in the act, she told me they classified it as a misdemeanor false info to police."

"Like using a false name?"

"Yeah. Katharine said it's a misdemeanor if he makes up a name but a gross misdemeanor if he uses someone's real name."

"Mac, I think it's time we heat things up with the Stewart's right after we run the name Guthrie. Pete should be at the station now. We're hauling all their drunken asses in. I want 'em believing we've got something on each one of them. I'll call Travis and tell him to keep an eye on Michelle. I'm sure he can figure out what to do with her."

*　　*　　*

They disagreed on many things, but Gage suspected the sad expression in his father's eyes came from wanting direct involvement in solving the Madeline Island murders. So he asked, and Frank readily swapped Sunday afternoon football to assist at the office. When they hauled the Stewart brothers in, they came willingly. Josie, on the other hand, berated them with wildcat screams. She then required restraints following several ferocious swings at Mac. Gage assumed the black-eyed gleam in Mac's eye a telltale sign that he actually enjoyed the act of cuffing her. While his dad and Pete sat with three, he and Mac drilled one at a time in the conference room.

Deciding to make Josie sweat it out the longest, they started with Mark, then Curtis, and released both after taping their statements. Mark's story replicated the first time Katharine and Mac spoke to all of them. Both stated they knew Derek Gunderson only by that name. Curt fessed up that everyone at work was aware of Cole then enlightened them to something they didn't know. Josie stayed at the bar with Maryann the night Mac broke up the argument between the married couple a few weeks back. Curt had had enough of Josie's bitching he called it and left the Tavern to go home to sleep off his drunk. He apologized for not remembering Maryann's name and explained that he just met her that night when Derek brought her to the Tavern. He admitted he had too much to drink to recall much else. He then informed them that Maryann and Josie were friends before she was killed, but couldn't understand why his wife wouldn't mention it. He frequently tuned out her constant ragging and probably missed hearing the name somewhere.

When Mark and Curt were released, Josie cut loose with a mouthful of profanities screaming they couldn't hold her without legal representation.

"You're not under arrest, yet," Mac told her.

"Why am I handcuffed?"

"Assault on a police officer. I'd love to lock you up and charge you, but I'm giving you the opportunity to tell us what we want to know about Maryann Graham and then you'll be free to go."

"I'll have your badge before I tell you anything!"

"Put your pen to the wind," Mac said. "Pete, the mouthy lady's getting three hots and a cot on the County." Facing Kevin, he demanded, "You gonna talk to us or you wanna join her?"

"I've told you what I know," he blustered.

"Well, I want to hear it again. But this time you're going to tell me everything."

"You can't charge me. I didn't kill her."

"I've got you both on parties to crime. Your sister-in-law doesn't know it but we're seriously considering charging you both with probable consequence to the Graham woman's murder besides assault on a police officer."

"I never touched you!" Kevin shouted.

"How?" Josie yelled.

Nicole may not want to keep them out of the tavern, but she made one hell of a witness. With Michelle's info and Nicole's recent statement they had enough suspicion to bring them in for Mirandized questioning. But the truth be known, it was too early to make any arrest for murder.

"Kevin you were the last one seen with Gunderson the night the Graham woman was murdered. Josie, we have witnesses who put you with Maryann shortly before her death. What's it gonna be, talk or jail?"

Kevin caved first, and Mac said, "Josie?"

"I ain't telling you shit!"

"Your choice. Book her Pete. Kevin, you're up. In the backroom now. Frank you wanna take a ride with Pete?"

"Absolutely. I can chat with some of my old cronies."

When Pete and Frank ushered a screaming Josie out the door, Mac was relieved Frank understood the need for a witness enroute to the jail. He trailed Kevin into the conference room and read him his rights after Gage inserted a new tape.

"Thought you said I wasn't under arrest."

"We're making this official," Gage told him.

Kevin declined legal representation. Done with the preliminary statistics and seated five minutes, thunderous pounding diverted their attention.

"Mac, go ahead without me." He went to check the back door and discovered Josie's father, Bert Hanson, standing on the other side. Opening the door, he began, "Bert—"

"What the hell you doin' questioning my daughter?"

"We're not. Right now she's on her way to jail for assaulting a police officer."

"Why you son—"

"Bert. That wouldn't be a threat you're about to make to a police officer, would it?"

"You son-of-a-bitch. You don't have a mark on you. What the hell you questioning my little girl for?"

"Bert, your 'little girl' was the last one seen with Maryann Graham before she was murdered. She lied to us the first time we talked to her about knowing the Graham woman then fought us today when we tried to bring her in for routine questioning."

His cheeks puffed up with heat flowing into them instantly drained of color.

"Now if you'll excuse me, Bert." Gage slammed the door shut. Fisting his hands to his hips, he heaved out an exhausted breath. No doubt, he'd hear from Carter Taylor shortly about this incident. He didn't give a shit since he was positive Kevin and Josie knew more than they were telling.

Why, wasn't—he stopped. Another idea fastened itself inside his mind. Something very obvious but no one ever considered until now. He'd check out his instincts on the Q-T, glanced at the fax machine spewing out paper. Pete had run the name Derek Guthrie through dispatch for both Wisconsin and Minnesota before he left. The dispatcher told him the computer was spitting out a mile of charges, which was coming in now. Further checks also showed Minnesota wanted Guthrie for a gross misdemeanor Driving Under the Influence—same as Wisconsin's OUI. The warrant out of Hennepin County in Minneapolis listed a physical description closely matching what they already knew about Gunderson. Hennepin County had N-P-A for the address. A street person Gage mused. Added remarks indicated there was an active misdemeanor assault warrant as well. Pete also contacted the Hennepin County Jail to find out if they had a booking photo of Guthrie. The jail said they'd pull it and fax that as well before the day was out.

Newer criminal technology could now match names to vehicles, but neither state had the scumbag listed to a red Honda in either name. And somehow, prints had slipped through NCIC on a match between both names. Not unusual, however extremely frustrating when the warrants were issued a little over a year ago.

The phone on the fax rang again and Gage waited until the machine emitted the Hennepin County Jail photo with the name Derek Ralph Guthrie. It was Gunderson all right and Gage recalled what Cole passed on from the Profiler about increased hostility of the serial killer. Things were looking up. All he had to do now was check out a hunch, prove it with tangible evidence, and find out which, Guthrie or Gunderson, was the real name. With a little more luck, Kevin Stewart might just confess that he knew Patriot. Unfortunately, Gage already knew the likelihood of that luck.

CHAPTER 21

His EYES FLEW open. He sat up even quicker. His ragged breathing came rough in his throat along with a numbed horror pulverizing the inside of his chest.

Michelle was in trouble.

Snatching his cell phone from the nightstand, Travis punched in a number and waited. Early morning, the Saturday before Thanksgiving, the grueling nightmare awoke him. He drummed his fingers as if possessed by a neurotic condition. "Come on, come on."

When Michelle finally answered, her voice sounded groggy and muddled. Travis exhaled slowly, attempted to control the master throb inside his chest.

"Good morning. Did I wake you?"

"Travis."

An idiot he was, but the dream was too real. He could still see the images, feel the fright engraved on her face as distinctly as he heard her cries for help.

"Travis," Michelle said yawning. "It's six in the morning."

"I know, Milady." Okay, so he overreacted and silently acknowledged she was tucked safely in bed. "I just wanted to hear your voice."

"Oh, isn't that peachy," she responded with mild sarcasm then came to life. "Travis Baines, I still think you're insane."

She laughed softly upon saying it, and with relief Travis propped the pillows to lean back. "Men do daft things when they're in love. Other than being wakened by a crazy man, how are you feeling this morning?"

"Much better. As much as I hate admitting it, you were right."

He grinned as if she could see him. "Since you're big enough to admit it, I won't say I told you so. Grandma-ma and I are going over to the old cemetery today. She wants to visit the graves of her ancestors. Come with us."

"I can't. We're baking pies at Paula's house for Thanksgiving. In fact, I thought you knew that since your mother will be there."

"Yeah, and I think I like the idea of you baking me a blueberry pie."

"Blueberry? What makes you think I'm gonna bake a blueberry pie when it's traditional to have pumpkin?"

"Because it's my favorite," he said with confidence. "You'll want to do it."

"You think so, eh?"

"I know so. Did you invite your sister and her family?"

"Yes, and Paula is more insane than you are. She's playing hostess to nineteen people. But no one could argue with her when she was so emphatic about it. I think she misses the way we used to hang out there as kids."

He already knew the list included his family, the LeNoir's and Dobarchon's, along with Nicole and the motherless child. "I thought there were only going to be seventeen people. Who else is coming?"

"Katharine's aunt and uncle from Bayfield. It's her dad's brother, Garrett and his wife Suzanne. Their kids aren't coming home this year."

"Are your parents going to be there?"

"They go south every winter and left already, but my sister's coming."

Detecting sadness in the tone of her voice it bothered Travis that any parent would accuse their child of failing. "You eat a good breakfast and I'll call you later."

"I will. Just don't wait until I'm sleeping to call again."

"Milady, the next time I feel the urge to wake you, you'll be by my side. And it won't be to know how your tummy is feeling. Later."

He laughed and disconnected before she could respond.

Obsessed by the all-too-real nightmare, the graphic picture in his head persisted. The panic he awoke with had been radically alarming. In that horrific moment, waking Michelle was the least of his worries. Nevertheless, something still didn't feel right. The haunting sensation came from the dream and she would really think him nuts if he showed up at her front door like he first considered doing. He scrambled out of bed headed for the shower.

An hour later Travis cleaned up his breakfast mess. Somehow, he needed to convince Michelle not to stay alone until Gage and Mac caught this monster. Since figuring out the dream of his weeping lady, and hearing Michelle's ghost, he wasn't about to ignore last night's version of the dream. The dead woman he discovered at the lagoon had definitely invaded his sleep, too. Clearly, he heard Michelle sobbing. While he stood helplessly watching, rivulets of tears poured out of her over the blood-covered woman as her ex snuck up readied to kill her. In the dream, he yelled her name in warning, tried to reach her, but he was too late.

Inhaling deeply through his nostrils, he let it out. All he had to do this week was figure out a way to harbor her from the vibes he felt deep inside but never neglected.

A second hour had slipped away when Travis stopped the Ferrari in front of a rusted speared, wrought iron fence enclosing the Indian Cemetery. Sliding out, he jaunted around the back end. Grandmama had already opened the door. Travis extended his hand to help her out.

"Thank you. You kids and these low-riding sports cars make it very hard for us old ladies to climb out of."

A smile deepened into subdued laughter. "You're just upset because I won't let you drive," he told her.

"I'll have you know I was driving before you were a twinkle in your daddy's eye."

Leaning forward and kissing her forehead, Travis teased, "It's the twinkle in *your* eye that scares me, Grandma-ma. I'll not have you committing hari-kari with the Ferrari."

"Hrmph."

Travis ignored her grunt of protest and shifted. The corroded iron fence stood strongly. He assumed, to deter thousands who passed through each summer. They walked toward an attached iron sign reading the inscription of Michel Cadotte, Sr. along with mention of his granddaughter, Julia, who was buried near his side. Superior bordered one edge with trees shading and protecting, and the marina hugged the other side.

"The fence is locked, Grandma-ma. We can't get any closer."

"Nonsense," she huffed, brushing her grandson aside.

"Where are you going?"

She ignored him and strutted with determination alongside the sturdy fence in the direction of the marina. Travis followed, caught up in long strides when Grandma-ma turned the corner post near a clump of penned in bushes. Or so he thought. Near the marina, she stepped up several large rocks to access the graveyard. It was his turn to grunt. She went ahead and entered whether it was right or not. He took her hand to assist then followed.

Maneuvering carefully through the unkempt grass, they read the inscriptions on each ancient headstone. Some were decayed and broken beyond readability. Others worn and marred while a few had crumbled from weather and time, perhaps even damaged intentionally. The decipherable years dated back to the 1800's on most. The faceless names were Native American, including the Chief of the Chippewa.

Cloudy skies and fog had consumed most of the morning making the location quiet in an eerie way. Scattered tulips and pansies misted over with dew graced grassy unkempt pockets in the November warmth. The colorful growth amongst markers of death was an odd contrast for the time of year. Just as odd, he thought, was the lack of straight lines with no rhyme or reason to the placement of the tombstones or other flowers inside the sacred burial grounds.

Grandma-ma gasped and Travis spun around. "What is it?"

"Nind anike-anike-nimoshomiss, Michel."

Carefully, he navigated a path to where she stood and definitely made out the carved name of her great-great-grandfather, Michel Cadotte. Quarters, dimes, nickels and pennies, some shiny, others inroads of time, all graced Michel's stone. Staring at the impaired primitive dates forced him to realize the brief space between the years was indicative of a man's time on earth. And right there next to Michel was a smaller stone protruding tragically for Julia Warren who died at five months. How sad he thought. There was little time for her abbreviated life to bare a fleeting thought. An honor, he decided, that his grandmother was named after the baby.

Travis shifted about. Upon arriving, curiosity got him. He wondered why shabby, broken-down red wooden boxes were scattered in the middle. "Grandma-ma, why are some of the graves covered with wooden crates?"

"Back in those days it was done out of devotion to the dead. Wooden crates were used to protect food the Native American's laid with the deceased."

Tossing a peculiar expression at her, he asked, "Why did they lay food out?"

"It was their belief that it took four days for the soul to move from earth to heaven, hence they believed the soul needed food for nourishment and laid it out inside the crates. It was also thought those crates would keep out evil spirits."

"Where's Michel's wife, Madeline?"

"Ah. It's unknown why, but Esquaysayway is buried on the north end of the island."

His stomach pitched him a curve ball. The thought of going through eternity without Michelle by his side split his heart in two as much as the notion of living without her now did.

"Some would say they were a superstitious people, Travis. It's been told that if one died of smallpox their skeletal remains were buried outside the Indian Cemetery." Julia looked from the stone to her grandson. "This would prove my thoughts on Julia Warren incorrect. I always assumed she died of that, or diphtheria."

Not appearing to lessen any, fog floated like ghosts in the air.

Travis moved on and studied a circle of stones laid ceremoniously around more slab tablets. He assumed those were in honor or for protection as well. In some ways, he felt like an intruder on their sacred soil, but had a compulsion to wipe away dried leaves and twigs. Further from their entry point, he discovered more headstones coveted by large trees and scattered brush. Life spans he thought dating back to the 1700's but couldn't be sure from the withered stone. More coins were strewn with dignity here, too. He thought it interesting that whether the coins were tossed or laid carefully, none blanketed the ground.

He glanced over his shoulder when the distant blast from an incoming ferry penetrated the misty air. The engine's hum carried across Superior at the same time he heard the familiar weeping of Michelle's ghost. He shifted toward his grandmother thinking she, too, heard Mikala. But Julia Perry stood erect like always in a belted, hip-length tweed jacket. He figured through the years she positioned herself upright because of shortness. He felt the tug of loneliness watching the dazzle fade in her eyes as she reflected on past memories.

"Kinawa akandowin nin, Pangi Ningo."

He shuffled uncomfortably. He wasn't just watching his grandmother. He was staring at her in admiration of her energy and integrity. For as long as he could remember, she frequently called him *Pangi Ningo*. It meant Little One, and thinking about it, he chuckled. "Grandma-ma, I'm not little anymore."

"That you aren't, nin kitchiogwissima."

He inched over near her side now. "You usually refer to me as grandchild. What was that you just said?"

"Grandson," she answered. "Something bothers you, Travis. What is it?"

They walked toward the area where they entered. "Nothing."

Julia stopped. "My eyes are open, and I see torment in both of yours."

"Grandma-ma, this is one problem there's nothing you can do anything about." He turned and faced her. "Even if you could, I'd never allow your involvement."

She reached touching his arm with frail fingers, and studied him. The common gesture was her way of fussing over him throughout his life. Generally, it preceded her perceptiveness.

"You're worried the ex is going to come after Michelle."

No longer surprised by her insights, Travis let out an audible breath. "How do you do that?"

Patting his arm now, she said, "Some day when you have your own, you'll figure it out. The same way we've been telling you your entire life you'd know when you met the right girl."

Walking away, he said, "Something tells me your intrusive insights have nothing to do with procreation since your own daughter lacks this gift."

"She takes after your grandfather," Julia tittered quietly. "But you, Pangi Ningo, are like me."

Travis halted a second time, spun around, and analyzed her words. He didn't know how to respond and shoved his hands into pants pockets.

"You're dreaming of the crying woman again, aren't you?"

"Not exactly," he muttered.

"Love's not easy when it's one sided."

"Come again?"

"Let's go," she said, walking away. "I want a ride in that souped up macho car of yours. You can drive me around the island."

Obediently, he turned, followed and assisted her past the entry they made then into the car. He revved up the Ferrari and drove where she directed. He didn't want to discuss the dream she mentioned, nor the one that had scared the hell out of him this morning. The last thing he needed was more needless worrying over her safety, too.

Silence loomed for a stretch of time before he finally spoke. "It's not one sided. We just have a roadblock we need to get around together. If she wasn't so . . . stubborn," he grumbled.

"Like your mother," Julia chuckled.

He pitched a vacant look at her.

"Travis, I love you with all my heart, but sometimes you take the cake on naïveté. Why do you think we all ended up in Boston?"

With little thought on the subject, he shrugged, slowed going around a sharp corner.

"Your mother was afraid to move away from us, away from the only home she ever knew. She returned one weekend from college insistently headstrong about breaking up with your dad because he was going out east after graduation."

"I don't get it. She left home for college and met Dad there."

"She was only two hours away. Boston was in another world for Rosemary. Your grandfather and I knew how your mother felt about your dad long before she did. We were aware of your father's plans for his future and knew she would never leave Wisconsin. So, we made our own plans and moved out there her last year of college."

"You're telling me Grandfather's job didn't transfer him?"

"Not until he requested it."

"Was Dad in on this scheme of yours?"

"Oh, I think he suspected something, but no, we never told either one of them anything. We let everything take it's course."

"Did you really?"

"Sometimes it's necessary to help the eyes see what the heart already knows. And I'd do it again if it were to help. Turn here."

The speed limited to forty max, Travis slowed a second time turning onto a dirt road. "How is it you all make loving someone appear effortless?"

"Travis Phillip! Wherever did you get the idea that love was effortless?"

"From all of you," he said with a frown. "No problems ever too big, etcetera."

"All our talking has been a waste of time."

"What's that supposed to mean?"

"First, there isn't a problem on the face of the earth that can't be resolved when it's shared with the one you care the most about. But loving someone is a far cry from being effortless. It takes patience, understanding, and digging deeply to find both when you think you can't take another second of the other's flaws. There's a lot of giving and days you'd swear your partner took more."

Travis gawked at her. "But—"

"Good Lord! Travis Phillip Cadotte Baines! Do you really believe your grandfather and I, or your parents, haven't had our difficulties? In my day, money was the root of many arguments. I wanted one thing, he wanted another, and we couldn't have either. You're very fortunate you'll never know that feeling, but there'll be something else. There always is. And it's devastating to love someone who won't love you back."

He fumbled silently for a response as an utter loss with defeat slugged him in the gut. *He wasn't wrong.* Then he remembered Michelle's words of falling instantly in love. That bastard had brainwashed her into believing love needed time to grow. He never had a confused day in his life. Glancing sideways at Grandma-ma, the core of his despair twisted itself inside of him with unmitigated frustration, and yes, confusion. He despised the fight. It was too closely related to the feelings of being a lonely child.

*   *   *

The day of giving thanks Michelle arrived at the LeNoir house early to help Paula prepare the feast. Feeling a great deal better both mentally and physically, she readily volunteered since Katharine hated cooking and Nicole had worked late last night. Wednesday's before this holiday, the Tavern was always crammed to the brim in pre-celebration.

A scrumptious aroma from the twenty-five pound turkey already stuffed and roasting filled the house. Paula greeted her at the door. Keeker dashed downstairs to rub her leg affectionately with his half cry, half purr. And the anticipation of sitting down to a turkey spread with friends and family made her feel fully alive.

"You girls are so gracious, Michelle. Nicole is bringing trays of hors d'oeuvres and Katharine said she'd bring condiments, along with ice cream and cool whip for the pie."

Michelle handed a large bowl of fruit Jell-O to Paula and picked up her kitty, hugging him lovingly.

"Mreow."

She stroked Keeker's neck and snuggled her nose into his fur. She missed him, but he jumped down and obviously didn't feel the same. "Believe me, Paula, making Jell-O was nothing compared to the work you're doing. We should be doing this at the Tavern."

"Rubbish. I wanted Thanksgiving dinner here and we're now up to twenty-one people."

"Twenty-one! Who else is coming?"

"Mac asked if he could invite his partner from Green Bay. The more the merrier I told him and I guess he's bringing a date."

"How are you going to fit twenty-one people around your dining table? I mean it's so small."

"Oh, honey," Paula chuckled. "That table belonged to my grandmother. It has six leaves. There's enough room for five more people if you want to know the truth."

"What about dishes and silver?"

"That was a problem until Rosemary suggested we borrow what we needed from the Tavern. Frank and Phillip went over and got more than we need last night. Ted had no problem as long as we have everything back Friday morning."

"Where is everyone?"

"Katharine went home since Mac and Gage called an early evening last night. Frank is stocking the fridge in the garage with pop and beer. Nicole went home after you left and the other two are still sleeping."

"Well, then, what would you like to start on first?"

"I thought we'd peel potatoes. Rosemary will be here any minute since she couldn't really bring anything and wanted to help. The rest will start traipsing in anytime. I'm sure the men will be glued to the Packer's game at noon. Dinner's at four. Did you let Sylvie know that?"

"Yes. She said they'll be here early so Harvey wouldn't miss any part of the game."

"Which reminds me, I'd better wake up Caitlin. I thought it best she sleep in this morning. I'm sure she'll miss out on a nap today."

Paula went upstairs and Keeker followed. Michelle found a

twenty-pound bag of potatoes, washed her hands, and searched for a paring knife or peeler. Upon hearing a car outside, she peeked through the kitchen window then went to the front door to let Rosemary in.

"Happy Thanksgiving, Michelle." She held up two potato peelers. "I came prepared, since I figured Paula would only have one."

"Greetings. Come on in. Paula's upstairs getting Caitlin and I've just found the bag of potatoes but no utensil yet." Michelle headed toward the kitchen, asking over her shoulder, "When will the other's be here?"

"Before noon. Phillip is still a true Vikings fan since he's originally from Minnesota. I've warned him Packer country is no place to be donning a purple jersey. He didn't care and went out and bought a Viking shirt just for the occasion."

Michelle giggled, aware of the battle of wills between the Packers and the Vikings. "If Phillip's smart, he'll keep his mouth shut during the first game today."

"Have you ever known a man to do that other than the moment a woman asks if she looks too fat? I'm sure Phillip will bet away the farm with all of them."

Michelle searched, found two pans and filled both with cold water.

"Are your parents coming today?"

"They go south every year with the other snowbirds," she said tersely. Setting the pans on the kitchen table, they laid out newspaper for the peelings and sat down together. "It's probably just as well they've already left."

When vicarious emotion filled Rosemary's face, Michelle regretted her comment. "I'm sorry. I didn't—my sister and her family are coming."

"Michelle, all parents make mistakes. Everyday is a learning process when you have children."

"I doubt you or Phillip ever made a mistake with Travis."

"Oh, I don't know. Sometimes it's not just mistakes but a lack of other things. Don't misunderstand. I love Travis with all my heart. He's my pride and joy, and everything I never was. Maybe he's what I didn't want to be because I love freedom. And that my dear is selfish on my part."

"But you're a close family. You share everything. Do you have any idea what it's like not . . ." she choked.

"He told us what you've been through. And no I don't know your pain nor can I fully understand your loss."

Michelle held the raw emotion in check. "You know, it took me awhile to figure out the problem. I'm not perfect either. I have faults. But I still don't totally understand some things myself."

She hadn't told anyone other than Sylvie of the recent confrontation with her mother, or her self-analysis of the situation, but oddly felt the comfort of this woman's presence. "Rosemary, like I did, my parents fell for Derek's charm. They saw him as the replacement for the son they lost. But why do they blame me for a bad marriage when Derek came close to killing me?"

"Did you ever tell your parents that?"

She stopped peeling the almost demolished potato. "No, not the last time it happened. I tried the first time he hit me. Each time it happened, it was not only physical but emotional. To admit to the failure was taboo. I was raised on stout beliefs. Marriage is forever. A month after my bruises heeled I could only tell them I was divorcing him. They accused me of being inadequate and refused to hear anymore let alone the truth. They told me to go home and make my marriage work. I finally found the courage to explain to them before they left for Florida. My mother doesn't believe me or that Derek killed that woman. She said if any of it was the truth then I really ruined the family name by marrying him in the first place."

"So what they couldn't visualize they didn't want to believe and by divorce they lost their son a second time."

Nodding, Michelle cut what was left of the potato and dropped it into the pan of water. "I guess I should've just stepped over my humiliation and let them see the damaged goods. But I never dreamed my own parents wouldn't believe me."

Grabbing another potato, she said, "Once I figured out I'd

made the same mistake, it made it easier for me to forgive them for not wanting to know what happened."

"Darling child," Rosemary said quietly. "Have you given yourself as much compassion and understanding?"

Michelle gaped wordlessly across the table at Rosemary. Caitlin burst into the kitchen giggling and squealing with Gage hot on her trail. Overwhelmed by Rosemary's question, Michelle barely heard something about a cookie monster when Gage cornered Caitlin and gobbled her up. Rosemary's question brought forth a rude awakening. The answer was still the same. If she found clemency for her mistakes, she would only be free to make the same one again. Even so, without giving herself the compassion she needed, and until Derek was caught, she could never be free.

The next sound came from her niece and nephew squealing out Gage's name. She watched both jump into his arms, hug and kiss him. He squatted to their level and introduced Shalee and Brendan to Caitlin. In the middle, Keeker had pulled up a chair for a ringside seat. Still pondering Rosemary's words, Michelle subconsciously wished she had a camera to snap a shot of Shalee taking Caitlin's hand. Her ex smashed the camera during one of his fitful tempers. Done peeling potatoes, she pondered another question. How deserving was she of compassion for herself? Frank came in from the garage and additional voices sounded from the living room. Michelle drained the potatoes and refilled the pan with water before setting it on the burner. Nicole had arrived and solicited Harvey's help to carry in large trays of breakfast.

"Where's my little blond cutie?"

Caitlin shrieked and Nicole scooped the child into her arms. "Happy Thanksgiving, my little sweetie."

The kitchen filled quickly with people and introductions were made. The atmosphere was charged with laughter and jocularity. Struggling silently with self-pity, Michelle observed another interaction for the first time. Gage leaned against vacant counter space, mug in hand, gazing with blatant desire at Nicole. And Nicole. Well, any attempt to hide the way she stole peeks at Gage were only self deceptive. How blinded by personal problems could she be not to have noticed this before now? Looking at Nicole and back to Gage, Michelle's heart swelled. These two had squabbled with each other their entire life and she suddenly realized every decision Nicole ever made for her future added up to only one thing. A man named Gage. If Sully's ghosts really did exist, Nicolina would have to work overtime in a hellish storm to get these two together.

"Paula, I thought brunch trays would be a great idea instead of you having to make breakfast. That way they can munch whenever they're hungry."

"Nicole, you're a gem. Gage, put the leaves in the table for me please. And the rest of you I'm giving the boot out of my kitchen."

Another round of Brendan and Shalee's gleeful cheers told Michelle Travis had arrived. Not far behind came Mac and Katharine along with Cole and his girlfriend. The razzing officially began when Phillip walked in wearing his Viking jersey. Bets were instantly wagered between the sea of green and the lone purple. Frank kept busy serving drinks and Michelle was thrilled that Harvey fit right in with the men. She couldn't decide between Katharine and Sylvie who was more interested in the game as both took their seats on the carpeted floor in front of the tube. Grandmama sat with Suzanne. Both helped the kids fill their plates and kept them seated at the table.

Michelle snuck her own peak at Travis when he boldly told the football fans the only way he'd bet for either team was against both when they played the New England Pats. Katharine threw a pillow at him. The others booed, including Phillip.

"Paula, tell you what," Michelle said. "After we get stuff ready here I'll get the kids out of everybody's way for a couple of hours."

"You kids go on and have fun. We've got it covered."

"Where're you going?" Travis asked, entering the kitchen.

"I'm taking the kids to the State Park so you guys can watch the game."

"I've been chastised from the room," he said grinning. "Mind if I come along?"

"I'm pretty sure I'll be outvoted again if I say no." Michelle shouted over the crowd, "I'm going to the State Park. Who wants to come with?"

The kids acclaimed their wishes loudly and the football crowd yelled, "Get out!"

Gage and Mac sent her fretful grimaces and she reassured them she would be fine. "Travis has invited himself to come along."

CHAPTER 22

THE WEATHER HAD cooled enough requiring lightweight jackets but not so much that the brilliant fall colors didn't riot around them under exhilarating sunshine. Brendan pulled Travis along as they hiked through the park. Shalee and Caitlin were less rambunctious and each held Michelle's hands.

"Auntie Michelle, tell Travis how the leaves change color."

"Brendan, I think Travis knows how and why the leaves change color."

"Bet he doesn't know Jack Frost does it. Do you, Travis?"

"I don't believe I do." Flinging a broad grin over his shoulder, Travis insisted, "Let's hear it Auntie Michelle."

As Shalee wigwagged the trail they were walking, she said, "Yeah. Tell Caitlin about Jack Frost painting the leaves."

"Who's Jack Frost?" Caitlin asked.

"Jack Frost comes at night when it starts to get cold." Brendan told her. "He's the one who leaves ice on all the trees because his fingers are made of ice. Right, Auntie Michelle?"

Skipping with Shalee, Caitlin said, "If his fingers are ice how can he paint the leaves different colors?"

Michelle chuckled. "It's true. Jack Frost does have fingers made of ice. At night after all little children go to bed, and the temperature gets cooler, Jack Frost goes from tree to tree pinching the leaves. Once he's touched them it brings bright reds and yellow and purples to the leaves in the daylight hours."

"But ice isn't colored," Caitlin argued.

"That's true, sweetie. But Jack Frost's fingers are covered with yellow, gold and brown paint. While you're sleeping, he paints the green leaves with quick broad strokes from his brush-like fingers. Then when old Jack Frost mixes the colors of paint on his fingers with the green leaves, it makes all the different shades of reds and yellows. He moves quietly through the forest, so not to wake us, and decorates every tree. In the morning, we see all the beautiful colors which is what season of the year?"

All three children bellowed, "Faaaall!"

"That's right. And what season comes next?"

"Winter!" They sang out.

"How come he doesn't paint the pine trees?" Caitlin asked gaping up and up to study a tall one.

"Oh, but he does. See that one up there," Michelle pointed. "With the brown tucked away between the larger branches."

"Uh-huh."

"That one's dying. Jack Frost didn't paint it," Brendan said.

"He sure did, dumplin'. Most people think it's dying but they really aren't. The needles just change more slowly and gradually. Tamarack pines like that one," Michelle pointed, "will change to all yellow needles and all it's branches change at the same time. You've all seen brown needles from the pine on the ground, right?"

"Yes," they chanted.

"Well, it's the same thing as the leaves falling off the trees. Pines lose their needles."

Travis stopped and turned. "I've got one for you, Auntie Michelle. I've been to Great Britain where they have trees just like here but the colors are dull and *uuugly*. Why's that?"

The children giggled at his description, and Michelle muttered, "Travis, you're going to wreck my Jack Frost theory."

"Tell us anyway," Brendan blurted.

Thinking, she eyed her nephew for a moment. "It's because warm sunny days with cooler nights slightly above freezing temperatures are needed. In Great Britain, they have warm fall nights and cloudy days making the colors dull and dingy."

Michelle grinned haughtily at Travis. "Jack Frost likes cool nights. So, he doesn't visit Great Britain like Travis does."

All three kids took off in search of pine trees with colored needles. Travis slowed for Michelle to catch up. "That's some story."

"I'm surprised Brendan didn't ask to hear the one about the Indian legend changing the color."

Intrigued, he said, "Tell me."

She eyed him curiously. "Do you believe in mythical stories and fantasies?"

"Milady, I'm hearing a crying ghost everyday of my life. Why wouldn't I?"

Sighing, she said, "According to an Indian legend, celestial hunters kill a great bear in the autumn sky. The blood dripping from the bear on the forest changes many leaves to red. The yellow colors come from the fat that splatters out of the kettle as hunters cook the meat."

"Somehow I think you cheated me out of the long version of that theory."

"Travis, you amaze me with your child-like enthusiasm."

"Finally," he said, laughing in a deep, jovial way then casually placed an arm across her shoulders. He leaned closer. "I hope that's not the only way I amaze you. I'll say this again."

With one eye on the children in front of them, Michelle kept one on Travis. "Say what again?"

"You'll make a wonderful mother."

Blood rushed quickly through her veins just before she called out, "Brendan Joseph Hood that's far enough into the woods. Get back here on the trail with us."

"Auntie Michelle, I just wanna see this pine," Brendan wined.

"Now, Brendan. Or we're going back to Paula's house."

"Let me handle this," Travis said.

He dodged branches and skirted low growth headed toward Brendan. Michelle caught up to Shalee and Caitlin, taking each by the hand.

"Auntie Michelle, how come we can't go off the trail?"

"Because your mother will be upset if you sit down to Thanksgiving dinner with dirt-covered clothes."

"I don't have a mother anymore."

Michelle blinked, looked down at Caitlin.

"Nicole said she's in heaven with the angels."

"What happened to your mother?" Shalee asked.

Clenching her free hand to her hip, Caitlin repeated, "I just told you, Shalee. She's in heaven. Right, Auntie Michelle?"

If she hadn't been shocked by the child's forthright words, the claimed relationship certainly surprised her. "That's right, sweetie. Your mommy is in heaven."

"Is it okay if I call you Auntie? Nicole said I had to ask you first and I forgot."

Large blue eyes desperately needing love waited for her to answer. Michelle squatted face-to-face with the girls. "Of course you can call me Auntie Michelle. And I betcha your mom is watching us right now and smiling down on you."

Caitlin's eyes widened. "Nicole said my mom would get angel wings and always be watching and protecting me. And when I'm lonely, I'm supposed to close my eyes and remember how she smiled at me. I do every night after I say prayers. I like Nicole. She's got pretty hair."

"Yes, she does, Caitlin. But you've got pretty hair, too." Brushing the child's fluff out of her face, Michelle said, "In fact it feels just like angel hair. All soft and silky."

"Does mommy have angel hair?"

"You better believe it," Michelle said convincingly.

"Auntie Michelle, can I tell you a secret."

"Darling, it's only a secret if you don't tell anyone. But Shalee and I promise we won't say a word if there's something you want to share with us. Right, Shalee?"

Her pint-size relative nodded her head vigorously.

"I haven't told anyone but that man who was staying in that room with us hurt my mommy."

Black fright pummeled Michelle. Her heart skipped a dozen beats. The last thing she expected from a three-year-old was an admission of this nature. "Caitlin, did the man—"

"Shalee, come with Brendan and me," Travis interrupted. "I want to show you something."

Once the three walked up the path, Michelle examined Caitlin as if there would be visible evidence. "Sweetie, this is important and I need you to tell me the truth. Did that man ever touch you or hurt you?"

"Hun-uh, but Derek yelled at mommy all the time. And once I saw him hit her and she was crying."

Michelle's heart jumped to her throat in several clawing strokes.

"I hope he never does that to Nicole. Will he?"

"*Caitlin.* Why do you think he'd hurt Nicole?"

"Auntie Michelle, he's mean and I love Nicole. And if I tell her about him, she won't love me. I wish she could be my new mommy."

Michelle tugged the child into her arms. "Caitlin, nothing's going to happen to Nicole, and anything you tell her isn't going to stop her from loving you the way she already does. Besides, Gage and Mac will make sure she's safe."

Leaning back, she said, "Now let's go have fun, and forget about that bad man for the rest of today."

"Okay. Can I tell you one more thing."

"You most certainly can."

"Well, two things."

Michelle nodded.

"Is Gage going to be mad at me because I didn't tell him when he talked to me?"

"No, darling. But I tell you what. I'll talk to Gage first and then you can tell him what you just told me. How's that?"

This time Caitlin wrapped her arms around Michelle and squeezed in response. "Will you be with me?"

Michelle reciprocated the hug. "Of course I will, sweetie. Now go catch up to the others and have yourself a good time."

"Okay," she said pulling away. "Auntie Michelle, Travis is a nice man and he's cute."

Michelle glanced up the trail at Travis walking between her

niece and nephew. Even a three-year-old saw the good in Travis. "I think you're right, Caitlin."

When Caitlin took off to catch up, Michelle followed and Travis hung back. He waited until the kids were chattering and giggling yards in front of them before speaking.

"If he did anything to hurt that little girl, I'll—"

"Travis, don't even think it. She says he didn't but I'm more worried because she named Derek. I believe she was honest with me and we agreed she would tell Gage everything."

"You want to go back so Gage can talk to her?"

"No. I told her to forget about it for today and just have fun. Thanks for taking Shalee so Caitlin and I could talk. She wants something that isn't possible."

"What does she want?"

Travis snuggled his arm around her waist and for once, Michelle actually accepted the comforting gesture. "She wants Nicole to be her new mommy and figured Nicole wouldn't love her because she hadn't been honest. She also thinks you're cute but that's a secret between us girls."

"Does her adopted auntie agree?"

Peering up at him, his pearl gray eyes sparkled. Tugging her in front of him, he held her close and gorged himself an early dinner with a mouth-watering kiss. Her insides glowed into a nuclear meltdown—

"Auntie Michelle, help! Travis! Help me!"

"*Omigod!* The Point!"

"Which way?" Travis barked.

"This way," she pointed frantically.

Brendan's scream was frantic, wild and Michelle took off catching up to Shalee and Caitlin. "Please, God, don't let anything happen to him."

"Brendan, hang on!" Travis yelled as he ran. "I'm coming."

Michelle picked up Caitlin and grabbed Shalee's hand making her run alongside. Travis yelled louder letting Brendan know they heard him. His cries sounded horribly frightful and thinking the worst, *he's fallen off the cliff into the water*, Shalee tripped. Michelle stopped, set Caitlin down to pick up her niece. "Dumplin' are you hurt?"

Nervously, she glanced toward the bridge unable to see the cliff on the other side, or Travis. Tears were leaking out of her niece's eyes. "Shalee! Where are you hurt?"

"I hurt my hand," she cried.

"Okay, darling. We'll take care of it in a minute."

Michelle scooped both children into her arms and ran toward Travis. When she got to the bridge, Travis had an iron grip on Brendan's arm.

"Let go. I gotcha, little buddy."

He pulled her nephew up over the railing and onto the bridge then checked a sobbing Brendan for injuries. Finding none, Travis picked him up, holding him tight in his arms.

"You're safe, little buddy. It's all right now."

Brendan clung to Travis with arms and legs until his cries turned to snivels. A large lump in Michelle's throat burned fire hot. Tears were streaming down her cheeks when Travis walked back to her carrying Brendan in his arms.

"Brendan Joseph Hood," Michelle cut loose. "I told you to stay with us! What if you'd fallen on the rocks and died!"

Travis pulled her and the two crying girls against him. "Michelle, he's safe. He's unharmed."

Hysteria churned into pure panic—*couldn't lose him, too*—she wept uncontrollably against Travis' shirt.

"Auntie Michelle, I'm sorry," Brendan sniveled through more tears.

Travis steered them to a large rock away from the bridge and one-by-one he set each child down. He made her sit next, checked Shalee's injured palm, kissing both until her cries subsided. Caitlin needed a hug out of fright, then Travis checked Brendan over one more time.

Sniffing, Brendan told them, "I wasn't going out to the Point. I slipped on the bridge because it was wet."

Michelle still couldn't respond when Travis took her trembling hands last, massaging both with his. Freaked out on her own guilt she cut loose screaming. "Brendan, how many times have I told you? You're never allowed on that bridge without me! I've repeatedly told you that and yet you—"

"Michelle."

She gaped at Travis. The quiet emphasis of his voice held a degree of concern.

"Omigod," she whispered, her hand on her breast. When the little tyke stood up to hug her, Michelle grabbed Brendan tightly in her arms. "You scared me so badly."

"I'm sorry, Auntie. I was scared, too. I'll never do it again. Travis saved me and I didn't get hurt."

Leaning away from her nephew, she inhaled, exhaled and bestowed Travis with an indebted look. "We both have something to be thankful for today. But, Brendan, you know we have to tell your parents what happened."

"Can't we just keep it secret," he begged through new quivering lips.

"Little buddy," Travis said. "Lying is never the manly thing to do. We'll tell them together since your aunt and I were distracted."

"I know. I saw you kissing and that's why I snuck over there. I thought it would be okay."

"Didn't we just have a talk about that when you went off in the woods?"

"Yes, sir. But if we tell Mom and Dad, they'll never let me come and see Auntie again."

"If we don't tell them and they find out, they won't let you come and see her either. Since it's just as much my fault, we both take our chances and do the right thing."

"But they'll yell at me for not listening to you guys."

"If you were my son, I'd discipline you as well. Right alongside telling you how much I love and would miss you if anything ever happened to you. Adults make rules because they care, Brendan."

"I know. You didn't do anything wrong, Travis. I'll tell them it was my fault because I didn't listen to you."

"A real man doesn't dump his responsibility." Holding out his

hand, Brendan's small paddy squeezed his back. "We're in this
together, little buddy."

Travis swiveled to the girls. "How's everybody else? No more
injuries, no more tears?"

They shook their heads, answering, "Good!"

"Then let's head back before the others gobble up all the turkey
dinner."

The kids chattered in the backseat as if nothing had happened.
Travis took Michelle's hand, caressing a thumb across her knuckles
as guilt ate away her insides. Her actions were irresponsible.

"Have you eaten anything today?" he asked.

Shaking her head, she muttered, "I overslept and there wasn't
time."

He removed his hand to shift gears, did it harshly before the
car stopped behind the last vehicle in the driveway.

"Everybody inside and wash up for dinner," Travis said.

Michelle didn't move when the kids piled out on driver's side.
The anger she felt coming from Travis was nothing compared to
her carelessness at the park. Rosemary's words came back to her
and she wondered how she could forgive herself when she kept
screwing up—kept failing. Brendan almost died because of her
foolishness. She'd never make a good mother. Because of her, Caitlin
was motherless, but Mr. Baines Incorporated was perfect at
everything, including the way he handled all of them. The pathetic
mess she made—

"Michelle."

She glanced over when Travis stuck his head inside the car. She
wiped the tears away from her cheeks unaware that she'd been
crying again. He wedged himself back into the seat next to her and
took her hand, kissing the back.

"Milady, don't cry. Everything came out fine and you're not to
blame."

"I screamed at him. I've never raised my voice to either one of
them before."

"Michelle."

She yanked her hand away. "Travis, I was responsible for Brendan. I'll talk to Sylvie about what happened."

Raw hurt glittered in his gray eyes.

"How do you think it made me feel when Caitlin stood there telling me she knew about Derek and what he did to her mother?"

"Michelle, Caitlin didn't witness the murder and for God's sake you are not responsible for everyone's actions."

"No, but she did witness the abuse!"

In that tense-filled moment, she had no idea why something else clicked from the day she fainted inside the construction trailer. "And tell me why is it that you haven't told Mac and Katharine about the extra cost they're going to owe for the repairs to their house?"

The unspoken pain was alive and glowing in his eyes. His mouth took on an unpleasant twist. "That's between me and them. Neither does it have anything to do with the real issue that's bothering you right now."

"Travis, if you screw them over on their house, I swear—"

"Michelle! I do not intend to do any such thing! Stop avoiding the real problem here. You can't run forever from the blame that you seem so insistent upon placing on yourself. You have no right to condemn me or any other man for what one bastard did to you and Caitlin's mother, and God knows how many others."

"Have no right!" she blurted. "You're so damn perfect you can't understand or know what I suffered let alone know what I am responsible for Travis Baines!"

"Damn it!" he growled.

Thrusting the door open, Michelle bailed out, slammed it hard then stomped off headed toward the house and went inside. She found Sylvie and quietly invited her upstairs where they could talk. "Sylvie—"

"Michelle, stop. Brendan came and told Harvey and me what happened. My son has pulled the same stunt on us. He also feels horrid for making you cry because you were so afraid. He told us how Travis had talked to him once before about running off then said he deserved to be punished for not obeying the rules. If you want to know the truth, Harvey and I are more surprised by the impact Travis has on our kids."

"But, Sylvie, because of my stupidity Brendan could have died like Brian did."

"That's about the dumbest thing you've ever said, Michelle. Brian's accident was not your fault. Do you think for one minute that I didn't see the way she took to Derek because he reminded all of us of Brian? How do you think it felt that Mother has never doted on Harvey the same way she did Derek? How do you think it feels to me knowing they've never seen their grandchildren? Sure it's fine for her to call and fill me in on gossip, but she and Dad have no desire to see their own grandchildren."

"Oh, Syl, I'll never understand that one."

"I do. They don't like Harvey. I really don't care because as far as I'm concerned, the sun rises and sets with him. He's the best thing that ever happened to me after Brian died. Do you honestly believe that because I'm the baby of the family I can't see what Mom's doing to you?"

Michelle examined her sister, fought back new tears. Sylvie moved closer wrapping her arms around her.

"Big sister, Mom's the fool and I told her a long time ago what Derek did to you. She doesn't want to believe it."

Pulling back, the shock of her sister's news caused her tears to spill over. "You knew? And you never said anything?"

"Of course I knew. The first time I saw bruises on you and you blew it off as klutzism was the day I realized. I started to worry about you until you showed up at the house looking the way you did and told us you were divorcing that son-of-a-bitch. You should've seen Harvey—he wanted to kill him."

"How come you never said anything to me about it?"

"I was raised by the same parents you were. We weren't allowed to be failures especially at marriage. As much as I wanted to reassure you, I knew the humiliation was difficult."

Sylvie's soft hazel eyes were always so soothing. Michelle caressed her sister's hair lovingly. "Oh, baby sister when did you get so smart?"

Sylvie grinned back. "I've always been smart. Now tell me all about the man who's wild about you. I'd love to hear the adult version instead of a five and six year olds translation."

Michelle grabbed a Kleenex and wiped her eyes then blew her nose. Travis Baines *was* insane—and in love with her. Suddenly, everything he said, everything he did hit her at once. "Baby sister, I love you so much." Michelle hugged Sylvie, "But, I have to talk to Gage first. I promise I'll fill you in."

Michelle dashed out of the bathroom and down the stairs. She saw Travis out of the corner of her eye with Katharine, Mac and Cole. He was watching her as she barreled into the kitchen where she found Gage removing the turkey from the oven. Julia and Aunt Suzanne were engrossed in an earnest debate about something. She went over to Gage and quietly spoke. "I have to talk to you outside."

Gage placed the pan on a sideboard and stuffed a piece of crispy meat into his mouth. "Okay, kiddo, let's go."

Michelle led out the back door and walked through the yard toward the swing set. A blast of wind blew through the trees and she pushed her hair out of her face. After glancing around like she thought someone might be listening, Michelle told Gage everything Caitlin said and watched rage torch his pale blue eyes.

His voice remained calm and steady. "Do you believe Gunderson didn't hurt Caitlin in any way?"

"I think she would have told me. She was more afraid you were going to be angry with her for not telling you in the first place. Gage, I'm worried about the fact Caitlin witnessed the abuse to her mother. She can identify Derek. "She's just a baby. What if—"

"Michelle," he cut her off. "Caitlin is safe here. Mac and I are concerned about you. We know he's on the island."

Her eyes widened alertly. "How? Where?"

"We got a call from Kevin yesterday because Mac and I suspect he's known something all along. We've been harassing him hard. Don't know if he was calling to get in our good graces, but he told us he saw the red Honda parked on the dirt road about a mile from the Pine Cove Retreat."

"That's where Travis is staying."

"I know and when we checked it out, the car was gone. We cautioned Travis to keep his eyes peeled. Michelle, I wish you'd come back and stay here until we catch him."

"And put your family in jeopardy? I can't do that."

"Michelle—"

"No, Gage! He needs money and he's after Brian's car because my stupid mother told him he deserved it as settlement for the divorce."

"Your mother?" Gage said with surprise. "When did she talk to him?"

"Apparently before they left for Florida. He told me the night he threatened me at the construction trailer he went to see her. I'm not sure when he did that, but Gage, my parents used Derek as a replacement for Brian."

"Michelle, do you have a key to their house?"

"No but, Sylvie—Gage! You don't think he's—they wouldn't!"

He placed his hands on her shoulders to steady her. "Listen to me."

"How could they let him stay in their house?"

"Michelle, we don't know that they did. Go inside and quietly get the key from Sylvie. Give it to Mac and tell him I want to talk to him out here."

Katharine yelled out the back door. "Hey you two. Dinner's almost ready."

"We'll be there in a minute," Gage yelled over his shoulder. "Go on, Michelle, and don't say anything to anyone."

Her mind reeled with furious thoughts as she hurried into the house. She pulled Sylvie aside and got the key to their mother's house then gave it to Mac.

*   *   *

Fifteen minutes later, Mac and Gage parked out-of-sight of the Callihan house. Cole pulled up behind and all exited the cars. Since Sylvie had a key and handed it over, they were more or less given consent to search without a warrant. Gage had fleeting thoughts of what Carter's response to this would be. Especially when the Town Board Chairman indeed didn't call the morning after they booked Josie in jail, but marched into the station demanding answers to all the 'w' questions. He blew Carter off with rhetoric of an active case. Gage still hadn't had a chance to check into a theory formulating in his mind from that day either, but he strongly suspected something was definitely awry. He also resented the strange way each had of blaming him for the increasing crime on Madeline Island.

"How you wanna handle this, Gage?"

Flushing his thoughts, he said, "Cole, there's a mandoor on the back of an attached garage where the red Honda could be parked inside. They've got sliding glass doors that open to a deck kiddy-corner to the water. It's a three-bedroom house with no basement. You and Mac cover the back and I'll go in the front."

"Gage, you can't unlock the door and cover yourself. Cole, can you handle the back?"

"No problem."

"Then, I'm with Gage at the front door. We'll let you in the glass doors once we've gained entry."

"Are there any windows on the garage?" Cole asked.

"Can't remember," Gage answered.

"Let's do it," Cole said. "I'm hungry. Mac knows my whistle. If I see the car parked in the garage, I'll signal. Once we get up there, give me two minutes to get around back before you open 'er up."

"Gage, the minute you unlock the door, I'll kick it with my foot and go high. You go low."

"Got it."

Quietly, with weapons drawn, the three men snuck up on the shingled rambler that appeared serene and vacant. Cole signaled two fingers just before he ducked around the side of the garage. Mac checked his watch as he and Gage lurked quietly toward the front door. Windows were draped on the front of the house and they positioned themselves, waiting.

"No whistle and that's two minutes." Mac aimed his forty-five when Gage inserted the key with his right hand while holding his Ruger in the other.

Mac kicked it open as both stood side of the door. He went in first and Gage dropped down clutching his gun with both hands. Neither announced their entry. Gage covered Mac then followed him in. The glass doors off the dining room to the right were shaded. Directly in front of them were a half bath and kitchen. Both rooms empty of humans, they slithered across the carpeted living room with their backs against each other. Mac unhitched the lock to the sliding door letting Cole inside.

"No red Honda," Cole whispered.

After a search of the entire house and attached garage, they discovered someone definitely was staying in the Callihan house. Men's clothes, and not Aidan Callihan's size, were strewn across a bedroom and one bath. Dirty dishes were piled in the kitchen, empty beer cans had been tossed and stashed everywhere along with butted smokes in ashtrays. The once neatly kept home was literally a disaster. Not to mention one fact Gage knew, the Callihan's were non-smokers.

"Mac, should we have the crime lab go over it?" Gage asked.

"We didn't find the murder weapon nor has a crime been committed here that we know of. I doubt they'll find anything we don't already know. No, Gage. I think we should sit back for now, wait for the slimeball to return, and pinch his ass when he does."

"Good idea, assuming that's who's staying here," Cole said. "Let's lock her up and go eat."

They returned to the house, learning everyone chose to wait for them before sitting down to Thanksgiving dinner. Gage told Michelle later they didn't find Derek but someone was definitely staying in the house. He asked her if they could hang onto the house key to keep checking the premise. Her and Sylvie's verbal agreement provided the necessary authority.

CHAPTER 23

FRIDAY AFTER THE Pilgrim's holiday the women went shopping including Sylvie, Shalee and Caitlin, and Cole's new girlfriend, Mona. They drove three cars with high expectations of finding excellent sales. Suzanne and Garrett were the only two who returned home Thursday after dinner. To avoid the biggest shopping day of the year, husbands gladly handed over credit cards and cash. Before the ladies went one way and the men the other, Rosemary extended invitations for dinner at the Tavern Friday evening. She was feeling quite generous since Phillip had cleaned out pockets when the Vikings whomped the Packers at home.

Dishware returned to the Tavern and the Callihan house checked a fourth time, the men met at the marina with guy plans. The perfect weather for a boat owner's dream, neither Frank nor Gage had stored their watercraft for the winter yet. Since Pete had volunteered to work on his day off for Gage and Mac, both accepted a much needed indulgence break. Dispatch would notify them via pager if Pete required assistance.

Ronson, Phillip and Harvey rode with Frank in his boat with the intent of seeing all of the Apostle Islands. Cole, Travis, Mac and Brendan went with Gage headed for the sea caves at Devil's Island.

"A cold beer and fishing pole's all I need now," Cole said.

"Gage says drinking isn't allowed on a boat," Brendan boldly informed him.

"That's right buck-a-roo. It's not."

"How'd you meet Mona?" Mac asked.

"Believe it or not, she works for Ashland County driving a dump truck."

"Thought the frail feminine type was more your style," he said with a significant lifting of his brows.

"I did, too," Cole said dryly.

"What're you gonna do when you go back to Green Bay?"

"Dunno. She's a stubborn ox and we're still *dee-scussing* it."

"She has to be to put up with you. Hah! If she's the right one, you'll find yourself doing stupid shi—"

Brendan's wide-eyed expression stopped Mac. "Things. And talk about obstinate. Sorry, Gage. But your sister was the most inflexible person I'd ever met."

"I warned you, Mac."

"You did. Anyone care to wager that Cole goes job hunting before Mona," Mac goaded.

"That won't happen, partner. Women are bullheaded."

"Tell us something we don't know," Travis muttered. "Wait til you start hearing a crying ghost."

Laughter floated up from Mac's throat.

"What's the catch, partner? What's he talking about?"

"Ex-partner to you."

Gage anchored the boat near the sea caves and plopped down next to Brendan flanking Travis. "Brendan, my man. If you listen to these idiots next you'll find yourself arguing with a woman about who's right and wrong."

"Yeah. What's that about anyway?" Cole asked.

"Yeah, what is up with that?" Travis wanted to know then snatched a seven-up from the cooler. He guzzled it to obscure the desperation he heard in his own voice. When the others shrugged, Travis decided that to debate the subject of love with single men, a newlywed and a child was ludicrous, but he was tormented by a gamut of perplexing emotions. Michelle had good reasons but enough was enough. He could never hurt her. Never would hurt her. The fact that she believed he might made him sick inside. He didn't believe Grandma-ma was right about Michelle's incapability to love him either. Couldn't Michelle see all he wanted to do was love her for the rest of their lives? Fifty years or more, he thought miserably. The revving of the motor distracted him and Travis looked up. A grayish-black, ominous sky was as bleak as his emotions.

"Got a storm coming in," Gage said. "I'm heading back."

"Gage, will Frank see it?"

"I'm sure he's already back at the marina, Mac. He's overly cautious."

When Gage steered into the marina, Frank was docking in a slip. While the others secured the boats, Mac checked in with Dispatch. Nearing the dinner hour, Travis offered to show Harvey and Cole the ballroom.

They arrived at the Tavern and Travis gave the others a tour of the ballroom's construction while Phillip and Ronson pulled tables together. A short time later, Brendan, the only male not tossing back alcohol, sat between the most conservative drinkers his father, Harvey and Ronson. Mac, Phillip and Frank debated impolitically correct government theories on one side. Travis thought, what the hell, one drink won't hurt and hunkered between Cole and Gage who were promoting their own happy hour. All three toasted one agreeable subject, headstrong women and ordered another round.

Guzzling his scotch, Cole leered at Travis. "I want to hear more about this ghost you mentioned?"

"He's crazy as a woman with a bedbug," Gage said, slugging back his beer and ordering one more for everyone.

Travis finished his bourbon and smacked his lips. "Gage, your sister said there's three."

"My sister's hormones are whacked out. You can't believe anything she says."

"Three what?" Cole asked.

"Ghosts! Mac heard Katrina," Travis answered and hailed the waitress for yet another round.

"Tha' right?"

"Yep. Meeekala's h-hunting me."

"Wha' for?" Cole asked, snatching his drink off the server's tray.

"Some stupid legend 'bout Mad'lin Cadotte daughters murdered on their wedding nights," Gage told him.

"Hun-uh. Night 'fore Michelle sez. Three exactly have to marry to put 'em to rest."

"I'm arrestin' you alongside Sully if he keeps spoutin' that stupid story to every body crossin' S'perior!"

"You jus' wait, Gage. Yessirree. Yer day's a comin' to be hunted by Nicole." In afterthought, Travis added, "Ina."

"No damn ghost's gonna hunt me."

"Got tha' right." Travis pointed. "Gonna be hunted by dat one der. Jus' like I'm being possessed by the one next to 'er."

Each man at the table turned with deliberate movement. Eight women and two little girls stood glaring at them, or so they all thought. In front, Katharine, Michelle, Nicole and Mona each had their eye on one man.

"Soused."

"Pickled."

"Smashed."

"Inebriated."

"So much for dinner dates," Julia huffed, stepping forward.

"I think dinner's what they all need," Rosemary countered. "Ten bucks says we get stuck with the tab."

"You're on," Katharine snapped. "My old man is not getting away with this one."

Sylvie whispered, "What have they done to my Harvey? He doesn't drink."

"Wait until next month when the credit card bills come," Julia chuckled.

Groans filled the room except from the three drunkest who sat in a ridiculous stupor, enrobed with silly grins.

*   *   *

Friday night and into Saturday, rain came down hard and heavy. Shopping had been therapeutic for Michelle. The company gave her an opportunity to muddle through her situation without living in fear. Since Derek's return, she hadn't been able to do that. She and Sylvie also had a long, private chat regarding their mother's actions. They agreed to deal with Elisabeth Callihan when she returned in the spring.

Michelle peeked out through an undraped window. Breathtaking described the woods surrounding her place during a rainstorm. Spraying showers stroked the green pines with light gray mist. The soothing ambiance was as tender as the droplets that touched every living thing. Thunder rumbled harshly in the background over some other island, and Michelle inhaled a deep breath. Katharine had asked the question first, then, Sylvie.

Why couldn't she fall in love again?

The moment Sylvie asked it, Michelle realized she had never loved her ex. In fact, Travis Baines was the extreme opposite of her ex. She observed that firsthand Thanksgiving Day. Derek never would have allowed children to skip alongside of him. He wouldn't have saved Brendan's life either. She battled with many emotions inside of her at the bridge that day. So scared, grateful, angry, in love, she never—her thoughts came to a screeching halt.

Do I really love him? All he's asked of me is a chance to prove he's worthy.

With the culmination of events, he'd done more. He calmly provided compassion during a crucial moment. As smoothly as correcting a jobsite mishap, Michelle mused. She was uncomfortable with the fact that he'd spoken the truth, too, and had no right to condemn him or blame herself for Derek's actions.

Michelle grabbed her jacket, purse and a gift she had for Travis. She locked the door and jumped into her car bound for the Pine Cove Retreat. Fifteen minutes later on the north end of Madeline Island, she braked at the end of the long drive inward, thinking, cogitating, muttering, "Now or never, Callihan."

Tortoise-like she turned and negotiated the soggy two-track road then stopped, spotting the Ferrari. The cabin was unlit in the middle of the dark dreary day.

"Probably sleeping off a hangover from last night," she grumbled, feeling nervousness slip back to grip her. Two-thirds of the way into the drive, she changed her mind and started to back out when the Mustang lurched hard. "Oh shit."

Michelle shifted into forward and gunned the engine. Brushwood scraped the side and bogged the car deeper into a furrow. Rocking the Stanger back and forth resulted in a loud clunk at the backend.

"Damn, that can't be good."

Michelle thrust the gears into forward, cranked the wheel a hard right and gunned the engine a second time. The car wasn't going anywhere without a tow, and no way could she exit the driver's door when it was eye-level with the forest floor. She sat motionless for a moment, chewing her bottom lip before she carefully maneuvered and crawled over the counsel to the passenger seat. She swiped the keys out of the ignition, grabbed her purse and thrust the door open with her shoulder to climb out. The door slammed shut with an exuberant crash. Although the tires still touched the ground, the car was almost on its side. While checking the backend of the Mustang, rain spit hard and the ground caved underfoot. Michelle slid into the trench, landing on her butt.

"My ex wants to kill me and God won't even give me a break today," she grumbled climbing onto solid ground and wishing she owned a cell phone for the first time in her life.

Wiping her hands on the front of her pants, she stared hopelessly down the road at the tail end of the Ferrari then ran toward the rental in the pouring rain. She scaled the stairs of the huge ponderosa porch and was shaking off excess water when the cabin door swung open.

"Michelle!"

She looked up and froze. Stood there tongue-tied. Travis stood barefoot and shirtless. The top button of his jeans was undone and his hair was wet. The shock hit her full force. She never considered he might have someone with him. Humiliated now, she muttered, "Okay, this is awkward. I'm sorry to interrupt, but I need to use your phone."

A miserable flush heated her face when a wily grin tipped the corners of his mouth.

"You're not interrupting anything," he said pulling her inside and shutting the door. "I saw you running down the road. Where's the Mustang?"

"It's stuck," she said with a fleeting look to the bedroom.

"Where at?"

"You're busy. Just let me use the phone to call a tow and I'll leave."

"Milady, the last thing I am is busy. I've been nursing a hangover for the better part of an otherwise wasted day. Neither is something I plan to do and I'd just stepped out of the shower when I saw you out there."

"Then what's so funny?"

"You are."

Laughter floated up from his throat. Her embarrassment quickly turned to annoyance.

"You think I have a woman in the bedroom."

"I do not!"

Travis leaned, placing both hands against the door on either side of her. "You do, too."

He stood so close she could feel the heat from his body. Trapped between him and the door, those butterfly things flitted wildly inside her stomach. "Do not."

"Your face tells all," he said, brushing his lips against hers.

Her pulsed raced frantically. A hot ache grew in her throat. Nothing but his mouth touched her cheek and jaw. Although shivers lingered along her flesh, he found a way to stoke the cold fire inside of her to a full blaze. The feather-like kisses amplified the urges hidden inside of her.

"Why did you come here?" he asked, lingering at the hollow of her neck.

Her body now felt heavy and warm but her reply only came out in a sigh.

"You're getting excited, Milady."

Her lashes flew up and Michelle pulled herself out of the heat of the moment. His overconfident expression maddened her. She cleared her throat with an ineffectual pretense and tried to shove Travis back. He didn't budge, just kissed her some more.

"Why do you need to call a tow?"

"The Stanger doesn't like to go baha'ing."

Travis stopped, focused on her eyes. "Say again."

"I backed the damn car into the damn ditch and now I can't get out!"

"Why are you covered with mud?"

"Because Travis, it's raining. Or hadn't you noticed? When I climbed over the console to get out, I had to check the backend of the Mustang."

His eyes never left her, just studied her, waiting. The look on his face said that her sarcasm amused him.

"I slipped and fell," she muttered.

"Why were you checking the backend?" he asked with a trace of laughter.

She really wanted to slug him, but said, "You're gonna make me tell the whole story, aren't you?"

He stepped back, nodded.

"Fine," she snapped. "I tried rocking the car to get it out and hit something. I just buried the left side deeper. The only way I could get out of the car was to climb over the console and go out the passenger door. I fell on my ass when I checked the backend for damage. The car hit a pile of rocks."

"You still haven't told me why you came here. Or why you were backing out?"

Her pulse skittered alarmingly. Her heartbeat throbbed in her ears. *This was a mistake.*

"Well?"

Michelle looked away, letting out an audible breath. "I was coming to talk to you but I chickened out halfway down the road. I was afraid you'd see me if I pulled in all the way and turned around, so I backed up. That idiotic grin tells me this is a mistake and right now I'm sorry I decided to come here at all."

"At the moment, all I want is to hold you and comfort you, Michelle, but we have things to resolve."

She looked at him in surprise then innocently asked, "What things?"

"Did he make you apologize for every breath you took?"

The thought of it shocked her while a critical expression replaced the laughter in his eyes. "Why would you ask me that?"

"Because you apologize for everything you say and do."

Travis took her keys, slid the purse strap off her shoulder and placed both on a nearby table. He removed her sopping wet jacket and hung it. Goose bumps layered her bare arms and Michelle hugged herself.

"It didn't matter what I did I always apologized for it later."

Travis drew her in, held her snug then rubbed his hands along her back. Comfort and warmth flowed through her into her blood.

"Milady, your skin is ice cold. You need a hot shower and dry clothes."

"What I need is a tow truck," she replied, withdrawing from his arms.

"Go take a shower," he insisted. "I'll find something dry for you to wear and put them on the floor by the door before I go out to check the Mustang."

Miffed, Michelle toed off her muddy shoes and headed for the bathroom. "Travis Baines, I hate it when you're right."

He studied her thoughtfully for a moment then told her, "Get used to it."

When Michelle thrust the bathroom door shut, his smile deepened into laughter. Travis went to the bedroom, finished dressing then dropped dry clothes on the floor next to the bathroom door. Pulling on boots and a rain jacket, he went out to check her car. She'd buried the left side to the window in mucky red clay and brush. He checked under the backend, muffler intact and observed no visible damage. Even if he could drive it out, there was no way he was getting into the 'stang the way she climbed out. She needed a crew of strong men. She hadn't locked the door and he opened it and pushed the knob then surveyed the woods judiciously, not forgetting Gage and Mac's warning.

Back at the log cabin, Travis removed his boots and jacket

outside on the porch. Inside, his clothes had disappeared from the floor. A chicken casserole that he whipped up before his shower was in the oven. He made herbal tea then tossed a salad together.

The scent of Irish Spring passed under his nose and he turned. A lurch of excitement stunned him into blankness. His white work socks were stretched up to Michelle's knees. The tails of his flannel shirt covered her bare thighs. She'd rolled the shirt sleeves several times midway to her elbows. Jutting breasts protruded the pockets. Her wet dark hair hung in a tangled mess over the open collar of his shirt. A smoldering flame in her immense green eyes glowed and pierced him, broke right through his entrancement, and Travis swallowed hard.

"The jeans were too big," Michelle muttered faintly.

Nervously, she moistened her lips and his heart thudded rapidly inside his chest.

"Do you have a washer and dryer?"

The prolonged anticipation was unbearable. Travis moved closer until he left her no room. Michelle stood motionless, gazing up at him with longing in her eyes. He touched her cheek, felt the movement of her breathing and gathered her into his arms. Her hands wound round his neck and he hugged her close. When she molded softly against him, he whispered, "Milady," into her tangled mass.

Michelle took a deep, unsteady breath. The flush of sexual desire rippled beneath her heated flesh. Months had slipped away since she once felt anything. He brushed his lips against hers and showered kisses around her mouth and jaw. He tasted the pulsing hollow at the base of her throat then nibbled her earlobe. It was slow and thoughtful until she quivered and drew his mouth to hers. Sweet, soft, moist.

Their lips pressed together, Travis took her mouth in a renewed embrace. She responded eagerly and he devoured her, their tongues twisting in greedy urges. He locked his hands against her spine and explored the hollows of her back. He slid his hands under the shirt, skimmed her hips and thighs. The ache inside of him was a driving force to love her. But his need that had been building for two years on the fate of a dream and a weeping ghost could never be forced. He would never have her if she wouldn't give herself completely to him.

Blood pounded through Michelle's brain. Her knees went weak from his hot, penetrating mouth. Personal desire skated through her body and fulfilled the yearning. She sighed out his name when he slid his hands across her belly, stroked his fingers over her flesh. Shocking jolts riveted right on through her when he gently cupped her breasts. Her head fell back and Travis descended on her with open mouth kisses burning trails into her flesh.

"Michelle, I want to make love to you."

"Oh, Travis," she sighed.

He pulled her up. Studied her for a sign of objection. The thump of her heart was rapid against his chest while her green eyes illumined with excitement. That darkened sparkle was all it took and Travis lifted Michelle into his arms. She blanketed his neck and shoulders with her arms and buried her face against him. He moved, flicked the oven off and carried her to his bedroom.

"Travis," she murmured quietly. "What about my car?"

Momentarily speechless, he finally chuckled and eased her down in front of him. "It's buried."

Her heart now dancing with renewed eagerness, Michelle studied every feature of his face. He held hers gently and kissed the tip of her nose. He planted a series of kisses on her face and neck and grazed her earlobe until, finally, their lips met. It was slow, drugging, urgent and exploratory all at once. Then he devoured her. Her thoughts spun. Her knees felt floppy. Her restraint exploded within the hunger as he slid the shirt off her shoulder. Her breasts surged, he caressed her taut nipples and Michelle inhaled a hard gasp. She grabbed his shirt and removed it, letting him sear a path with his hands down her abdomen. The heat of his hands, the stroke of his fingers sent deep cravings racing through her. His gentle touch elevated her to renewed fervor and she couldn't wait a moment longer. She reached to unbutton his jeans.

Raising his mouth from hers, Travis gazed into her jade eyes.

So compelling and magnetic, his own heart now pounded loudly over his uneven breaths. He tugged her closer and slid his hands to the swell of her hips and thighs. He held her, wanted to let the scent of her flesh soak into him before he knelt and slowly rolled his socks off her feet then shucked the last garment from her body. His breath stuck in his lungs when she stood before him, the shapely beauty of her naked body taunting him. She stared wordlessly at him, the silence charging up between them. Then she breathed one word and Travis pulled her body against his. She inhaled sharply at the contact, but her soft perfumed flesh molded to him and Michelle wrapped her arms around his neck. She kissed him with a thirst that belied everything about her. He moved to the edge of the bed and drew her into his lap. She inhaled several more breaths as she straddled his thighs. Travis picked up a lock of her damp hair and gently caressed it.

Gathered against his warm pulsing body, their mouths connected once more until they were rocking back and forth. A succession of slow kisses, sensuous trails along her waist and hips, the virgin touch of his hands along the length of her back all quickly turned into lust-aroused exploration. Whispering his love for each part of her body, Michelle softly moaned when he caressed her swollen nipples. She explored the tendons in the back of his neck, delicately dragged her fingers up and down the sculptured planes of his chest, arousing his desire. Taking her hand, he guided it to himself. As their eyes met, control was lost and she fantasized an even deeper thrill.

He lifted her out of his lap and laid her onto the bed then stood to rid himself of his jeans. Michelle stared tongue-tied, gazed at the length of his sturdy legs, his hard muscles and tufts of bronze hair. His heavy breathing matched her hammering heart. But it was the tenderness in his expression that amazed her. Michelle discarded her fear and reached out to him.

Travis took her hand, joined her, and the anticipation boiled over inside of her. Gathered in his arms, she buried her face in his neck and breathed a kiss there. He drew her face up, traced her lips with a finger. He kissed her slowly, thoughtfully, over and over, searing a path down her neck and shoulders until her body began to vibrate with liquid fire. Desire flamed hotter inside of her. With an aching need for another kiss, her lips instinctively found their way to his.

Travis recaptured her soft mouth, demanding more. As he aroused her passion, his own grew stronger but he still abandoned himself of the sensation. He fondled one milky-white globe, then the other. Her breasts surged as he caressed the fully swollen buds with his tongue then made a path down her stomach, skimmed either side of her body, explored her thighs, moved up, roamed and probed eagerly. She panted breathlessly, arched urgently like a fine bow. His own blood flowing fiercely, he paused to kiss her. She pitched excitedly, and he whispered hoarsely, "Let it go, Milady. I've got you."

Michelle groaned. It was an awakened response of dormant sexuality. It came from deep inside of her. And it shook her universe. To yearn to this degree shattered her into a million fiery stars, freed the deadened sensation inside of her. She soared higher, yielded to her scorching need, felt flooded with desire. Hurtling far beyond the point of no return, Michelle cried out, "Travis, *I want you!*"

His own breath already rugged and fast, her declaration sucked the air right out of his lungs. Travis clutched her hips and slid inside. She welcomed him, encircled him and tightened her legs around him. Flesh to flesh her eager response matched his. Electrical energy flowed between them while the virginal pleasure exploded and rejoiced. It scorched through them with a tempo that bound their bodies into one.

"I'll always love you," he spoke in a hoarse whisper.

Michelle's carefully constructed casement shattered. Her brain clouded as his hands and lips continued a hungry search of her body. Then she saw the reality, his truth and virtue in the emotion of his eyes. That was all she needed for the fire to ravage within and spread to her heart. And she let everything go, giving it all to him.

Travis sensed the change and watched Michelle with hope.

Passion was alive inside of her. It danced in her eyes like exultant angels. He plunged deep, deep, deeper sending both over the edge. The deadened flame within her soul had been torched and their united bodies vibrated in the blazing wake. The turbulence of passion swirled around them. He needed her, he wanted her, and he loved her.

Gasping breathlessly, Michelle cried out, "I love you, Travis Baines."

He replied with a raw act of possession and drove himself further, deeper, harder, emptying himself of everything he possessed in exchange for her heart. Then, Mikala's mantra cry echoed throughout the room. Travis stopped. Michelle looked. They waited. He refocused on Michelle beneath him. She lay panting, her chest heaving. Her damp hair was messy, wild and thick. Her eyes were a dark glaze. Across her pale and beautiful face, a dim flush raced like a fever. He kissed her lovingly, held her tenderly and embraced her closely. Surrendering to the only woman he had searched his entire life for, he spoke it richly, "I love you, Michelle."

She gazed at him with the knowledge that she would never be the same. Had never felt more alive either. Never had the vibrant chord of her soul struck so hard. The dread of living had burst inside of her. The burden of failure and fear had all dispersed and been strewn to another world and life. Never wanting it back, Michelle now clung to the man who had changed it. She pressed her open lips to his and curled into the curve of his body as their legs entwined. The pace of their hearts returning to normal, their panting subdued, she was too emotion-filled to speak.

Travis nestled closer to her and gently drew figure eights on her shoulder. Her head rested against his chest. He peeked at her and smiled. Never saw euphoria on her face before either. He planted kisses on her shoulders, neck and face. While nibbling her earlobe, he said, "Tell me again, Milady."

She had said the words to him—couldn't believe how easy they came out of her. She'd never been more certain of her feelings either. Michelle stirred slightly, coveting her own smile.

"I'm hungry."

"I know you're hungry." Travis snuggled her closer. "I can hear your tummy growling. Tell me what I've waited all my life to hear."

"I need to call a tow truck," she said straight-out.

Travis stroked an exposed hip, a thigh, a leg and kissed her again. "Please."

Michelle moaned, arched, felt the growing excitement. He shifted and enclosed her the same way when he kissed her that night in her kitchen. He tasted and teased, caressed and fondled every inch of her flesh inflaming her with mere kisses.

"Tell me," he whispered.

"Ahh!"

Nibbling on her, he said, "Say it, Milady."

Lordy, she thought, what he could do with a mouth she had never paid attention to before. With her heart pulverizing the inside of her chest, Michelle thrust toward his sleek body and hung tightly to the new experience. She quivered and vibrated wildly, rose higher and higher to the mighty peak of exhilaration then shrieked, "Travis Baines, you're insane!"

"Tell me."

"Travis, please!"

As their bodies rejoined, her words came unhindered in a declaration. "I love you!"

She drained him, dulled all his sorrow and anxiety, and voided those desperate feelings of solitude when she exhaled the words to him once more.

"I *do* love you, Travis."

CHAPTER 24

HOURS BEFORE DAYBREAK he cast several suspicious glances over his shoulder. Then it registered with him. He was alone inside the rambler. But the unbelievable distrust Gunderson felt, when gray turns to dark, swept through him. It tortured him. He swung around seeking out those who wanted him dead. His junkie eyes narrowing to twin slits then fiercely bulging with the phobic growth of another crack attack. Depleted of sleep, jittery without a hit, he was coming down. He shifted tautly, and weaved and wedged non-stop about the entire house. He dragged heavily on a day-old Marlboro like he was seducing it, leered into corners and drawers searching for valuables. He needed money to feed his habit. He crushed out the cigarette he just lit from the week-old accumulation, and dug in the ashtray for another. He lighted that one with unsteady fingers.

Crank desires had him by the throat. He needed a hit. Sweat gushed out of his clammy skin and he sucked the nicotine into his mouth hard. He sold everything of any value in Elisabeth's house. *They* were still after him. He needed to crank up—plunder away the illusive shadows always on his tail—*they* were out to get him. The love of meth provided the reason—big scores to pay. He hated everyone and would kill 'em all before they got him. He'd be free then. Knew how to snuff them out. He'd done that with the coyote-ugly bitch last night. Vaguely remembered the act of taking care of business when she lied to him. Promised him a crack gallery—

didn't come through. He showed her, just like the first bitch. There was a kid, too, and he nervously wondered where the brat went. The kid knew him. Could finger him.

He felt like screaming now, and he did. It didn't help.

He needed to smoke a crib, just to get by. The crack would relax him then he'd go finish off the bastard shacking up with his wife. They didn't know he was there lurking. He knew what they were doing. Elisabeth said he should have the car, too, and his slut wife owed him that much. Now, he'd rather have the black spider. That souped up Ferrari was worth a lot more. As if his brain had unfried itself, Gunderson counted on—no. He schemed one sure way of repaying those gambling debts. He'd have a shitload more money than the Mustang was worth.

Grinding out the Marlboro, he lurked quietly, looking over his shoulder and sneaked his way back in the grayed dawn to leave his mark. Just a little longer, just a bit too cocky, he'd sit back and wait. Soon he would be flying down easy street.

*   *   *

A glorious smile filled her face as Michelle gently stroked her flesh with a soapy washcloth. The weekend over, it had been the best holiday celebration in years. She and Travis spent hours talking between cuddling and intimacy Saturday night into Sunday morning, and again last night into this morning. She shared childhood thoughts of loving parents with a mother who put Band-Aids on skinned knees, wiped her tears away and taught her the difference between right and wrong. Sturdy Catholic beliefs made her parents count upon perfect children and high degrees of impossible success. She talked about Brian's fatal boating accident, her sense of deep loss, and the way her mother had slipped from life then stopped attending church. It contradicted the teachings. But her father became despondent, amputating himself from caring, their family values and his nurturing ways. He stopped giving sound advice. Simply put, he ceased living and their perfect little family had suddenly disintegrated.

Travis listened then explained how sometimes parents provide all of life's materialism alongside their beliefs on family value. Their undying love for each other is exposed but without realization of the impact it will have on their children. It seemed like an odd combination to him when the only thing he ever wanted and needed the most, but didn't have, was brothers and sisters. After a long silence, he unburdened to her that a rich kid's lack of siblings made for a large, empty house. No matter how much parental love surrounded him, there was always a hole inside of him. He didn't know why he felt that way. As he grew up, he discovered the enjoyment of business success. The feeling didn't last when the loneliness followed him all the way to the top. He compared it to the despair he felt the day he went to the cemetery with Grandmama. Told her that he stared at baby Julia's grave with new feelings of shame because she never had a chance to live. He wondered that day what right he had to complain.

Michelle figured out quickly that he was fond of his parents and grandparents never disputing his love for them. Nevertheless, he believed children needed other children not just adults to fill their days and nights. Her tears leaked out when he spoke of isolated walks on busy streets in strange cities, sleeping in empty hotel rooms many days a year, only to return to Boston and his own alien house. She realized his lack of siblings was just as bad as the loss of a brother.

He gave up his search for the right woman, believing one didn't exist . . . until he met her. Her heart soared when he said he wanted marriage and a large family neck and neck with the daily problems of both. When she asked him why he never married, he hesitated before confessing he was meticulous. The women he knew cared more about his bank account than they did him. Then he looked at her and said 'besides I've just met the only woman I'll ever love.'

She looked at the closed bathroom door now. Travis was clanging around in her kitchen for the second time. His whistling was music to her ears. She sunk into her tub and reveled in the minty-smelling suds, wondering if what she felt this moment was true love. Though she couldn't identify with the feelings, it sure felt good.

A crew of musclemen had bailed out the Stanger and a tow truck would hook and haul the car sometime today. She giggled, recalling how her jaw dropped when six men picked her car up like a feather in their hands and placed it back on the road. She removed the forgotten gift and later handed it to Travis. Last summer Katharine had drawn individual sketches of her and Nicole on the boat. Friday while shopping, she had hers framed with the sole purpose of giving it to him. Unknown what had possessed the vain act, his bona fide expression was followed by a perpetual study of the portrait. And if the love emerging on his face weren't enough, he told her no other gift ever meant as much to him.

This morning, she was meeting Gage and Mac with Caitlin to go over what the child had told her. Michelle looked up when the bathroom door opened and Travis entered. He bent over to kiss her.

"Breakfast is ready and you look like a very sexy prune."

"I never thought of prunes as being sexy but I'll trade you favors for a good cup of coffee."

He laughed whole-heartedly. "Nope. Your order is waiting. Hurry up before it gets cold." Playing with the hand towel he carried with him, he said, "I was just thinking of something."

"What's that?"

"I don't know your middle name or your birthday."

"It's Noma. I'm not sure why my parents gave me a Native American name when we have no Indian blood whatsoever." Michelle propped her arms and leaned against the tub's edge. "I was born on June second. When's yours?"

"I only celebrate mine once every four years."

"Travis Phillip—" she stopped when the phone rang.

"Hold that thought."

Returning minutes later, he spoke solemnly. "Michelle, that was Jerry."

She sat up in the tub. "What is it? What happened?"

"Someone broke into the Tavern last night. They found another body inside."

"Omigod! Nicole!" She clutched the tub edge with both hands.

"No!" Travis dropped to his knees, holding her to halt her shaking. He grabbed a bath towel, helped her out of the tub and wrapped her quivering body.

"It wasn't Nicole. It's another adult female like the one at the lagoon. Nicole wasn't there. She's fine."

"Thank, God. Travis, I . . ."

"It's all right. Nicole is safe."

Michelle clung to him until her breath caught up. "Did Derek do it?"

"Jerry didn't say. Gage and Mac need me over there. I'm guessing they won't be talking to Caitlin this morning."

She looked up needing support, but his eyes were darkly alarming. "When's it gonna stop, Travis?"

"Michelle, I don't want you there. Will you stay home and I'll be back within an hour to pick you up?"

She nodded and he kissed her then left.

*   *   *

Travis parked the Ferrari near one of the squads and rushed into the Tavern. Broken liquor bottles lay amongst shards of the gray-smoked mirror behind the bar. Worried over leaving Michelle alone, bringing her here wasn't an option either.

Mac and Gage met him at the entrance to the ballroom.

"This one's brutal, Travis. It's like he totally lost it."

"How much damage to the ballroom?"

"Mainly sheetrock," Gage told him. "The victim's blood is smeared everywhere. It's gonna take awhile for the crime lab to go through it all."

"Can I go in there?"

Gage nodded. "We'll need a list of all damage and stolen property. Don't touch anything and watch where you step."

"Have any of my crews been in here yet?"

"No. Jerry discovered it first."

"Where's he?" Travis asked.

"Out back. This one got to him."

Moving into the room under construction, Travis stopped, grimaced, inhaled a deep breath. This parasite hadn't just lost it. He was a psychotic lunatic. A woman's mutilated body lay in pools of blood. Blood smeared on floors and ceilings splayed across every wall in all directions. Gage told him to watch where he stepped and it seemed utterly impossible. There were gruesome blotches everywhere. He felt ill. He glanced at the victim again and wondered if they would be able to identify her. A sickening wave of terror welled up from his belly. His queasiness was nothing compared to the price she paid. Scanning the room quickly, every crewman's tool had been destroyed. He thought one electric saw, saturated with blood, might have been the murder weapon. Damage estimates would come in around five figures.

Travis turned and exited the tavern inhaling grievous amounts of fresh air. He made his way around back and realized early in the morning, he needed a good stiff drink to erase the ugliness from his mind. He found his general contractor leaning over a sawhorse.

"Jer, you okay?"

"Jesus! I've never seen anything like it. They know who she was?"

"I didn't ask. Gage says it'll take awhile. Give everybody today and tomorrow off with pay."

"Travis, how the hell are we gonna clean up that mess?"

"I'll start calling around for cleaning crews. You re-order whatever supplies and tools need to be replaced."

"Mac said the crime lab is gonna take everything. We can have the sheetrock here tomorrow but it'll take awhile to replenish all the tools."

"I know, Jer. What about you? Can you replace them faster from your office?"

"Normally, but with the extra work, all my guys are using them at other sites."

"Do what you can. Send the bill to headquarters and I'll call and have them cut you a check for whatever it costs. We'll need two lists of the loss. One for insurance and one for the police."

"You think we should call Range Security and get them back here?"

"Travis, come 'ere," Mac yelled.

"I'll let you know."

After they enclosed the ballroom, Travis thought they wouldn't need armed guards anymore. He shifted and headed in Mac's direction by the construction trailer. "What've you got?"

"Where's Michelle?"

"I left her at her house. Why?"

"Take a look."

He studied the words written in blood on the side of the trailer.

A million Baines or she's dead!

White-hot rage coiled in his throat in front of panic then erupted like a volcano inside of him. Travis yanked the cell from his pocket, glanced at his watch and punched in Michelle's number. No answer. Inner torment gnawed away at him. He dialed his parents next. "Dad, I need you to get over to Michelle's immediately."

"Why? Your mother and grandmother just left and went to visit. What's wrong?"

A guttural scream cut loose inside of him. Travis explained then said, "They couldn't possibly have made plans. Michelle had an appointment."

"Your grandmother wanted to visit. I'm on my way. I'll meet you there."

Travis disconnected and headed for his car.

"Where you going?" Mac yelled.

"Michelle's not answering."

"I'm right behind you," he shouted.

Travis revved the Ferrari's engine, squealed the tires and cursed himself for leaving her alone. Now his mother and grandma-ma—couldn't think about that, and thumped the steering wheel with a clenched fist. He could never forgive himself if anything happened to any of them. Moment's later he jerked the car into park, bailed and left the door open. The rental car was empty as he ran by. Travis burst through the front door and came to a hard halt.

"Michelle!"

Someone had inhumanly annihilated the inside. Books lay everywhere. Ripped from the wall, the shelves were broken. Hanging plants that draped the windows now lay upside down on the floor. Cut and smashed furniture was overturned. His footsteps thundered down the hall to the bedroom while he repeatedly called out. "Michelle!"

Each room empty of human life and in worse shape then the previous, Travis rushed to the kitchen and sucked in a deep breath. He stood numbed by horror in the middle of the room, eyes transfixed on the kicked in back door. Splintered wood lay on the floor.

"Travis!" Mac yelled from the front door.

"They're gone," he responded in a voice as cold as death.

"Who else?"

"My mother and grandmother. I'll kill the bastard."

"Gage and I will take care of this," Mac said, keying his mic. "I'm betting Gunderson took them to the Callihan house."

"Where's that?" he demanded then began yanking unopened kitchen drawers and cupboards in search of a phone book. The third drawer he jerked open contained one. He located an Aidan Callihan then tossed the phonebook to the floor and rushed out of the house.

"Travis! Shit!" Mac aired the situation into his portable.

Travis didn't stop and went on by his father and grandfather who had arrived out front.

*   *   *

Anticipation enlarged Gunderson's fantasies. Three wealthy bitches was a gold mine. He lit a cigarette from a pack he found stashed, and rechecked the rope he used to tie them up. Those puss faces would pay anything to get 'em back. His breathing rugged with the expectations, Gunderson paced the room around

them. Bringing them here was good. The shocked expression on
his wife's face when he used a key filled him with extreme superiority.
Nothing like shooting up—*I really need to shoot up*. Needed to ease
the crisis for a crank injection and lighted another cigarette.

"Young man, you have the intelligence of a two-watt light
bulb!"

The old biddy was driving him nuts with her goddamn
gibberish. He puffed hard, whirled around violently and got down
in her face. "Shut the fuck up you old hag!"

"Or what, you demented snot. You'll kill me? Kill all of us?
You won't get your ransom," Julia taunted.

"Mother!" Rosemary shrieked. "Do as he says."

"Grandma-ma, don't provoke him," Michelle pleaded.

With an adventurous toss of her head, Julia replied, "The man's
already provoked. Nothing I do or don't do will change that fact.
And since my life is near an end, I deserve to pray in my native
tongue if I so wish."

"Praying is done silently," Gunderson shouted. "Shut the fuck
up! All of you."

"Young man, if you had an ounce of brain in your head you
would know Native American's chant their prayers aloud. You could
use some spiritual guidance yourself!"

"Whiskey gives me all the spiritual guidance I need," Gunderson
exploded.

Michelle gaped at Julia. With her heart pounding, she could
hardly breathe. Did Grandma-ma understand Derek was going to
kill them? "Julia! Do not goad him further."

"Shut up! All of you shut the hell up!"

"You worthless degenerate. I'll bet your parents are disgusted
with you."

Michelle held her breath and watched Derek's face redden.
His fixed eyes mutated into the uncivilized rage she recognized.
One fist clenched, Derek dragged heavily on the cigarette with the
other. When he leaned closer to Grandma-ma, his eyes cold,
thirsting for blood, electrifying shock reverberated through
Michelle.

"I don't have parents you old bitch."

Michelle finally exhaled when Derek backed off. He stood motionless now near the dining room table before he jerked abruptly, circled all three of them, spun and was gone. Michelle swallowed hard. "Grandma-ma he's serious. Please stop annoying him."

"Mother, Michelle's right. I'm far from ready to meet my maker." Leaning to her right, Rosemary spoke sternly. "I'm only going to tell you once, Mother. Keep your mouth shut."

Julia managed a shrug.

How would they get out of this? Would they survive, Michelle wondered. The morning events came abruptly. One minute while daydreaming in the tub of a possible future with Travis, the phone call came. Barely dressed, all hell broke loose at her house when she heard the splinter of wood at her back door. Julia and Rosemary arrived at the front door not sixty seconds later. With no time to warn them, Derek took both hostage before he made a destructive venture through her house searching for money and valuables. Tied to chairs with hands bound behind their backs now, they sat kiddy-whompus in Elisabeth Callihan's dining room. The only consolation came with the knowledge that Gage and Mac had a key. The dilemma was that they were all at the scene of Derek's latest victim. It could be hours before anyone discovered them missing. Thanks to Elisabeth Callihan, they were going to die in the house Michelle had come to detest. It'd be a righteous ending for the mother she loathed this very moment. But she couldn't dwell on that now.

An examination of the visible rooms told her most of her parent's personal possessions had disappeared. Her father's expensive art and electronics from the living room, along with other tangibles, all sold or traded for money to feed an addict. She wondered about the bedroom safe where her mother kept expensive jewelry. Had her ex found that? Couldn't think of him as her ex any longer. In fact, she couldn't think about anything. Her hands were numb, the rope around her wrists was tight, and her head throbbed with pain.

What she did think about was how fully alive she felt for the first time since Brian's death. Travis woke her senses up. He removed her previous wishes not to have been born. He wanted the same things she did. Bittersweet tears stained the jeans of her lap before Michelle realized Travis was her reason to fight back.

She inhaled slowly and let calm strength find its way into her soul. She thought of Katharine trapped in that burning bungalow and dynamic, iron control began to grow inside of her. One way or another she would swap stories with her courageous best friend. It could be hours, it could be days, but Michelle toyed with the rope binding her wrists. *Success was of the utmost importance.*

She stopped when a loud crash came from the bathroom. Watched, waited. Rosemary squirmed nervously. What was Derek doing? Didn't matter. The more time he spent out of this room, the more time she had to plan their escape. Her body pulsated with new energy. She knew exactly how to get away and worked faster on the knotted rope.

"Both of you listen carefully to me," Michelle sternly said. "When he comes back, keep your mouths shut. Do not react to what I say. Do not respond to him at all. Do you both understand me?"

They nodded simultaneously. Her mind and body finally working together, she felt the rope loosen. She quickly massaged her fingers to relieve the numbness then manipulated the rope ends for several more minutes. A terrible tenseness in her body forced her to stop, relax, and take a deep breath. Nervously biting her lip, she continued to manipulate the rope. Julia and Rosemary watched her as a tense silence enveloped the room until the rope loosened more and slipped to the floor. Jumping up, Michelle yanked a buffet drawer open, hitting the back of the chair. She glanced over her shoulder but continued rummaging through the drawer. The silver was gone and she dug for her long-gone grandmother's brass letter opener.

"Come on, come on. Where is it?"

"What the fuck are you doing?" Derek shouted, coming around the corner of the dining room.

Michelle's head swung about. She met his wild, glassy expression and eyed him with cold triumph. Her hand still in the drawer, she touched the cool brass and gripped the handle as Julia stuck her foot out. Derek flew through the air landing with a thud in front of Rosemary who then toed him in the head with the point of her shoe. So much for obeying orders, Michelle thought.

Derek hissed, screamed then grabbed a leg of Rosemary's chair flipping it backward. "Fucking bitch! I'll kill you!"

That's it! Rage absorbed Michelle. Right arm raised, letter opener in hand, she lunged. Derek lifted himself up as she rammed the brass point into his shoulder with a forceful thrust. His blood-curdling scream filled the air and Derek dropped to his knees. Michelle backed up, fell over Rosemary, sending the letter opener across the room. Panic swept through her like a growth of cancer inside of her.

"You slut!" he howled, stumbling to his feet. "I should've killed you when I had the chance!"

Savage death crept into his eyes. Derek hurtled over Rosemary, dove and landed on top of her. Her breath blew out. He seized her shoulders, shook her brutally then swaddled her neck between his large hands.

Her breath quickened. She choked and gasped before it came raw in her throat then her air supply was cutoff. Her pulse roared in her ears. Terror rioted within. She flailed her arms frantically, got a hold of him and gouged hard with her nails. The light dimmed, she felt the cold fist squeezing her heart from the weight crushing her chest. Wheezing, she called out, "Travis . . ."

The last thing she saw was her ex's hateful expression.

CHAPTER 25

LOVE WAS SLIPPING through his hands.

He must have been mentally unbalanced to leave Michelle alone with that raving psychotic still on the loose. His heart raced painfully while perspiration pooled across the upper part of his face. Their time together had been too brief, and images of baby Julia's gravesite flashed through Travis' mind. Snuffed out too early like Elton John's candle in the wind. Or was it rain? Who cared—nothing would matter if he lost Michelle. Life would be over and true love would evade him forever.

His own nightmare from a week ago took a tawdry route through his mind. He stood and watched Michelle die in that dream. Lucid visions of the truncated woman lying on the ballroom floor mingled with the dream and his internal dread. Involuntary tremors ruptured his insides. He could have shielded Michelle from viewing what he saw. If he'd just brought her with him—*Dammit! I screwed up!* Made one thoughtless mistake because . . . he didn't know what he was thinking when the call came from Jerry this morning.

Right now he needed to find Michelle, and blew out an exasperated breath. The idiotic map with roads making no sense and side roads unmarked was impossible to decipher. Slamming the brakes, shifting, Travis bit a sharp turn down the third drive. Dust blew high and far out of the backend of his low-rider. He recalled the comment Michelle made about baha'ing and attempted a lame smile. Saturday's mental picture of his drowned rat standing on the porch of the rental reappeared in his mind. It faded quickly when he swerved around a forest critter and veered sideways before stopping in front of another house. Travis bailed out the car and rushed to the front entrance. Ramming his fist against the door he waited five seconds for an answer then took off checking the circumference.

No cars.

No life.

No luck.

And no Michelle.

Hurling himself back into the Spider, Travis squealed the tires in a wide circle, convinced he peeled a layer of skin off them. Back on the main road, which was still dirt, he spotted the fourth driveway. Shifting harshly, the Ferrari hugged the corner, raising more dust in a quiet-looking scene. He lost his dad somewhere.

Where the hell was Mac?

There were no visible cars and no garage. Another dead end, but he leaped out skirting the perimeter of the building, checking doors and glancing into windows. Why was it so hard to find their damn house?

Again, nothing. And the minutes were ticking away. He ran back to his car, stopped abruptly, listened. It was Mikala's cry. He scanned the area hurriedly.

"You brought me here, old girl. Don't let me lose her. Where's she at?"

The muffled sound came again and Travis shifted.

That's not Michelle's ghost.

It was Grandma-ma's uncompromising voice. Travis popped the trunk, snatched the crowbar then darted swiftly across the yard thrashing savagely through hedgerow. He heard the grating sound of racing tires on the main dirt road, but couldn't wait.

*   *   *

"You greasy piece of filth," Julia screamed. "Let her go!"

Hunched over Michelle, Derek was strangling the life out of

her. Rosemary swung her legs up over and winced with pain when the chair's back crushed her arm. Lifting her head, she managed to twist and look. Saw a direct shot and with both feet together, shoved her legs as hard as she could into Gunderson's rear. He howled and fell forward ripping one shoe off her foot. The slender heel now hung from the seat of his pants.

"Run, Michelle!" Grandma-ma yelled.

Michelle wheezed and coughed violently. Slowly, she rolled to her side choking and gagging. She wished she could run, shift, get up, move or do something, but breathing was impossible. Then the letter opener caught her eye. She took in a lungful of air and willed herself to move. It was exhaustive and came with difficulty. She rolled slightly, inched forward, and stretched to reach for the weapon.

Derek grabbed her ankle, yanked her back and flipped her over. Ripping the heeled shoe from his pants, he bellowed, "You're dead, bitch!"

Evil filled his eyes before he dove over her and grabbed the letter opener. What little energy she had left drained out of her completely. A mixture of hope and fear swamped her mind when his arm went up in attack mode. Michelle tried to scream but nothing came out.

"You slimy rat!" Julia screeched. Get off of her!"

*   *   *

Grandma-ma was yelling at the top of her lungs, but Travis couldn't understand the muffled words. He raced along the outside walls leaping bushes and wintered flowerbeds, peering into windows and turning door handles. He uncovered no openings or entries on the east or south sides of the house.

He came flying around the southwest corner of the house, crouched beneath a draped window, climbed a set of wooden deck stairs three at a time and stopped suddenly. His heart ceased beating when he heard Michelle's faint scream. The muffled sound came from near the covered sliding glass doors. It would take more than one whack to fracture through the expensive, double-panes. With a two-fisted grip on the crowbar, Travis swung viciously against the panel. The first layer splintered and he swung with full force a second time. The third whack destroyed the sheet of glass. It sprayed universally, crumbling to the deck and inside the house. He punched away the jagged shards near the handle with his clothed elbow and cleared the remaining debris with the crowbar. He stuck his hand inside, flipped the lock and propelled the door open with drive, knocking away the ruins. With one good yank, the drapery tumbled from the rods into a heaping pile. He stormed in, glass crunching underfoot.

His mouth crimped, tightened. Veins bulged from his neck in livid ridges. He swung the crowbar battering Gunderson in the back. The lunatic never flinched. Travis then seized him by the neck, yanked and tossed him over Michelle into a buffet. He eyed the murdering bastard, crowbar raised—

"Drop it, Travis!" Mac yelled from the point of entry.

With weapons drawn and aimed at the bundle in front of the buffet, Gage coaxed, "Put it down, Travis. Don't do it. He's not worth it."

Travis swallowed hard, lifted his chin and boldly met Gunderson's half-open eyes.

"Son, listen to them. He's not worth it," Phillip said.

"Travis, don't," Michelle whispered hoarsely. "I'm okay. Your mother is hurt and needs help."

He looked down at her, tossed the crowbar and dropped to his knees. He lifted Michelle off the floor and cradled her delicately into his arms. Her neck was marred with red marks and he throttled back a massive lump of hate trapped in his throat.

"He's hurt you."

"It's not your fault," Michelle said, struggling for breath.

Travis hugged her. "It is my fault. I shouldn't have left you alone. I didn't . . ." he choked into her hair.

Michelle wrapped her arms around him and held on. "I love you, Travis."

"But you—"

She put a hand gently to his mouth and shook her head.

Mac and Gage slapped cuffs on Gunderson, stood him up and removed him from the Callihan house. Travis helped Michelle to her feet then turned to assist his father untie his mother. Ronson untied Julia and Michelle staggered cautiously over glass toward them.

"Grandma-ma, you and I are going to have a very long talk about today," Michelle said hoarsely.

"Hrmph. In case you've forgotten, I got in a darn good lick myself."

She offered a forgiving smile then hugged Grandma-ma. Ronson bundled both of them into his arms.

Rosemary told her husband and son as they eased her out of the chair and off the floor. "I think my arm's broken, but the three of us put up a damn good fight."

Phillip kissed his wife. "There's an ambulance outside, sweetheart. We'll get you to the hospital."

"Good, because Phil, darling," she took his arm. "I think I'm going to faint now."

Phillip took a strong hold of his wife and Travis grabbed a chair for his mother to sit down. When two paramedics entered the room, Travis told them, "Check my mother first. She thinks her arm is broken and is about to pass out."

Travis shifted about, hugged Michelle then his grandmother. "Are you okay? Did he hurt you, Grandma-ma?"

"I'm fine, Pangi Ningo. But what in God's name took you all so long to find us?"

Travis forced a smile and exhaled, "It's a long story, Grandma-ma."

"Michelle, we'll need to get a hold of your parents," Gage said returning inside. "The crime lab will have to go through their entire house. It could take a couple of days."

"I'll get a number, if you'll call them."

Gage brushed her cheek tenderly with a finger. "No problem, kiddo. Are you okay?"

She nodded.

"I'll need pictures of your bruises then you can go home." Addressing the others, he said, "We'll get statements from all of you tomorrow."

"Travis, I'm going with your mother to the hospital. Ronson can take the rental and bring your grandmother back to their bungalow. I'll call you later."

He nodded, handing Michelle his cell phone to call her sister and get their parent's number in Florida.

*   *   *

Mac Mirandized Derek Gunderson first then paramedics examined his injuries. They cleaned and bandaged the superficial wound in his shoulder. Their diagnosis, *"He's coked and complaining of pain in his back,"* wasn't enough to swap a jail cell for an ER stall.

His days as a Green Bay street cop taught him to turn on the recorder. He stopped at the station to retrieve same and called his wife with the good news. He realized repeatedly how much he needed Katharine. Hearing her voice relieved the internal anger. Today was no different as he told her everything. And afterward, he reread Gunderson's rights to him with the tape recorder running. Gunderson repeated that he understood his rights and chose not to lawyer-up. He left the tape on during the transport across the big lake on the ferry and to the County jail. Mac didn't have to question the now self-effacing, doped-up dirtbag as he gave a detailed account of what he did to Maryann Graham and their victim from this morning. Booking charges were listed as murder and kidnapping.

When he returned to La Pointe, he found Gage at the Callihan house. Three additional investigators from the Crime Lab were well into processing the scene.

"Any problems, Mac?"

"We got 'im," he said waiving the miniature cassette tape.

"A confession?"

"Yep, with a recorded Miranda warning. He kept referring to

this morning's victim as 'Jeannie'. Said he had to kill her because she lied about getting him crack. The guy's a dopecase and kept rambling on about how he had to kill everyone before they got him."

"I'll be damned. Unbelievably, Del found ID in that mess at the Tavern. Her name's Jeannie Bell from Ashland. He was definitely making the rounds."

"Was she staying here or don't you know?"

"Dispatch is calling around and will let us know."

"Where'd these guys come from?" Mac asked pointing.

"Gus and the others are still at the Tavern. He called and got this bunch over to do the house since it'll take them the better part of the day and night to process the Tavern. We got the murder weapon for the Graham woman out of the Red Honda. Also found a spool of fishing line and no poles."

"You found Michelle's pruning saw?"

"Uh-huh. They'll have it analyzed for our first victim's blood. We suspect he was down to his last injection. They found paraphernalia, couple of crack rocks and needles they're pretty sure have traces of crank."

"How are Michelle and the others?"

"They're okay. Travis took her home after we snapped off pictures of her injuries. Rosemary went to the hospital with a broken arm and Julia was a little shaken up. I got a hold of Michelle's parents and they're flying back today."

Glancing around, Mac said, "Appears he cleaned them out even more since Thanksgiving."

Gage nodded. "I doubt the Callihan's will be happy when they see what Travis did to the doors over there."

"It's their daughter for God's sake!"

"I know," Gage muttered. "It's a long story. Gunderson didn't by any chance mention any paraquat or the serial killings in the course of his confession?"

"Not a word. But he kept saying his real name is Guthrie, not Gunderson."

Gage massaged his temples briefly. "Oh, yeah. Dispatch called about an hour ago. They have something for us but said it could wait. Check it out. I told everyone we'd get statements from them tomorrow."

Mac used his cell phone to make the call instead of the Callihan phone since it appeared not to have been dusted for prints yet. While waiting for a supervisor due to shift change, he finally got the message a little past three. Sanders, his ex homicide captain back in Green Bay wanted to talk to them. Mac called Sanders, informed him of the events then learned the identity of their eighth serial killing victim. He disconnected.

"Gage."

"Yeah, what've you got?"

"My captain back in Green Bay said somehow a runaway report slipped through the cracks. Anyway, our eighth victim is a Sharon Marquette from Green Bay. C student, no priors, and raised by her mother."

Gage fisted his hips. "How the hell did she wind up dead by our serial killer here on the island?"

"You think Kevin brought her back with him?"

"Doesn't jive. We hauled him in and questioned him. Somebody, somewhere on this island would have known. We've checked his house. Where the hell is he hiding the deadly chemical?" Gage asked more of himself than Mac. "When did the mother report her missing?"

"That's the really bizarre part. The day *after* she was discovered here," he answered. "Sanders said the report literally slipped between two desks and was never entered into NCIC."

Gage didn't respond.

"There's one other point that's different. Whether it's important or not, I can't say."

"What's that?"

"This is the first victim who didn't live with both parents. Mother's divorced and the father lives out west but hasn't seen his daughter since the age of five."

"We'll work on it after we wrap this up. Go back to the station and start on the reports. Get Cindy to transcribe that tape. I'll call if I need help here."

*   *   *

I actually lied to her! He told Michelle he needed to get back to the ballroom. Jerry had everything under control. Travis took a long deep breath and shifted gears on the Ferrari, increasing his speed beyond the forty max. His hands tightened on the steering wheel as the black Spider whizzed past vacuous scenery.

He needed time away. To think. Every emotion, muscular twitch and chest-pounding chill replayed through his mind. It was positively a blueprint. He would have killed a human being in cold blood if they hadn't stopped him. Thousands of times, the headlines loomed—*Mass Murderer Slain by Police—Four Dead in Ohio—Oklahoma Bombing—Columbine Shooting—9/11*—senseless destruction in a world that escaped him. It had always been difficult for him to understand the workings of a criminal mind . . . until today when he encountered deep-seeded hatred for someone. When all the intense events switched over to him, he became confused and joined the ranks of world scum. If Mac and Gage hadn't been there to stop him, he would have gone through with the ghastly act of murder. Michelle's cowering horror was crystal-clear to him now.

Travis braked the car behind Katharine's beater at the new house. He didn't remember turning. Construction was moving smoothly. Siding, windows and doors fully enclosed the house. Katharine opened the front door and jumped to the ground to greet him.

"Travis, what're you doing here? Is Michelle okay?"

He exited and stood by his car. Nodded briefly. Her red hair was wild. Her belly was growing with life inside, and her face was radiant. Looking at her now, no one could ever tell that she had taken a man's life. Tragedy had etched composure and dignity into her face. Why didn't failure bloom out of her eyes? Why didn't she feel the defeat? He faltered in the silence that now engulfed them, and finally asked, "How's the house coming along?"

"Good."

"You hear what happened?"

"Yes. From the man I love more with each passing hour and day. Come on. Let's take a walk. The doctor says I need to keep exercising."

Travis stuffed his hands into his front pants pocket and followed her. He wondered, too, if Katharine felt remorse for what she did. Did she fall asleep each night with culpability and wake up every morning with self-blame? Did this feeling ever go away? Could he be trusted never to hurt Michelle? He knew he loved her. What he didn't know was if the hatred he experienced today was more powerful.

". . . and we'll be in before Christmas." Katharine stopped as Travis kept walking. "Travis."

He shifted about to face her. "How do you live with it?"

"The fact that I shot and killed two men?"

His muscles quirked, but he could only stare at her. After several moments, he said, "Two?"

"Michelle didn't tell you."

He shook his head and they continued walking.

"The first time was a domestic. We'd been there many times. He was crashing. Cocaine blues we call it when they're coming down and going into depression. He'd stabbed his girlfriend and their baby before I arrived then came at me with the knife. The aftermath is what almost killed me. I couldn't function on the street anymore. That's when I resigned."

"Don't you feel any guilt about taking a human life?"

"Daily," she told him. "I just don't dwell on it anymore. Both were ruled justified homicides and Mac helped me to understand the rest."

"How does justifying murder make what you did right? How do you know you'll never have those same feelings of pent-up rage and do it again?"

"I don't know." She rubbed her belly lovingly. "What I do

know is the difference between protecting and serving the innocent from the guilty. I know self defense versus intentional maiming. Travis, the emotion you're dealing with is normal. You wanted to instill injury on a scumbag who'd hurt three human beings. People you love and care about. But you didn't. That's what you need to keep telling yourself. In that crucial moment, whether consciously or not, you backed off because you knew the difference between right and wrong."

"Katharine, I didn't *want* to back off. I lost control. I've never done that in my entire life."

"Welcome to the human race, Travis."

"It wasn't until Michelle spoke that I dropped the crowbar. What if she'd been unconscious or dead? What if I forfeit my restraint and hurt someone else . . ." he paused. "What if I hurt Michelle?"

"Travis, you're not a man who lives with what ifs. And you certainly are not a man with a begrudging heart. You can't torture yourself because of an isolated incident revolving around the love you feel for another. That bastard already killed two women and you stopped him from killing three more."

"I screwed up by leaving her alone. I shouldn't have done that. None of this would have happened."

"You're wrong. Gunderson would have found another way and others might have died in between. But they didn't because you stopped him. Things happen the way they do for a reason even when reason appears senseless at the time."

Travis stopped. He gaped at her, suddenly felt a strange numbed comfort. If the dream hadn't plagued him for many months, or he hadn't heard Michelle's ghost, he probably wouldn't be in La Pointe. If Michelle hadn't buried her car in mud, the weekend would be just a rainy day hangover. And he wouldn't have been with her this morning when the call came from Jerry. He never would have known of the impending danger to her. Michelle's voice, her words, her courage and strength were the real reason he didn't go through with the heinous act. The tortured guilt he placed on himself came from mingled feelings of hatred and love. Although filled with hatred in that final moment, the deep love he felt for Michelle is what ultimately stopped him.

He smacked a big kiss on the spunky little red head's mouth.

"Aw geez!"

"Mac is one lucky man."

"Why do you say that?"

"And you're one hell of a woman, Katharine Dobarchon. I have to go."

"Michelle's right," she muttered as he took off. "The man *is* insane."

Katharine grinned as the black Ferrari sped off just before she felt a movement in her tummy and rubbed it gently. She couldn't wait to tell that lucky man of hers the news.

CHAPTER 26

MISERABLE, SLEEPLESS, THE night enfeebled her. Travis never called. He never returned. Tossing and turning, Michelle laid awake reliving the previous day's events. Wanting to put all the pieces together, she asked herself a million times. Why would her parents give Derek a key to their house? She stared at the darkness for a long time wondering why her mother hated her for divorcing a man who came close to killing her. At 4 A.M. when her thoughts veered to the possibility that there might be other victims, she got up and brewed a desperately needed pot of coffee. To hell with her stomach, she needed to clear the fuzz off her brain. She then finished what she began yesterday afternoon. Cleaning up Derek's destruction. She had done it so many times it almost felt normal.

Now hours later, she sat in the police station conference room, yawned and rubbed her eyes. She didn't understand, but if Travis needed time and space away from her who was she to dispute it. Perhaps the tables had turned. He couldn't love her. It'd make sense. Because of her two women were dead. Julia and Rosemary almost died because of her. That alone would chase any man away. Maybe Travis finally realized what she'd been telling him since day one.

She traded those thoughts with the non emotion she felt about facing her parents any second. When Mac called last night asking her to come to the station at ten this morning, the idea of being in the same building with her mother was repulsive. At the end of her tolerance with Elisabeth Callihan, she forced herself into deadness until she agreed.

Propping her elbows on the table, she covered her mouth as another yawn seeped out. Her head came up when Gage entered the room. Travis followed him and she nervously moistened her lips. His weak smile was without malice, almost apologetic. Confidence had replaced the blazing anger and hatred she witnessed yesterday. He slid out a chair and sat next to her. A probing query came into his eyes and she watched the play of emotions on his face. Michelle offered a hand. He broke into a relief-filled smile and linked his fingers with hers.

"Michelle, there's a few things I want to go over with you before we get started," Gage said.

"Okay."

"There's nothing to worry about but I thought you should know. Gunderson's real name is Derek Ralph Guthrie. He's twenty-nine, originally from the Twin Cities and has a revoked Minnesota drivers license."

"Everything was a lie," she said with quiet meekness.

"Well, he *was* raised in foster homes. We were able to confirm his ID with a Minnesota birth certificate and fingerprints against outstanding warrants for his arrest. We also found your pruning saw in the red Honda. The car was stolen from the Cities in Minnesota. The lab's processing both, and we're positive the pruning saw is the weapon he used on our first victim from the lagoon. He used fishing line as well not that garden tool of yours. We'll be getting that back to you in a day or so. But, we'd like to keep the book you lent us."

Michelle nodded unsure why what Gage was telling her came at her in blunt force. She glanced at Travis. He pressed her hand reassuringly, massaging his thumb across her knuckles. *What must he think about this mess? About her?*

"Michelle, Mac's talking to your folks right now. They'll be in here shortly. Travis asked to be here and we didn't think you'd mind."

Travis said nothing, nodded agreement and kissed the back of her hand. She had no response to either one of them.

"Julia gave us her statement," Gage continued. "We'll get Rosemary's later today. We're going to record yours and will be asking you several questions. All you have to do is tell us the way you remember it."

"Then what will happen?"

"Guthrie will be tried and most likely convicted, then jail for life without parole."

"Why do my parents have to be here at the same time that you question me?"

"Michelle, this isn't going to be easy, but it seems they don't believe what has happened. I gave them an ultimatum."

"But—" she began and was interrupted when Mac entered the room with her parents.

"Have a seat," Mac said to the couple.

Michelle shifted uncomfortably when her mother's steely eyes grazed her with an awful slant. Generally, they were soft hazel, a deceptive color, until their flecks of green miffed you with a deadpan expression. Her cheeks up tilted, her upper lip might, too, when disgust was foremost in her mind. Elisabeth Callihan had once been a pretty person before she traded in her curvy feminine garments for dark colors and tailored lines. Michelle was only seventeen but her mother's romantic style and flair exchanged places with dominance and authority for protective armor. But behind all her mother's intentional cover up, her upper lids continually tensed with sadness and bereavement.

Her father was spiritless, older, and withered like a piece of worn out rawhide. Wrinkles of misery consumed his gaunt face. Never noticed Brian had had his pale green eyes until today. Deep sunk temples looked as if death had knocked and eaten Aidan Callihan alive. Neither moved with Mac's order. They just stared at her until Mac nudged them both to chairs.

"Gage, we're ready?"

"Okay," he began.

"This is absurd!"

"Mrs. Callihan, you heard Derek's taped confession," Gage said.

Elisabeth flung a scalpel stare at Michelle. "This is all your fault!"

"I'm not the one who gave a dope-crazed murderer a keyed invitation to steal you blind."

"If you hadn't failed in your marriage, we wouldn't be here now. He told me how you refused to perform. He wanted you back and you refused to speak to him."

"*Omigod*," she screeched in extreme anger, and yanked her hand away from Travis. "Mother, he's brainwashed you! He beat me until I was almost dead!"

"I don't believe you. Derek would never do that!"

For the first time throughout the last fifteen years, Michelle saw the flicker of shock as life returned to her father's eyes. He'd been caught unaware. On the other side, fury filled her mother's eyes. She clenched her fists as if she were waging war with them. A hurtful exchange passed between them before Elisabeth lowered her eyebrows and picked imaginary lint off her suit.

"This is a trick by a daughter I've disowned in order for her to gain sympathy for her failures."

"Oh, well, that's rich," Michelle blew out. "I forgot Brian is the only one who ever mattered to you and you used Derek to replace him. Do you know how much it hurts Sylvie the way you ignore Harvey?"

Elisabeth squared her jaw. "Harvey is feckless. But *you*! You disgraced this family name with divorce. In the eyes of God, that's a sin. And if that weren't bad enough, now you're shacking up with the likes . . ." Elisabeth threw sparks at Travis. "Of him! You think I don't know. Well, I do know. And someday you'll have to answer for your sins."

Michelle heaved her body upward, slamming her hands on the table with a loud smack. "That's a bit too damn high and mighty coming from someone who hasn't set foot inside a church since Brian's death! In all your righteous arrogance, you can't deny the fact that you wished it had been me instead of Brian who died! Can you, Mother?"

A revealing glare confirmed her mother's guilt.

"You have no right to speak to me that way!"

"That's where you're wrong. I do have rights. And a lot more rights than you have at this moment. You aided and abetted a criminal knowing he killed that first woman. But you chose not to listen to me!"

Elisabeth shrieked and sputtered.

"If I were Gage I'd throw your sick, pathetic ass in the slammer right alongside that murdering piece of shit. You deserve each other, Mother."

"How dare you!"

"Elisabeth, shut up! Just shut your mouth!"

She shrieked a second time as her eyes expanded with abomination. Michelle fell backward with an ungraceful lurch onto the chair. Taken aback by the sudden vibrancy of her father's tone, her father never raised his voice, let alone to her mother.

Travis clutched her trembling fingers, squeezed and held snugly while she just sat there gaping at her father. She glanced from her father to Travis, wondering what must be going through his mind now. Why would he want any part of this complex screwed up family?

"Gage, is this true?" Aidan asked.

"Mr. Callihan—"

"I asked you a question. Is everything Michelle said true? Yes or no?"

He did not intend to book Elisabeth Callihan for stupidity, and muttered hopelessly, "Yes."

A bulge appeared above Aidan's brow, his eyes glazed over and his lips trembled.

"Aidan, I am not charging your wife with any crime. We're here to take formal statements and learn exactly how and why Derek had access to your home."

Staring at his wife, Aidan said, "I'm afraid we're to blame for that. I didn't know."

"Aidan, you're weaker than that pathetic excuse Sylvie married," Elisabeth berated. "This is ridiculous!"

"Mrs. Callihan, that's enough," Gage said.

"You're right and I'm leaving."

"No you're not," he responded tersely. "Moments ago when I watched the two of you listening to that tape, it was crystal clear to me that Derek replaced Brian for both of you. I relived my own heartache over his death. I do everyday of my life. But I thought, rather, I had hoped that by insisting you return here, you would be able to see what your own daughter has suffered because of Derek. I was obviously wrong to have any hope of that and right now I have this demon inside me that wants to shake sense back into you."

"I don't have to sit her and listen to this."

"I'll only say it once more, Elisabeth. *Shut up!* Gage, it's true. We gave Derek a key and told him he could stay there. I'd heard rumors, but my . . ."

Aidan's face soured, scrutinizing the woman sitting next to him.

He looked at Gage. "Elisabeth reassured me. I know ignorance is no excuse. My daughter's right. Elisabeth is wrong."

The air was silent as each person sat motionless. Her father looked straight at her.

"Baby, I'm sorry. I lost one child and I can't lose another. I had no idea. Can you ever forgive me?"

"Oh, Daddy. Yes."

Father and daughter ignored Elisabeth's guttural objections as each watched the other across the table through blurred vision. His bottom lip twisted in agony, her sobs racked up inside with a painful longing that had squeezed on her heart entirely too long.

"I'll not sit here and be part of this rubbish," Elisabeth spat and pushed her chair back.

"Mrs. Callihan! Gage may not choose to book you for aiding a felon, but guaranteed I won't bat an eye at the thought. Either sit down and keep your mouth shut, or you're getting a free bed on the County tonight," Mac ordered.

At that, Michelle stood, skirted around the table and met her father half way. Gathering her into his arms, Aidan held her tightly, rocking her gently the way he once did.

"Baby, I'll find a way to make everything up to you and Sylvie," Aidan promised through tears.

"Oh, for God's sake!" Elisabeth thrust her body off the chair.

That's it! "Mrs. Callihan, I've sat here quietly and listened to you disparage your daughter, ignore the law and scorn your husband," Travis calmly said. "It seems to me that you're the one shirking your performance as a mother, a wife and a decent citizen. My mother and grandmother were kidnapped as well. Anyone who messes with either, or Michelle, will have to deal directly with me. Now, if you don't sit down and keep your trap shut, I'll sic every high-priced lawyer in the country on you until I've bled you so dry you won't have a pot to piss in."

She grunted then Elisabeth Callihan roosted herself snobbishly, but quietly. Michelle and her father returned to their seats. Travis took her hand, holding it throughout her detailed account of the kidnapping over the next hour and a half.

Her father explained how Derek came to them with eyes bloodshot from crying he told them. His voice quivered as he pleaded, begged them for help to get Michelle back. Aidan admitted he didn't understand until now why Michelle had divorced him. Derek had them convinced Michelle was the problem and begged to stay in their home until he got a place and could work things out with her. They missed their son so much, they readily agreed.

"Michelle was right. Gage, you're right. Derek did remind us of Brian." Looking into his daughter's eyes now, Aidan said, "All these years, I've been wrapped in personal grief and suffering. I blinded myself to life, to my daughters and to my grandchildren. Baby, we've made a grave mistake."

"I-I know, Daddy. I did, too."

"We—I'm sorry." Aidan swiped at his eyes. "I wish you would

have come to me first and explained to me what he did to you. I'm sorry your mother has lied to cover her grief. I guess I knew it. Still, I let it shut you and Sylvie out of our lives. The boating accident tore this family apart. Neither you or your sister is to blame. Will either of you ever be able to forgive me?"

Lifting her wretched body, Michelle went around the table a second time and squeezed her arms around her father. Tears gushed out as her fifteen-year ache dissolved. "Y-yes. D-daddy, I love you."

"I love you too, baby."

The interview over, the Callihans were ushered out. Wild horses couldn't have moved Michelle at that moment. Her lifeless limbs anesthetized, the shocking confrontation had immobilized her. With her parents out of the room, Gage told her to take as long as she needed. Hours ago, she walked into Town Hall unfeeling, but her father not knowing her ordeal, her mother lying about it, Derek's deceit, everything had turned into an emotional revelation. And right now, she didn't have the energy or the strength to lift her head and face Travis.

"Are you okay?" Travis asked.

She shrugged, unable to speak.

Travis leaned over and wrapped his arms around her. He held her snugly. Her mind in tumult, she felt bereft of hope. The grief and despair engulfed her body. With nothing left but raw sores to mar her aching heart, Michelle caved. She covered her face with trembling hands and bawled uncontrollably from the agony of her loss. Travis lifted her into his lap and Michelle buckled into him. She wept compulsive sobs until drained of all the agony. He held her against him, stroked her cheek, and rocked her back and forth soothing her shredded soul until her body calmed.

"I love you, Michelle," Travis said then took her home.

*   *   *

The story made front page headlines in the Island Blazer. An invigorated smirk twisted the serial killer's mouth.

Murder Mania on Madeline

Reported by Ed Harris

Green Bay Police first identified David Patriot as the Green Bay Serial killer upon discovering a fingerprint left at the scene of their sixth homicide. Lured in with drugs and alcohol, Patriot tied up his victims and fed them lethal poison known as paraquat. Paraquat is a chemical used on highways to kill roadside weeds. He then waited eight months and killed three more in the same months of July, October and December the following year by the same means.

The case took an ambiguous turn with La Pointe's first murder when police discovered Sherry Martin in the woods off the Old County Road at the end of July. An autopsy revealed the cause of her death came from the deadly poison abrin. Abrin comes from the abrus precatorius plant, a twisting perennial vine grown in tropical climates. The one inch pod of the abrus precatorius plant is what harbors the poisonous seeds, commonly known as rosary peas. The rosary pea has a bright red outer shell with black spots and has been used by some for centuries to ward off evil spirits.

Jennifer Wicket, La Pointe's second homicide victim, was discovered on Michigan Island early August. Her autopsy revealed death by abrin poisoning. Wicket and Martin's death faults law enforcement's original theory; that these murders are the work of the Green Bay serial killer. La Pointe's third victim, Jessica Henderson died of the same poison that took the lives of the six teenage girls in Green Bay. She, too, was murdered in August, throwing another wrench into the case.

Police believed the case was resolved when David Patriot was shot and killed by ex Minneapolis Police Sergeant Katharine (LeNoir) Dobarchon. The morning construction began for the Red Rock Tavern ballroom crews for Baines, Incorporated found Sharon Marquette, another sixteen-year-old dead. An autopsy revealed the abrin poison caused her death.

The Green Bay Serial Killer is still at large and police seem to be no further ahead with two additional and unrelated murders. David

Ralph Guthrie admitted to stabbing and killing Maryann Graham, a Duluth, Minnesota resident at the Island's lagoon. Fingerprints left at the scene of the murder identified Guthrie who is wanted on an active warrant in Nevada for felony assault with a weapon and in Minnesota for gross misdemeanor driving under the influence. Guthrie also murdered Jeannie Bell inside the Tavern's unfinished ballroom sometime late Sunday night early Monday morning. Bell was a resident of Ashland, Wisconsin.

"It was necessary to close down until the mess could be cleaned up," said Ted Evans owner of the Red Rock Tavern.

Police also said they took Derek Ralph Guthrie into custody midday Monday inside Aidan and Elisabeth Callihan's house after he kidnapped Rosemary Baines, Julia Perry and La Pointe's Town Board Supervisor Michelle Callihan. Their abduction followed the murder of the Bell woman inside the Tavern. Police said construction crews reported to work and discovered Bell's body. A reliable source was quoted as saying, "It was the most ghastly thing I've ever seen."

Guthrie was charged with two counts of murder, three counts of attempted murder and three counts of kidnapping. Police Chief Gage LeNoir told reporters criminal damage to property charges are pending.

The killer reread the article a second time. Green Bay Serial Killer was a worthy label! An auspicious title indeed. It was a prize with a ring of amorous overtures. It was also extremely gratifying to revel in public fame. Almighty One expected the notoriety. Feeding the soul of death in a tribute such as this provided erotic, carnal feelings for the killer. Gunderson proved helpful in the plight, rather than a hindrance like once thought. That asshole wanted ownership of the Divine Creator, but possession was impossible. No one owned the Divine Creator. It was good they locked him up. It was better the Tavern's doors had to close for three days. The delay of the ballroom's construction was an unexpected reward.

Eagerness stimulated the killer in anticipation of the game. Impatience also gripped tightly like an addiction. There were twenty-seven long days before the next sacrifice. Sixteen days after the autumn harvest another soul would be given in a ceremonious pledge. It was commitment. It was devotion to the act. Loyalty to the cause. Murder did away with the heavy burden of hatred.

The killer fed off private thoughts of doing in the conceited slut alongside the next official death. Hers would be a savage death. Poison was too good for her. It was necessary to dispose of her existence quickly, brutally. That would provide additional fame. Self-recognition.

Pondering the plan to lure two more sacrifices consumed the killer with electricity now. Infectious as a cancer claw, the blond slut's death would have to occur at the commencement of the New Year. Planning a method to manipulate her into capture took imagination. Perhaps poison to seduce her into the ultimate truth, but it was too good for her death. Living out the act in mind and body almost had a sound to it, too. Like a chime. Or the hum of energy but on a much higher level. If one were walking through a minefield, the feeling might match Pandemonium of a serious world event. The killer thought it, felt it, let it exhilarate, thrill and chill through to the bone. It had always been about passion's revenge. That brazen slut and her honey-gold hair would relinquish her soul to the New Year then all would be right. Punishment for the damage she committed would become the killer's glorious beginning.

"Commitment to the cause be pure and white. Repugnance for the past be foul and black."

Laughing obnoxiously now, they really had no idea how simple it was to murder.

CHAPTER 27

 T RAVIS NUZZLED MICHELLE closer, soothing her, caressing her hair. She'd been through it all and he had never witnessed anything like what he observed yesterday at the police station. He didn't understand with one loss, why Mrs. Callihan chose to shun both her daughters. He could only imagine the depth of her pain, but suspected Elisabeth Callihan would never understand her mistake. Still, her actions made little sense to him.

Michelle snuggled closer to him wrapping her arms around him. Travis just watched her sleeping. When he brought her home from the police station yesterday, she collapsed into a comatose sleep. He watched her for several hours then, too, until fatigue finished him off. Lying here together for the past couple of hours, they discussed the events of the previous day in between dozing. He didn't know how Michelle had found the courage to forgive her mother, but she did. She told him that his own mother had pointed out she needed to forgive herself as easily as she forgave Elisabeth. By doing so, she was able to go forward. Michelle explained that forgiving someone didn't mean she liked the outcome, but she could accept it. The fact that she could overcome such a tragic event and still find room in her heart to care consumed Travis with a mountain of emotions. All this time, he thought she was the one who needed to learn how to love when in fact, she taught him something about the power of love, and of hate. She certainly changed his life forever.

She moaned slightly when he kissed her forehead. He had more love for her than he could ever hate anyone. She shifted, fluttered her eyes open.

"Two pennies for your thoughts," he said smiling.

"I'm sleeping."

"Only half sleeping," he teased softly.

"You were right, again," she mumbled.

"Of course I was. About what?" he asked caressing the tip of her shoulder.

"I've fallen in love for the very first time in my life."

It might have been lightning that struck him. Except the sky was blue and cloudless. Perhaps another dream but he knew they were wide awake.

"Well, this is a first," she said coming to life. "Insane Travis Baines, speechless. I'll repeat it. I've fallen in love for the very first time in my life. With you, Travis."

He let his breath out slowly, not knowing why he thought anything different. He readjusted himself and propped an elbow into the pillow before he kissed her nose. He brushed the strands of tousled hair off her face. So beautiful and everything he wanted, he couldn't stop his love for her.

When he didn't respond, she said, "Oh-oh. I'm not sure I want to hear the answer but I'll ask anyway. What are you thinking about?"

"When did you decide this?" he finally asked.

"Sometime around last Thursday. Shopping Friday with everyone gave me the needed time to think without having to look over my shoulder. I was coming to tell you that on Saturday."

He chuckled letting it turn into laughter until he was laughing so hard he couldn't hold himself up on his elbow.

Michelle sat up and gawked at him. "I'm making a buck-naked declaration to the man I love and he lays there laughing at me."

"Oh, Milady, I'm not laughing at you. Either the good Lord above or your ghost, I don't know which, but one of them is watching after us."

He sat up. Puzzlement filled her faced and he wrapped his

arms around her. "Milady, you chickened out and went *baha'ing* instead. But you still ended up at the Retreat with me. It was fate that drove you into the ditch."

"Fate? More like dumb luck."

He took her face between his hands. "Lovely lady, I don't care what it was that brought you to me. Will you become my wife?"

"Travis! I knew—I mean—but—"

She yanked the sheet from the mattress corners and slung it around her body as she scrambled off the bed dragging the extra to the floor. His grin stretched from ear to ear as the excess bundled around her ankles. *Absolutely the most beautiful creature he had ever seen. And oh, what that messy dark hair did to him.*

Amused, he waited, watched her pace up to her usual cadence while muttering unintelligibly. After the third flyby, Travis climbed off the bed and went to her.

"Michelle, I love you. I want to spend everyday of my life loving you and taking care of you if you'll let me. I want fifty years and more with you beside me along with a dozen children to fill our days and nights so they'll never be lonely."

He wanted children with her! "B-but, but, Travis."

He took her in his arms, kissed away new tears and soothed her quivering lips. "Milady, tell me your doubts and I'll make them vanish."

"Trav—" she stopped.

Both looked up, scanned their surroundings when Mikala's cry echoed throughout the bedroom and the house.

"See," then recanting, "I mean hear. Even your ghost is telling us that we're meant to be together forever."

"I just didn't expect it this quickly."

"Why not?"

Michelle embraced his neck and stretched on tiptoe to kiss him. "As crazy as this will sound later—"

"You mean to our grandchildren?"

She nodded, "I don't have any doubts. I know it sounds absurd that a tourist guide, a ghost, an insane man, and my heart are all saying the same thing, but I guess they can't all be wrong. I want more than anything to spend the rest of my life with you."

He gave her a slow, drugging kiss. "Let's plan the wedding for the very near future. I'd like to take you to Boston for a quick couple of days."

"You just want to show me off," she teased.

"I want you to see and feel the sights, the sounds, the excitement of a large city. I want to show you everything and yes, show you off. After Grandma-ma's anniversary party, we'll honeymoon for as long as you like anywhere you want."

"Travis, that party is only a little over a month away. Where will we live? What about your business? And mine?"

"Not to worry. I can't take you away from here."

She quirked her eyebrow questioningly.

"Michelle, you belong here. I see it in those jeweled emeralds of yours every time you talk about the Apostles, Madeline Island and my heritage."

"But how? Where will we live? How can we get married when you're in the middle of construction on the ballroom? How can we get married so fast?"

"Jerry can handle the ballroom. I can work from here as well as Boston with those fax machines and cell phones you're so crazy about. You can keep your business, but we'll maintain the house in Boston for when it's needed and reside here on Madeline where our children will be raised."

"You'd do that for me?"

"I'd live at the North Pole if that's where you wanted to go."

"Again. Where will we live?"

"I'll build the house of your dreams. Now, let's eat some breakfast and you can tell me all about the kind of wedding you want to have."

"You mean you don't care?"

"I have only one request as long as everything else makes you happy."

"What's that?"

"I want to marry you immediately. The sooner the better."

With a twinkle in her eye, she said, "Deal, with a condition."

"Ask and you shall receive, Milady."

"I want two dozen children."

A diabolical grin filled his face. "I'm thinking you better pick a date quickly so we can get started."

It felt good for her to be able to reach out to him and Michelle did.

He drew her in, bopped her on the nose then kissed it. "Who are you going to call and tell first about our news?"

She slid her hands across his bare chest. "No one. I want you all to myself."

"I knew there was at least one other reason I loved you," he said, backing out of their embrace.

"Where are you going?"

"It's a surprise," he tossed over his shoulder walking out.

"I'll tell you the date I've picked if you tell me what the surprise is."

He stopped, hesitated then turned and leaned inward against the jamb.

"I knew that'd get your attention," she teased.

"I do not need to be bribed to be attentive to you."

She grazed him up and down with the same come-hither expression he was giving her. When his heart skipped a couple beats, Travis turned and fled. He returned shortly with a small square jewelry box in hand. "I was going to give you these at lunch today. Grandma-ma wore them when she married, and my mother wore them at her wedding."

Michelle took the box, opened it, and whooped, "Diamond earrings! *Omigod!* Travis, they're stunning! And huge!"

"Someday our daughter will wear them for her wedding."

"Or daughter-in-law," she said, eagerly removing them from the box.

"I'm almost positive out of two dozen babes, one will be a girl. And that tells me we'll need a very large house."

She didn't hear him but he didn't care. It was positively pleasing to watch her eyes sparkle with new life. Even if at the moment, she was gaping deliberately at a pair of materialistic karats.

"Can I wear them now?"

"Milady, they're yours until the next wedding. He leaned down and kissed her.

"Stop that. I want to try them on."

Literally, the woman of his dreams, he thought, let the sheet drop to the floor as she gingerly slid first one diamond into her lobe, then the other. "Now this is something I never thought I'd see."

Admiring herself in the dresser mirror, she hummed, "Wha's that?"

"My wife to be standing nude with the diamonds my mother and grandmother wore at their wedding."

She cocked her head, catching his fiendish expression in the mirror. "Travis Baines, you're insane and don't you ever repeat what you just said outside these four walls."

He laughed loudly. She rolled her eyes before flipping hair away from her ears and went back to doting on the karats gracing her lobes. He inched up behind her to caress her intimately, nibbled on one earring then her neck. "When, Milady?"

Leaning against him, she moaned, "A week . . . from . . . Saturday."

"You're on. Tomorrow we're going shopping for a ring."

Then he lunged to fulfill his need.

*   *   *

Michelle sat in front of Katharine's bedroom mirror at the LeNoir house. This time, she didn't care about horse-drawn carriages and flawless Venise lace. She was in love and love was very important. The swiftly made arrangements created a different memory in an uncomplicated way. Paula offered the use of her house and Michelle asked Father Napoli if he would marry her and Travis in the LeNoir home. To which he readily agreed. Her best friends since they were little girls were still her bridesmaids, and Brendan would carry the rings. Shalee and Caitlin were flower girls. Travis had asked Gage and Mac to stand up with him. And her father and Sylvie would walk her down the stairs. Tragic as it might have seemed her mother refused to participate. The ceremony would be straightforward with the exchange of vows, but this time she knew they would be forever. Tomorrow the leer jet would take them to Boston for a couple of days.

"Hon, sadness isn't allowed on your wedding day."

Michelle touched up her makeup in the mirror and looked up at Nicole's reflection. "Oh, I'm not. I've never been happier. I was just thinking about my mom, wishing things could be different. She's missing out on so much in life."

Katharine moved over and stood on the other side of Michelle. "Girlfriend, as long as we live and breathe there's always hope."

"True. I may have lost one parent, but I'm gaining four more. I consider myself very lucky to be surrounded by so much love from so many people."

Michelle stood up and faced them. "You both are absolutely beautiful today and I love you more than anything."

"Ah, geez. Don't go getting all mushy on us. The saucy twit's gonna start bawling and wreck her make-up."

"I can't help it," Nicole said, dabbing her eyes. "You two are the luckiest women in the world."

"Your day's coming," Michelle told her then giggled.

"I doubt that," Nicole responded flatly. "The only way any of us can find true love is to be rescued by a hero. And I sure as hell don't need rescuing."

Katharine and Michelle exchanged conspiratorial grins. "You may not need to be rescued, but just wait til you start hearing Nicolina."

"That's right," Michelle said. "It's going to happen and I've got a gut feeling very soon."

"Please do not tell me that you're referring to Sully's ghost," Nicole shrieked.

Heads together, Michelle and Katharine nodded.

"Don't even go there. There's no such thing as ghosts."

Both women sighed before Katharine said, "I've got some news."

"What?" the other two asked in unison.

"I went to the doctor last week for my check up. Found out Mac and I are having twins."

"Great balls of fire! Are you serious?"

Smiling, this time Katharine grabbed a tissue and dabbed at her eyes. "You guys, I almost fell over when the doc told me."

"What did Mac say?" Michelle asked.

"Before or after he passed out?"

Michelle squeezed her arms around Katharine and Nicole enveloped both of them.

"I'm delighted for you and Mac. Congratulations," Michelle said.

Paula stuck her head inside the door after knocking. "We're all—Oh! What's going on?"

Without waiting for an answer, she entered the room to examine each one. "You all look magnificent! What a gorgeous bride you make, Michelle. We're ready to start. But first there are two who have asked if they could come in and talk to you."

"Okay, send them in."

Katharine and Nicole left as Paula steered Brendan and Shalee into the bedroom.

"Oh, Auntie Michelle, you're pretty."

"You're beautiful, Auntie Michelle."

"Why thank you, dumplin's. Shalee, you're dress is very pretty, and Brendan, you're a very handsome young man all decked out in your suit. What did you want to talk to me about?"

Her niece and nephew shuffled their feet, hemmed and hawed for a moment. Their little faces were filled with worry and concern. Michelle squatted gently in her gown to meet at their level.

"Auntie Michelle, are you going away forever?"

"Brendan, why would you think that?"

"Shalee and me heard Travis tell Gage you're leaving tomorrow. Are you coming back?"

"Auntie Michelle, we don't want you to leave. Or Travis," Shalee whined.

She hugged them both. "Dumplin's, Travis and I are taking a trip tomorrow. We're going to Boston for a couple of days but we're both coming back here."

"Where's that?" Shalee asked.

"It's by the ocean. Travis and I have to get on an airplane and fly to get there. But you know what?

"What?" they asked in unison.

"After Father Napoli marries Travis and me, Travis is going to be your new uncle."

"He'll let us call him Uncle Travis?" Brendan bounced.

"That's right and he'll love you just as much as I do."

"As much as our new grandpa said he loved us?" Shalee asked.

Somehow, Michelle believed Grandpa Callihan was going to be making up for lost time, and said, "As much."

"Wow cool! A new grandpa and uncle at the same time, Shalee."

"Okay. Is everybody happy now?" When they nodded their heads, Michelle squeezed both and told them to go get in line.

She took one last peek in the mirror wondering how her mother could choose mourning over living. Her hair swooped up beneath her veil she smiled as her diamond earrings caught the light. She walked out, waiting in the hallway for her father and Sylvie. The music played and Brendan went first, her flower girls next, then her two best friends.

"Baby, you're beauty stuns me," Aidan whispered to his daughter as he kissed her cheek.

Sylvie held back tears, giving her sister a hug, and they each took her arm as the Wedding March began. Flowers and candles garnished the living room. Attendance was minimal, but it was everyone who mattered.

As they reached the bottom step, Michelle's breath caught in her throat. Travis stood there noble and handsome in a black Tux. An easy smile played at the corners of his mouth until he turned and looked. When his face brightened prominently at her, Michelle saw everything she would ever need or want in his devoted gaze.

Travis sponged back a gulp. Once his nemesis, all he saw was her sparkling emerald eyes. They were brighter than the diamonds on her lobes. His ladylove moved in a slow graceful walk. Her hips swayed with more than a hint of self-confidence. Warmth and love replaced the cold bitterness he once observed and he knew her love for him ran deep.

He stepped forward as she approached then offered his hand for her to take. He waited while Aidan kissed her cheek and Sylvie adjusted her veil. Thereupon, he tucked her arm in his and they inched toward the priest. She smiled at him as he gazed down at her. Father Napoli performed the sacramental exchanging of their life-long vows. Just before he pronounced them husband and wife, both Travis and Michelle looked at each other. They swapped their secret smiles when Mikala sang out jubilantly. In that moment, neither realized they would never hear their ghost again.

"I introduce Mr. and Mrs. Travis Baines to you," Father Napoli then announced.

Friends and family clapped.

Travis took Michelle in his arms, and before he kissed her, promised, "I'll love you forever, Mrs. Baines."